DAUGHTERS

of

BRONZE

ALSO BY A. D. RHINE

Horses of Fire

DAUGHTERS
of
BRONZE

A Novel of Troy

A. D. RHINE

DUTTON

DUTTON

An imprint of Penguin Random House LLC
penguinrandomhouse.com

Copyright © 2024 by Ashlee Cowles and Danielle Stinson
Map copyright © 2024 by Olivia Hinebaugh
Penguin Random House supports copyright. Copyright fuels creativity, encourages diverse voices, promotes free speech, and creates a vibrant culture. Thank you for buying an authorized edition of this book and for complying with copyright laws by not reproducing, scanning, or distributing any part of it in any form without permission. You are supporting writers and allowing Penguin Random House to continue to publish books for every reader.

DUTTON and the D colophon are registered trademarks of Penguin Random House LLC.

LIBRARY OF CONGRESS CATALOGING-IN-PUBLICATION DATA
has been applied for.

ISBN 9780593474808 (paperback)
ISBN 9780593474815 (ebook)

Printed in the United States of America
1st Printing

Title page art: Horse line drawing © Lesya Gridneva / Shutterstock
Interior art: Sculpture silhouettes © Olga S L / Shutterstock

BOOK DESIGN BY ALISON CNOCKAERT

And Priam and his fifty sons
Wake all amazed, and hear the guns,
And shake for Troy again.

RUPERT BROOKE,
FRAGMENT OF A POEM WRITTEN AS HE
APPROACHED CAPE HELLES IN 1915

But the effect of her being on those around her was incalculably diffusive: for the growing good of the world is partly dependent on unhistoric acts; and that things are not so ill with you and me as they might have been, is half owing to the number who lived faithfully a hidden life, and rest in unvisited tombs.

GEORGE ELIOT, *MIDDLEMARCH*

To our husbands, Jordan and Joshua, and to our children:
Isla and Jack; Uriah, Isaac, Daniel, and Caleb.

You are our everything.

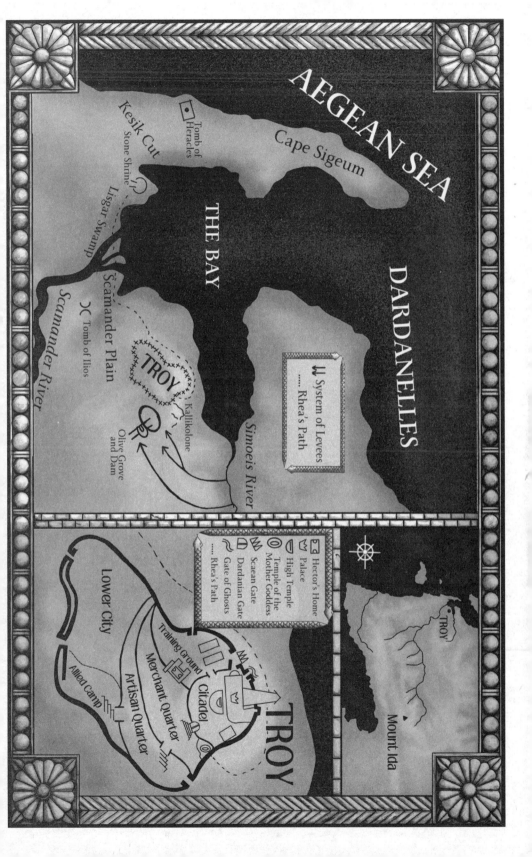

DAUGHTERS

of

BRONZE

THE SHADE

A sorrow wind
that batters walls.
A quiet shadow
through quiet halls.

Who hears the wind
and discerns a cry?
Who sees the shadow
and does not hide?

Silent screamer;
forgotten dreamer;
upon the rocks
where bones still lie.

Now hears the Shade
a desperate call.
The Horse of Fire
pacing his stall.

He feels it slither
across the moon.
A touch of ice.
A whispered "soon."

Song not yet written
notes rearranged,
choices and fates
might still be changed.

The Shade's red tears
leave little doubt.
So many ways in,
just one way out.

BOOK
I

1

RHEA

A CRY PIERCES the night.

My bones absorb the jagged note.

I press myself flat to the ground as a winged army erupts from the tall grasses all around me. They take to the air above the Lisgar Swamp. *Birds.* A hundred feathers blocking out the moon. Only when they melt into the darkness do I see what flies high above their wings.

It burns across the night. Head of fire and a tail of flame. Glowing scales of molten color only the gods can name.

A serpent in the sky.

Half-remembered stories from my childhood rise up in the silence. Pieces of Phrygian prayers and old Hittite songs that spoke of eternal winters. Of sheets of ice that became floods of rain to drown the world. Death and rebirth that left even the mountains scattered as dust upon the wind. A shudder runs through me despite the sticky summer heat.

I rise from the grass. This time, the warning is not a sound, but a feeling.

Movement to the west. Tall reeds swaying in the opposite direction of the wind. One shadow separates from the others.

He is not wearing armor, but the outline of a spear is visible over his shoulder. A mane of long, lank hair tumbles down his back. He stands, staring at the place where the fire serpent lingers on the horizon.

I count two hundred twenty-seven breaths before the sentry melts back into the shadows of the Scamander plain.

A hundred breaths more, and I slip over the hill that overlooks the Achaeans' camp on Sigeum Ridge, where the invaders have been camped the ten long years of this war. The moon drifts back behind the clouds, drenching the swamp and hidden lattice that forms a secret path across it in darkness, but every one of the steps I take is part of a dance I can perform now with my eyes closed.

A hulking monolith takes shape out of the gloom to my right. The stones sing to me with their own beguiling magic, but I force myself to move past the ancient shrine to gods long forgotten without looking back.

My basket waits in a clump of bushes just before the latrines. Tucking it under my arm, I step out into the camp and blink against the brightness of a hundred fires.

On my way to the bathhouse, I pass Agamemnon's settlement. Then Menelaus's. One after another, I list off the names of the Achaean kings until, finally, I draw near the camp closest to the Kesik Cut.

The gates outside Odysseus's settlement are barred to outsiders, as they've been since the Ithacans' failed attempt to trap Troy's people behind burning walls last spring. The Lower City would have fallen then but for my mistress, Harsa Andromache, wife of Prince Hector and the mother to Troy's future heir. That day when Odysseus's arrows rained fire, it was Andromache and her allies who saved Troy from destruction. I know because I was there. From my hiding place upon the Trojan plain, I saw everything.

Even if nobody saw me.

A low groan rises from my right, where a swaying Achaean relieves himself against a nearby hut. A short sword glints in the war belt at his waist. I myself carry no weapons but the small blade strapped to my thigh. Despite Andromache's best efforts to teach me, I am no warrior. Nor am I a leader whom others would follow as they do her and Prince Hector. Instead, my talents lie here, in the shadows, where I gather bits of information like straw and bring them back to those who might *do* something with them. Only, lately there is no straw to be found.

I approach Odysseus's settlement. The walls have been built high enough to block out prying eyes. There is only the sound of cracking wood, smelting metal at all hours, and a subtle shift in the air. One that tells me that Odysseus's men are building *something* behind those gates.

Whatever it is, it can only mean trouble for Troy.

It is the conviction that brings me back here, night after night.

The smell of livestock grows stronger the closer I draw to Odysseus's settlement. A few men stripped down to kilts work just outside the well-constructed gates. Most of the Achaeans deride Odysseus behind his back for these extra precautions he has taken. And why wouldn't they? Since the fighting resumed on the summer moon, the gridlock on the plain remains unbroken. Men bleed and men die, but the lines that mark the spaces between them do not move. Without Achilles and his deadly Myrmidons to bolster their ranks, the Achaeans have made no ground. But neither has Prince Hector and his army.

In the common places where the men gather after long days on the plain, words have taken the place of spears. The men mock Hector for the same reason they do Odysseus. Because they do not glimpse the higher stars that guide them, each along his own path. Hector's refusal to press is born not of weakness but of duty to a king, a council, and a hundred years of tradition that bind his hands. As for Odysseus . . .

Unlike the other warriors on Sigeum Ridge—men who drink and quarrel to drown their homesickness and their fatigue—Odysseus knows that danger is much closer than they realize. Even now, it walks among them, waiting upon their tables and lying beside them at night with open eyes while they drift away to sleep.

A clump of wet earth lands in my path, drawing me up short. A man lifts himself out of the trench to my right. The young warrior nods in apology. I nod back, storing his face in the memory that uniquely qualifies me for this dangerous role I play. The same memory that assures me that while the Ithacans are here digging day and night, their trench somehow never gets any deeper. I watch them work with calculated laziness. Like the sentry on the plain, their gazes are trained not on the tools in their hands but on the Kesik Cut.

Searching. Waiting.

The moist heat of the bathhouse rolls over me. I hardly spare the naked men in the pools a glance as I move toward the back where Ven, my closest ally in this camp full of enemies and one whose scarred face I had a hand in making, supervises the washing. Her brows draw together as she watches me approach.

"What's wrong?" she demands.

"Hello to you too." I lay down my basket and bend to help her with a load of dirty tunics.

"Never mind that," Ven snaps. "You're white as moonstone. What's happened?"

"The serpent in the sky."

"So I heard," Ven says grimly. "The men are agitated. They say Agamemnon's priests are holed up in his hall trying to divine some meaning in it." She shrugs. "It is not the first warning sent by the gods and it will not be the last. If it makes the Achaeans anxious, all the better for us."

I nod, but Ven's frown only deepens. "There is something else," she says. "Out with it."

I let out a long breath. "I saw another one."

Ven puts down her load and turns to face me fully. "Where?"

"Southeast of the Lisgar Swamp."

Ven's scars are an angry red in the bathhouse steam. "How close?"

"Close."

Neither of us speaks. Since the summer began, I've seen Odysseus's men moving in the dark on my nightly trips back to Troy's walls. Ven and I have tried to track their movements, but they change with the wind. This isn't the first time Odysseus has sent scouts to the plain, but it is the first time they've strayed so close to my well-worn path.

Ven reaches for the tunic I wear when running errands for the Achaean healer Machaon and loops it over my head. "Did they see you?" she asks, tying the material with brisk, efficient movements.

"No."

"Are you sure?" The belt at my waist cinches painfully.

"Yes." I draw back. "They were too focused on the Kesik Cut and then the sky serpent."

"They are getting closer."

I say nothing. There is nothing *to* say. Odysseus's silent retreat into his settlement is not the type of quiet that feels like surrender. No, this silence has all the markings of a trap being laid.

Ven regards me with midnight eyes. In them, I glimpse the truth I can no longer deny. Every night I step out onto the plain might be the night the Mother goddess's favor finally runs out.

It is the risk that I take. That we are all taking.

"He knows," Ven says simply. "He knows, and he is hunting us."

I swallow and nod.

Odysseus hasn't forgotten the failed attack on Troy, or what it cost him. Nor is he oblivious to the shift in momentum that has followed. Since our network of shadows has come to these camps, every raid the Achaeans have undertaken against the coastal settlements of Anatolia has been met with resistance. Some of the cities have held. Others have fallen. None have been taken without a price.

While most Achaeans blame their woes on the gods' ill favor, Odysseus is too shrewd not to see the work of other invisible hands. And so he has drawn inward just as we have extended ourselves.

"If he suspects treachery, we must take extra care," Ven says. "It might be time to pull back on your trips through Troy's walls."

Panic rises inside me, but I swallow it down. "We've come too far to abandon our work now." My mind conjures up the image of the ancient shrine and the broad-shouldered silhouette waiting for me there. Guilt pricks at me, but I shove the feeling away and meet Ven's gaze. "He suspects a traitor, yes, but he is looking in the wrong place. He can't imagine his informant could be anything but a man."

"Are you sure we aren't in danger of making the same mistake?"

I glance up sharply.

"To catch more information for your mistress, we've spun a wider web," Ven says carefully. "At last count, we have twenty-three women acting as eyes and ears for Troy. Ours is a delicate weave. One loose thread may send it collapsing down around us."

"Each one of those girls was specifically chosen," I say. "I trust your judgment, Ven."

"Don't you know by now?" She presses the basket into my hand. "Trust *no one*."

She turns before she can see the way her words leach the color from my face. The reality is that every unlikely soldier enlisted to our ranks comes with a hundred secrets that might open doors to a thousand invisible dangers.

Nobody knows this better than me.

I tighten my grip on the basket and leave to make my rounds. The night is crystalline. Bright stars salt the black sky, adding flavor and texture to the rough outline of Cape Sigeum with its high ridges gently dropping down to white beaches lined with rows of black-hulled ships. I spare the Ithacans outside their gates a final glance.

Chopping. Sawing. Hammering in the dark.

What is Odysseus doing behind those walls? And if he knows there are Trojan spies on Sigeum Ridge, why hasn't he sounded the alarm?

I quicken my pace.

"What is it, girl?" asks the guard outside King Idomeneus's settlement. Just as he has asked me dozens of times before.

"Delivery from Machaon."

The sour-faced Cretan scrutinizes my basket. He jerks his head, and I make my way into King Idomeneus's compound. In my months spent in the camps, I have learned to distinguish the factions by their looks and manners as easily as by their separate settlements. The men of Crete take particular care with their appearance, unlike the hard-nosed warriors of Mycenae and Sparta. Or the rangy, clever soldiers of Pylos. Or even the perfectly sculpted giants of Salamis and Phthia. So many divisions in the ranks of these men.

Every last one of them at the ends of their ropes.

"Poultices from the infirmary," I tell the pretty girl who greets me at the door to King Idomeneus's house.

The hall behind Zeyra is crowded with Cretan soldiers, drinking and laughing too loudly. It is the laughter of men who are worn thin and trying hard not to show it. The fighting on the plain was fierce today. Or so I gathered from the number of newly filled pallets in the infirmary.

Zeyra glances over her shoulder before stepping all the way outside.

A soldier brushes past us. We wait for him to walk away. Instead, he loiters.

Zeyra stiffens. I shake my head subtly and shift the basket onto my hip while I mark the man for Ven. Tall. Middling build. With three twisted fingers on his left hand. I don't recognize him. Which means he could take his orders from anyone: Odysseus, or Agamemnon, or even old Nestor.

Either way, we are being watched.

"Thank you." Zeyra's voice is steady. "The women here have no need of cleansing herbs at the moment. Perhaps check on us again in a few days?"

No new information from the camp of King Idomeneus.

The Cretan spits and leans against the wall. Talk of female cleansing often sends battle-hardened soldiers running. Apparently, not this one.

"I'll let Isola know." I force my gaze to remain fixed on the young woman in front of me. "She'll make up a fresh basket, and I'll return in a few days."

"Rhea, wait." Zeyra chews her lip and glances at the idling soldier. "I've heard that women in King Diomedes's settlement may require some sage and wormwood."

Sage. News from Lissia.

Wormwood. Death or injury.

"Thank you." I offer the girl a smile to let her know she's done well. "Tell the other women to take care. The marsh sickness is rampant."

It takes all of my willpower not to run as I make my way across the crowded camp. None of Ven's recruits have been more helpful than Lissia and the girls in King Diomedes's settlement. The young Argive king likes his women almost as much as he likes to boast about his exploits. What Diomedes doesn't realize is that those women bear long memories and even longer grudges.

Heat slicks up my back. The moon is drifting across the swirling blue of the Aegean as I finish the last of my rounds. Soldiers brush past me, but there are many women too.

Zamna. Dawiya. Adomeni. Kallwi.

Some of them call out greetings. Others wave. More ignore me as I pass.

Lissia. Zeyra. Manatta. Balan.

Who were they before the Achaeans sacked their homes and turned them into slaves? I suppose it doesn't really matter. I'm trusting every one of these women with my life, just as they're trusting me with theirs. We were born in different cities, but over these many moons, we've become sisters of the Troad bound together by Ven's careful organization and Andromache's plans, dedicated to a single purpose. To that end we have been tirelessly working.

I pass the tidy settlement that belongs to Ajax the Great just as he strides through the wooden gates. The warrior flanking him looks like a boy beside the giant.

Ajax's tunic is rolled up to his elbows. Sweat glistens on the hard ridges of his collarbones, and his beard is freshly trimmed to his square jaw. He rubs the golden stubble absently as he listens to Agamemnon's chief herald, Eurybates. They stop just beyond the huts built by the men of Salamis, and Ajax listens with an expression that should be unreadable but isn't.

Not to someone who knows his tells.

Tidings dutifully imparted, Eurybates drifts into the river of people flowing between the settlements, leaving Ajax to roll his shoulders under the weight of whatever new task has just been placed upon them.

I am widening my path around him, hoping to avoid notice, when a shout rings out directly behind me. My basket slips out of my hands. I bend down to retrieve it. Another warrior approaches the settlement of Salamis. The man is as finely made as Ajax, though on a more moderate scale. He is also easily recognizable by the longbow slung across his back.

"What did that weasel want?" Teucer asks loudly enough for the retreating herald to hear. Eurybates makes a rude gesture over his shoulder before heading off toward the Cretan settlement I just left behind.

"What does Eurybates usually want?" Ajax asks.

"So you've been summoned like a dog to Agamemnon's heel." Teucer sighs. "And here I thought we might pass a pleasant evening roaring drunk in the weaving tent with some of its warmer offerings. Not that you seem to have much interest in banal pleasures lately. My company included."

Ajax shrugs. "Perhaps if you paid the occasional visit to the bathhouse."

"Show a little respect." Teucer reaches up to grab Ajax by the back of the neck and pulls him into a headlock no sane man would attempt.

Ajax pushes him off, expression lighter. The smug grin on Teucer's face suggests this was entirely the point.

"Meet me on the beach for a swim before sunrise?" Teucer asks, seriously this time. "It's been too long since I gave you a proper trouncing."

The golden strands of Ajax's hair gleam molten in the firelight when he shakes his head. "I have plans."

The thudding at my temples becomes just a little louder.

"You always have plans," Teucer laments. "And they never include me." He studies Ajax with an intensity that belies his easy tone. "If I didn't know better, I'd think you'd finally found yourself a woman."

The space between us is crowded with people, but Ajax looks up and our eyes connect.

I stand quickly, the blood in my head too slow to follow, and I hold up the basket as if it might somehow hide me.

The corner of Ajax's mouth curves upward. Teucer follows his gaze. The archer's brow furrows when he sees me standing there, dozens of clay pots containing poultices and tonics scattered at my feet.

Ajax jerks his eyes away. "Not all of us are ruled by our loins, Teuc."

I quickly bend back down to retrieve the contents of my basket.

"Our esteemed King Telamon would agree," Teucer says with a shrug. "Which is probably why he thought you the better choice to lead his men." There is no envy in the smile he levels at Ajax. Only affection tinged with a trace of something else . . . worry? It's hard to tell. "You've been quiet lately."

"And this surprises you?'

"I know your moods, Ajax. You saw the sky serpent, same as every man here. The battle will soon break one way or another. When it does, you need to have your head on straight." Teucer lowers his voice so I must strain to hear it. "You don't sleep anymore, and when you do, you toss and turn, keeping me up with your endless muttering." A slight pause. "I haven't seen you like this since Alashiya."

Something pricks me at the sound of the woman's name. Whatever Ajax's reaction, I don't dare to look. Instead, I bite my lip and take my time reloading my basket.

"That was a long time ago, Teuc. I'm not that same boy."

"True. But some ailments we never outgrow." Teucer lowers his voice again until it is only the obliging wind that carries his words to me. "We can't afford another incident. Not with Achilles and his Myrmidons already relegated to the sideli—"

"Leave it," Ajax snaps with uncharacteristic harshness. "My problems are the same as every other man here. The nights are hot, these Anatolian bugs hungry, and the cursed plain grows wearisome."

"One sweltering, pointless day does bleed into the next," Teucer agrees, but something in his expression says he doesn't quite believe Ajax, even if he isn't willing to push him. "The only cure is an equally pointless night of heavy drinking. Come on, Ajax. We'll find you a strong, steady girl, and then we'll have our charming physician Machaon describe in proper detail exactly what you're meant to do with her."

Ajax looks up at the sky as if asking his gods for deliverance. "Believe it or not, Teuc, I know how to find my own amusement. But I'll take you up on that swim if it will shut you up." He heads toward the beach, but not before casting a pointed glance toward the shrine of the old gods.

A flash of dimples, and Ajax is gone.

Teucer spares me a brief look before ducking down the path traversing the western side of the ridge.

I force my legs to move and tell myself that it is nothing. Just a look. I've gone fifteen paces before it occurs to me that I'm headed in the wrong direction.

For that is the unfortunate truth about secrets. In keeping them, we often run the risk of losing ourselves.

Trust no one.

Ven was more right than she could ever know.

I make for the latrines and pointedly ignore the ancient monoliths they hide. The night before Odysseus's attack on Troy, I'd let myself become distracted in those stones. Because of that, innocent people died. People who *trusted* me.

When I finally returned to the Achaean camps after the fires in Troy burned out, I'd kept my distance from the shrine. To go back felt like a betrayal. But then Agamemnon flew into a rage, and the rifts between Achaean factions grew more rigid than ever. The men's tongues quickly followed suit. Even with Ven's swelling numbers of recruits, it became harder and harder to glean anything worth reporting back to Troy.

In the end, I was left with no choice but to return to the one place I swore I wouldn't.

So many days had passed since our last meeting, I'd assumed Ajax would not be there, but he was. He did not ask me where I'd been, and for my part, I didn't volunteer an explanation. The ease between us was gone. My fault. Not his.

I don't know what he took from our early nights sitting together in the stones, but he must have taken something, because he returned again and again. Whenever my speech grew stilted, his flowed freely.

It's been no easy task hiding the source of my information from Ven and Andromache.

Half of Troy's successes have come directly from the things Ajax has told me, but that is not all I've found in the ancient shrine to gods long forgotten.

All those moons ago, Ajax told me he wished us to be friends, and despite my best efforts, it has somehow become so. Ajax's easy warmth and surprising generosity when coupled with his crooked smiles have made him impossible to hate.

And the Mother knows I've tried.

Ven would never understand how I can consider Ajax a friend. Nor would our other sisters in the shadows, Salama or Isola. And Andromache...
I know exactly what Andromache would say if she knew how I spent my time away from Troy.

That it was impossible.

That it was dangerous.

Scurry, scurry, little mouse.

Only, take care not to scurry right into a trap.

One that you have set for yourself.

The next stop I make is at King Meriones's camp. Then King Nestor's. Then King Eurypylus's. Finally, I pass King Thaos's seat. At every door the women turn me away, signaling that there is no need for my basket, and therefore, no news. Nothing but gridlock and distemper and growing resentment.

My path cuts west, bringing me closer to the beach. As I pass the women's weaving hut, the skin prickles at the back of my neck. I glance sideways to find a figure watching me intently from the open doorway. Calis's wiry frame and sharp features are as unmistakable as her severely plaited gray hair.

I glance away quickly, before she can signal me over. Calis runs the weaving hut while Ven runs the bathhouse. Calis despises Ven, which means she also despises me. She is mean and bitter, and she lords what little power she has over others without mercy. Worse yet, I suspect she is also clever. Maybe even clever enough to be dangerous.

I force myself to keep an even pace. Only when I pass out of sight of the weaving hut do I speed my steps.

The sharp odor of excrement intensifies as I make my way past the latrines toward the last three camps before the Kesik Cut. I place a cloth over my mouth and head toward the encampment belonging to Diomedes. Lissia is standing at the door, already waiting for me. She grabs my hand and pulls me inside just as a scream erupts from the rooms behind the empty hall.

"What happened?" I ask when she's sequestered us in a quiet corner, far away from the two other servant girls, who are busy grinding molded barley into flour.

"Diomedes has been injured."

My heart leaps. Though the battle has been gridlocked all summer, Diomedes, the young king of the Argives, has spilled more than his share of Trojan blood.

"How bad is it?" I ask.

"Nothing fatal. More's the pity. Still, it's making him testy." Lissia's smile is feline.

We stop speaking when another girl enters the kitchens with an armful of bloody rags. She dumps them by the hearth with a huff. My spirits lift at the sight of a face I haven't seen in weeks.

"Salama!"

Her expression stops me before I can do something foolish. Like embrace her.

"Ven sent me to retrieve the laundry. There was also the matter of a special salve required by the Child King of the Argives."

"How is he?" I ask.

"Bleeding lightly." Salama smirks. "And loudly lamenting every drop."

"He's a poor patient." Lissia grins. "Something that hasn't escaped the other men's notice." She says something else but my mind is only half listening. It's nearly midnight. My heart beats faster as I reach for my basket.

"Where are you going?" Salama demands.

"I need to head back to Troy."

"So early?" Lissia frowns. "It's hardly past the second watch."

My hand twists the edge of my tunic before I force myself to let go. "Andromache will want to know about Diomedes as soon as possible."

"Fine," Salama snaps. "But first take these down to the beach. You can leave them to dry on the rocks, and we'll fetch them in the morning." She dumps the bloody rags on the ground at my feet. "The salt stiffens them so it's easier to remove the shit and blood. Or so Ven says. The gods know how she loves ordering me around."

"I have to—"

"I don't care." She glares at me. "While you run back to Troy to be doted on by Andromache, the rest of us are here breaking our backs and gritting our teeth whenever one of these grunting animals decides to take a fancy."

Her words silence any protests from me.

I reach down for the rags and recognize the long strips Isola fashioned for use in the infirmary. By now, I've grown well accustomed to the sharp perfume of latrines, and still, the smell of this bundle is enough to make me gag. Salama raises a dark brow, drops down onto a worn pillow, and makes a show of putting up her feet. Lissia shakes her head but presses a bowl of dried figs into the other girl's lap. Salama's grin is wicked when I duck out of Diomedes's hall and set off on the narrow path leading down the west side of the ridge.

The beach is steeper here, and therefore empty. To the south where the shore lies flat, the harbor holds rows of staggered ships, the raised gangways between them a web of timber. I move north, away from the ships and toward Kesik Tepe and the mound the Achaeans say was built by the hero Herakles. I've never come here before. There has never been a need. It is almost tranquil with the low rumbling surf drowning out the sound of men nearby. The waves wash up on the shore in silky folds of white foam that spill across the sand.

The night is clear. The summer moon unusually bright. I can see for miles across the dark smudge of sea toward distant Euboea. It is the kind of night when I almost forget to miss the sun.

Only the faintest tail of the sky serpent remains visible on the northern horizon.

I glimpse a shallow pool of water a few feet from the shore, drop the disgusting rags inside, and begin to scrub. Salt stings the cuts on my fingers that never fully heal because of my nightly travels through the rough passageway that is my secret pathway in and out of Troy. The pain is sharp and bright, quieting my mind for once. My gaze runs back to the endless water dancing under the full moon.

"What is it like?" I'd asked him once.

My father was raised on the steppes far north of Achaea. Horses were in his blood, but the way he spoke of his days sailing across the Aegean always echoed with a longing he didn't bother to hide.

"*What is what like, my little mouse?*"

"*The sea?*" I'd said.

"*Ah. Nothing rides like the waves,*" Papa had replied. Entire constellations of stars shone in his eyes. "*And only the wind runs faster.*"

I'd dreamed of the sea my whole life. Now it is never out of sight, and I hardly bother to look at it. Maybe that is a mistake. Staring at the endless plain of water and stars stretching out before me, all the worries I carry suddenly feel . . . small.

A breath fills my lungs. Deep and pure. The kind of breath I only ever seem to draw when I'm—

I stand abruptly and kick off my sandals. Slowly, I approach the surf. The sand is warm and grainy between my toes. One more step and the waves tickle my skin with strings of foam hung with pearls by the moonlight.

"Peaceful, isn't it?"

A yelp escapes as I spin to face the mountain hovering over my shoulder. Ajax claps two hands over his ears and staggers backward. "Gods, woman. Every wild dog in the Troad will be headed this way."

"Wh . . . what are you doing here?" I stutter, though the answer is quickly obvious.

Ajax is bare to the waist. Streams of dried salt glint off the hard slabs of his chest and stomach. Despite the sheer size of him, the playfulness in his expression as he stares down at me makes him look less the fearsome warrior than the young man of twenty-odd summers I know him to be.

"I went for a swim," he says.

My eyes cast out to the midnight sea. It is beautiful and dark and no doubt teeming with sharp-toothed creatures lurking just beneath the obsidian surface.

"Is that safe?"

With his broad back suddenly blocking the moon, I cannot see the smile in Ajax's eyes. But that doesn't mean I can't hear it in his voice.

"The old women back home are fond of saying Teucer and I were born with fins for arms. Besides, the sea is warm." A flash of teeth is the only warning before he leans over to shake his head like some breed of giant, golden dog.

I yelp again.

"It's only a little water," Ajax says, highly amused.

"Yes, but it is so very wet."

Chuckling, Ajax bends down to grab his tunic and throws it back over his head. He comes to stand beside me, and together, we watch the moonlight dance across the waves.

It suddenly hits me that this is the first time we've ever met outside the protection of our stones.

Wind gusts over the beach, tearing at my headscarf. A reminder that we are completely out in the open. Where anyone might see us.

"Don't worry," Ajax says, reading me easily. "Teucer and I are the only ones who come here."

Even so. "I should go."

When Ajax doesn't answer, my eyes glide sideways to find him staring out over the water. For a few breaths, every sharp line of his body seems to round; every hard ridge softens. "I've always loved the sea," he says. "The way it makes all the noise in my head go quiet. Even as a boy, the water was the one thing that could make me feel . . . weightless."

His words are such a perfect echo of my earlier thoughts, I forget all the reasons I shouldn't stay.

Ajax gently bumps my shoulder with his side. "Perhaps one of these days, I'll teach you how to swim."

The idea is so ludicrous it draws a snort from my lips. "Thank you, but I prefer to keep my feet on solid ground."

"I did not take you for a coward, Rhea."

After all our nights spent in the stones, the man knows just how to bait me. "In that case, I'll learn to swim the day you learn to ride."

Ajax's eyes widen. We both know his size would be the end of whatever poor beast he tried to mount. He holds up his hands in surrender, and for a moment, we both stand there, smiling at each other.

The moment lingers.

"I really should go," I say.

Ajax nods. We don't touch. Not even to say good-bye. That is not the sort of friends we are.

As I turn to leave, Ajax drops down onto the sand. His arms reach around his knees in an oddly childlike gesture. He stares at the water as if he might read the waves the way my papa once read the stars.

My steps slow without permission. Andromache will want to know what I've learned about Diomedes, but Lissia wasn't wrong. It's early yet. Besides, something is troubling him.

Trouble for the Achaeans means opportunity for Troy.

I drop down beside him. "What's wrong?"

I don't pretend not to read his body language, and he doesn't pretend to be surprised by how easily I manage it.

"Diomedes is injured."

"I'm sorry to hear it," I lie.

Ajax snorts. "Don't be. Diomedes is a spoiled boy playing the part of a demigod. It was only a matter of time before it caught up to him." He tips his chin to the stars. "He's been telling anyone who'll listen that the gods favor him ever since Achilles refused to fight. It seems Pandarus's arrow has neatly punctured that illusion."

Pandarus. Andromache's archer.

"You don't believe the gods have taken Diomedes under their protection?" I ask, eager for any kernel of information I might take back to Andromache.

"Oh, I'm as reverent as any man," Ajax says. "But I don't know of a single god in any pantheon who'd favor that pissant." He runs a hand over the blond stubble already darkening his jaw, and I marvel at the way the bristles catch the moonlight. "Diomedes is out for Pandarus's blood. And he is being loud about it."

"It is not your problem." A frown bends my lips as I study him more closely. Even in the dark, I can make out the red threads woven through the whites of his eyes. "You should rest more," I say before I can help myself.

A lopsided smile. "Says the girl who never sleeps."

"I'll sleep later. For now, my duties keep me busy."

The smile slips as he studies the rags floating in the pool behind me. "Duties for Odysseus?"

When we first met, I stupidly told him I was a slave of the king of Ithaca. At this point, I can hardly contradict him.

"Does he treat you well?"

A small rush of air leaves my lungs. Since our first meeting, Ajax has never again spoken Odysseus's name. Our ancient shrine has become a retreat from more than just the war. But we are not in that shrine now. I don't know why that changes things, only that it does. Or maybe the change isn't the place so much as Ajax himself. He seems bigger outside the confines of the stones. Like the sea he loves, wild and vibrant and maybe even a little unpredictable.

My eyes dance across the beach, suddenly anxious to assure myself that we are still alone. "He's a good master. Better than most."

"You respect him."

I glance up in surprise at his insight. "Yes, I respect him." And admire his cunning. And also fear him. Especially his silence, for it makes me wonder what he and his men are building out of the reach of our eyes.

"Does he return that respect?" Ajax's gaze tangles with mine. "Don't," he says when I start to speak.

"Don't what?"

"You have that look you get when you're choosing your words as carefully as Teucer chooses his arrows."

He seems so earnest. As if whether I'm well treated makes a difference to him. In all the nights we've sat together, talking about everything and nothing, he has never once pressed me like this. In that ancient shrine beneath towering stones where we talk mostly of past memories, our present roles outside them never seem to matter.

At least, that is what I thought.

"I am a slave, Ajax. He doesn't have to respect me."

Ajax looks away. His throat bobs once. "I have to go."

There is something in his tone. It rubs against the grain of everything I know to be true about him. Since the battle resumed, Ajax has occasionally fallen into somber moods. He is always kind. Always eager to take in whatever I'm willing to share and return the favor with a laugh at his own expense. But on the days when the darkness holds sway over him, even his smiles are haunted. He wears that look now.

"Where?" I ask, though I was there when Eurybates came calling.

"A meeting of the kings at Agamemnon's settlement."

"In the second watch of the night?"

His fingers adjust the neck of his tunic, helpless to fit the wide expanse of his shoulders. "Odysseus insisted."

A chill runs up my spine. "And Agamemnon agreed?"

Ajax nods. "The serpent in the sky has left everyone unsettled."

"What do Agamemnon's priests say?" I ask.

"That it is a sign the end of war is coming fast. There's also talk of gray ships sighted off the shores of Ugarit in the south all the way north to Crete and Pylos. Cities that Nestor and Idomeneus cannot defend while they languish here. The other men grow restless and hungry since our own raids haven't been as successful as we'd hoped."

No. They haven't.

Not only because of Andromache's warnings to the villages based on the information we've gleaned from these camps, but because the Achaeans are no longer the only raiders in the Aegean. There have been whispers of Sea Peoples lying in wait along the coasts. Bands of seafaring tribes of dubious origins. Mysterious men in masks who inspire fear wherever their gray ships land. Rumor has it they have already sacked multiple cities along the Egyptian coast, and now they have turned their sails north.

"Our time on these shores is nearly up." A pause. "Either we take the Citadel and all its riches now, or we go home."

My spine becomes an iron rod. "How does Odysseus propose to take Troy when his earlier attempt failed?"

"He would use Diomedes's feud with Pandarus to draw out the one Trojan asset that kept him from sacking the Lower City the first time around."

I frown. "The Trojans will see you coming and have their line of chariots waiting before you make it halfway to their walls."

"Troy's greatest strength is not her walls or her chariots," Ajax offers in a tone that suggests the words are not his own. "Chariots and walls can be rebuilt."

"I don't understand," I say.

"Her horses," Ajax says hollowly. "The Trojan army without horses is like a fleet of boats without oars."

Cold spreads through me. "No."

"I don't like it either." Ajax's mouth is grim. "But very little about this war feels right to me. At least this has a hope of success." His shoulder brushes mine for a moment as he leans back onto his elbows. "We'll use Diomedes to draw out Troy's horses."

"And then what?" My heart is beating so hard at my temples I can barely hear myself speak.

"Odysseus has been tight-lipped," Ajax admits. "All I know is they will engage the chariots and, with any luck, bypass them to move our army right up to the walls. Then it'll only be a matter of time." The haunted look returns as he sends his gaze my way. "It may be a few days before I return to the shrine."

"Days?" I ask hollowly, my mind a stone skipping over his words.

"Will you worry for me, Rhea?" A ghost of a smile touches his lips. It only heightens the strange sorrow in his eyes. One that pulls at me like the sea, filling me with the sense that I am caught up in forces far beyond my control.

"Why would I do that?" I try to make the words light, but that is not how they sound.

A strand of hair comes loose from my headscarf, lashing my face. I reach to push it back, but Ajax gets there first. His calloused finger skims my cheek, tucking the hair behind my ear.

His skin is hotter than I imagined it would be. It burns across my face and though I'm seated firmly on solid ground, somehow I feel myself slipping.

The wind catches my sharp exhale and sends it swirling all around us.

Ajax stands and then reaches down to pull me to my feet. "Until I get back, try to tend to yourself as diligently as you do everyone else." Something moves in his eyes before his smile returns. He backs away slowly, lopsided grin fixed in place, and I decide I must have imagined the tenderness in his expression. "Until then, take care of our stones for me."

He disappears around the mount of Kesik Tepe. I raise my fingers to my face, where I can feel his heat trapped inside my skin. My hand is still pressed there when I sense the unmistakable weight of eyes on me.

Farther down the beach, a lone figure stands, arms loaded with tunics and head turned in my direction.

Even the shadows cannot hide the angry scars on her face.

Ven lifts the rags from the water and starts back up the beach.

2

ANDROMACHE

OVER THE ILIUM plain, a serpent of light streaks through the purple haze. As the tail burns above me, the winds below change. No longer do they sail off the Aegean in the west. Now they blow in from the Dardanelles in the north and Mount Ida in the southeast, carrying the faint scents of honeysuckle and pine.

My footsteps across our balcony come to an abrupt halt. I lower my eyes from the strange stars to a floor showing signs of wear, its stone polished smooth by my slippered feet. Pacing has become my early-morning ritual since this belly made sleeping impossible—and the child within it came to regard my bladder as a sparring bag.

I almost always wake at the same time. Near the end of the third watch.

The hours when Odysseus is most likely to spin the web of sabotage Rhea watches for but hasn't yet been able to unravel.

It is more than that, though. There is an unearthly heaviness at this hour, a weight that these signs in the sky have only intensified. An ominous presence seems to be always at my back—like a shade who has returned from the Great River to warn me of some evil to come. I walk through my own home feeling the constant need to glance over my shoulder. Palms sweating. Heart racing. Eyes forever searching dusty corners bathed in shadow and uncertain outcomes.

Searching for her. For *them*.

In reality, there is no need. Not when *they* visit me each and every night.

A sea of innocent faces crying out to me in my dreams. The hollowed-out gazes of a hundred children—Troy's children— submerged in a pit of flame.

These were the innocents Helen gave her life to save.

These are the children who *will* burn, along with my own child, if my strategies and Hector's execution of them do not succeed. My hands clench into fists, willing the fire snake above to tell me its secrets.

One thing I don't need a sign to know—we must win this war, and win it soon.

A crash rings out as something falls to the floor behind me. I spin toward my bedchamber, forming an X across my round middle with both arms.

"Sorry," Hector grumbles. He punches his pillow twice before flipping over, my own side of the bed long cold.

My lips twitch toward a smile even as my legs shake. I'm not the only one who has stared down restless nights. But whereas I'm startled from nightmares that leave me ready to begin the day, Hector merely tosses and turns—taking out any objects on the bedside table in the process. Tonight, it is a defenseless depas cup.

"Unable to sleep again, my *alev*?"

My fire.

Hector's muffled voice reaches for me across the dark expanse between the balcony and our bed, and I can feel his compassion in it. Along with his sadness in knowing this is one area where he can do nothing to ease my discomfort.

And the one woman who had the skill is gone.

I push the thought of Helen away, as I have a hundred times before, banishing the memory of her bruised and beautiful face.

"I will go ask Bodecca to warm some milk," I say.

If our indomitable cook is even awake. I approach the bed and reach out to clasp the soft flesh of Hector's ankle, sticking out from the blankets right where I know it will be. Lately, he only allows his feet to remain un-covered and exposed while he sleeps. It makes me think Hector has also sensed some shift in this war. New vulnerabilities forming in the dark despite our recent victories.

"Go back to sleep, Hector."

His breathing has grown heavy again by the time I release his ankle.

More memories of Helen follow me to the kitchen, as they do most nights. Sometimes Bodecca is awake, preparing the household's bread for the day, but most of the time she is not. Especially when there is less einkorn wheat to grind with each passing week, and what remains is often flecked with mold.

It is on the nights Bodecca does not preside over her hearth that I feel most haunted. Most alone, with only my regrets and the shadows at my back for company. Wraiths that hiss whispers of harsh words spoken in haste. Of actions taken too late.

But then the babe, who has become a part of me in ways I never expected, gives my ribs another hard kick, and I'm reminded that I am never alone. Bodecca likes to tease that I may never have the luxury of being alone again.

"Not until you're my age and have no more use for solitude."

A faint smile touches my lips as I enter the kitchen. I am grateful there is one woman in this household willing to tell me the truth, now that Rhea is gone more often than she is here. As I step into the faint light of the oil lamps, I'm met with the musk of simmering goat's milk and an even thicker sense of relief.

"You're more reliable than any sundial," Bodecca says with a grunt, not bothering to turn from the fire where she stirs. "Or maybe it's that acrobat you will soon give birth to. Likes to keep to a fixed morning routine."

"Then in that, he is like his father," I say on a slow exhale, easing myself into the closest chair. Now that the Lower City is mostly habitable again, Hector has returned to his daily exercise with morning runs around Troy's walls.

A quick scan of the kitchen, my favorite room in our modest house, has me frowning. Bodecca's workstation is empty. Not a grinding slab in sight nor any sign of rising bread. "And you, Bodecca? Why are you awake at this ungodly hour?"

She harrumphs. "Blame the serpents."

The old woman turns her ice-blue eyes my way. Despite their cloudiness, they are eyes that have always seen more than the practicalities that have been her life's domain.

"I'm relieved I'm not the only one bothered by them," I say. For as devoted to the gods as he may be, Hector has shown a distinct lack of concern whenever I've mentioned the stars that seem to be falling right out of the sky. He has enough earthly concerns, so he leaves the higher matters to his temple priests. Normally, I also prefer keeping my gaze fixed to the ground in front of me. And yet . . .

"A light like this, one that falls slowly . . . It's an ill omen, Andromache," Bodecca says with a visible shudder. "The last time we saw such lights in Troy, I was but a child. Nearly the entire city gathered at the High Temple, where the priests burned the sheddings of a hundred snakes, speaking strange prayers in an old language we did not understand over the ring of serpent stones in the courtyard. Just the thought of the rite gave me nightmares for months, and I've done my best not to dwell on it since. But now . . ."

Yes, why *now*? Why have the sky snakes returned?

"These serpent stones," I say, chewing my lower lip. "What do they mean?"

For they are flat paving stones—modestly decorative, but nothing sacred. I'm sure I've walked over them countless times on my way to King Priam's palace, and yet I never thought to consider their significance.

"There are rumors, of course. Some say the stones cover a great cistern that would provide water to the Citadel in the event of a siege." Bodecca pours hot milk into a cup, and I try not to gag on the strong aroma rising with the steam. "But no one really knows. No one except the king and his high priest."

I nod, churning the possibilities. It comes as no surprise that whatever these stones conceal, it is meant to benefit only the Old Blood who take refuge behind the Citadel's high walls. Another reason we can't allow the Achaeans to come so close to taking the Lower City ever again. Where would our people even go? We already learned the hard way that shelter in the higher rings of Troy is limited.

And there are many who prefer it that way.

"Though ask any commoner who has lived long enough, and they will tell you . . ." Bodecca shrugs like such matters are far above her pay in grain. "Those serpents guard some grave secret. One as old as Troy herself."

"Then it is too bad that entertaining bygone legends is a luxury of peacetime," I say, rising from my chair after one sip of the sickly-sweet milk. There will be no more sleep for me. Not when there is much work to be done before my body takes on more primal labors. I stare at my round-ness, eager to have a full range of physical prowess back but also terrified at the prospect of having no control over the process it takes to get there.

Still, there are other ways I might wield some influence.

"Will you try to worm your way into the council again?" asks Bodecca, hands planted on her wide hips as I reach for the cloak hanging by the kitchen door. "Or did I say something that would send you on another fool's errand before the sun is even up?"

"Set your conscience at ease, Bodecca." I give her a teasing smile. "The imminence of giving birth has simply left me feeling . . . pious."

Bodecca snorts and raises the wisp of an eyebrow. As one who bows before life's many mysteries, the old woman respects the untamable ways of the wind as much as I. But she also knows I have little patience for ani-mal sacrifices made to gods greedy for the mindless devotion of whatever new people they happen to conquer.

"I'm meeting Aeneas at the High Temple. Hopefully *his* piety and sense of decorum will go far in persuading the council to admit me this time." Because they must. Now that the Lower City's walls are nearly repaired, Hector's army is ready to be unleashed. Unfortunately, those who benefit most from playing it safe must still be convinced.

"While you're at the temple, you could light an incense brick." Bodecca's eyes soften when I meet them. We both know who I ought to pray for, as well as the many reasons I have for atonement.

I nod and swallow hard, Helen's face filling the space meant for a re-sponse.

Having none, I leave the kitchen and my past failures behind, stepping into the muted lavender of a coming dawn. The uphill walk from my threshold to the inner gate would normally take a few minutes, but not today. Not when Troy's future queen must waddle through her own city like a maimed duck.

It isn't long before I'm forced to stop and catch my breath. To ease the strain on my pelvis, I lift my midsection like a basket of laundry and press on. The bricks of the surrounding homes sweat with the kiss of midsum-mer. Though the sun hasn't yet appeared over the walls, the sky above is the deepest blue of Egyptian glass.

With one fist pressed to my lower back, I breathe in the city's rare silence until it no longer feels like a colt is sitting on my chest—though it will come as no surprise to anyone that Hector's child kicks like one.

By the time I resume my trek, swollen feet screaming, the streets before me are painted in the gold of the Great Tiwad. It is a nearly perfect dawn.

But perfection is almost always hiding something; the city's gilded sheen is a mirage. An oak tree at its most stunning, just before its leaves catch fire and die one by one, to be carried away by the wind.

That wind lashes the fabric of my robe against my legs as it stirs the tapestries hung over the windows of the nearby houses. Tapestries bearing woven designs with the antlers of Runtiya, god of the hunt and protector of mortals. Sworn enemy of the serpent.

My mind spins Bodecca's words like a spindle winds wool. We have always known the Citadel hides secrets. I owe it to Helen to find out what they are, especially if they might aid those she gave her life to save. But right now, there is only one viper's lair I am worried about accessing—the innermost chambers of the King's Council.

I wrap my hands around the unbearable fortress my body has become. A sanctuary that will soon be vacated. Another child who will soon be at risk.

My gaze shifts to my right, and I imagine the sturdy houses of Troy's most prosperous merchants standing in judgment of my recent mistakes. Linen canopies once shielded these balconies, providing shade for the women who stood at their outdoor looms for long hours, weaving their husbands and children tunics made of the finest thread. Eating sweet melons imported from the Nile in the east while sipping honeyed wine from Illyria in the west.

There are no more canopies. No more mead or melons either. The winter rains destroyed what few crops we had, and Tiwad's harsh sun took care of what remained. While we managed to thwart Odysseus's attack and save our herds, the Achaeans refocused their efforts on disrupting our major trade routes. Troy is now cut off from the world in a way we have not been in all these years of war, and it seems man cannot live by cattle alone.

Still, the shortages are felt more keenly in some rings of the city than in others. I pass through the gate leading into the Citadel and dip my hand in a bubbling fountain on the other side, wiping cool beads across my brow. Another reminder of the water the Citadel alone has in excess, thanks to ancient springs below the city. Shallow canals carved into the terraced walls carry the effervescent water to gardens that encircle each of the palaces belonging to King Priam and his children. I am always startled by the shock of green among so much stone. Not even the oldest Trojans can recall a summer this dry. The Ilium plain has become scorched earth in more ways than one.

It does not seem a particularly auspicious summer to be born.

My eyes fall back to the babe who somehow continues to grow despite repetitive meals of dried beef strips. Sweat drips down the column of my spine as I strain against the road's grade. The pressure is almost unbearable—it's as if Hephaestus's anvil hangs between my legs.

Despite this heaviness, my heart lightens as I think of Bodecca's fussing these past few months. Perhaps I shouldn't have been surprised to find her waiting up this morning—the woman watches me like a hawk. Monitoring my eating and harping on all the hours I spend on my feet with Troy's allies.

It is both humbling and maddening to be loved so fiercely.

The infant in my womb voices its agreement with another violent kick. A laugh chases my wince. Not even born, and a warrior already.

The short-lived smile fades. This is not what a normal mother should wish for.

It is the reason I am here. To give my child a future that isn't war. It is why I have made more trips to the Citadel in recent weeks than I have in all my previous years in Troy.

The cry of a bird lifts my gaze to Cassandra's tower, its gold roof gleaming in sunlight the same color. The long shadow the tower casts lands on the thick exterior door to Paris's palace, lined with guards and draped in mourning tapestries of midnight blue.

Helen's body was never found.

Not before our battle for the Lower City ended, nor after the flames were doused. That is the turmoil that threatens to overtake me most of all. It has nearly made this pilgrimage to the High Temple genuine. The entire Lower City served as Helen's pyre, so I pray her shade is at rest, but it still feels wrong that Helen's ashes should lie in Troy rather than with her beloved daughter, Hermione.

Grief and guilt take to brawling within me, though there is little room left for either. Helen was present at the battle because of me. Because she was a healer and I asked her for help. Aid I refused to grant *her* until it was too late. Bodecca is right—an offering to her Achaean gods is the least I can do.

It is all *I can do.*

But it is not the only thing I can do for the living.

A few more twists and turns and the High Temple appears before me, three stories of white limestone. The sanctuary is stunning but also daunting. As unapproachable as its deities. Only Cassandra's tower rises higher. Hector once told me the temple was rebuilt after the death of the Imposter King from Hattusa in gratitude to the gods for placing Troy back into Luwian hands. And yet there is precious little of Anatolia to be found in the arched entrance, framed by repeating patterns as garish as the stones they adorn. To me, they are hollow. Lifeless decorations lacking substance. Chaotic forms that feel random and inscrutable.

An apt summary of all the High Temple stands for. Beauty without meaning, rather than the meaning that gives rise to beauty.

Some say they have seen the Shade of a veiled woman wandering the path between Cassandra's tower and these temple grounds whenever the moon is full.

Some even go so far as to claim that it is Helen.

Normally, I do not entertain their tales. Not because I don't believe in wandering spirits, but because if Helen were one herself, the Citadel would be the last place she'd choose to linger.

I hear a throat clear behind me, and my reverie is interrupted.

"I'm late. My apologies, Harsa."

Aeneas joins me in the sunlight bathing the High Temple's walls. The tension that radiates from his jaw makes him look years older than his thirty summers. His polished breastplate is shiny enough to pass even Bodecca's inspection, despite being put to good use. My eyes land on that armor's declaration of his Dardanian ancestry, the simple pattern of a snake eating its own tail. Symbol of life devoured and then reborn.

Is that what these strange stars are trying to tell us? That it is time for Troy to transform into something . . . else?

I swallow the lump in my throat. It has been some time since I last saw Hector's cousin, given that the son of Anchises has been splitting his time between Troy's regular army and my allies. A part of both groups while never fully belonging to either. It may be the only thing Aeneas and I have in common. Both of us destined to dwell on the threshold between two rooms.

"Another late night, Captain? Is Creusa well?"

The shadows of exhaustion that dance across Aeneas's face make the hollows of his cheeks even more pronounced. Hector's sister Creusa is carrying Aeneas's second child, and she has spent many weeks in bed, her body still weak from last autumn's plague.

"It was the falling light that kept me up. Did you see it?"

I nod, though the brighter the day grows, the more I feel my natural skepticism toward signs and wonders rising with the sun.

The gods may strive to plan our course, but we determine our own steps.

"They are trying to tell us something," Aeneas says grimly. His eyes fall to the emblem on his chest in a way that makes me suspect he believes the gods are speaking directly to *him*. "And yes, Creusa's lungs seem to be getting worse as the child grows."

"What do the palace healers say?"

"They bring her remedies and blessings."

"But?" I press. If even the devout Aeneas is second-guessing the temple, then Creusa's condition must be worse than I have been led to believe.

He surveys the morning sky with a wild look I've never witnessed in the nearly flat emotions of Aeneas. "The ways of the gods are mysterious, yes. But I wonder if they are angered by something we have done . . . or failed to do."

On that, Aeneas and I may be in agreement. We *have* failed—failed to advance this war and break a stalemate that has gone on for months.

His shoulders sag, a small crack in his normally impenetrable defense. "As for Creusa, nothing seems to help her. She can't keep their bitter brews down for more than a few minutes."

I recall the pot of rancid salve the priest Laocoon delivered on the last full moon with instructions to rub the balm all over my belly—a gift Bodecca promptly threw over the ledge of our balcony. If only we had a true healer.

"I will visit her soon," I promise. Something I should have done long before now. My recent efforts to change the climate in the Citadel have kept me occupied, but not so busy that I should forget a friend who has never forgotten me.

That has happened once already, and I fear the shame will never leave me.

Sensing Aeneas's discomfort on this intimate ground, I change the subject. "I appreciate you accompanying me to the council."

Though I also suffer no illusions. Aeneas is here out of loyalty to Hector rather than any confidence in my diplomatic methods or way of leading our men. Or faith that I should be leading at all.

It is somewhat ironic that even though Aeneas was born beyond these city walls, his respect for Troy's rules makes him better suited to life in the Citadel than even Hector. Aeneas has always tried to prove he is as much a Trojan as any of Priam's children—so much so that he volunteered to serve on the lower council in addition to his many other duties.

I fear his efforts are in vain. Despite long family ties, the icy bedrock between Priam and Aeneas's father, Anchises, has existed for as long as I have lived here, and I see no sign of it thawing soon. Still, the king needs the support of his wealthy Dardanian cousin, which is why Anchises sits on the inner ring of the Five. "I would caution you against high hopes of making much progress," Aeneas warns. Caution is the name the gods should have granted him.

He does not have to tell me that as a woman born of Thebe under Mount Placos and not Troy, I am not permitted within the council's innermost chambers. Not unless I am extended an explicit invitation, the kind of summons that has never been good news for a woman.

Which is why I need Aeneas.

"Regardless, we must try," I insist. "If we do not press the Achaeans now while Achilles and his Myrmidons sit on their shields, they will be right back at our walls. Next time, we can bet their fighting force will be made of more than Odysseus and a handful of his men."

Aeneas's grim face grows grimmer still. "What makes you think we will succeed with the council where Hector has not?" he asks earnestly. "It's not as if they are ignoring the threats. They are merely debating which strategy will prove the most prudent."

"Oh, I have no doubt countless arguments have been made. That's what the Old Blood are here for, is it not? To debate in a ceaseless circle that never fails to keep their bellies full of food and their chests lined with gemstones. To pontificate their strategies until even Hecuba's Mycenaean gods are surely leaking ichor from their ears."

Aeneas frowns. "This is how wars have always been fought, Harsa."

"Perhaps. But it is not how wars are won."

And unlike politics, warfare is what I understand. Charges and retreats and feints to draw out the enemy. But here in the Citadel, the rules are different. Priam's palaces are not an open plain where men move and chariots advance; they are a maze that leads to a pit of stagnation where motives remain hidden. A realm where words, not actions, are judged and ultimately hold sway. Well-crafted arguments that are bandied about, leaving nothing accomplished but the feeling that one has forgotten the direction of true north. Even when there is some fleeting victory, it vanishes as soon as the council holds another session and the self-indulgent process can begin all over again.

Hector once said that all parts of Troy made her who she is. Who *he* is. Even the tireless windbags who debate the fates of braver men from the safety of their Citadel. Laocoon. Antenor. Tumaeus. They are mere names to me. Little more than strangers. I have never cared to know them, nor they me.

Still, these are the men we must convince.

Five seats. Five votes.

Polydamas, Hector's friend and cousin, along with Aeneas's father, are the only ones among them I can count on. The council remains gridlocked on how the war should proceed, and the king will make no move to overrule them without a verdict from the Five who make up the council's core.

"You managed to convince your father to vote with us," I tell Aeneas as we start toward the gates to Priam's complex of palaces. "Why not Tumaeus? His trade dealings have been greatly hampered by the war. Of the three men with votes who still remain, he is more likely to join us if it means reopening the routes to the east sooner rather than later."

Aeneas ducks under a low-hanging trellis covered in jasmine, strung between the palatial houses belonging to Troy's oldest families. "Self-interest takes many forms, Harsa. It does not always signify that we stand to gain, if others gain *more*."

He is right about that, and it irks me. "But if we do not press the enemy now and end this madness, our people will soon starve. What good is an army of bones?"

Aeneas keeps his gaze fixed straight ahead. "The fact remains that Antenor, Laocoon, and Tumaeus are all dead set against launching an offensive. They believe the army should focus on defending Troy's walls, and I cannot see any of them changing their opinions."

"We must try," I repeat, seeing no other option.

And we must start with Tumaeus.

Aeneas does not reply, but his doubt is as palpable as this unrelenting heat.

Before long, we reach Tumaeus's house. When I knock on its ornate door, a distinctly unpleasant expression comes over Aeneas. He rubs his bloodshot eyes as if seeing me for the first time. "It has occurred to me that we are not suitably dressed for the occasion."

And by *we*, he means me. I stare down at the flesh-colored tunic that could easily double as a tablecloth. Or perhaps a galley's sail. The garment I now live in because nothing else is comfortable.

"Has Tumaeus's wife not borne him any children?"

"She has." Aeneas breaks my gaze, but the lines around his mouth remain pinched. "Three girls, I believe."

"Then he has seen a woman on the verge of birth and knows how little patience she has for pointless fineries," I say more curtly than I mean to. "Not when her feet are too swollen for sandals."

At that, the Dardanian looks down at my bare toes, wiggling in the dirt like five overfed piglets. He releases a faint sound that resembles a wheeze.

"Out with it, Aeneas."

"It is just . . . how well do you know Tumaeus and his Harsa?"

"About as well as I'd like to know the Achaeans' guard dog Cerberus."

Aeneas seems to choose his next words carefully. "Tumaeus is an Old Blood from a family that made the mistake of entrenching themselves in trade with the Hittite Empire. It gives Tumaeus's shady business dealings with our powerful neighbors a stink no temple sacrifice can mask. The Old Blood are unforgiving about such things. It has made Tumaeus insecure and thus highly sensitive."

"Meaning?"

"He might take your casual appearance as a slight to his status."

"You seem to know him well." It pleases me that in choosing Aeneas as my ally, I have chosen a man who considers every angle before he acts.

"Not personally, but that doesn't mean he won't presume everything about both of us before we even walk through his door." Aeneas releases another long exhale. "Some of us are judged more harshly than others, Harsa. Which is why even the customs that seem silly or shallow matter."

. The door opens before I have time to consider the wisdom of Aeneas's words.

Kohl-lined eyes widen in shock that is about as authentic as the Phoenician purple tint to the woman's tightly curled hair.

"Harsa Andromache," gasps the finely dressed woman who must be Tumaeus's wife. Behind her, three adolescent girls stand at their looms. Two send us scowls while a third stares blankly out a window, seemingly unaware that she has visitors.

"Good morning, Harsa Kalawashi," Aeneas begins with stiff politeness.

But I have no time for pleasantries. Not when serpents in the heavens and shadows haunting the earth seem to scream that this war is reaching its apex.

"I've come to speak with your husband." I step into the cool home at the woman's signal. The two animated daughters follow my movements with ardent curiosity. "I sent a servant yesterday to let Tumaeus know I would be calling on him."

"My apologies, Harsa Andromache. To my knowledge, we received no such messenger." Kalawashi's smile is sharp. "Or maybe our servants simply forgot to mention it."

Lies. And not even clever ones.

"Is your husband available now?" I ask, wishing for a chair and one of the sweetcakes Bodecca hasn't had enough honey to make in months.

"I'm afraid not. He has gone to meet with the council."

"So early?"

"They have much to discuss these days," says the woman demurely. As if this might be news to a Harsa strange enough to live beyond the Citadel's walls by choice. "Perhaps you can find him there."

I force my jaw to relax. She knows as well as I that admittance doesn't come so easily.

"Or maybe the Harsar can deliver your message?" Kalawashi opens her door wider for Aeneas, though she might as well slam it in my face.

"Seeing that you made the journey up that ghastly hill, can we at least offer you some refreshments?" Kalawashi continues. "Many expectant mothers say melon is the only thing sweet enough to coax a babe from its cocoon." The look on her round face is alarming—shrewd and placid at the same time. She gestures to a table behind her that somehow overflows with fruit in the midst of famine. My mouth waters despite myself.

Ever courteous, Aeneas bows to the Harsa and her daughters. "Thank you, but we will trouble you no further."

"Of course, Harsar. You are a busy and important man." Kalawashi shrugs carelessly. "Yet it will not be said that Harsa Andromache graced my threshold and left without a gift for Troy's future prince. Or princess, if the gods are as kind to you as they have been to me."

As she turns toward the fruit platter, she gives me another razor-edged smile to soften the obvious dig. When Kalawashi returns, she is holding a melon as large as my middle. The woman thrusts it into Aeneas's arms.

"Long live Prince Hector and his Harsa," she says before slamming the door.

"ANDROMACHE. WHAT HAPPENED?" Open arms reaching for me, Hector crosses the room in three large strides.

"Melon," I groan, tossing the fruit onto our bed before I follow.

A small smile rises in the corner of Hector's mouth as he lies down beside me, resting a warm hand on my middle. "I take it your visit to the Citadel did not achieve the desired outcome?"

"It did not."

When I appeared before the Five, the men looked upon me like pregnancy was a condition that was catching. They would not permit me to stay for the council session, no matter what tales of sky serpents and ill omens Aeneas used to try to persuade them.

Hector sighs. "There is only one way to redeem this day, then." He grins as he slips down the length of my aching body, pausing at my feet. They are covered in dust, but he doesn't seem to care. His firm grip as he massages each toe sends a warm tingle up my legs.

"Hector, I can't . . ."

For I fear I've become immobile like the melon I so resemble.

"Your mind is in the latrine, my *alev*." Hector switches to the other foot and rubs the throbbing sole. Deliciously hard. "I've had a tiresome day myself. I wish to ease your burden."

A small whimper escapes my lips as both pleasure and pain spread through me.

"Did your cousin make any inroads with the council on his own?" I ask once I'm able to speak. Aeneas has surely reported back to Hector by now. After I left the man sputtering apologies over the council's dismissal, I spent hours working in the bathing house to dull the sting of the slight.

Thankfully, there were no new bodies to prepare for the pyre, but getting down on my hands and knees to scrub bloodstains from the stone helped to expel my frustrations. And perhaps move the child within me if Kalawashi's sweeter remedy does not take.

"You can ask him yourself," Hector says. "I've invited the allied captains here for a war council."

"What? Why?" I try shooting up from the bed, but my infuriating belly makes that impossible. How many more actions will feel impossible going forward, after my arms cradle a newborn instead of a bow?

Yet new ways of being will appear in their place.

The unbidden thought is just the kind of comfort Helen would offer if she were here. A woman born to be a mother. A woman who was everything I am not.

"You're like a poor turtle washed up on shore." Hector laughs heartily as I flop backward onto the pillow again.

I smile up at him. "Careful. I've heard the female turtles are not only larger, they also have the sharper bite."

"No doubt," Hector chuckles. "The gods do not make mistakes."

And that is all it takes. One reminder of the higher duties he is bound to, and a thousand worries overtake the laughter in his chestnut eyes. "What is it, Hector?"

"Rhea came back to the city while you were away."

Grief at having missed her stabs me between the ribs. "And what news did Rhea bring?"

Hector's face falls. "It is Diomedes . . ."

He proceeds to tell me what Rhea reported and what the Achaeans are plotting. How they would use Diomedes to draw out our chariots, only to dismantle them. How they would slay Troy's horses without mercy.

"But for what?" This is not how Achaeans fight. I extend my hand so Hector can pull me up from the bed.

The answer comes to me with the rush of blood to my head.

Siege.

Perhaps not yet, but they are preparing for it. The Achaeans would use our defensive strategy against us, barring us behind our gates once and for all. Until we either surrender or starve. And the first phase of their plan to close in on Troy's walls? Destroy the other safeguard we possess that they don't—a superior chariot fleet.

Standing eye level with Hector now, I can see there's no need to tell him what I've surmised. He already knows what the Achaeans intend to do. He knows because it's exactly what *we'd* do if we were them. He also knows there is only one way to prevent this siege from coming to pass, and it is the last thing the unchanging council wants to do.

Unleash the full strength of Troy's army, down to the last man.

My hands run across my belly, as if the touch might erase this new and unfortunate development. I turn to the cradle positioned beside our bed. Empty. Waiting. Its smooth wood carved and then sanded, over and over again by Hector's hand.

How does one *begin* to raise a child in a world that is crumbling, let alone prepare him to rule what might well be rubble?

Hector's brow furrows and he finally speaks. "What are you thinking, my *alev*?"

That the king and his unimaginative council can never be counted upon, even if we manage to gain the allegiance of the Five.

That if I hope to spare my child and the rest of Troy's children in the long run, I must do what I have always done—make an inroad of my own.

But I cannot say this to Hector now. Not when his mind must remain fixed on thwarting this underhanded scheme and the siege meant to follow on its heels.

"This plot reeks of Odysseus. I'm thinking that if Agamemnon is willing to let his most gifted strategist take the lead, then the king of Ithaca will no longer find it necessary to move under the cover of night."

Which means we have nearly run out of time to initiate first.

Hector nods. "Rhea did report that Odysseus is up to something."

I grunt. "When is he not?"

"Yes, but she says it feels different this time . . . bigger."

Then a large-scale attack must be imminent.

Hector gives me his arm. "Come. We will break this news to our captains."

Holding one another, we head downstairs, where Bodecca has managed to scrounge up enough lentils to serve a heavily spiced stew. The allied captains fall silent as we enter the dining hall. Their sweaty faces glisten and their eyes travel up my length. What I find in their perplexed expressions has me lowering my gaze.

Ah, yes. The bare feet and sweat-stained tablecloth. A far cry from finely woven gowns and the breastplate of Queen Penthesilea, the Amazon garb I once wore to Hector's war councils. It doesn't help that my husband is, despite the heat, wearing his best lion-skin cloak over bare shoulders.

Even still, the hazel eyes of Sarpedon, captain of the Lycians, flash as I take my position by Hector at the head of the table. The prince of Troy wastes no time telling his men the reason for this impromptu gathering.

"Why the alarm? Odysseus has tried such tactics before," Hippothous says, swirling his wine cup as he smirks. The Pelasgian captain no longer questions every decision I make. Though he pointedly ignores my requests that he wear more than a short kilt that does little to cover the gifts the gods gave him. "As I recall, it did not work out so well for him."

"Yes, but Odysseus's last attack was made with only his own men," I say. "Given the damage caused by a handful of Ithacans, imagine the cost if he had the full strength of the Achaean army at his back."

All movement around the table ceases.

I study each of the men before me. Next to Sarpedon is Akamas, his former Thracian rival who now sits so close, the two warriors could share a dinner plate. On the other side of the table are Aeneas and Pandarus, brothers in an even truer sense, having spent every summer of their youth together on the slopes of Mount Ida. Hippothous is on my left beside

Nhorcys the Strong, who has recovered from burns sustained during the attack on the Lower City. Peirous and Glaucus sit shoulder to shoulder on my right, the oldest and wisest of the group. And seated behind all of us by the cold hearth is Cyrrian of the Two Shadows, Hector's chariot driver and our dearest friend, strumming his lyre like he has no other care in the world.

But I know better. These bonds forged in fire have been strengthened by the recent skirmishes that managed to thwart the Achaean raids, yet we will need even more fraternity for what is to come.

"Why attempt a siege now?" Glaucus asks, breaking the silence.

"The Achaeans grow weary of dying for the sake of that fat pig's honor," Peirous suggests. "As well as his lust for a woman's gold."

"If only it were that simple," I say. "Threats by the Sea Peoples against our enemies' homelands have their eyes drifting west to the kingdoms they left undefended. Their patience grows thin, and Odysseus is seizing upon it to make his final play."

Murmurs move up and down the table as Sarpedon reaches for the last piece of day-old bread, dipping it into what remains of the olive oil. "And what does our Alev plan to do with this information she's learned by her most clever means?"

I give the Lycian a warning glare. Thanks to our successful campaign against the coastal raids, it has become obvious to the allied captains that I must have a spy in the enemy camps. Be that as it may, they must never learn *who* that spy is. If word ever made it to the Citadel that their fate rested in such small hands . . .

Hector gives me a reassuring nod, his full trust bringing on a tightening across my belly. While I also trust our foreign allies, what I am about to say comes with risks. These captains can never fully enter the private chamber Hector and I share with Rhea alone. But perhaps the time has come to open the door to them a crack.

"The Achaeans will not attempt a siege straightaway. Not until they weaken our forces significantly," I explain. "Furthermore, Diomedes has taken the place of Achilles as the Achaeans' most fearsome warrior, but he is hotheaded and fights only for himself. Pandarus's arrow succeeded in wounding him, yet that victory has had an unintended consequence." I turn and give the archer a pointed look. "He is coming for you, Pandarus."

"You are marked, brother," Hector affirms, making it clear we are of one mind. Pandarus's confident expression does not shift, but he nods to show he understands that he is a walking target.

Glaucus breaks the tension yet again. "Then we must use the petulant boy's talent for marking men to draw him deeper into the fray. Where we'll be waiting for Diomedes ten to one!"

"Normally that would be enough, Glaucus." I must tread carefully to avoid revealing details that might expose Rhea. "But we also have reason to believe Diomedes himself will serve as the bait. The Achaeans hope we will use our chariots to run him down, which is when they will spring their trap."

"What kind of trap?" asks Nhorcys, running a hand over the discolored patches of flesh where hair will no longer grow.

"Its exact nature is unclear," I say. "But Odysseus knows that even the strongest wall can be cracked, given enough time and the right tools. Thus, he intends to wipe out our horses and our chariots first, removing the final roadblock to a total siege."

Aeneas clears his throat. "I mean no disrespect to my prince and his Harsa . . ."

"The Alev," Akamas corrects.

Aeneas swallows. It seems there is nothing this controlled man fears more than a fire that cannot be contained, and our morning walk to the Citadel did little to change that. "Troy's chariots are her greatest weapon. Why would we attempt to deflect a major attack without using them?"

I study Aeneas closely. The man who questions my judgment is not a swindler like Sarpedon or an agitator like Hippothous. He is a man who has been given much responsibility and yet fails to believe he was born worthy of it . . . though he will shed his last drop of blood trying to *prove* that he is.

"A fair point. Only Troy's chariots are not her greatest weapon." I look to the rest of the men. "This trap may be a grave threat to our city and thus a danger to your homelands. But perhaps it is also an opportunity. *Now* is the time to demonstrate what we've been training for. And we start by breaking the Achaeans' morale while all of Troy looks on."

I can feel Hector stiffen beside me. He meets my eyes with a gritted smile for his captains, though his eyes scream, *Caution, woman.*

"Ever since the fighting on the battlefield resumed, it has been the same old song," I continue. "Meet the Achaeans on the open plain so the best of our warriors can get in their licks from the comfort of their chariots. Then when we force the enemy back, instead of pressing onward to their camp, we retreat to our own walls."

Sarpedon, Akamas, and several other captains nod in understanding. It is a tired approach to warfare that turns common foot soldiers into dispensable fodder, just so the most powerful heroes can put on their show.

"I believe this strategy is known as *defense*," Aeneas says dryly.

"And after ten years of stalemate, it is working brilliantly," I return in kind.

A few men smirk, and the Dardanian's neck reddens in spite of his stone-cold face.

But my battle is not with Aeneas. I clear my throat. "The council must *see* that unleashing Troy's might is the only way we'll send the Achaeans back to the crumbling cities they call kingdoms."

And if we don't, the council will only realize their mistake when it is too late. For if Troy falls, there will be nowhere to flee. No neighbors to take in our refugees. The gate to the Dardanelle Straits will have been breached. Then there will be nothing to stop the Sea Peoples from sailing all the way to the Baltic Sea, razing every settlement as they go. Hector releases a slow exhale. One that tells me he is about to issue a warning meant for my ears alone. I suspect it will be the high priest Laocoon's stately voice I hear behind his words, urging Hector to remain close to the walls the gods bid us to defend with the last drop of Trojan blood.

To my mind, the reality is less lofty and smells more of earth than incense.

"Let us first save our horses to avoid a siege," Hector says measuredly. "Then we can discuss launching an offensive. The Lower City still has vulnerabilities from the last attack. Our priority must be defending it by avoiding Diomedes's trap at all cost."

"Forgive me, Alev, but how do you know the information you have received is even reliable?" Pandarus asks.

I open my mouth, scrambling for some excuse that will protect my source. "I have good reason to—"

"It does not matter. I will slay Diomedes, son of Tydeus." Aeneas's somber voice fills the chamber like a ceremonial gong. He turns, placing a hand on Pandarus's shoulder.

It is a small gesture, but one that allows me to read their bond in a new way. For it is a bond that goes beyond the sharing of an idyllic boyhood. If Aeneas feels barred from the innermost circle of the Citadel because he is not Trojan born, then it is Pandarus who stands beside him outside the gates.

"No."

The word drops like a stone, forcing all eyes to the head of the table, where Hector presides. "Like Andromache said, we cannot let ourselves be drawn into the Achaeans' trap." My husband turns to Aeneas with softening eyes. "Patience, cousin. We will fight this battle as *one* and guard our weakened walls above all else."

This is truly Hector speaking now, not the council that tries so hard to turn his head. For only Hector would care to defend what is vulnerable and still in need of repair instead of what is already strong. His devotion to all levels of his city are why his men love him. Why *I* love him.

But love does not win wars.

A faint tightening seizes my middle again.

"Diomedes cannot keep breathing!" Aeneas says with uncharacteristic rancor. Again, I glimpse the frantic wildness I saw outside the High Temple when he spoke of serpents and angry gods.

"Do not underestimate Odysseus," I say, hoping to redirect Aeneas's frustrations back to their proper source. "We cannot send our chariot fleet charging onto the plain after Diomedes. No matter what happens. That is what he *wants*, and it would be a grave mistake to give it to him."

Aeneas straightens like I've issued a direct order. One he disagrees with vehemently. "You speak as if you know Odysseus personally."

The silence that falls over the hall is stifling. In the echo of discomfort, I hear what these warriors are really asking. Our allies, men I have fought so hard to unite, want me to reveal where my information is coming from. If this were the King's Council, they would have pressed me to the wall until I named my source. And then they would feed her to Odysseus's pigs in the vague name of some greater good.

"I know men," I say simply. "Do any of you have the stones to deny it?"

"No. But some of us have larger stones than others."

Sarpedon's wit is both reliable and contagious. A mirthful murmur cuts through the weighty atmosphere.

But Aeneas's face still simmers with the anger of a man who has been trained from birth to subdue his passions. At least until there is a spear in his hand. "Then enlighten me, Prince Hector. How do we protect Pandarus from our enemy's most proficient killer? Or is *bait* how you regard a lifelong friend to Troy?"

Cords stand out along Hector's neck. His eyes flit between Aeneas and Pandarus. Does he fail to see what I can so clearly? That Aeneas's resentment isn't directed at Hector, whom he loves. It is aimed at King Priam, who has always treated the Dardanian captain like a Trojan imposter. If Aeneas thinks we view Pandarus as expendable, then he must wonder if that is also how we view him.

Before I can mediate this rising tension, Hector steps out from behind the table and marches toward his cousin. Aeneas rises from his seat in turn. As the two men stand chest to chest, it becomes undeniable just how similar they are. These two descendants of Ilus, founder of Troy, are the same height and have an eerily similar build. Though Hector has more charisma and manages to crack an occasional grin, the gods could not hope to find two more loyal sons.

The trouble is, there may only be room for one of them in this hall.

Hector's fists clench at his sides. But in the very next breath, his hands open. Raising his right arm, he grips Aeneas's shoulder. Just as Aeneas did to Pandarus a moment earlier.

"No one is bait, Aeneas. Every man here *is* a friend to Troy. But as a friend, he is free to stay and free to go." Hector pauses, his earthen eyes holding up the stone walls of Aeneas's gray. "Diomedes will mark Pandarus. There is nothing we can do to stop that, but we can make him come *to us*. To bring Diomedes down, all of our best fighters must overtake him. Not one man fighting on his own."

Sarpedon meets my gaze again, and for once there is no hint of ardor dancing in his eyes. "Do you agree, *Alev*?"

I feel another deep fluttering, one that seems to announce everything I long to say but never will. Not with our most trusted men looking to Hector for leadership that has already been questioned by Aeneas, his right hand. Leadership that, regardless of the affectionate titles these captains give me, ultimately comes from Hector, prince of Troy and commander of her army.

Hector and I have much to discuss behind closed doors, for this opportunity the Achaeans are giving us cannot be wasted. If Odysseus senses there is a spy in the camp like Rhea has claimed, then we are running out of time. The trajectory of this entire war must change. We need to move. *Now.* Before the Sea Peoples visit our shores and rival the Achaeans in their raids. Before the serpent rules the entire sky and every kernel of wheat has shriveled beneath the Anatolian sun.

We cannot use our men as bait, but Odysseus's trap is still our chance to silence the council and take this battle back to the beaches. Back to where it should have been put to rest ten years ago.

All of this I will say to Hector in the privacy of our chambers. Until then, I have little choice but to offer up the first lie I have ever spoken to the captains in my charge.

"Yes. I agree."

3

CASSANDRA

I STARE UNBLINKING at the door of my tower.

It stares back.

Wooden. Heavy. Locked from the outside by order of the woman who bore me. By the father who loved me until he came to know me.

As if love were a box that could be opened and closed.

As if I had any choice in the matter.

Strange child, they called me. Back when I was a small girl and the things I saw were mere sketches layered over the world that shone through my eyes. Helenus couldn't see them. Not until I gripped his hand and showed him. At first, my twin was as eager as I to watch the colors dance. But slowly, slowly he began to pull away. Too frightened by the shapes he saw moving in my vision.

The shapes never scared me. Neither did the Light. I would marvel at the pictures it made. I would babble my delight to anyone who would listen, and then I'd watch as their expressions changed. From indulgence to confusion. Amusement to discomfort.

So too did change the names they called me.

Gifted became *Grotesque*.

Charming became *Cursed*.

Strange became *Broken*.

All these things and more the world will never know. Truths interwoven with lies. Lies spun out of truths until they were indistinguishable. Until there was no room left in the tapestry for *me*.

Strange girl, they said, and so I am. So *we* are.

Trapped.

Inside the prison of my head.

Inside the cage of this room.

At least, that is what they say.

I take a single step toward the door. A sharp pain spears my abdomen, sending ripples down my legs. My breaths are jagged slashes in the silence. I wait for it to pass before I take another step.

Roots sprout through my feet straight down to the floor. The Hawk cries out. His wings blossom in my chest in answer to the call of the wind.

Fly, the wind howls. *Fly. Fly. Fly!*

Away from this tower. Away from the ache in your guts, and the door blocking your way, and the death bird smiling at you from the corner wearing a skull's face.

I look sideways, and there it is.

Lurking. Leering at me with a smile that is also a grimace. Teeth and bone and gray flesh crawling with maggots.

I close my eyes, but still, I see it. Squatting as it has done every day for nine cycles of the moon. Taunting me from the corners of my cage before it lights out of the window, climbing the night on black wings, circling my tower three times before coming to rest on a single roof in the second innermost circle of the city. My Hawk has tried to fight it off, but the Raptor always melts into the shadows before he can reach it.

The Raptor stirs again in the corner of my vision. It has been sitting there for hours. Ever since the Serpent appeared in the sky.

The last piece. The final sign.

Events set into motion that can no longer be stopped.

The only question now: Who will strike first?

I take another stumbling step forward, and the Raptor makes its move. It streaks across the floor of my chamber and throws itself into the air. Black robes sprout into feathers as it falls. Landing on that roof I know well, for I love the people it shelters. People too consumed by the threats outside to see death hanging by taloned feet above their very heads.

The death raptor screams as it has every night. But unlike every night before, it does not remain on the roof where I can watch it just as it watches me. Tonight, the shadow melts. Black blood pouring down golden walls. Seeping into the stone of the house it has marked.

Hector's house.

Pain draws a low groan from my lips.

Let me out! Let me help you! I do not fear the pain. The Fury's scream echoes up the well inside me.

She would bear this walk for me if I let her. She would take my pain and turn it into rage unleashed upon the world. As she did the morning the false god paid a visit to my chamber and the Fury drove him out, knife in hand. Red blood spattered upon white sheets.

Even now, the blood sings to her.

Let me out! she screams. *Let me right all the wrongs done. Let me carry this for you!*

She would carry it. For me, they all would. The Crone. The Wraith. The Child. The Hawk. Every shade that lives within me would gladly spare me now. As they have spared me since I was a sad, broken girl who first stumbled upon the secret well inside her.

The place where they live.

Where did you come from? I asked on my second visit to the well.

We were forged in blood and born of pain, the Crone rasped. She lifted her chin, and I knew.

My blood. *My* pain.

You are not alone, said the Child, taking my hand in hers. *Not anymore.*

We can bring you safety, added the Crone. *We can be your shade when the light gets too bright. But only if you welcome us.*

As much as they frightened me, the choice they offered was the only one within my power to make. And so I did. One by one I let them out of the well. They have been my shield against a world that has forsaken me. They have been my friends when those who were meant to love me left me here to rot.

But this walk I must make is one I can trust to no one. Not even them.

I fix my gaze upon my brother's house as memories swirl through my head.

Hector as a young man, sneaking me honeyed nuts from the pockets of his robes.

Lifting me onto his shoulders. Running. His arms holding mine up to the sun so that it felt like we were flying.

Sitting at my side, listening to the stories that made the others run from me. Hector never ran. He always stayed, and it was never duty that bound him fast, but love.

Hector.

Troy's hope. Andromache's husband. Favorite son and soon-to-be father. Before he was any of these things, he was my brother. A boy who offered secret smiles that felt like treasures. A protector who would have guarded me against every threat, if only he could see it. But he couldn't see the threat that broke me. Just as he cannot see this one. But I do. I see it.

For Hector, I face down the door again.

Another step. Another wrench in my guts. It's not the pain that stops me. It isn't even the lock on my door. No, I've walked out of this tower many, many times, but tonight is different. For the first time in twelve years, tonight I must leave this tower as myself.

The Crone. The Child. The Fury. The Wraith. The Hawk. They have all taken their turns to spare me from what lives outside. They have each protected me from the man who walks my father's halls. Twelve years, and still the thought of him shatters me. Slivers and fragments of pottery and bone.

I can't face him, but I also can't hide here. Not anymore. The Raptors have seen to that.

The sharpest pain yet racks my stomach. A stream of green bile pours out of my mouth to spatter the stones beneath my feet.

Now. It has to be now, the Crone commands.

Quick. It must be quick, the Child whispers in my ear.

The Wraith merely points.

Yes, I know. The path I must take. The task to accomplish and how it should be done. So much knowledge. So much truth, and what good has it ever done me? What value are my visions and my warnings if nobody else can hear them?

I grab fistfuls of hair and slam my back against the wall.

No man will ever take your word over mine.

How true the words the false god spoke to me that morning have proved themselves to be. No man has ever believed me. No man except for one. And if I don't find a way to leave this tower, the raptors will rend the soft flesh of everything he loves, picking my brother clean.

I bite back a moan, cross the last few feet to the door, and rap my knuckles against the wood. Three sharp knocks followed by two thuds.

The door opens to reveal the dark silhouette behind it.

The Wraith cries silently at the bottom of my well at the sight of the grizzled man. Like the Master of Keys, the Wraith lived in this tower long before I came here. She belongs to the Master just as he belongs to her. And though we've never spoken these words out loud, I think a part of him has always known it.

It is why he guards this tower. Why he helps me now.

He ignored her voice when she still had one. Blocked his ears to her words when they might have made a difference, and as penance for this sin, he now lives in silence. It's through those silences that we have learned to speak.

The Master of Keys watches me with broken eyes. I want to smile. To give him some comfort for the Wraith's sake, but it is whispered in the streets that my smile could make Cerberus cower.

One step. Two steps. Three. I pause on the stairway with both palms pressed against the wall.

Tap. Tap. Tap. My knees knock. The world is still, but somehow, I am spinning.

Pressure on my shoulder. Warmth.

I look into the face of the Master of Keys. His arm is a bridge, connecting me to solid ground. I stare at it in wonder. His hands. Calloused. Covered in age spots and white limestone dust from drawing.

I raise my eyes to the drawing on the walls. A maze of twisting lines and doors leading to darkness. Circles within circles. Rings stacked upon rings. Each one with its own guardian. Some are clearer than others. Hector before the Scaean gate. Priam and Hecuba in the Citadel. Laocoon and the council before the temple of lies. On and on they go, but none of them are the ones that I am searching for.

A Weaver trapped with her loom, her outline gently scrubbed out by sorrowful hands until only the barest traces remain.

My eyes skate across other lines. Thicker than the rest. New.

A small shadow scurrying across the plain.

A Shade wandering Troy's walls.

A lone Hawk sitting on a tower.

Language of shapes and lines the Master of Keys and I share just as we share the Wraith. I find the figure I am searching for and rake a bloody nail across it.

The Master of Keys nods. I hold out my hand, and he places something on my palm.

An iron key.

I reach into the satchel hidden under the folds of my robe. A curved edge of the sharpest bronze flashes in the moonlight. I grip the knife in one hand, the key in the other. I start down the stairs.

Halfway to the landing, the pain strikes again. So sharp. I press my shoulder into the cold stone to keep from tumbling face-first.

Careful, whispers the Crone deep in the well inside me.

But not too careful, giggles the Child, deeper still.

The Wraith watches and the Fury rages, and the Hawk banks in the clouds as I pick myself up and descend to the main palace.

After all this time, my feet still know the way. They skip down the wide corridors. Dodge behind the columns and across the offering tables like the specter some claim me to be.

Every moment that passes, the pain inside me grows stronger. The shadows deeper.

If I don't hurry, soon it will be too late.

Hallway after hallway.

Corridor after corridor.

Door after door, until at last I find the one that I need.

I take out the key. It slides easily into the lock.

The door swings open. I walk into a room flooded with moonlight. In the far corner, a lone figure stands at a loom, weaving many shapes.

Shapes I have already seen once tonight, drawn by a broken man's hands.

The woman turns. She eyes the open door behind me with longing before she rises. Fear floods the room. I open my mouth, and then I force myself to speak in the voice I rarely use.

Mine.

"Come, Helen. It is time."

4

HELEN

"CASSANDRA?" I STARE at the young woman standing in the doorway. Gate to my prison—the weaving hall that was once mine, yet that no longer exists to those outside it. Just like the woman concealed within. "How?"

It is, I suppose, a ridiculous question to ask a prophetess.

Yet saying the word out loud may be the only way to assure myself I am flesh and blood, not the ghost they all believe me to be.

For I have heard their cries on the wind. A city mourning the many dead that fell the night Odysseus's fire arrows rained down. A city that mourned *me*.

Andromache's rich alto rose above the rest as she sang her lament for a woman who would be forgotten long before I ceased wandering these halls. Once again a prisoner in my own palace, the chains of invisibility bound even tighter than the fitting of my old veil.

The unfortunate thing about being dead is there is no hope because no one has reason to look for you.

No one, it seems . . . until now.

Behind Cassandra, the door slams before I can get a glimpse of the corridor beyond. Paris draped the passageway in deep blue textiles. No one would dare disturb his shrine to his dead wife, one that will hold me in its dark cocoon until . . . what?

"The serpent has come to swallow the stars," Cassandra intones. "It is time, Helen."

Time for what? The war wages on, that much I know, for I have heard the clash of metal on the wind. I'd hoped that once the Achaeans thought me dead, they would finally sail home, but that was foolish. My dowry treasure remains within Troy's walls, and that has always mattered more to Menelaus and his brother than me. Agamemnon will never abandon the Kesik Cut until every piece of blood gold is his. "The world has changed," says Cassandra. She is right. Yet the only person in this palace who seems to recognize the change is Paris, who never ceases to remind me of the seafaring spies he has hired. Men who bring him reports of what is happening in the lands of Troy's rivals. The old days of strong palaces that lord over the fates of those tending their fields are dying as rapidly as the overworked land. The coffers of Mycenae and Sparta were nearly empty when I left them years ago, and now those debts are bottomless. Whatever slander Menelaus and his brother may spread about my role in causing this war, the truth will be revealed by circumstance soon enough.

The Achaeans need new sources of wealth and even better sources of trade.

They need the vast array of minerals buried beneath the Anatolian earth.

They need *Troy*. Along with the gateway to the east she guards.

"You did not know it when you came to our shores," Cassandra says, inching toward me, "but you know it now."

I nod. Ten years ago, I wove my guilt into elaborate designs until my fingertips went numb. Now those fingers tingle with the promise of something new.

Cassandra smiles.

It is strange to stare into the eyes of another who sees the truth, however unnerving those eyes may be.

She knows that I carry no guilt for this war and never did. If the Achaeans had not left their shores, uniting against a common enemy in the process, the farmers and craftsmen who fight for them now would have countless causes for insurrection back home.

These are the spinning thoughts I have had so much time to weave.

Cassandra's lips stretch farther, as if she can see the threads pulling together in my mind. I wait for the face of the Fury. For the Wraith. For an expression that is mad or sinister or at least explains what she is doing here. How she knew *I* was here—alive, but silenced. As I have always been. Yet for once, the face Cassandra wears harbors no outward signs of inward torture.

She takes another step into my hall. Then another. When she is standing directly in front of me, Paris's sister does something she has never done. At least not in kindness. Or as herself.

She touches me.

An icy hand runs along my cheek. My heart beats rapidly as Cassandra tries on another expression I do not recognize. She seems amazed. Perplexed, even.

I do not blame her. Not after the portrait painted by Paris's fists, one revealed to all of Troy at last spring's Festival of the Divine Twins.

Those cuts and bruises have long healed, but my hair remains shorn, barely grazing my chin. I flinch as Cassandra reaches for a thick plait, gently tucking it behind my ear.

"Poor, poor Helen."

Tears prick my eyes. "He . . . he has not laid a hand on me. Not since . . ."

Since the day the Lower City walls, along with the small alliance I fought so hard to build, went up in smoke.

It is the hardest part of being trapped here again. Almost as disturbing as when Paris returned to the Lower City to find me as flaming arrows rained down. I will never forget the look of animal fear on Paris's soot-streaked face as he pulled me from that burning building. Not fear for himself . . . but, inexplicably, for me.

As if he truly cared.

Cassandra arches a thin brow. "He knows you are no longer a victim, but rather a threat that must be contained."

I suppose it is something Cassandra and I have in common.

Yet it is also the truth, one I cannot fully explain. Throughout the days and nights I have languished here like a ghost, Paris has not put one finger on me. Not in lust and not in wrath. If he visits me at all, the only thing he does is watch me as I weave a new design. It is as if I have become his personal goddess whose existence is known to no one else, this empty hall his private temple.

"Please say what you came here to say, Cassandra," I whisper. "He will return soon. He must not . . ."

"Come. It is time," Cassandra says again.

Anger at her cryptic speech swells within me. "Time for *what*?"

"He needs you."

A frail bird flutters in my chest, fanning the flames of frustration. *"Who?"*

"You already know." Cassandra grabs hold of my arm. Her pale skin feels warmer now, pressed against the delicate blue veins inside my wrist. "You have made greater sacrifices for him than this."

Memories swirl.

A hawk's shrill warning cry of a coming storm.

My veil—stained with my child's tears as my dreams of the life I might have lived caught fire. It all disintegrates into bits of ash that hover above the flames until they are carried over distant mountain ranges by the wind.

Rhea high on a horse. And a baby . . .

Andromache.

Before I can speak, Cassandra seems to shrink into herself, clear eyes turning to crystallized honey. I wait for her face to change. Instead, she stares toward the hills beyond my balcony. As if she can see something far, far away. Getting closer and closer . . .

Familiar footsteps echo down the hallway.

"Hurry. The loom," I hiss.

Cassandra disappears behind my half-finished tapestry without a word.

I position myself in front of it, hands clasped, ready to greet him with the demureness he has come to expect since he saved my life. If I can guide Paris toward the sofa, the spot where he likes to pour out his troubles, he may not notice the feet fidgeting beneath the row of fieldstone weights that hang from the loom.

"Is now a good time?" Paris asks when he enters my hall.

"All time is good when used for a good purpose," I say with a forced cheerfulness, gesturing to the sofa. "What is troubling you, husband?"

Because something is always troubling him, now that he is isolated from everyone. Including the frequent visitor I used to overhear in his rooms next door. A low voice I did not recognize, but that for once was not female. Paris and the stranger had a heated argument several moons ago, and now even that voice has fallen silent.

Which is why Paris visits his dead wife instead. Not for my body or my embrace, but for something that is almost worse.

My confidence. My counsel. My *comfort*.

Paris's rage against me has burned itself out, only to be replaced by a wounded man whose needy moroseness is somehow harder to stomach.

A man who has lost everything. Except for *one* thing.

The mother he longed for but was never given. A woman made entirely for himself that no one else can even see.

Clearing my throat, I turn away from the loom and cross the floor to fetch Paris a cup of wine. He stares into the blackened rubble of the cold hearth. "Is little Aléxandros still unwell?" I ask him cordially.

Paris's son by his servant Clymene arrived a few days ago but weeks early, and the child is a sickly thing. Because Clymene and her mother Aethra are the only ones who know of my existence, they brought the babe to see me right after he was born. I instructed Clymene to drink a tea of fenugreek and blessed thistle to awaken her breasts.

Yet I did not give them false hope.

Clymene, transformed from selfish girl to anxious mother overnight, looked at me with tears in her eyes. From sleeplessness or grief or both. *"Paris has not even asked to see him."*

No. He wouldn't, I thought but did not have the heart to say. Not when Paris lost his chance of taking Troy's throne after Hector was officially named the heir at last spring's festival. Paris no longer needs the boy. Or his bastard's mother.

A sentiment that is only confirmed when Paris waves his hand in the air at my mention of Aléxandros now. He downs his entire cup of wine.

"Diomedes has marked the archer Pandarus for drawing his precious blood." Paris's lips twitch. "When the battle begins at first light, Pandarus and his protector Aeneas will be walking targets." Paris looks at me expectantly, as if I might believe he actually fears for the competent duo.

Out of the corner of my eye, I glance at the small feet that have stopped shifting, trying to think of what response will keep Paris's attention focused on me. He is clearly fishing for something.

I rest a hand on his shoulder. "Creusa. Your poor sister. She must be distraught for her husband."

Paris sneers. "If Aeneas is cut down, it serves him right. Driving a chariot is a step above being a servant."

I nod because agreement is what he expects. "Yet he is a good man and an honorable warrior."

Paris's eyes snap up to mine. "You admire Aeneas, then?"

A warning coils inside me.

"Are he and Creusa not family?" I say with a shrug.

"Family." Paris's laugh is full of scorn. "When have any of them ever treated me as family?" He stares off again, traveling a long road of past grievances.

I try not to stiffen as I follow his gaze. Past my unmade bed. Past the loom where Cassandra holds her breath. Past the balcony and up, up, up toward the Hill of Kallikolone, over which I have watched the strange streams of light. Each night they fell, I begged the Unnamed One—my name for an inner voice I have known since girlhood—to tell me what they mean.

"She told him, you know," Paris says.

I frown. "Who told what?"

"Cassandra."

My body tenses as I will the many voices inside her to remain silent. It takes all my strength to keep from glancing at the loom, the direction Paris's eyes are already moving.

I place myself in front of him, pursing my lips into the slightest pout. "What has your sister done now?"

"It is what she *did*. He told me everything. And he wouldn't lie."

He?

The phantom stranger.

The one I overheard in Paris's rooms right after the Lower City fires. The man Paris argued with who has since left him. Just like everyone else.

"When she was small, Cassandra told Hecuba I was still alive. Alone. Out there." He lifts a hand in the direction of Mount Ida, his face falling as if this betrayal from long ago is somehow fresh. "Even then, they did not search for me. I was never stolen from my cradle like they all claimed. That's only the story she told people. And yet Hector still has the gall to call that harpy *mother*. He answers Hecuba's every demand as eagerly as he grovels at his Amazon's feet. As willingly as he tolerates Cassandra's ravings." Paris shakes his head with mock pity. "It is the love of inconstant women that makes men weak."

He lifts his shining eyes to mine. "A deficiency I am starting to understand."

A chill rips through me. In all the years I have known Paris, feared Paris, *loathed* Paris, he has only spoken of how he was abandoned as a baby to die on the slopes of Mount Ida once. Yet he has never revealed that he wasn't really stolen from the city, or that he believes it was Hecuba herself who got rid of him. All because she had a dream that while her firstborn would be a blessing to his city, her second son would bring about its destruction.

A dream horrible enough to make the queen do something no mother should be able to imagine. If only some faceless friend had not rescued Paris, carrying the infant to the mountain shepherd's hut where he was to be raised. If only that same phantom, a man whose identity Paris has never revealed, had not brought the boy back to the city—once he was old enough to do the damage he was always destined to unleash.

If only . . .

Paris's hand closes around my wrist. Gently. He pulls me down to the sofa, resting his head of black curls on my shoulder. As if I alone might help him sort through the deep wounds his own mother caused.

"You are all I have left, Helen," he whispers, stroking my bare collarbone.

My insides lurch more than if he'd issued his worst blow.

"But there is hope," he says suddenly, lifting his head. "I have reason to believe this war is about to take a turn. The throne Hector stands to inherit will not be worth the precious stone it is carved from." Again, he looks across the room toward my balcony. "The future of Priam's line lies beyond these stifling walls."

He turns back to me with a smile bordering on the delusional. "And *we* must carry it there."

Every muscle stiffens. Paris's face is as earnest as I have ever seen it.

"When that day of reckoning arrives, you must wait for me, Helen. Do you understand? I will come for you. I will *always* come for you, just as I did in the Lower City. Believe me, I am the only person who can guarantee your safe passage." Gently, he takes both of my trembling hands in his. "And *I will*. I promise you that."

The only response I can manage is a weak nod.

Satisfied, Paris rises from his seat, eyes grazing my loom with a fleeting interest that makes my heart stop. "Why don't you weave as often as you used to? You once loved it so."

Another tremble of warning skitters up my spine. "It is . . . with our supplies dwindling . . ." I follow Paris over to the loom so I can redirect him back to the sofa. "I no longer have thread that warrants the quality of the garments you are accustomed to."

Paris smiles and strokes my cheek. "That is a problem I am capable of solving. It seems one positive outcome has resulted from Andromache's free rein over her foreign pets. With the Achaeans no longer raiding our coastline, the Sea Peoples are on the move once more."

He turns to my door, then pauses. "I have an errand, Helen. It may keep me for some time. Do not fret if I don't return until late tomorrow."

As if I ever wait up.

He locks the door after him.

As soon as Paris's footsteps are a faint echo, Cassandra steps out from her hiding place. She pulls me to the balcony, which hangs over the Citadel's most exterior wall built into the rocky plateau. Though the fall would be a long, unmitigated drop, the balcony has the best view in Troy with the exception of Cassandra's own tower. Distant Kallikolone rises to the east and the Aegean Sea waits in darkness to the west, with nothing but an open plain drenched in shadow between.

"It's of no use, Cassandra. The ledge is too high for an escape. And thanks to the wind, it is too far from the city streets for anyone to hear our cries."

Believe me, I have tried both.

Yet when we reach the balcony's railing, Cassandra simply says, "Look."

I follow her gaze down, down, *down*.

Down a fall that would mean instant death to anyone who made the leap. Suddenly, the cliff face begins to move.

Cassandra does not speak as a gate opens far below us, a gate that somehow blends into the wall of the plateau itself.

"The Gate of Ghosts," Cassandra whispers. "Known in Troy by only a few." She gives me a look pregnant with more meaning than this moment could ever deliver. "And now, it is also known by you."

Hooves pound in the distance as a single chariot pulled by a team of midnight horses exits the gate. Galloping toward a plain that will soon be drenched in the fire of the rising sun. And shortly after that, the blood of countless men.

I immediately recognize the dark green cloak the rider wears. I should know it, since it was woven at my loom. The black stallion's head in the middle of the garment was an intricate design that took extra planning and care.

A horse of Troy for a prince of Troy.

Paris spoke of Diomedes and the coming attack, but that is not a fight he or his archers would engage in. So why is he leaving the city alone at this early hour?

"He was not born this way, you know." Cassandra tears at the skin around her dirty nail beds with her teeth. "To make good choices, you must first have good options. Not all the decisions that determine our options are made by us alone. In this one matter, the stallion prince spoke the truth."

I turn, knowing that the sage voice speaking now is one of many that live inside her. "How so?"

Cassandra bypasses my question with one of her own. "Does Paris leave his palace by this hidden gate every night?"

"I, I . . . don't know. He has spoken before of . . . errands."

Illicit trade deals with the Sea Peoples that keep the Citadel alone supplied with rare goods.

"Then the ending is not far off," Cassandra says with a solemn look. "Even as this night of lies marks a new beginning."

I frown. "But you just said Paris—"

"Spoke the truth. Yes. I *did* tell my mother he was alive." Cassandra nods like a strange little bird. "But not so the boy might be brought back home."

Her darker meaning sinks in with the potency of saffron dye.

"Come, Helen. They will be waiting for us." Cassandra turns on her heels and marches toward my chamber door.

Not knowing what else to do, I join her. I rest my forehead against the door's smooth wood. A full breath of cedar I have inhaled a thousand times before. The scent of the bridal bed Menelaus's father gave as a wedding gift. The bed where my Hermione was born, and where I nursed her late into the night. And even further into happiness.

Sacrifices made in exchange for ashes.

"There is no point, Cassandra. It is locked."

And railing against reality does not change it.

Cassandra slowly lifts her hand, revealing the iron key. Her smile promises to banish the darkness from these halls, along with any ghosts who wander them.

We cover our heads and make our way through the Citadel on the heels of the dawn. When we reach the courtyard of the High Temple, Cassandra stops suddenly, golden eyes flitting through columns and over carved stones.

A sound in the distance builds. Has the day's battle begun already?

As it becomes clear the repetitive drumming is a horse's hooves, a look of delight brightens Cassandra's sallow face. She turns to me, clasping her hands. "He has arrived earlier than expected."

"Who has?" I turn in circles.

Before Cassandra can answer, Hector's fire horse bursts into the courtyard, a streak of smoke and tail of flame.

"Atesh! Atesh, come back!"

I recognize the boy chasing the wild stallion at once, a servant in a stable hand's tunic that is most out of place in the Citadel. Rhea's friend Larion.

Cassandra's body goes still, but her head nods, slow and steady. As if all is as it should be. She gives me a small smile.

"The beast has escaped so he can greet his new master."

5

ANDROMACHE

A TRANQUIL SUNRISE in the east meets the massive army marching from the west—a force led by every Achaean leader, save the one Myrmidon who sits in his hut by the sea.

That so many kings have presented themselves in person is itself an affront. A taunt meant to assert that these invaders are so superior to us on foot, they need neither the speed nor the protection of their chariots.

How I long to tell these kings their plot was spoiled by a girl of seventeen summers whose height barely reaches their studded war belts.

My eyes follow the spread of the sun's gold up the Ilium plain. At the other end of the rampart, King Priam stands in the company of Antenor and his cousin Anchises, along with Laocoon and Tumaeus, a man who smacks his jowls like he is chewing something.

"Melon, perhaps," I mutter through gritted teeth.

I stand on this rampart alone, but it is no accident that the Five—minus Polydamas, who is among the ranks below—huddle around the king. Word of my futile trips to the Citadel must have made the rounds. These powerful politicians are here to pressure Hector, ensuring he obeys his king's will. If Priam even knows what that is anymore.

Sweat drips between my breasts as Anchises whispers into one of Priam's ears and Laocoon takes the other. It is a risk for the king to watch the war from the Lower City, in range of an expert arrow and far from the protective rings of the Citadel. But this positioning is the only way for

Priam to exert his control. Which is apparently something he feels he must do.

A flash of bronze and my gaze falls back to Hector. He marches to the head of the line, horse-tail plume swaying as his men form a long but thin barrier along Troy's outermost wall. My allied captains stand in the center with him. Only a handful of chariots sit among the Trojan ranks, since the Achaeans must see a few chariots if they are to believe their ruse is working. Aeneas and Pandarus occupy one, while Cyrrian drives Hector's usual team. Every captain has received the same command: the chariots do not move.

At the rear of the army, near Pyraechmes and his Paeonian archers, Akamas sits on a spotted stallion surrounded by a small team of ten Thracians, also on horseback, slings in hand and leather shoulder sacks filled with stones. On one side of the Thracians, Sarpedon and his Lycians wear their light armor, ready to unleash their speed the enemy. On the other side, Hippothous and his Pelasgian tribes hold their long spears steady. A row of Phrygians stand in front of them, prepared to use their man-sized shields to defend the spear warriors, since the nimble Pelasgians refuse to fight with any of their own.

The expanse between the two armies pulsates in the silence. The potent desire of my allies to launch such an attack after months of deadlock tightens around me like a coil.

My eyes fall back to Hector, basking in his element. Doing exactly what he was born to do. Not just fight, but *lead*.

As the Achaean force moves closer, I can almost smell their confusion on the wind, a gale carrying the stench of sweat beneath unwashed armor. *Why aren't their chariots riding us down? Where are the famed horses of Troy? Why are they just standing there like fools?*

The wind blows hard against the plateau, and the way the dust kicks up between the two armies almost gives the sense the gods are on the move. If that is the case, there is one man from the Achaean line who believes he has been anointed to do their bidding.

Diomedes steps into the swirling dust. He swaggers like a fighter who is good, though perhaps not as good as he believes.

As soon as Diomedes stands at an equal distance between his men and his enemy, he raises his round shield and beats it with the shaft of his spear. Slowly at first. Then faster and faster, until every Achaean behind him has joined in the frenzy, filling the killing fields with a thousand drums and a collective roar. At the signal of Diomedes's raised fist, they fall silent.

Here comes the bait we will not take.

One by one, the allied captains look to the ramparts for reassurance.

All except for Aeneas and Pandarus. They are looking at each other. Aeneas says something to Pandarus, then raises his finger in the air and streaks it across the bright sky. It is a long, slow arc we have all seen.

My breath becomes a dagger in my lungs. There are few things as dangerous as a man who is certain he is obeying the gods.

The first slice of the knife rips through me when Aeneas turns to Priam. The king looks down on the young Dardanian, but I cannot read the older man's expression.

Aeneas, on the other hand . . .

His jaw sets in a rigid line. Rage ripples across Aeneas's face. I see all the warning signs I should have heeded earlier. The months of training for a war that starts and then stalls, then starts again, with little progress being made. Aeneas straining against his leash only to be jerked back by the council over and over, always striving for the honor and respect that should be his birthright.

And now, sky serpents granting signs of certainty from above.

"Aeneas!" I shout over the harsh gale. *Don't.*

If he hears me, he pretends he doesn't. Aeneas turns his back on the king, on Hector, and on me. If the Five will never accept him, then what does his allegiance matter? He has the favor of the gods. Aeneas has marked Diomedes, and he will not let his oldest friend risk a maiming or worse to draw that enemy close.

The sharp snap of the reins ripples from here to the sea. Churning wheels drown what Hector shouts as Aeneas and Pandarus charge toward Diomedes. The Achaean plants both feet firmly on the earth, raising his shield while Pandarus lifts his bow from his dominant position on the chariot.

I grip the wall's weathered stone.

Diomedes drops his shield to the ground, but he does not turn and flee. No, what he's after is leverage, along with the full rotation of his arm.

Fools. You're giving him exactly what he wants!

Diomedes releases a growl as the spear sails through the air, striking Pandarus in his helmet's small gap just below the nose.

An explosion of blood.

I stifle a scream when the wooden spear shaft splinters, iron colliding with bone, the force of Diomedes's direct hit enough to send the archer flying from his chariot.

A sharp pain wrenches through my middle. Pandarus greets the infinite darkness before his body hits the dirt.

Nothing moves across the Ilium plain but another cloud of dust. Pandarus's demise came about so fast that neither army knows what to do. But then Diomedes begins his celebratory strut, moving up and down the red clay like a rooster.

Do not be wooed, Aeneas.

Another rumble of pain has me doubling over. Out of the corner of my eye, I see the council's composure begin to crumble. Of all the men who might defy them, the dutiful Aeneas is the last they'd expect.

They do not know that Aeneas harbors a long-nursed resentment at being undervalued and overlooked. That he will die for Pandarus and his gods without a second thought to what they think.

The council also doesn't know that Peirous snores like a wild boar. Or that Sarpedon adores his mother with a devotion that rivals the cult of Hera.

But I have trained these men, and *I know.*

Aeneas pulls hard on the reins, halting the horses midcharge. Turning the team, he circles back to Pandarus's body and jumps from the chariot, spear in one hand and a broadsword glinting at his hip. The horses, Aeneas's own and two of the finest in Hector's stable, take off toward the Achaean line as soon as their master disembarks.

Aeneas lets them go.

He looks down at the body of his friend for a long moment, arms outstretched like he might gather up the corpse to cradle it. But then Aeneas stops, lifts his spear again, and straddles Pandarus's body.

He waits.

"My king. Please." The plea on the wall comes from Anchises and it couldn't be clearer.

Please send men to save my son.

Priam turns from his cousin as easily as Aeneas turned away from his command.

Across the battlefield, Diomedes boasts of his kill in a manner that does little but betray his youth. But it provides the men around Hector with enough time to stir. Just below the outer wall of the Lower City, Akamas canters his horse to the back of the line. He jumps down beside Glaucus and Sarpedon, who speak to Hector in a flurry of gestures I am close enough to make out. As their voices grow louder, the winds of the Troad carry their words up to the ramparts.

"Are we to just stand here until the Achaeans have circled the entire city?" Akamas points to where Aeneas is crouched over his friend, waiting for Diomedes to try to claim Pandarus's body so he can steal the armor and insult it further. "Aeneas is a man as noble as *you*, son of Priam. And he awaits his death alone. We can spare him, but we must *move*."

Listen to them, Hector. Attack. Only do so without *the chariots.*

All the words I can't say burn up my throat. If I speak, the council will view Hector's defiance as a consequence of my meddling and nothing more.

No. This command must come from Hector. Priam's heir and the ruler of Troy in spirit if not yet in name.

Sarpedon joins his Thracian friend, lean limbs shaking with an anger I've rarely witnessed. "Where has it gone, Hector? That highborn courage you always carried? How many friends of Troy must die for a city that isn't even ours before you'll shrug off the grip of those who watch from cushy thrones? They do not know the stench of sand soaked in the piss of frightened boys. But *we* do. And so does she." He turns and points back to the wall. "Look at her, Hector! *Look at her.*"

Hector's helmet shifts in my direction, but I can't glimpse his eyes. I cannot see if they've been humbled, or if they've ignited with a rage that will sweep through our allied ranks like a wildfire, destroying every bond of unity I have worked so hard to forge.

"Is the Alev and the child she carries worth fighting for? Tell me now, for I've sailed from Lycia to aid you in your cause, leaving my wife and son behind. Not to mention riches that were the envy of our neighbors." Sarpedon opens his arms wide, as if walking in for an embrace. "And I *miss* them, Hector."

The Lycian captain takes a knee. "I long for my family with an ache I pray you'll never know. But to make that so, my men must run to Aeneas *now*. Even as you stand here, waiting until the Achaeans pound on Troy's gates again." Sarpedon rises to his feet and spits into the dirt. "Your precious walls can never claim victory. This war will not be won by hiding. You know it, my prince." He looks to me again, eyes alight. "And *she* knows it best."

Hector's gaze leaves my face as he scans the ramparts, searching for his father. Laocoon says something that causes Priam to shake his head. *Stand firm*, the gesture commands. *Hold the line, son. Let them come to us. Do things as we have always done them.*

My hands clench around a spear of air.

Only this *isn't* how things have always been done.

From the moment the first arrowhead was crafted out of rock, men have used the strengths of their people and the tools of their own soil to protect what is theirs. It is the oldest and most basic way to fight—not for eternal fame or everlasting glory. *Those* are the innovations.

Men fight for what they love. By whatever weapons are at their disposal.

Hector removes his helmet, eyes looking for mine. I already know the turmoil I will find in their endless depths.

This is where Hector's battle must be fought. A battle between Old Blood and new allies. Between loyalty to his father and his wife.

Between what is safe and what is right.

On the field beyond, Diomedes makes his way toward Aeneas. His revelry transforms into a lust for more spilled blood. The rest of the Achaean army marches on his heels, shields gleaming in the sun.

Do it, I tell Hector with everything I have but my words.

Sarpedon rests a hand on my husband's shoulder. "Love demands risk, do you deny it?"

Hector weighs Sarpedon's words. Then he turns and gives Akamas, waiting in the wings, a firm nod. The prince of Troy spins on his heels, pulling two spears from his chariot as he moves through the ranks. Raising the weapons high above his head as he releases a low roar, Hector rallies his men. Until their war cries are loud enough to shake the High Temple.

Scorn rains down from the ramparts where the king and council watch.

There will be a price to pay for this disobedience. But whatever the cost, it has no weight against the loss of Aeneas's life.

For better or worse, Hector has made his choice.

With a loud whoop, Akamas races to Sarpedon. They bang their shields—both marked with the symbol of my burning flame. Akamas grabs Sarpedon by the back of the neck and presses their foreheads together. When he lets go to turn back to his troops, the Lycian lifts his eyes to the wall one last time.

Sarpedon brings a hand to his lips and kisses my signet ring.

The solid line of the allied ranks breaks into smaller units at once. Akamas and his Thracians grab their rock slings. The tribes that follow Hippothous drop their Trojan swords and reach for their spears. Pyraechmes urges his Paeonians to raise a wall of longbows, ready to make a storm of arrows that will assail the Achaeans before Hector begins his charge.

An allied captain stands at the head of each unit, each a man whose name and lineage I know. Each a seasoned warrior who has shut the gaping eyes of a hundred sons, sent down into darkness by his commands. They know what awaits them now, but I have faith they will rally. Because their friend is in need. And because I stand here, hands cradling flesh within flesh, the promise of an actual future. One that will not happen on its own but that must be *taken*.

My allied army advances toward the enemy's line.

How strange to think I was once desperate to stand among them. To fight within their sweaty ranks and die among their numbers. My grip on my middle tightens. There is honor in their sacrifice, but there is dignity in this sacrifice too—a calling that brings order into chaos. Life instead of death.

Not a burden, but a power. One no man will ever know.

The Paeonians release their arrows just before Hector gives the signal, and forty hooves vibrate across the Ilium plain. Out in front, Akamas rides hard toward Aeneas, only a few breaths from Diomedes and his bloody spear. The Thracians' riders are faster than a clunky chariot team, but ten warriors on horseback won't hold off the Achaean army for long. Unless Sarpedon and his troops follow at once, these riders are dead men.

It is a move that requires risking everything for the sake of one. And it will bring the wrath of their fathers and the entire council down upon their heads. But while men owe their fathers honor, they also owe their sons a fighting chance at a future.

Sarpedon and Glaucus raise weapons to the sky before releasing hoarse cries as their charge becomes a sprint, every man behind them adding his own voice. Until there are no more Thracians and no more Lycians. No Pelasgians or Paeonians or Phrygians. There are only *men*.

Fighting for their brother.

When the small cavalry has nearly reached Aeneas, I startle at the sound of a different roar—the howl of angry flames as a wall of fire rips across the open plain.

Odysseus's trap.

My mind whirls through limited possibilities as the picture forms. Our enemies have set fire to an oil-drenched rope and raised it high from a dug trench. If we'd sent clunky chariots like they wanted us to, they would have crashed into the flames, burning horse, warrior, and driver alive.

The Thracian stallions squeal at the blast of heat, but they've too much momentum to stop. Akamas buries his face in horsehair as the beast leaps across the wall of fire at such speed that the tongues must hardly taste the animal's hide. Through the billowing smoke, I see Akamas rise up tall on his nimble horse. The pounding in my chest slows as his men follow the same path, their horses leaping through the flames and over the trench.

Diomedes, seeing that the trap has failed, lowers his head, charging Aeneas like a bull bearing down. Akamas shouts a command and the line of horses breaks in two, half his men darting left and the other half veering right as they encircle Aeneas and Pandarus's body.

Diomedes skids across the dirt in an effort to stop himself as Sarpedon and his foot soldiers sprint toward him. Behind Diomedes, the full might of the enemy army keeps moving.

Then comes the cosmic crash as the two armies collide. It is not the usual game of heroes facing off to fight for personal glory while their troops hang back, waiting for the signal to engage. No, this all-out brawl is something new from the beginning. Every muscle in my core tightens as Hector's helmet disappears into the fray of flying dirt and flashing metal. How many of these men won't return to their homes tonight? Are there even enough river stones in the Scamander to pay the fares for them all?

Ripples of pain shoot across my belly and up my back. I inhale sharply and press both hands against the wall's ledge, my eyes fleeing this battlefield for a new war that is about to begin.

For a few short breaths, I gulp down air before another assault charges through my core with the strength of a thousand men. My eyes squeeze shut. The far-off sound of my moans swirls with the clash of weapons and the cries of dying men, all pleading to their own gods for a quick end. It cannot be a promising omen to be born during such a storm, but there is no stopping it.

Hector's child is here.

6

HELEN

THE FEW OTHER times I have been inside Andromache's home, it smelled of overboiled tea leaves and the rosewater that forever trails behind her.

Tonight, it smells of blood and sweat.

A musty, animal scent that barely prepares me for the moaning creature I will find writhing on a pallet behind a privacy screen made of thin papyrus.

It feels like coming home again.

Eyes of ice widen as an older woman rounds the screen to refill a jug of water. The pottery that falls from her steady hands breaks into a dozen shards.

"Helen," Bodecca gasps. She approaches on wobbly legs. "You've come back."

Gnarled hands trace the blessing of the Mother over me and then, more fervently, over herself. Is this movement a prayer or a banishment? It is hard to tell.

"She has indeed returned, but not from the dead." Cassandra steps in front of me. "Helen is here to help as only she can. This is no time for questions."

Bodecca seems at a loss for words. I don't know the woman well, but I gather this isn't typical. The silence lingers, until it is interrupted by another cresting moan.

"Who is it?" Andromache's voice is saturated in pain. "Who's there?"

"I'll check."

Rhea's small form appears from behind the screen.

She freezes at the sight of me. Time stills with her. And then she *runs*, throwing herself into my arms.

"Helen! How?" The girl's astonishment is sliced in two by a guttural scream.

"*Now.* It must be now, Helen." Cassandra's nostrils flare.

"The full tale will have to wait," I tell Rhea as we move behind the screen. Dread grips my gut as soon as we do. "How long has she been like this?"

Rhea's hands clutch a stack of clean linens. They are as pale as her blood-drained face. "She's labored all morning. But it's only in the past hour or so that she became . . . like this."

"We should have arrived sooner," I say.

The city was so crowded with people heading to the ramparts to watch the battle. Cassandra and I had to move carefully through the streets to remain unseen. Now I regret that caution.

While Rhea presses a cool compress to Andromache's forehead, I pour undiluted wine into an alabaster basin to wash my hands and forearms. The wine stains one of the linens as I dry off, its red mottled fabric making me shiver despite the day's heat. Just the thought of being up to my elbows in blood makes me hesitate.

It has been a long time. Too long.

And yet I know these moans and what they mean.

"Cassandra is right. We must hurry," I say. "She is growing too weary."

Fresh terror sparks in Rhea's eyes. For who would ever think that Andromache, battler of men, might succumb to the fate every woman fears? What Rhea doesn't yet know is that the road to motherhood always demands a little death. One way or another.

A serving girl I do not recognize enters the room. She lets out a startled cry, then backs into the corner, as far from me as possible.

"Pull yourself together, Faria." Bodecca's order is as abrasive as the coarsest salt.

The girl's cheeks do not regain their color. "The stories are true, then. Her shade haunts the city."

"Helen is no more a shade than you are a queen," Bodecca snaps. "Find some nerve, girl, or leave us and free up space."

"It's all right, Faria," Rhea urges. "Helen is alive. She is here to help."

"But . . . but we already have a midwife." The servant girl gestures to Bodecca, who has moved to crouch before Andromache's fluid-stained shift.

"Not the right midwife," Cassandra says, pushing me toward the pallet. Bodecca grunts but does not look up from her task.

Rhea casts me a pleading look. "We're thrilled to see you, Helen, but I . . . I fear your sudden presence may distress Andromache."

She is right. And yet I take a step forward anyway.

With Andromache, it is always the truth.

"We're out of time." Cassandra's eyes dance around the room. Her far-away gaze seems to perceive only the invisible threads that lie beneath and beyond. "This is the work you were meant to do, Helen. So do it."

Work. The lack of it is why Troy's Citadel may crumble even if the city walls stand. Among the Achaeans, kings and queens do not sit in lofty positions of idle comfort. Odysseus is a pig farmer. Menelaus had his vine-yards to tend. And I had my herbs and my midwifery, a knowledge passed down from my mother before me. A divine gift bestowed by the Unnamed One that could be neither demanded nor returned.

You, Helen, must be my hands in a world of hurt.

I turn to meet Cassandra's glare. She nods.

Rhea stands from where she has tried to prepare Andromache for my arrival with a soft word and another cool compress, but neither can relieve the fevered sweat pouring from the woman's face. Nor prevent the shock. Andromache's eyes flash as I remove my veil.

Her expression holds no surprise. Andromache's face is solid stone.

"You." She flops back on a pile of pillows, heaving shallow breaths.

"It is a long story."

"Am I dead, then?" Andromache says on a long exhale. "Is this torture the Underworld?"

"No." I laugh in spite of everything. "We are both very much alive."

Andromache's face fills with a shining relief that says more than words ever could.

"Too bad for me." Another grunt followed by a dozen short breaths. "But good for you."

I reach for her hand as another wave begins to build.

Andromache winces but seems determined to talk through it. "And Paris? He'll see justice for what he—"

"Hush," I say. "There is a more important prince of Troy to concern ourselves with now."

"And if he isn't?" Andromache forces herself up from her reclined position, her eyes red spiderwebs. "Everyone assumes this child will be a son, but last I looked, daughters still walked beneath half the sky."

"And any disappointment you are expected to feel when you hold her will flee as fast as the east wind." I place a hand on her shoulder. "Trust me."

Andromache grits her teeth as another swell pummels her.

Cassandra rocks back and forth, rubbing her raw hands, as if the many pieces of her fractured dreams are coming together in witness to this single moment.

"May I look?"

"Do what you will." As Bodecca stands, she turns to me with a grimaced mouth and says in a low voice, "The babe is stuck. Stuck in a bad way I've seen before. If the child refuses to change positions soon . . ."

The poor woman cannot bring herself to finish.

"Quiet, Bodecca. Ill words bring ill outcomes." Cassandra urges me forward again with eager gestures bordering on the ridiculous.

"There are ways to turn a baby," I say as I crouch between Andromache's splayed legs. What I fail to add is that most of these methods are excruciating—for the mother. My examination confirms that while Andromache's birth pains are strong and regular, she isn't nearly as open as she should be. Her body is fighting this natural process just as it fights against everything else. I rest my hands on her stomach, feeling for the different bulges that tell me how the baby lies.

A thigh . . . a spine . . . and yes, there it is. The head.

"What is it?" Andromache whimpers as she anticipates the agony of another birth pain.

"The baby is turned the wrong way. That is why it's having trouble emerging." I turn to Bodecca and Rhea, adding in a low voice, "And if it *does* emerge, such a delivery isn't without risk."

"Just tell me what to *do!*" Andromache cries.

My eyes scan the room, stopping on a piece of yellow fabric hanging from Andromache's loom. "Cassandra." I give her the command with a single nod.

Like an eager child, the princess fetches me the cloth. Its length is perfect but the weak stitches are too loose. Though that may serve our purposes in the end.

"Andromache, I need you to crouch on all fours and ease yourself over the edge of the bed. No, not like that. Headfirst, so both hands are pressed to the floor with your head hanging in between. Yes, that's right."

Once Andromache is on her knees, I stand on the bed behind her, raising her hips high in the air. With a deep breath, I brace myself as the crest of another birth pain surges through her, the muscles of her quivering arms flexing as she strains to hold up the weight of her rear.

"What are you doing?" She pants before expelling another low moan.

"Try to stay calm." I drape the fabric around the front of her belly, holding one end in each hand behind her to create a kind of sling. "I'm going to twirl this fabric like it is the yarn and you are the spindle," I say in the most upbeat tone I can feign.

With a firm, sifting motion, I lean back while pulling the broad fabric across Andromache's middle, gently rocking her belly back and forth. I pray this movement will be enough of an upset for the baby to flip on its own.

Andromache releases pitiful little noises beneath me, followed by sighs of temporary relief, her splayed hands pressing deeper into the floor as I try to tempt the baby into a head-down position. Rhea watches carefully as I work. All the women do, silent witnesses to a magic as old as life itself.

By the time I'm finished, sweat cascades down my cheeks. "Now, let's see if this child is as headstrong as his parents."

"There's little doubt," Bodecca snorts. She takes one of Andromache's arms while Rhea grabs the other. Together, the two smaller women manage to lift Andromache back onto the bed.

Where she promptly begins to scream.

Like a cat crouching before a leap, Andromache flips from lying flat on her back to a table position on all fours. She arches her spine high into the air and moans.

Back labor.

I press my hands into her hips. Pushing hard like I am kneading bread. "Does that help?"

Andromache does not speak, but she nods. Vigorously. We remain in this position for at least another hour. Me leaning into her back with all my weight whenever a labor pain takes her, and Andromache moaning as she sways from side to side, lost in that faraway realm all women must travel to in order to keep breathing through such an ordeal.

It is good that Hector's wife was trained to be a general. Most of giving birth is a mental game, and usually it is a long one. The pain comes and goes but it can be lived with—it's the exhaustion that leaves a woman without the strength to push and makes widowers and orphans. Yet despite our efforts to coax him, the heir of Troy will not come.

"I can hardly blame him," Andromache says with a shudder during a moment of lucidity. "Who would want to inherit such a miserable kingdom?"

"Any child of yours will be up to the task. Now brace yourself, Andromache. I need to check the baby's position again." I help her onto her back once more. "It will only be for a moment."

When I lift up her shift and feel her belly, my racing heart seems to stop all at once. "He is lying sideways now. I may be able to move him by hand the rest of the way. But we must hurry. Before he drops even further and tries to emerge feet or shoulder first."

"And if he does?"

I swallow what feels like a mouthful of sand. "We can't let that happen."

A flash of fear in Andromache's eyes. "How will you do it?"

I hold up my pale hands. They are still. Steady.

"There could be complications. I may unintentionally break your bag of waters," I explain, knowing she will want every detail. "Or the pressure of my hands could sever the cord and cause excessive bleeding. All the same, we are running out of options."

Andromache is trembling all over now, the way many women do once they have finally delivered. And the fear isn't merely for herself.

"Do what you must."

A small scream escapes me when Cassandra races toward us, holding her dagger high. Andromache crosses her arms over her core like a shield, but Cassandra merely holds the wooden handle of the blade to Andromache's lips.

"Bite down," she commands.

Andromache obeys. Rhea pours olive oil over my palms before she and Bodecca each grab one of Andromache's arms to keep her still. I feel along Andromache's stomach until I find the baby's buttocks on the right side of her body.

Then, I twist. With all the strength of my weaver's hands, I press my weight against her until I can feel the baby turning. Andromache grits her teeth behind the blade as I work her flesh like dough, but she does not cry out.

Something gives under skin pulled taut.

"There," I say after one more turn, smiling with relief. "I think that did it."

I pray I'm right, because when I stand back, the front of my tunic is soaked from the bursting water sac. I kneel in front of Andromache, searching for a good omen between her knees.

My hope sinks to the floor. The baby has turned, but he is lying face up. I know because Andromache has opened fully, and I can feel the soft pink flesh of the cone-like head.

There will be no stopping him.

"What's wrong?" Andromache gapes at me with wild eyes. "I need to push. *Please.*"

"Slowly," I warn. "Very, very slowly."

I do not want to tell Hector's beloved that pushing in this position will be excruciating. Her grimace tells me she can already feel the stirrings of a new and specific pain she has never known.

"Should I get Hector?" Rhea asks. She paces the room helplessly, just like the prince would if he were here.

"No," Cassandra says. "This is our domain."

"And there is no time." I turn my full attention to Andromache as Bodecca's recitations to Hannahanna rise with the burning incense. "I must . . . reach inside. To guide the baby out."

I lick my sandy lips and pray to the Unnamed One for the healer's hands once promised me.

Fighting the urge to bear down, Andromache meets my gaze with eyes cast in iron. "Do it, Helen. Let's see if you can bring us both back from the dead."

7

ANDROMACHE

THIS IS NOT how I want to die.

In a sweat-drenched bed instead of a battlefield. In a state of helplessness. *Weakness.* Not from pain but from utter exhaustion.

"Let go," I hear Helen whisper from far away. "Your body knows what to do. It is a wisdom much older than you are. Surrender to it."

Surrender? I want to laugh, but that isn't possible. My traitor lips release another beastly moan.

In the gasps that follow, Hector's young face flashes before me. So hopeful. So good.

When we were first married, Hector once took me swimming in the Aegean. My mere presence must have upset Poseidon, for the waters grew rough as soon as I entered the sea. A shield of tall waves rose from the black depths. The harder I fought, the deeper they drove me into the rocky seabed. I had to go limp. Let the wall roll over me and carry me up to the sky.

Giving birth is much the same.

"Be pliable, Andromache. Yield. You will find your strength in weakness," Helen repeated like an incantation during the worst of the pains.

"Come back to me," that same voice orders now. I blink as the swirling room sharpens into focus. Helen splashes water on my face and slaps my cheeks. "No more leaving us, understand? It is time to work."

"*Work?*" I gasp, wondering what it is that I've been doing. "But I have no strength left."

Helen cracks a small smile. "That is the way of all births. Deliverance arrives only when we have nothing more to give." She pushes the matted hair away from my face. Her eyes cradle the same timeless wisdom she spoke of earlier, and in this moment, I *want* to trust it. To trust *her*. More than I trust the heart that beats furiously inside my own chest. "You do have the strength, Andromache. And even greater courage. When the next swell washes over you, you must summon both and push Hector's child into this world."

"Hector." My whisper becomes a desperate cry. "I want him! Where is he?"

Rhea stands by my head, ready to pass Helen whatever tools she asks for. It is only when Cassandra appears by the foot of the bed that I realize they've been in this room the entire time. The concerned glance they share does not escape me.

A man in the birthing chamber would be unusual. A prince, unheard of.

"Hector has gone to be with Aeneas," Cassandra says simply.

"What? Why?"

"Quiet!" Bodecca hisses. "You'll only upset her more."

Possibly moved by voices inaudible to the rest of us, Cassandra approaches the bed and grips my hand. "Aeneas was injured. But he will live." Her grip tightens along with her voice. "We will *make* him live." Her eyes land on Helen with a weight even I can feel.

Bodecca rocks back and forth on her feet. The look she gives me is one of unwavering confidence. And faith that I have not yet lost my grip on reality. "I'll fetch your husband."

I want to thank her, but another pain surges. One that threatens to splinter my spine. It's all I can do to plead with my eyes that she be quick.

I am going to die.

"Stop it, Andromache. Remain *here*. With us."

I can't.

Hector's bronzed face. Bent over a cradle made for a child he never thought he would hold. I will never forget how his strong hands gripped the oak stump gently as they carved each bend and curve.

Let him make it in time.

"Andromache, look at me," Helen commands yet again. "Don't even think of saying good-bye."

She grabs one of my knees and calls Cassandra to the other. Rhea presses a damp cloth against my forehead, her own hand shaking as a shudder passes through me. My legs spasm uncontrollably. The herbal smell of the compress makes me want to retch as another yawning groan erupts from my core. Rhea drops the rag and clings to my hand like it's the mane of a horse set loose.

Hector. Please. Hurry.

"Yes, that's it. Don't fight it. Now, as the next wave builds, I want you to use the power of the swell to *push*." Helen holds my gaze with a resolve I've witnessed only in Queen Penthesilea. She forces my knee back toward my head. Eyes widening, Cassandra mirrors the same movement. I can see their lips moving, but I can no longer hear their words over the roar of the sea. All I feel is this unimaginable pressure . . .

It *burns*. But it also promises relief.

Leaning into the spasm, I bear down with all the strength I have left. Moan upon moan. Rising into a scream.

The brutal might of the ocean recedes.

"Good! That's it, Andromache. The head is coming!"

My joy at Helen's words shrivels like a dying leaf. Another wave builds as I gasp for air.

Tired. So, so tired.

"I can't, Helen. I can't do it."

It isn't just the pain. It is this constant pummeling, over and over.

"Yes, you *can*." Cassandra's hot words lick at me like flames. "If you don't push again, everything we've done to reach this moment will have been for nothing."

"You're nearly there, Andromache," Rhea adds, her small fingers tightening around mine. "The baby needs you. You must fight just a little while longer. Fight so your child can live."

"Once more," Helen promises. "Give us one more hard push, and the child you have waited for, *battled* for, will be here."

"He . . . already . . . is . . ." The urge takes me so suddenly, I've hardly begun to push when I feel the baby emerging without any effort on my part, riding a wave of tense muscle and bloodied water that is all his own.

Startled, Helen drops to the floor in front of me. She catches the slippery body as it falls.

There is no crying.

"What's wrong? Show him to me!"

The sound that finally pierces the silence is laughter. Helen stands, her eyes filled with tears. I'm waiting for her to announce that the son our city expects is in fact a daughter—and I find that Helen is right.

I do not care. So long as the child lives.

Relief seizes me at the flash of pink flesh. It's quickly followed by a desperate need to see my daughter up close. I open my arms, too weary to speak.

"I have delivered many babies . . ." Helen says as she places the red, squirming infant onto my bare breasts. "Yet I have never seen a boy with so much hair."

Everything building inside me overflows.

Hector has a son. I have a son.

My laughter bubbles to the surface as I clutch the child against me, hot tears splashing his dark little head. The baby indeed wears a crown of thick curls. A sight that is truly comical, as the amount of hair makes him appear much older. He gazes up with blinking eyes that search eagerly for my face.

My voice.

My heart.

Everything else burns away in an instant. Everything but for the chestnut eyes holding fast to mine. I collapse onto the pillows, my former agony dispersed like ash upon the wind.

The baby begins rooting for my breast. Rhea helps him find it as I fumble over his tiny body, which I'm unsure how to position. Once we figure out the mechanics and the child is suckling, Helen touches my shoulder gently.

"Now you must deliver the afterbirth."

"There is *more*?" My eyes flit from Cassandra to Rhea and back again, but the two younger women are as shocked by this news as I am. "Why did no one warn me?"

The ghost of a smile lingers on Helen's lips. "In the coming days, you will feel as though no one has told you much of anything. Yet that is the way of it. Some moments can never be prepared for. Only lived."

The second delivery is thankfully much easier than the first. After it is over, Helen raises a long purple cord. It's strange to see her pale goddess hands covered in so much . . . humanity. Blood that stains her nails, as my work in the bathing house so often stained mine.

Only this time, it is in the service of life.

The disheveled Helen before me has never looked more mortal, and yet she wears it well. Her clear eyes search the room for the tool she needs.

"Here." Cassandra fumbles through her robes, producing a slim crescent blade.

Helen casts me a cautious look before returning her gaze to Cassandra. The younger woman's eyes shine at the sight of her nephew—with tears of joy and of triumph, but also with a clarity that suggests the voices within her are silent for once.

"Should the new auntie do the honors?" Helen asks. Her tone sings with unspoken gratitude, though I'm not sure why.

Cassandra's hawk eyes fly to mine. I nod my permission. Her face blanches as her hand tightens around the knife's handle. With one swallow, Cassandra does what needs to be done.

The cord is cut, but the threads binding those in this room are now a single strand, sealed with the strength of bronze.

"Would you like to hold him?" I ask Cassandra.

Her lower lip trembles as a questioning hand falls to her chest.

"Yes, *you*." My smile grows. "Though it would be less stressful for all of us if you'd put down the knife."

The bloodied tool clatters to the floor. Cassandra laughs as she gathers the child into her arms. A foreign sound as crisp and pure as the rushing waters of the Scamander.

"He's so small," she says with wonder. "And look, he has your kiss from the gods. Your *alev*."

Cassandra leans down so I can see the copper streak that has appeared now that the baby's hair is beginning to dry. The tendril is a flame sprouting from his forehead, in the same spot as mine. A strange sight in an infant so new.

"It means he will be bold like his mother," Rhea says.

"With the quiet strength of his father," adds Helen, a reminder that the babe still hasn't cried, for all the intensity of his birth.

"He will be the best of both." Cassandra rocks the child back and forth—not like a tortured wraith, but like a woman born to hold babies. A distant look overtakes her again. "He will be all those things. And more."

A fierce wail erupts from the baby's chest, as if Cassandra has issued a battle cry of her own. Humming a little song she could not have possibly learned from Hecuba, Cassandra walks the child around the room, lost in another world. A world that is real and good.

My eyes meet Helen's. I can see she is bothered by memories she may never speak of, but I think I finally understand. Who she is. All she has done. Tears welling, she opens her mouth to speak.

The door to my chamber bursts open as Hector enters the room.

Or rather, Bodecca pushes him in.

"Andromache." The desperation in Hector's voice betrays his fear.

I can't help feeling a twinge of satisfaction. Now he knows what it is like. To wait. To not know. To sit helplessly on the side. The spark of relief in his eyes turns to cinders when they fall to my empty lap. To the blood-soaked linens by my feet.

"Is it . . . The child . . ."

". . . has a healthy pair of lungs," Cassandra says as she reappears from the balcony. Hector's beaming sister places the boy into his hands, and suddenly our son seems even smaller.

He doesn't say a word, but that isn't a surprise. What is shocking is that Hector—a man who has birthed a hundred foals and who carries himself with a confidence all men crave but few feel—cradles the infant like he is made of glass.

When he joins me on the bed, the trepidation in his eyes gives way to a mystery whose depths no poet can name. Not if he sang all the earth's songs for a thousand years.

It makes me think of something Bodecca said on one of my sleepless nights, her honeyed milk served up with a humble prophecy. "*The first time you see your husband holding your child, you will not know how you ever thought you loved him before. How you ever loved* anyone. *What was left unfinished without you even knowing it will seem whole, and your heart will hardly be able to withstand the anguish of this strange new joy.*"

Anguish and joy.

Two strands spun so tightly they can never be undone.

They wrap themselves around me now, threatening to turn my world black as I watch *this* man with *this* child, knowing that my heart's capacity to pump out something *this* true will never surpass this moment.

When he finally speaks, Hector's voice is hoarse. "Thank the gods you are still here."

"Yes. I am." I lay my weary head on his shoulder as he kisses the baby's bronze streak.

Eyes rising to mine, his voice deepens so as not to crack. "It seems we are not alone."

I follow his gaze to Helen. Hector's grip around the baby tightens. In fear that she is a ghost? Or merely at the shock that she isn't? "The gods have given us more than one miracle today," I say quickly. "Let's enjoy them and seek explanations later." Still, the thought of miracles and the omens that proceed them has me sitting up with a wince. "And the Achaeans?"

"Have been pushed back for now. No small part thanks to your men." Hector runs a thumb across my cheek. Something dark stirs in his eyes, but I do not want to see it. Not yet. This moment is for us alone.

I look down at the son between us. "What shall we call him?"

Hector's eyes drift toward the balcony where we have watched a thousand sunrises, and where I hope to see a thousand more. They soar across the plain to a river that, despite the drought plaguing these lands, pulses with melted snow from the peaks of Mount Ida.

"He must have a name fit for a strong ruler but a good man," I say.

"Scamandrius," Hector whispers as the wind flutters the curtains. "His name is Scamandrius."

THE ROOM IS quiet. Filled with the soft sounds of my sleeping son and the woman in the corner who saved his life. And mine.

Helen stares toward the balcony and the sea beyond.

"Thank you." My lips twitch at sentiments still foreign. "For everything."

Helen casts me one of her man-leveling looks. She seems . . . surprised.

"I am . . . sorry," I continue. "For failing to keep my promise. To protect you."

"There is no need," Helen says. "The risk was mine. The choice to help the Lower City was *mine*. You told me to stay in that courtyard, and I didn't. It is not your fault Paris found me first."

Her assurances do little to lift my guilt. Still, it is hard to find fault with a woman who acted according to her own mind. Only what did these actions cost her? For all the months Paris kept her imprisoned, she appears as well as she's ever been.

"Regardless, I am in your debt. And debts are something I always repay. If Paris ever . . ." I hesitate, overcome by emotion. "If you need to call on me again, I am bound by blood and water to answer."

"Then I would call in that debt now."

I laugh softly. "Name it."

"I would have you listen," Helen says firmly.

"Listen?" The word is an echo of a distant memory.

"Yes." Helen focuses her weary gaze on the infant sleeping on my chest, our breaths rising and falling as one. "Paris has been working to undermine Hector's position. From the beginning," she says in one forced exhale.

As if she's rehearsed the words countless times.

I nod. "I expected as much. Ever since we traveled to Cyzicus—"

"No, Andromache. I mean from the very *beginning*." She sighs. A sound of many regrets. "I should have told you the day of the festival, but for so long you *hated* . . . I thought I had more time. I never expected . . ." Helen rises from the chair, her hands wringing. "Paris is the one who started this war. He *always* meant to start this war."

Helen's eyes are lucid, clear as a mountain spring. The light they cast is one that can only illuminate.

My chest burns, but not with the ache of my milk coming in. "How would he manage to do such a thing?"

"Through my daughter. Hermione." As soon as Helen says her name, the tears fall. A thousand jewels sliding down velvet cheeks. Helen is beautiful even when she weeps.

And then she tells me her story.

How Paris snuck into her palace rooms in Sparta wielding a crooked dagger, prepared to take any queen or princess he could find as his ransom.

How Helen willingly traded places with Hermione, sparing her daughter the ill-timed fate that falls on too many girls of royal blood.

How for nearly ten years, Paris bought Helen's silence with threats that his seafaring spies would bring harm to Hermione, should she fail to co-operate with his schemes.

And what base plot was at the root of them all? Inciting a futile war with the Achaeans that Hector—fighting on the front lines—had little chance to survive. Thus opening Paris's path to whatever remained of Troy's throne.

My sorrow for Helen's sorrow—for all that I never knew—plunges me back into an ocean of pain. And rage. For Hector. For her. For all of us, who have lost so much to a war that need not have been.

I look down and want to weep. My son has been in my arms for less than a turn of Tiwad's crown, and already I can't fathom how Helen could bear it. How she survived all these years, knowing her decision to take her child's place also meant she'd never see that child again.

As for Paris . . .

Helen has confirmed, without a shred of doubt, what I have always known about the monster I must call a brother. Still, for some reason, the desire for revenge I feel at her revelation does not overtake me all at once. Not in this small sanctuary where life has clearly defeated death. Where the scales of justice feel balanced for at least one day.

I do not wish to abandon this threshold yet.

"We must decide how to explain your miraculous reappearance to Troy's people, while also finding a way to keep you out of Paris's grip," I say, mind whirling like a chariot wheel. It screeches to a halt. "Aeneas."

My throat closes around his name. It was Aeneas's decision to break ranks, but the road that led to that choice is one that many others, myself included, had a hand in paving.

"Rhea says he is in need of a gifted healer," I say. "No one will think twice of you staying with your sister-in-law to tend to him."

Even more than an effective solution, it is a plan born of my guilt. All the times Helen reached out to me and I cut her down. The baby stirs on my breast, his wrinkled face strangely like Bodecca's when she is furious. It makes me wonder. Will I do the same thing to this sweet boy of mine? Will I silence him with my wrath? Lash at his shame with the whip of my temper and my tongue, forcing him to bury his darkest moments even deeper?

Two hours. I have been a mother for two hours, and already my former strengths feel like detriments.

"I fear the danger has grown beyond Paris," Helen says. "After the Lower City attack, I began hearing a strange voice in his rooms. Paris does not act alone. I am starting to wonder if he *ever* acted alone."

It makes sense. Paris is a resentful creature who lashes out when poked. He is not a cunning architect who patiently plans an entire war.

"What makes you so sure?" My face furrows as the baby attacks my tender nipple.

"It is something Cassandra said. Someone from the Citadel brought Paris back, Andromache. Brought him back to Troy when his entire family believed him dead."

"Then that someone brought him back for a purpose." I sigh, inhaling the newness of my son. Born in innocence, though it seems we are about to be plunged back into a broken world. "We must determine who the voice you heard in Paris's rooms belongs to. If only the council would admit me."

"Why won't they?" Helen asks, perplexed. "You are Troy's future queen."

"It was a difficult task before, but now I must wait until the time of ritual cleansing has passed before I can set foot inside a temple . . ." I lift my nose from my babe's sweet head. "But not you."

Helen frowns. "What about me?"

Her hair has grown back some since the spring festival. Soft ringlets of spun gold kiss her delicate jawline. With her other injuries healed, Helen is once again a picture of feminine grace. She is also a miracle. A woman thought lost who must be blessed by the gods in ways we never dared to dream. The kind of guest the wives of the Five would love to have adorning their homes. The kind their Old Blood husbands would never suspect capable of anything but idle chatter.

Helen's is a subtler power, but it is a power nonetheless. One I am coming to respect. And quite possibly envy.

A slow smile spreads across my face. "Perhaps there is more than one way to infiltrate a Citadel."

8

HELEN

PRESSING DOWN ON the stone mortar with all my strength, I grind the rosemary leaves and pink mallow flower into a thick paste. The tangy aroma fills the stale room, the herbs' healing properties—and power—released.

Cassandra stares at the pestle in my hands like it is an enchanted implement. It was difficult for us to leave Scamandrius and Andromache behind, but there is another patient for us to tend to who has an even greater need.

I turn toward the bed where he waits. Unlike Andromache with her deafening labor, Aeneas does not writhe in pain. He does not groan or cry out. He does not make any noise at all.

I wish more than anything that he would. Green and purple bruises cover Aeneas's hip where Diomedes struck him with a boulder, but it is his head that worries me most, the tender flesh disguising the graver injuries hidden beneath. Yet I can only mend the wounds that rise to the surface. Those that remain buried are beyond the healing arts of a Paeana.

Though perhaps they are not beyond a prophetess.

"He will find his way back to us," Cassandra murmurs over my shoulder.

"Are you so confident he will live?" Gently, I spread the herbal paste across Aeneas's forehead, hoping to reduce the swelling. Grief squeezes my throat. Though Cassandra has been right before, I have never seen anyone with such serious injuries survive.

"He *must* live. The serpents have confirmed it."

It is unnerving. How long Cassandra has remained lucid. How she continues speaking as herself. Might she finally be free of the traumas that have haunted her for so long?

Which isn't to say Cassandra is a portrait of peace. She paces the room in agitation before stopping beside me again, so close I can smell the honey on her breath.

"Keep him alive, Helen," she whispers in my ear. "Bring him back to the surface. Aeneas must live to see the light, or the sun will set in the west. Never to rise again."

My hands, busy wrapping Aeneas's head in fresh bandages, go still. I do not understand what Cassandra truly means—can anyone?—but I can tell she is traveling to her thousand-foot view. To that place in the sky where she can see much further than the rest of us.

Where she can see the things unseen.

"Helen?"

Cassandra's question is lost in the commotion behind us. I turn to see her sister Creusa trembling in the doorway. My heart sinks. There are some women who take to pregnancy like they are exchanging one tunic for another. The weight of new life adds a robust dignity to their already strong frames.

Andromache was one of those women.

Creusa is not.

"The whispers are true, then. You're alive."

"She is, sister." Cassandra thrusts herself between us as Creusa moves in for an embrace. "Helen's time evaporates like water in the desert. Do not squander it if you want your husband to wake."

"I'm glad to see you all the same," says Creusa with a gentle smile. A child emerges from behind her skirts. Her only son, Ascanius, is not even five summers old, though the expression he wears is that of one much older. He has the fragile disposition of his mother coupled with the seriousness of his father. An odd child. One who speaks fewer words than he should and who is more likely to be found in the company of the Citadel elderly than among those his own age. Yet I have never felt as if this distance was driven by fear or simplemindedness. His silences are full of hidden understanding, rare in a child so young. Like his mother, Ascanius tunes himself to the emotions of others, quietly going where he is most needed.

If only Aeneas could see these gifts of the gods as strengths, instead of focusing on Ascanius's weak lungs and lack of a warrior's spirit. Yet I can see that this boy is the heart of Creusa. The woman who has taken my apparent resurrection in her characteristically gentle stride.

A coughing fit that is anything but gentle racks her slight frame. "How is Aeneas?" Creusa asks when she is able to speak, her voice quivering with frail hope.

Sadly, I have little hope to give. "He is no worse than when I first arrived."

Cassandra paces again, hands wringing. "He is not of the oak, but he will carry its seed. He is not of the oak, but he will carry its seed . . ."

Creusa doesn't pay attention to her sister's cryptic chanting—she is too distraught at the sight of her husband lying motionless. I give her hands a squeeze before grabbing a basket by the room's entrance. "Are you able to sit with him for a while? I need to return to the bathing house. Mallow flower would do wonders for your cough, so I'll fetch you some while I'm there."

Creusa's eyes fall. "What good are plants at this point?"

"Plants are of the earth. As are we." I hold her gaze with as much warmth as I can offer. "I am able to help Aeneas's body heal with plants. To a point. But the part of him that is spirit, the part wandering through a dark night we know little about . . . well, all we can do is wait for his return. But do not lose faith, Creusa. Your prayers and your love are potent. They may well lead him home."

For while a woman's humble pleas may be overlooked by mortals, I believe they hold cosmic weight. The gods did not grant Creusa relentless strength like Andromache, or the far-reaching sight of Cassandra, or Rhea's keen perceptiveness. Yet they did grant her a gift that might surpass them all in the end: knowing her very human limits.

Creusa drops my hands and kneels before the small altar at the foot of Aeneas's sickbed. She places a black pellet of incense in a clay censer painted with Minoan swirls. The dense but distinct aroma of pine resin, mint, cinnamon, juniper berries, raisins, and camel grass fills the space.

"*Kapet*," I say, surprised at the distinct scent of Eye of Horus. An expensive blend that hails from Egypt, known for its healing properties. Strange, I did not think there was any of this sacred incense left in Troy.

"The scent has always calmed me," Creusa says.

"Why do you think that is?" The ancient and rare recipe was intended to appease even the most fickle gods. And Creusa is far from fickle.

"It reminds me of my childhood. Of the golden days before the war." An expression of innocence overtakes Creusa's features, bringing a flush to high cheekbones that have turned gaunt from constant worry. "Father used to let me sit in on his trade dealings. I dreamed I would one day sail up the Nile on a grand ship. Perhaps marry a handsome pharaoh." Creusa's sad gaze drifts back to Aeneas like his body has all the pull of the moon at high tide. "I've always wanted to see the world beyond Troy's walls. But even as a girl, I think I knew it was only a dream. Aeneas will never leave Troy."

Cassandra makes a strange noise behind us.

"Be that as it may, the ability to dream is worth holding on to," I tell Creusa as I move to leave. "It is a gift few in this city still possess."

And I can glimpse those dreams in the lines of her compassionate face. It makes me determined to keep Aeneas by Creusa's side. He is the only dream she was granted, even if he has failed to return her love with the same affection.

As I reach for the chamber door, Cassandra jumps up from her prone position. She grabs my wrist and hisses, "Remember. He must wake. For dreams to live, so must the body that carries them forward." Desperation twists her features; it makes the same sensation travel up my arm. Why so deep a fear for Aeneas? If Cassandra can see all ends, I don't understand why she resists revealing them plainly.

Cassandra's lips twitch as her fingers tighten around my wrist.

"Come, I will walk with you," she says suddenly, calm once more. "It is not yet time for you to be alone."

My breath catches on the final word. In many ways, alone is all I've ever been, yet never in the way I have longed for. Isolation is not the same as solitude. The closest I've come to real solitude within the Citadel is inside the enclosed herb garden beside its bathing house. If there is any hope of healing Aeneas by human hands, the remedy lies there. Before we depart,

Cassandra and I cover our heads and faces with heavy veils, layers of gauze and silk I haven't had to wear in months.

Now our every step requires secrecy. Though we are safe within Creusa's or Andromache's household, word will have reached King Priam and Paris that we have escaped our respective prisons. And so Cassandra and I move through the Citadel like the shadows we were always intended to be.

In silence, we slip beneath the trellis of jasmine and enter the walled garden. It is like stepping into a secret world. A serpentine moat of silver water winds through rock like a river made by men. Islands of green connected by stepping-stones lie in the swirling pools, home to so many plants that few know the names of them all. We quickly fill our baskets with all manner of medicinal herbs. Once we have enough and are ready to leave, Cassandra lifts her angled chin. Listening for words not yet spoken.

The only sounds I hear are the soft crackle of growing things and the trickling of water. Whispers of the Unnamed One I have rarely heard since the hillside encounters of my girlhood. Whispers now limited to the wind.

"What is it, Cassandra?"

"You must remain calm." Her hands flex toward the stained knife at her belt, and my heart races at the plain fear on her face. "They will not harm you if you stay calm."

My mouth goes dry as Cassandra leads me out of our hidden oasis and back into the street. It doesn't take long for the source of her warning to materialize.

An infantry of at least twenty Citadel women marches toward us up the incline in a swirl of silk gowns, the varied scents of what remains of their imported perfumes floating ahead of them.

"Kalawashi's entourage of bored wives?" I say lightheartedly, even as my skin goes damp with sweat. "That is what worries you?"

Cassandra releases a sound that can only be described as a growl.

The Harssi are almost upon us, and the women's ardent strides suggest they know exactly who we are, veils or no veils.

"We hoped we might find you here, Helen," says Tumaeus's wife upon reaching the garden's gate. She lowers her veil, revealing a mouth pinched in disbelief. I do the same, seeing no reason to keep up the ruse. "It is true, then. You've returned from the grave."

"Or simply survived death," Cassandra clips at my side.

Kalawashi smiles in a manner that almost seems genuine. It radiates the confidence of one who is more clever than she would have others believe. "Such a thing does not come to pass unless one is uniquely blessed by the gods."

"Or is beneath their hateful curse."

I rest a hand on Cassandra's tense forearm, which wields her basket like a shield. "It is all right," I say before turning back to the company of Trojan women. For once, they do not look upon me with contempt.

It would be less unsettling if they did.

"Why do you seek us out?" I ask.

"Because you have the favor of Hygeia, goddess of good health," says a woman whose eyebrows are drawn on so thick, she looks permanently enraged.

"And don't forget Aphrodite," adds the younger Harsa beside her. "That you have become a channel of her mercy is the only explanation for why Aeneas lives."

A prickle of warning travels up my skirts as this throng of voices, so rarely heard, takes to the wind.

"The temple priests keep turning us away!"

"They say there is no help for us unless we return with better offerings."

"As if we have any gold or goats to spare!"

"You are a healer." Kalawashi thrusts a young girl toward me, pulled from the swarm of robes. The girl looks to be about thirteen or fourteen summers old. "You must help our children. Most were born to a world at war, but the walls have never closed in on us like they do now."

I look into the child's hazel eyes and see it at once—the look of a caged bird that spends its days pacing in distress. In the early days when the battle still felt as distant as the crash of Poseidon's waves, these women of the Citadel took frequent expeditions beyond the walls with armed guards; that way their servants could wash clothes in the Semiosis River to the north while their children played in its calmer waters. For years, this extra room to roam had been enough to keep the inner disquiet at bay. The kind of illness that cannot be seen as it slowly wraps around the mind and heart like the most enterprising vine, bringing on a despair not easily shaken.

"How would you describe what ails you?" I ask the flat-gazed girl.

Her mother speaks before the poor thing can form a word. "She's become lazy and does nothing but mope around the house, and yet she never sleeps. She hardly touches what little food I manage to serve."

I crouch down to the child's level so it's clear I am speaking to her and her alone. "Are you experiencing any pains, dear?"

The girl nods as she touches the muscles between her neck and shoulders.

"Upset stomach?"

Another mute affirmation.

I hand the mother a bushel of yellow star-shaped flowers from my basket. "In Sparta we call this plant *Hypericum*. If you have your daughter drink it as a tea throughout the day, it may improve her mood. You should also make sure she is taking daily exercise outside the house."

Thin eyelashes bat as if I have spoken a foreign word. "Exercise?"

"Yes. A daily walk to the High Temple should suffice. Preferably first thing in the morning when the sun is brightest." I hold the girl's gaze, willing her to see that she is capable of more than she's been allowed to put to the test. "Or, if you have the energy, you might take a servant and walk down to the Lower City. The streets there are wider and there's nothing like a long walk to clear the mind."

The Citadel women bristle like I have recommended that their daughters march straight into the Achaean camp. Or a brothel.

Even still, Kalawashi accepts the flowers and murmurs her thanks.

"We cannot linger," Cassandra hisses, grabbing my arm as woman after woman shouts her ailments over the next. "Aeneas is the one you must heal. *He* is who matters most."

The intensity of her words startles me. How can Cassandra give preference to one man when there are so many in need of help? Such a thing would never happen back in Sparta, but here in the Citadel, mothers have not taught their daughters even the most basic of the healing arts.

I frown at the wasted potential. It appears an excess of comfort is not only the death of long-held traditions, it is the death of common sense.

And yet, *I* can help them. I can help all of them.

"No." Cassandra pulls me away from the women, her eyes darting this way and that, as if a new adversary waits around every corner. "You are needed elsewhere."

"I am needed wherever there is healing work to be done," I snap, wrenching myself from her talon grip. Even if Cassandra is worried for her cousin, I am tired of my gifts being a tool for others to use. "Besides, I told Andromache I would drop off some peppermint to help soothe the baby's stomach."

"It is your choice, Helen." A faint smile. Her eyes scan my face, searching. Always searching. "Helen of the unnamed god."

My growing unease coils into a knot of fear.

"What did you say?" I gasp.

Cassandra just shrugs. As if she has not referenced something deeply personal. Something I've never spoken of to anyone. "There are no powers above or below that will make us a vessel against our will." Her lips peel back in an unnerving grin. "Not unless we welcome it. Welcome *them*."

One hard swallow and it's all I can do to avoid racing down the hill to Andromache's house. Cassandra is on my sandals the entire way, yet I am no longer sure if her companionship is a comfort.

Is that the true explanation behind the many faces she wears? Not a sickness of the mind, but specters whose aid she has welcomed?

I was never permitted to pursue my girlhood dream of becoming a priestess on some silent mountaintop, yet I do know this—the realm Cassandra has access to may not be one we were meant to tamper with.

A few more paces and we exit through the Dardanian gate that leads into the Merchant Quarter. We round a corner and Andromache's courtyard comes into view.

A crowd has packed the wide streets in front of Hector and Andromache's home. Dozens, if not hundreds, of people clamoring to be let in. A line of armed soldiers forms a wall in front of the door, keeping the crowds from cutting down the narrow alleyway that runs past the kitchen and into the training grounds. As soon as the people see us approaching, an old man starts banging on the mudbrick wall with his walking stick. A woman lifts her baby high in the air, shouting, "Mercy! Mercy!"

Her hair long and loose, Andromache stands behind the guards, watching the crowd. Bodecca's stout outline fills the side doorway of the kitchen, a tightly swaddled Andrius nestled in her arms. The old woman's gaze lands on us.

"Andromache!" Bodecca points.

Andromache turns and sees us. So do the people waiting for admittance. Their desperate cries increase. My hands shake in a way they haven't since I gave up my tinctured wine.

Cassandra releases a small noise. "Perhaps you've welcomed them after all."

I don't understand what she means, but the shouts of so many in pain, of so many *needs*, reverberate through me as the mob presses in our direction. What happens next occurs at an unfathomable speed. Somehow, Andromache's guards manage to reach us first, forming a tight ring around our bodies until Cassandra and I move as one. As they push us through the throng toward the main entrance, the soldiers' commands and the pleas of the people swirl together like a thunderstorm. Hands reach for me, grasping for my hair and tugging at my robes. As if a single touch might bring them healing. Or the favor of gods who have thus far ignored their cries.

"Praise Aphrodite for this miracle!"

"The Spartan queen is not a curse. She has been sent to save us!"

I squeeze my eyes shut as the guards shove back bodies with their shields, my head throbbing as the roar builds and I wait for it to be over.

When a hand stronger than the rest clasps my wrist, my eyes snap open and I find I can breathe again.

"Let's get you inside." Concern clings to the faint lines of Andromache's face.

Cassandra and I follow her through the front room to the kitchen, yet I can't help but glance over my shoulder toward pleas no wall can block out.

"Please help us, Harsa Helen. Have mercy!"

A hundred fervent requests land like a hundred daggers, each causing my chest to tighten. Each a reminder of the last time a crowd gathered when I first came to Troy, rushing the temple steps for the chance to glimpse my face up close. Given Andromache's tight expression, she is reliving the same moment—one that brought her shame and me terror. "What is this? An uprising?" My voice trembles. Though if growing hunger in the Lower City has pushed these people to their breaking point, then maybe we *should* be afraid.

"Of sorts. It seems word of your blessed presence has spread." Andromache gives me a small yet loaded smile.

I do not return the gesture.

"You have gone from Whore of Sparta to Troy's most treasured miracle . . ." she continues.

A familiar dread builds and spreads as she studies me in that calculating way I have come to know well.

"Miracles, my friend, are a currency we can play with."

9

RHEA

"WHERE HAVE YOU been?" The voice stops me cold at the edge of the darkened swamp.

When I glance up, he is sitting on the crumbling outer wall of the shrine exactly where he was the first time I ever saw him.

My stomach clenches at the sight of firm lips, pressed flat. Agate eyes ringed by golden lashes and set within dark circles. It's been three days since Ajax left me on the beach to attend the meeting with the other kings. A mere scattering of hours between then and now and yet, somehow . . . I had forgotten.

His cheekbones are chiseled granite in the starlight. The rough weave spanning his shoulders strains at the slightest movement. Before I can fully adjust to the sight of him, his massive body is sailing through the air. Ajax lands in a crouch in front of me. He straightens slowly, and the hairs on my arms dance on an invisible wind.

How long has he been sitting here? Long enough to see where I've—

He shifts and the shadows obscure his face. For one terrifying moment, every lie I've told burns bright as the stars above us.

"Where have you been?" he asks again. The edge in his voice holds me fast. Not sharp so much as brittle.

He shifts his weight as if to take a step toward me before rocking back on his heels. The hesitation in that simple gesture pricks at me. As does the way he stands there. With his shoulders rounded, arms tucked in close to his side as if to take up as little space as possible. It's a look I haven't seen him wear since the night he led me into these stones and showed me the mark he'd carved into his own skin. Because he could never remember the lines, and because that forgetting shamed him.

"I was gathering herbs in the swamp." I hold up my basket. A flimsy excuse and an even poorer shield. "How long have you been here?"

"Not long. It took me forever to slip Teucer's guard. I've been waiting for you every night for three days. *Three days*, Rhea."

He doesn't suspect.

The relief coursing through me dies the moment I get a clear view of his face. He looks as if he hasn't slept since I left him last.

"There was a difficult birth. Mother and child were almost lost."

The words flow past my lips with hardly any thought. It's second nature to me now. The delicate dance between truth and falsehood as familiar to me as those steps over the darkened swamp. It's how I'm able to face myself each day when the long nights end. The real reason I could never explain to anyone all the hours passed within these stones . . .

For every secret Ajax gives me, I give him one in return. Bits of seafoam clung to tangled weeds that only become strings of pearls in the moonlight.

I've never betrayed a word of the truths we share about the things that matter. A trade dealing not in kings or the movements of men, but in flavors and textures. In the sights and sounds and smells baked into the clay of who we are. My father's and my sister's laughter along with the trembling notes of the aulos my mother loved to play. The lilac scent and quiet humming of Ajax's older sister, Irene. How she'd pretend not to notice the boy who hid at the foot of her bed, carving small figures while she worked her loom. The way she made him feel seen without ever once glancing his way.

I remember the night he told me how it felt like part of him had vanished when Irene left to be married. She'd died during her first labor soon after, and he'd refused to speak for a year. Grief too vast to pass the throat. I knew it well; saw it ripple across his face as he spoke calmly of his father, King Telamon of Salamis. A man who insisted to anyone who'd listen that this was what happened when the gods chose the strongest of vessels and joined it with the weakest of minds.

There are joyful things too. Stories of Teucer and Ajax terrorizing the local fishwives in their youth. Races through the warm waters of Salamis that ended on hot, sandy shores. Long nights in the stables and short rides to the edge of the plains where they kissed the mountains that had watched over me most of my life. Endless skies and wind in my hair. Or the way Ajax sings off-key when he is truly happy, which makes the silences of his occasional sadnesses all the louder.

Joys and sorrows. Memories and moments. These are the offerings we lay upon this ancient shrine to forgotten gods. Meaningless treasures to anyone but the two of us. And so, entire moons come and go where I find no need to lie. If I occasionally let Ajax believe what he will about who I am in the hours we're apart, that's no more than what most people do.

Even Hector and Andromache have secrets . . .

The words I tell myself.

Sometimes, I even believe them.

"Are mother and babe both well?"

Warmth radiates through me. "Yes." Andrius's squishy face boasts enough wrinkles to bear an uncanny resemblance to Bodecca. The mighty battle of his birth resulted in bruises that have turned all the colors of a sailor's dawn. That and the yellow tinge of his skin covered in rough white bumps has caused Andromache no shortage of anxiety. Luckily, Bodecca and Helen are there to assure her of the thing I knew from the very first moment I saw Hector's son fight his way into the world.

He is perfect.

When I left at sunset, Bodecca was showing Andromache how to mark the side she'd last nursed while Helen added a gentle word about proper latch. All the while Cassandra hunted the dark corners of the room for threats only she could see. It was hard to leave them, but I'd already stayed too long. Ven would be waiting for an explanation about what she saw on the beach. Whenever I wasn't reliving that moment, or basking in Scamandrius's newness, I was preparing my excuses to face her.

Somehow, I had not thought to prepare for this.

Ajax stands perfectly still. Even in the dark, I can feel some strong emotion in him rising up to flood the space between us.

It sings to me. Not in the whispers of horses, but in the roar of the sea just beyond the breaks. Music of crashing waves trapped in a spiral shell pressed to my ear. Notes of *pain*. Deep as any ocean. Sharp and cutting as salt air.

His breath hitches. The sound echoes through me on a peal of thunder. I've taken a step forward before I can stop myself. "Ajax? What's wrong?"

"I—"

Every rigid line of his body begs for relief from some wound I can't see. I want to run my hands over him until I find what hurts. I want to offer him my warmth and comfort like I would any one of my horses, but the rules of the stones keeping us safe forbid it.

Ajax grabs the basket from my arms and presses it to his chest. Wicker groans.

"I thought I'd scared you away."

Realization hits like a slap of cold water. He thought I'd made the choice not to return to our shrine. Because he'd approached me outside the stones, blurring the lines we've carefully drawn around ourselves. Because in a playful moment that meant nothing, he'd broken the rules of the game we played.

Because he'd touched me. And, so doing, had shattered any illusion of control I had been clinging to.

His eyes search mine, and mine search back. "You could never scare me, Ajax."

So many lies I've told him. This is the truth.

Shadows stir in his pupils. Shades that greet me now whenever I stare at my own reflection. Ghosts that haunt the spaces between words I speak and the ones I could never say. Between the seeds of information I plant and the crimson leaves they reap.

"I should scare you, Rhea. I scare myself sometimes."

He stands there, a man drowning in his own shadows. The shades in his yawning pupils scream at me, begging to be dragged out into the light.

I know I shouldn't. That I have no right. But his loneliness pulls at me, and like the tide I am powerless to stop it.

"Alashiya." I say the name that has been stuck in my head since the night I heard Teucer speak it. "Who was she?"

How did she hurt you?

The wounds must have been deep. What else could explain her tie to the darkness that sometimes clings to Ajax the way mists shroud the mountains?

A muscle tics in his jaw. "Alashiya is not a woman. It is a place. A land rich in copper. It was where my father brought me on my first raid." His gaze goes distant. "I remember when he called me into his hall. How excited I was. How badly I wanted to make him proud of me."

"You didn't fight?" I guess.

"Oh, I fought. And I killed." He grows hollow as a skin of wine emptied from the inside. "With a talent that went beyond even my father's wildest hopes." His throat bobs. "For a time after, I was not myself. I . . . I was angry. Confused." A shadow of that confusion flashes across his face. "I was a danger to myself and anyone who came near me."

"What happened?" My heart hurts for the boy he was. Lost and alone. Frightened of the world.

Of himself.

"Teucer," Ajax says. "He left to find Chiron, the man who trained me, and brought him back to Salamis. I don't remember much about that time. I just know that one day the darkness lifted." His eyes sail back to mine. "But it is always there, waiting. And on days like today . . ."

"What?" I ask. "What happened today?"

His pain is so stark, I can't bear it. I want to take it away, to ease it in any way I can, but all of that is impossible unless I know what it is.

"The truth." I repeat the words he said to me on the beach. "The truth is what I'm asking for."

His face sets in an expression of resignation and some other emotion that bears no name in any of the languages that I speak.

"I killed a man today. No, not a man. A boy." His lips twists. "A child who should have been home, hiding behind his mother's skirts."

His words sent me hurtling over the cliff's edge. "Who?"

"I don't know his name." Ajax stares at the outline of stones, his eyes glassy as mountain lakes. "He came right for me. Stupid boy, waving a sword that was too damn big for him. I tried to push him back, but he wouldn't run. He lunged. Another day, I might've found some other way, but I haven't slept in so long . . . and I . . ." He turns on me with red-rimmed eyes. "I killed him, Rhea. I caved in his skull with the handle of my sword."

Sickness swirls in my gut as Larion's gap-toothed smile flashes through my mind. A dozen other faces. Boys led by hollow-cheeked mothers to Hector's stables. Small hands gripping large swords. Chins raised in a desperate effort not to shame the men who once bore these weapons.

I stare at Ajax, and I find it is easier to see the boy he must have been than the man in the stories whispered through the stables. Stories like the one he just told me.

"If you want me to fear you, you'll have to try harder."

His nostrils flare. "You deserve to know the kind of man you are meeting in the dark."

I think of my father. Of Hector. The weight he carries on those strong shoulders. The goodness inside him and the quiet strength he lends to others. Hector kills. Just as much as Ajax. And perhaps the part of him that was born on the plain—the darkness he expunges each night when he washes his own armor in the dim light of the stable—perhaps that part even enjoys it. The moment of power. The seal stamped with life and death held in his hands. As close to a god as any mortal will ever be in this life. Except . . .

Andromache rises up in my thoughts. The expression that overcame her as she gritted her teeth and bore down on the day of Andrius's birth. Pain and exhaustion and sheer determination. The power she held in empty hands. Not to take life. But to *give* it.

My head whirls with thoughts and ideas. Half-formed shadows. I refocus on Ajax, and I see it burning right there below the surface. A similar desire. To give, not just to take. A fight like the one Hector wages with himself as fiercely as he does Troy's enemies. Perhaps even more so because the battle raging within him is one that never ends.

"Wars are ugly and so often pointless, but that isn't true of all the men who fight them."

Especially not you, I think, though I do not say it.

His expression grows fierce. "If you knew the things I've done, you would run from here without looking back."

If you knew the things I've done, would you do the same?

Air saws through my lungs. "Let us agree that it's not what we've done that matters, but who we are when we are here."

He studies me, and for a moment, I want nothing more than to know what it is that he sees. "It isn't safe to ask you to keep meeting me, but every time I decide not to come back, the next day here I am." He jerks his hands through his hair, and my heart aches with the need to do . . . *something*.

"We are being careful." Truth. "There is nothing to fear." Lie.

He draws a breath as if steeling himself. "When you didn't come, I got it into my head that something must've happened to you."

The hairs rise on the back of my neck. "What did you do?"

"I went looking. I had to know that you were all right."

Cold washes over me. "Where did you go?"

"The infirmary and then the bathhouse. The woman there—the one with the scars."

Ven.

I flinch. I can't help it.

"She said the sickbeds were overrun with marsh sickness. That you'd barely stopped to sleep." He looks at me, pleading for . . . what?

My heart races in my chest. I can't avoid Ven anymore. I have to explain what she saw on the beach as soon as possible.

But if Ajax had found Calis instead of Ven; if he had found nearly anyone else . . .

So close. So close we'd come to disaster, and all because I saw a friend where I should have seen only an enemy.

Impossible.

Dangerous.

And now there is no going back.

"You can't come looking for me again. You know what would happen if anyone found out about our meetings. If Odysseus—"

"I know," he says. "He'd put his spear between my eyes, but I can't promise I won't do something stupid if you go missing again. Next time, leave me a sign. Anything so I don't imagine the worst."

His bronze skin glows pale in the moonlight. And the thought strikes me like one of Yarri's arrows.

In his own clumsy way, he is only trying to protect me. For that is what friends do.

A lump rises in my throat even as an invisible blade twists between my ribs.

"I wasn't thinking . . ." he says quickly. "I should leave this alone, but I . . . I can't . . ." The words are blocks of wood on his tongue that could be turned to beauty if only they might fall into his giant hands. "Each day is a new storm," he tries again to explain. "The wind screams and tears at the sails. The waves crash high on all sides, and as strong as I am, it's never strong enough to keep her steady." His hands drop, and he looks at me. "I think . . . I think it is the way you listen. That settles the sea and makes the wind go quiet."

His words echo through me. It is the magic, not of the shrine, but of Ajax. The simple way he has of putting names to truths I could never find, no matter how many words I gather. No matter how hard I try to outrun them.

"I value your friendship too."

Low laughter floats through the night. It cuts through the dark like a ray of light breaking through the clouds.

"What?" I ask, unsure if he is laughing at me or himself and not really caring so long as he *laughs*.

Ajax scrubs a palm over his stubbled jaw. "I can't decide if the gods have sent you to comfort or torment me." The space between us disappears. "Either way, I wouldn't like it if something happened to you." The flash of his dimple is like the sunrise. "Who else would sew up my wounds with crooked stitches?"

I fight a smile of my own. For the first time tonight it feels as if my feet are planted back on solid ground. "Perhaps I've grown fond of you too, Ajax."

Truth.

The darkness he carried with him to the shrine lifts like mountain fog. Even his posture is straighter, and it fills me with such contentment that I don't notice Ajax's hand moving until his calloused fingers are wrapped around my wrist.

Every invisible line we've drawn blows away in the wind.

"Don't disappear again, Rhea. Promise me."

"I promise."

Lie.

And then words and rules cease to have meaning, because Ajax raises my hand and presses his lips to the soft flesh of my palm.

"Until tomorrow."

SHE FINDS ME at the stream behind the bathhouse, where garments hang to rinse on long lines in the clear water. I am gathering a handful of empty baskets to be brought back inside when her voice speaks up behind me.

"Where have you been?"

It is the same question Ajax asked, but the sentiments underneath are as distant as Ida is from Olympus.

"Andromache has given birth," I say, straightening to face Ven. "To a son."

Whatever answer Ven was expecting, it was not this. Her features slacken. The fabric of her robes rustles like mardi reeds as she walks away from me down to the stream. The moonlight forges the water into a silver blade sheathed in green silk. Ven's hands come around her waist.

"Ven."

"A boy?" One breath more and her hands drop back down to her sides. "He is healthy, then?"

"His name is Scamandrius. And he is beautiful."

She turns. "Scamandrius." It's as if years and lifetimes fall away with the scars to reveal the girl she once was. A new wife with a husband and an infant son. A girl who died long before I ever met her in that cart bound for Cyzicus.

"I thought you were avoiding me," she says.

"You weren't entirely wrong." I gather a breath, but all the excuses turn to dust on my tongue. "What you saw on the beach. It isn't what you think."

"I know what I saw." Her eyes are obsidian. "The question is: Do you?"

"What you saw was me helping Troy," I say staunchly. "Using every tool the Mother sees fit to provide."

"People are only tools for the gods. They can turn against you as easily as they are placed in your hands."

"I do not know why, but he has chosen me to trust, Ven. An Achaean prince." My voice rises. I take a breath and lower it. "He tells me things that I would learn no other way. How do you think we've been as successful as we've been these many months of Odysseus's silence?"

"Some rewards are not worth the risk," Ven says. "When the giant came looking for you, I was not alone. Calis had sought me out to complain about some new slave I sent her."

My stomach knots. "What did she hear?"

"She heard him ask after you. I told her that Ajax the Great was a man of unusual tastes."

"Do you think she believed you?" I ask.

"She has no reason not to. But she is watching us."

"I'll be more careful," I say. "There is no danger from Ajax." I don't realize how mad the words sound until they have already left my lips. "It is under control. I promise you, Ven. I know the risks I am taking."

Her eyes narrow on me. "No, Rhea. I don't think you do."

The sea wind swells and ebbs. Swells and ebbs between us.

"Will you tell the others?" My voice goes small at the thought of Salama finding out . . . or Andromache.

"We have already said everything that needs to be said."

The coil inside me unspools. "Thank you, Ven."

"Do not thank me." Her voice is sharp. "I fear you will come to regret this. I hope you are the only one." She takes the basket from my hands, leaving me utterly vulnerable. "Now, I need you to do something for me."

It shouldn't come as a surprise. Ven is cunning and determined. Nobody knows this better than I do. She has leverage over me now, and she will not hesitate to use it.

"What?"

"There is something in King Agamemnon's settlement I need you to see."

"Agamemnon?" His camp is the most dangerous ground on all of Sigeum Ridge. The king of Mycenae is suspicious of outsiders, while at the same time lax in governing the baser instincts of his own men. Worse still, it is well known that every king and prince on Sigeum Ridge has spies in Agamemnon's household.

"Go past the main hearth, toward the back rooms. To your left there lies the corridor leading to his private chambers. This time of night, the guards will be otherwise occupied with the girls who work there. You should not have any trouble, though I would not linger."

I swallow what little moisture is left in my mouth. "What am I looking for?"

"You will know it when you see it." Before I can object, she adds, "You cannot ask for trust you would not give."

I bite down on a retort and turn sharply toward the lair of the king of Mycenae.

"Rhea." She speaks up behind me. "There is one thing you should remember."

I glance back at her.

"The most dangerous lies are the ones we tell ourselves."

KING AGAMEMNON'S SEAT lies at the very center of Cape Sigeum. My pulse pounds at my throat every step of the way there. I approach the warrior at the gate and raise my basket. "From the infirmary."

The guard wastes no time letting me inside.

Agamemnon's hall is bigger than any of the others I've seen, as if the size itself is the point. It gleams with treasure pillaged from innocent cities up and down the Anatolian coast. I face the large hall, teeming with blood spoils and the remains of the nightly feasts Agamemnon insists upon despite the meager fare. Warriors sleep on the floor in drunken heaps. Others have servant girls pressed up to the walls. It is disorganized, reeking of wine and sweat and urine. I've been here only once before on an errand for Machaon and was lucky to escape without being dragged into some dark corner.

None of the women in the camp come here if they can help it.

A stocky warrior staggers past. Rough hands grip my shoulders. I tense before I realize they are merely searching for a stable anchor on their way. The man half falls out the door, and my knees go weak.

I lean against the wall and focus on the layout of the hall in front of me. A circular hearth surrounded by four wooden pillars sits in the center of the open space. Above it, the night sky pours in through the rough hole cut for ventilation. The scent of smoking fish wafts toward me from somewhere to the right. To my left there's a hallway leading back to a set of rooms just like the one Ven described. I've taken a dozen steps toward it when raised voices drift toward me from a room draped shut with a hanging curtain to my left.

Dozens of voices tangle together behind the cloth. One of them in particular stops me.

Odysseus.

I'm leaning forward when a soft tread echoes toward me from within the hidden room. A shadow stretches toward me from under the hanging curtain. There's no time to stop and think. Instead, I turn and duck into the first door I see. It isn't until I am inside that I realize where I am.

Agamemnon's private chamber.

I'm studying the large bed, draped in exotic furs and rich fabrics, when a voice speaks up behind me.

"You shouldn't be here."

A woman stands in the doorway. My eyes move from the mixing bowl of wine in her hand to her face, and I catch my breath. She is stunning, with a strong nose and dark eyes framed by slashing brows that make her both beautiful and utterly unique.

"Speak, child. Before I lose my patience."

"I . . . I'm lost. I . . . was looking for Grida. To deliver these remedies. From Machaon." My words are clumsy foals, tripping over themselves.

"In Agamemnon's private chambers?" A dark brow arches. "What is your name?"

"Rhea."

A flicker of emotion. "I see."

"I'll go." I duck my head. "I'm sorry to disturb you."

The woman blocks my path with one graceful step.

"You are lying, Rhea." She places her mixing bowl on a table.

"No . . . I . . ."

"Do not play games with me."

It is slowly dawning on me that perhaps this woman is the reason I am here.

"Who are you?"

"Once I was a woman. Now I am a slave." Her words are an echo of others spoken to me once. By a grieving mother in a cart bound for a distant city. A mother who has now become a slave to revenge and at whose request I have come here.

"I was once someone else too," I say.

The woman watches me as if she can read the truth in my face. Truth no one else can see. "And what are you now?"

What am I now?

I think of my journeys through the wall. The dances around Odysseus's men in the dark. My stolen hours with Ajax and those I spend sleeping at the foot of Hector and Andromache's bed while someone watches over me.

Not a mouse.

Not a lion.

"I am a shadow."

The beautiful woman snorts without delicacy, and yet it does nothing to detract from her loveliness. She closes the distance between us. "My name is Briseis. I am a soldier's prize. Perhaps you would care to switch places?"

A thousand thoughts run through my head. A thousand dangers.

"I speak in jest. *Breathe*, Rhea."

But I can't.

"You are the one Ven sent me here to find," I say finally.

She does not deny it. "I confronted your friend at the washing stream a few days ago. As Achilles's former prize, now Agamemnon's, I am not easily welcomed by the other women." Her smile is mirthless. "But while they are busy avoiding me, I am watching them. Let us say that your scarred partner and I have . . . observed each other on previous occasions." She shrugs. "I am in a position to learn many interesting things. I could help you both, but I cannot decide whether your efforts are brave or uncommonly reckless. What do you say to that?"

It is an accusation I have heard more than once.

I study Briseis in the light of the oil lamp. This is the woman who sleeps in Agamemnon's bed. The one who pours his wine and shares his pillow. She is also a daughter of Anatolia. One who, like the rest of us, has lost everything at the hands of these invaders.

There is not a single person on Sigeum Ridge who could be of greater assistance to our designs. But does she still burn with enough fire to avenge all she has lost?

If Ven sent me here, it's because she thinks I might somehow convince her. But how? Briseis may be a slave, but she was once a princess. The iron in her spine reminds me a little of Andromache, and Andromache would never respond to pleading. She could not respect it.

I raise my chin. "I'd say nothing great is achieved without a little bit of recklessness."

Briseis tilts her head. "There is some fight in you. That is good, for it is a fight that your mistress is after. I've never met Hector's Amazon wife, but I have heard of her. And yet, she is not the one in this camp, surrounded by the enemy. An enemy who will make Santa, the death bringer, seem gentle as the Mother if they find out what we've done." She moves until we are a breath apart. The scent of cinnamon drifts over me. "Tell me, little shadow, if all goes up in flames, will you run back behind your walls or will you fight for those who have stood and fought for you?

"I would fight for us all."

Her eyes turn piercing. "I will need a guarantee."

"What kind of guarantee?" I ask.

"A test. To prove you can do what it is you claim. And that you have the courage to carry it out." She moves to a low table and picks something up. A cylinder of carved ivory with a flat top pressed into the shape of a lion's head.

The personal seal of Agamemnon.

"Take this to your mistress and return to seal our bargain. I trust she will come up with something suitable."

I stare at the offering in Briseis's hand. Until now, it is only stolen words that I've carried across the plain, kept secret in my memory. The plain has always been a danger, but if I am caught in the camp with Agamemnon's personal seal, it will mean death with no way out.

And Calis is already suspicious.

The lion's head is made of solid gold that gleams in the firelight. I make no move to take it.

Briseis could be trying to trap me, or she might be telling the truth.

Don't you know better by now?

Trust no one.

But if I had trusted no one, we would not have saved all those cities along the coast. We would have never thwarted Odysseus's siege, or be growing our web of shadows by the day.

We would not have come this far.

My gaze slides past the door to the hall, where Agamemnon and his kings gather night after night to contemplate the destruction of everything I love. Then to the bed the woman in front of me is forced to share with him.

Yes, to trust is to risk, but without risk, there can be no gain.

I square my shoulders and take the seal.

THE SHADE

Mouth chokes on words
the Shade cannot teach.
Face pressed to doors
she cannot breach.

No eyes to see
nor tongue to speak,
trapped in the dark
no Light can reach.

Lines twisting
bending,
still descending,
endless as sand
upon the beach.

Shade leaves her haunt
of wind and stone,
drawn by the pull
of blood and bone.

A sleeping child
new mother at rest.
Memories of a babe
held to Shade's breast.

She finds him at the Mother's table
not a child, a man
she longs to cradle.
Aegean eyes
and curls of sable,

The Horse of fire rears in his stable.

The truth they share
unknown to all.
One hero will rise.
The other, fall.

Dreams made of dust.
All thoughts rescind.
Shade screams his name
into the wind.

BOOK
II

10

RHEA

"YOU ARE LATE. It is becoming a habit."

I blink against the flickering oil lamps and down into Cyrrian's face. I thought it would be the Master of Keys who'd be waiting for me in the Mother's temple. The old warrior has been my silent companion most evenings since Prince Scamandrius's birth. Six weeks that have passed in the blink of an eye. If he has questions about what keeps me later some nights than others, he does not possess the ability to ask. Cyrrian is a different story.

He looks as aloof and handsome as ever in the shadows of the temple. Once, that would have aggravated me. When I first saw Cyrrian in Hector's stables, I'd been struck by the beauty he wears as carelessly as Paris wears his finest robes. It was only when I got to know him better through our work with Andromache that I saw that beauty for what it truly is.

A shield. Against what or whom is anyone's guess.

"Briseis's guards are no longer easily distracted," I tell him. It is not an outright lie.

I hold the basket to my chest. The one hopelessly crushed by Ajax's hands when I returned to the camp after the prince's birth all those weeks ago. I quickly lower the basket in a vain attempt to look innocent.

Cyrrian scowls. "One of these days the sun will beat you back to the walls. You are growing careless, and I grow weary of waiting for you to get yourself killed."

"Your concern is heartening," I say through clenched teeth. Nobody has the power to infuriate me the way that Cyrrian does. I might feel guilty for that if the sentiment weren't entirely mutual.

"I'm not the one who should be concerned." He moves aside so I can emerge fully into the temple. For a moment, we stand on either side of the gentle face of the Mother goddess, staring at each other in hostile silence. It has been like this since Odysseus's attack. A chill has settled between us that my repeated attempts at civility have been powerless to thaw. Though he's never said it out loud, I think Cyrrian knows why I was late the day Odysseus's men attacked the Lower City. I feel it in the way he watches me when he thinks I don't notice. A grudging acknowledgment that he is no longer the only one in our uneasy partnership with secrets.

It is a novelty neither of us seems to enjoy.

Don't meet him. The words Cyrrian said to me the night before the festival when I went to find Ajax in the stones. *Ajax son of Telamon is no ordinary Achaean. He is easily the deadliest warrior to set foot on our shores despite the odes the bards heap on his cousin. More importantly, he is a man. I'm afraid you aren't so good at judging those.*

As far as Cyrrian knows, I've never gone back to the stones after that night. And yet I hear it echo in the tense silences between us.

Suspicion.

"You are relieved of your duties," I tell him hurriedly. "I can walk myself home." Cyrrian has been my silent escort since Helen's miraculous return from the dead and the attention it has brought. The crowds that gathered at Hector and Andromache's house, eager to touch Helen like she is an amulet from the gods, have become impatient, even dangerous on occasion. Helen has done her best to help where she can, but with so many growing malnourished, the need is greater than any one woman could meet alone.

"And if I want to walk with you?" He leans back against the stone wall, his expression unreadable.

I rub my cheek, too tired tonight for his games. "We both know you'd rather not. Go on. I'll make excuses so you can find the first warm, available bed to fall into."

A flash of something. Too quick to catch.

He pushes off the wall. "Because in your infinite cleverness, you know me so well. Is that it, Rhea?"

"I don't know you," I admit, suddenly weary to the bone. "That is an honor you choose to withhold from everyone."

"You speak of secrets as if you don't have any."

A trickle of mountain water down my spine.

"What . . . what do you mean?"

His smile is sharp as Phoenician glass. "You once told me I'm smarter than I look. Do you think it's escaped my notice how you come back later and later each evening, usually with nothing to show for it but tired eyes and flushed cheeks? Or that the information you do bring is not the kind any warrior careful enough to survive ten years of war would idly spill in a bathhouse?"

There it is. The true source of the anger that has turned the air frigid between us. As close as he can come to an outright accusation without speaking Ajax's name.

Fear crystallizes. Cyrrian is indeed cleverer than he'd have anyone believe. I should have been more careful to account for my time in front of him. If Cyrrian tells Andromache I've been meeting with Ajax the Great, she will never understand. She might even go so far as to stop sending me through the wall.

I cannot let that happen.

I square my shoulders because any sign of weakness now would be an admission of guilt I cannot afford. "You spend a curious amount of time thinking about things that are none of your concern."

"Tell me you aren't meeting him."

Silence falls heavy as shadows between us.

"I'm not meeting him." I make myself meet his eyes. "I am not a fool."

We stare at each other in the dim glow of the hearth fire. I don't know if either of us truly believes me, but it isn't about what Cyrrian believes. It's about what he can prove.

"You've changed since you first went through the wall," he says at last. There is something in his tone that almost sounds like . . . regret.

"I've become who Troy needs me to be."

"Haven't we all?" Cyrrian says. "But be careful, Rhea." More words from our past. "Tell the same lies over and over again and sooner or later you start to believe them."

Once, this condescension would have sent me cowering. Now, it fills me with anger because what right has he to judge me?

"Do you never tire of it?" I step toward him. "Using indifference as a shield? Laughing at the world and everyone in it when you're the only one allowed to know the joke?"

"Brave words." Cyrrian meets my step with one of his own. But he does not stop there. He advances until my back is pressed against the cold stone and the fire of him is all that I can feel.

"Is that what you really want? To know me? To collect all my secrets and store them away in the crammed amphoras of your mind?" He bends down and a curl tumbles over his forehead. I watch it fall, black strands shimmering in the firelight.

"What are you doing?" I ask, my voice panicked.

He smiles. There is not an ounce of humor in it. "Exactly what you asked for. Offering you truth for truth." A few more inches and we are breathing the same air. "Mine is right here." This close, the Aegean of his eyes is bottomless. "Are you feeling brave, Rhea?" His breath kisses my lips. "Brave enough to take it?"

My gaze dances over his face, searching for meaning and finding nothing but defiance.

Ajax said he liked the way I listen. It is the one small pride I've always taken in myself. My ability to hear and see what others don't. But the man standing before me is not one I recognize despite the many nights we have spent together in this damp temple. There is nothing cold or aloof about him; instead, he glows like the hottest part of a flame.

The room grows thick and close. Every second that passes feels like an open dare. I bite the inside of my cheek to keep myself from rising to it. I won't let him drag me into his anger only so that he can take it out on me. We have danced that dance before, and it always leaves me burned.

I lean back. "I have no interest in your games," I tell him. "Let me go."

The fire inside him turns to smoke, but still he does not step back. "I am not a horse you can command."

"No," I agree, smiling only because I know it will irk him. "I've never met a horse so ill tempered."

I step around him, and our shoulders brush. The glancing touch pulls me up short. The satisfied twist to his lips makes me want to push him directly into the hearth.

"If you ever grow a spine, Rhea, you know where to find me."

Digging my nails into my palm, I leave Cyrrian in the temple without a backward glance. I should've known better than to think he'd let me have the last word.

Dawn is breaking when I finally stumble down the narrow alley beside Hector and Andromache's house. I sag against the kitchen door. For once, the streets around the house are silent and empty of those seeking miracles. The nights are growing longer even as the days grow shorter, but I am not quite ready for this night to end. At least, not yet.

It's only been six weeks since the birth, but the hours I've stolen with Andromache and her newborn son are already a chest of memories gilded in gold. I wouldn't trade them for anything, despite the toll they've taken. I pause to catch my breath and sort through the meager offerings I have for Andromache.

When I returned to Agamemnon's hall after Scamandrius's birth with a gift from Andromache—a rough carving of the grandmother, Hannahanna—Briseis had taken it with a nod. Since then, she's been true to her word. The scene she has painted for us of Agamemnon's private world is that of a vain man who worships himself and has no tolerance for those who don't follow suit. It is why he hates Achilles. Why he keeps Menelaus close even though he loathes his own brother. Agamemnon is petty and proud, and as with most men, his insecurity is born of fear.

According to Briseis, he has been driven half-mad by reports of gray ships off the coasts of Ugarit to Mycenae. Ships full of masked men whose arrival has made every Achaean turn his gaze toward home. He distrusts the warriors at his back and the kings invited to sit at his table each night. He fears abandonment and humiliation. But mostly, he fears Achilles—the threat his open defiance poses to Agamemnon's carefully crafted image. It is not the death of thousands of warriors that keeps him awake at night, but the thought that he might one day be revealed for the jealous, petty man and poor leader he truly is.

Briseis says Agamemnon would rather die.

And so, he has turned to the one man who offers solutions instead of platitudes. A warrior whose gates remain closed and whose men are still hard at work at some secret project behind their walls . . . walls we cannot access no matter how many new girls Ven recruits to our cause.

Whenever Odysseus comes to speak with the king of Mycenae, Briseis is sent from the rooms.

"*He never took such precautions before,*" she confided in me earlier tonight. "*Something has changed.*"

The kitchen should still be empty at this hour, but instead, I'm greeted by a roaring fire and a gathering of women around the central hearth.

Creusa is sleeping soundly in a chair with a blanket drawn high over her swelling womb. Beside her, Helen rocks quietly, her fingers gracefully working a blanket done in fabrics too bright for the early hour. Between caring for Aeneas and trying to get close to the wives of council members on Andromache's behalf, it is a wonder Helen finds time for such things. To say nothing of the many others who seek her out. Even now, a basket of tinctures and salves sits next to her, ready for the dawning day. In truth, Helen is the only person I know who sleeps less than I do.

On the other side of the hearth, Cassandra sits alone. The princess's posture is as straight as a spear. Her hands tightly grip the object in her lap—one she puts down only on the occasions when she holds her nephew.

It is a crescent knife still stained with Andromache's blood.

I lift my gaze from the weapon to meet Cassandra's yellow eyes. "Don't worry, little mouse." Her voice slithers sideways through the air. "There's no need for more bloodshed. Yet."

Swallowing hard, I walk across the kitchen to where Bodecca is beating a mound of dough she has somehow managed to conjure from a handful of flour and a basket of shriveled acorns, all the while studying our guests with an expression that is the opposite of welcoming.

"They are still here." I state the obvious under my breath.

Bodecca scowls. "And it doesn't look as if they have plans to leave anytime soon."

The women haven't strayed far since the night of Andrius's birth. When I close my eyes, I can still feel the warmth in the room. A canopy of hushed female voices and infant coos. A cocoon of milky breath and the rise and fall of a tiny chest. A secret sanctuary for a little prince who commanded a force entirely his own—a battalion of singing women who rocked and hummed and paced all hours of the night.

A sudden urge fills me. To see Scamandrius and cradle his little body in my arms. But first, I walk up to Cassandra, whose narrow face in the hearth light is almost as haggard as mine.

"You should go home, Harsa. Get some sleep."

She blinks slowly at me. "I have been sleeping for twelve years. It is your turn now, little mouse." She shoos me away with her slender hands. "Rest and do not fear. I will guard the prince."

The flesh of my arms prickles. "Guard him from what?"

Cassandra's knuckles turn white against the bone handle of her knife. "The raptors."

Darkness stirs in her pupils. The kind that swallows every bit of light it touches. Fighting the urge to back away, I offer her a weak nod and walk out of the kitchen and through the main hall. Instead of turning toward the servant rooms, I keep going straight up the stairs until I am at Andromache's door.

The curtain that usually covers the balcony has been drawn back, revealing the river and the plains for which Hector and Andromache's son is named.

Scamandrius.

A name spelled out with the blood of a thousand warriors.

A name that cries out with the fury and faithfulness of the wind.

In the outline of the dawn, Hector stands in his armor, rocking his sleeping son in his arms. In the swimming shadows of morning, his stalwart face is laid bare. Every wall turned to rubble by the tiny being in his arms.

The sight fixes me in place. I don't know how much time passes. Enough for me to think of my own father. To wonder if he ever held me like this. If he ever woke early just so he could steal with me those hours before dawn. My eyes burn because I know in my heart that he did.

"Do you want to hold him?" Hector whispers in the silence.

I step all the way into the room. "I came to check on them. I didn't mean to intrude."

"You are never intruding, Rhea. This is your home."

Emotions rise in my throat. Sadness for all I've lost. Joy for all I've found.

"How do you always know when I'm there?"

"I imagine the same way the horses do."

Larion once called the way I speak to horses magic, but it isn't. Not really. It is less a practice than it is a place. A cavern that rings with the horses' whispers and echoes my feelings back to them. A place as real to me as the farm where I spent the first sixteen years of my life before men with swords and spears burned everything I loved to the ground.

"You have it." I voice the thing I've long suspected. "The *assussanni* gift."

"A touch. Though not like you do." He smiles, and like the most precious of stones, I cut the image from the air and fix it in my memory. "I knew it the moment I saw you."

His words bring me back to that slave market in Cyzicus where I first saw the prince of Troy. Hot sun beating down on my back and the coarse rope biting into my neck. The scent of sweat and salt and the silent terror of the girls bound beside me, because they knew the fate that awaited us. A fate the prince of Troy saved me from even before he knew who I was. The daughter of Haskim of Phrygia, a loyal friend who'd fought and died at Hector's side, only to leave his own wife and daughters defenseless in his absence. A man Prince Hector saw buried in the customs of my people, entombed in earth and beneath stone somewhere on the distant plain.

Even now, I can hear the cry of the fire horse as he ran wild in his pen in that slave market where the prince found me. Feel the strength of Hector's gentle hands as they pulled that rope free from around my neck.

Hector lowers his chin so that his jaw brushes the soft, dark hair with the copper streak crowning his son's head. "I wonder if the horses will whisper to him as they do to us."

"Not if he takes after his mother."

Hector chuckles low, and the child stirs against his broad chest. "I pray to the gods that Andrius takes after Andromache in all things." His eyes drift to his wife sleeping on the nearby bed, and the love that shines from their depths fills me with longing. But there is something else too. Something that looks almost like sadness.

"Andrius?" I whisper to distract him from wherever his thoughts have gone.

Hector grins, and it makes him look like the young man he must've been before the cares of a prince wrote their marks across his face. "As much as I love the name we chose for him, Scamandrius seems a rather large title for such a little fellow."

"It suits him," I say. "Though you must've heard what the people have begun to call him." For as long as I live, I'll never forget the cheers that rose the day that he was born. Men poured out precious wine to the gods. Women conjured feasts from nothing. Children ran wild through the streets, and for once, the tears in the old women's eyes were ones of joy, not sorrow.

Hector nods, his expression suddenly solemn. "To the people of Troy he will be Astyanax, lord of the city. But to us, the ones who love him best, he will be Andrius." Hector places the sleeping baby against my breast. The child burrows into me, unleashing a rush of warmth pure and bright as the first mountain snow. For a moment, all the ragged edges of the world are softened by his sweetness.

I am cradling him to me when Hector drops down to place a kiss on his son's head. Hector stands, but instead of leaving straightaway, he ducks once more, pressing a second kiss. This one to the top of my head.

A swell of emotion heats my face. "Are you leaving so early to make your run around Troy's walls?" I ask.

"No. My father has called me to the Citadel. The council has finally agreed on what should be done with an heir who so openly defied their wishes."

He means the day his men rode out to save Aeneas despite his father's commands. I steal a worried glance at Andromache, but she is still sleeping soundly. "They will punish you?"

"They will try." He smiles, but it is strangely sad. "I should have told you before," he says, glancing at the sleeping child in my arms. "Thank you, Rhea. For guarding them so well."

I don't know why, but his words send a whisper through my blood. Before I can question it, Hector leaves us. I rock Andrius to my chest until Hector's broad back disappears completely and the sky lightens. The sun rises, Andrius stirs, his little hand reaching to grip tight to my finger, and in that single act, I feel the course of my destiny shift, my life forever bound to his, just as his is bound to mine.

"My son is a morning lark. Like his father." Andromache's groggy voice rises from the bed.

I turn to find her watching us dance in the rising light. Immediately, I move to bring her the child, but she just shakes her head.

"He is a handsome boy, isn't he?" Andromache asks with a weary smile.

I look down at his squishy face, still covered in fading bruises.

Andrius.

"The handsomest," I say.

"In this, he is his father's son." Andromache leans back against the pillows. "I hope he will take after him in most things."

I smile at her choice of words. My parents loved each other. I often saw that fondness between them, but still, my mother had her world and my father had his. They loved each other well in all the places where those two worlds touched. What Hector and Andromache have is different. Like the moon and the sun, they share the same sky, lighting the world with the dance between them. Warming the sea and driving the tides.

Unbidden, my thoughts drift toward the circle of stones. Andrius stirs.

"Cassandra is still here," I say, pulling my mind away from dark and dangerous paths.

Andromache sighs. "I am starting to think she's forgotten the way back to the Citadel."

"Bodecca may soon take matters into her own hands."

"Cassandra makes her nervous. Though I can't say I blame Bodecca there." Her face sobers.

"What is it?" I ask.

"Cassandra is different somehow. It's almost as if . . . as if she is someone I have never met."

I nod. "I didn't realize the princess and Helen were close."

"Neither did I." Andromache rubs her hands over her stomach. "But Cassandra's vigil makes me wonder."

"About what?"

Andromache meets my gaze. "About what else she knows that we don't."

My grip on Andrius tightens.

"I met with Briseis tonight," I tell her. "She says Agamemnon and Odysseus often disappear behind closed doors. She thinks—"

"Shh." Andromache hushes me softly. "You are tired. Just this once, your news can wait until tomorrow."

Gratefully, I nod, and she holds out her arms. I place Andrius upon her chest and laugh at the way his mouth roots instantly for her breast. The smile on Andromache's face is almost painfully bright as she leads him to the thing he seeks. Motherhood has already softened every hard line, every angle, and I swear that no woman on earth could compare to her beauty.

I stand, but Andromache grips my hand. With a gentle tug, she pulls me back down onto the bed beside her.

"Lie here, Rhea. Your cares will still be here when you wake."

She strokes my brow, and I lean into her touch. Into Andrius's warmth and the feeling of belonging. Of home.

A moment later, Andromache's rich alto drifts through the room. I don't know the words of the song she sings, but I know it is a lullaby. Just as I know it's meant for me as much as it is meant for the child between us.

The earth falls away as I drift toward sleep. Andromache's voice reaches me from that place between waking and dreams. "I think I know why Cassandra is here. Why she can't bring herself to leave."

My eyes flutter shut even as my mind clings to her words. "Why?"

"Because in this house there is no death. Only life."

11

HELEN

"IT'S GOING NOWHERE, Andromache. How many more halls must I dine in?"

Andromache's brows narrow. "Most of the Citadel's Harssi have jumped at the opportunity to host Troy's talisman. Most, except for Tumaeus and Kalawashi, who have been reticent in extending an invitation. Doesn't that strike you as odd?"

"It does," I agree. After I helped her melancholy daughter, it was Kalawashi's enthusiasm that caused the other Citadel Harssi to act; that way they might be the first to boast proximity to the phoenix of the Lower City attack. Yet in six weeks, I have learned nothing from these tedious meals but the latest gossip.

"It's him." Andromache rises to pace the kitchen, but not before I slip a burp cloth beneath Andrius's sleeping head on her shoulder. "I can feel it," she seethes as her restless body begins to burn off heat. "Tumaeus is the roadblock on the Five. He wishes to prevent the army from making an aggressive assault. Total war would end what meager business dealings Tumaeus has left. He has made his wealth through trade, and any sea routes still open to Troy are controlled by Paris. Of course they would join forces to serve their shared interests."

I nod. "And if Tumaeus and Paris have recently parted ways, then I am the last Harsa he would want to dine in his home."

"Which means the best path to the truth is his wife," Andromache says.

"I ought to arrange to meet Kalawashi in public, then. Somewhere Tumaeus isn't able to prevent us from speaking candidly."

"The Citadel bathhouse?"

"That might work." The women of the Citadel spend long hours there to escape the heat, lounging in the spring-fed pools.

Andromache hesitates. "On second thought, that is close to Paris's palace."

"Paris will not move against me now. Not when the entire city considers me its charm of good fortune."

And I'm not sure which is worse: to be blamed or worshipped. Either way, distance from the palace has provided many gifts. I am no longer afraid of Paris, for one. Maybe that is the true miracle.

"Still, your personal guard must accompany you everywhere." Andromache nods to the Master of Keys, standing silently in the doorway. "This is dangerous work, Helen. Do you understand?"

She is serious, but I smile. To be within Andromache's circle of concern is to feel cared for with unrivaled fierceness. "No one has tried kidnapping me yet. At least not today."

Andromache chuckles. "Perhaps. But if Tumaeus is really the Old Blood who once pulled Paris's strings, then I am sending you into the belly of the beast." She sighs. "There is no helping it. We need to win over the Five. If we don't launch our offensive soon, the Achaeans will beat us to it with a siege. But no matter what doorway you darken, you must keep the Master of Keys close."

"As you say, Commander."

Andromache's mouth turns up. "These *are* deployments, you realize. Be they of a different kind."

I glance again at the Master of Keys, my silent protector. His expressionless face shows no sign he's heard Andromache's many revelations, though she's clearly not worried about the mute man sharing the information he is privy to. The Master of Keys' eyes rest on the baby dozing on Andromache's shoulder. Only I seem to notice the longing that fills them. When he isn't escorting me through the city or spending a night watch guarding the Mother temple for Rhea so Cyrrian can rest, the Master of Keys is here. You would not expect a retired soldier of the king's guard to look so at home in a woman's kitchen, but he does. Even Bodecca seems unflustered by the male infiltrator as she scurries about us, banging together pots and jugs.

The Master of Keys is not the only one who feels at home. Between the demand for my healer's hands and my efforts with the council, I have never been so exhausted.

I have also never felt so alive.

"The best way to sway the Five to vote in favor of launching an offensive is to sniff out the mole on the council," Andromache continues, bouncing Andrius when he awakes and starts to fuss.

Which is why I have placed myself in countless rooms where everybody speaks and no one listens. Yet these efforts have not borne much fruit. So why not climb to the top of the tree?

I look to Andromache as a new idea forms. "I could speak directly with Priam."

She grunts. "Do not pin your hopes there. They say the king's mind is drifting more with each moon. I know Priam once . . . cared for you. But he is not the same man he was."

"Be that as it may, I would like to try."

The king, after all, is the common knot among these tangled threads. If Tumaeus won't expose himself and Kalawashi has been ordered to hold her tongue in my presence, why not seek out the man who elevated Tumaeus to the Five in the first place?

"Fine," Andromache relents. "Let's pray King Priam gives more weight to your words than he has ever given to mine."

ONCE WE LEAVE Andromache's kitchen, the Master of Keys and I make a straight path to Priam's throne room. Unexpectedly, the old warrior insists on waiting outside its massive doors rather than inside where he can see me. As if he is afraid to take a single step into that great, yawning hall.

My slippered feet barely make a sound as they cross the throne room's floor, its plaster etched in elaborate designs. At the center of the hall is a large fire. Whirls of smoke exit through a circular hole in the roof. Though few burn fires in this heat, Luwian lore claims this flame has remained lit for as long as Troy has existed. Its warmth hits me like a wall, and the thick air tickles the back of my throat. Four pillars surround the hearth, painted in swirling designs of red, blue, and gold that guide the eye upward. Equally detailed paintings of griffins and winged horses cover the walls, floor to ceiling. It is a space so overwhelming, one would almost miss its entire focus.

The unassuming throne of stone where a man who might be mistaken for a statue sits.

"Helen." The king's face warms with life. Priam pats the empty chair beside him, usually reserved for Queen Hecuba. He is alone, thankfully, except for the guards stationed by the entrance and in front of the steps leading up to him. "Come sit, my dear. I have missed our talks."

If Priam has believed me dead these past few months or has received word of my newfound fame, nothing about his manner suggests it now. We are picking up right where we last left off. Given Andromache's warning about the state of his mind, that is not a good sign.

"I have missed you too, Father." I climb the steps to kiss the king's rough cheek. When I first came to Troy, I walked veiled through a misty world where every sound was muddled by the poppy flower's poison. None more so than my own voice. Yet I always heard Priam. Not because I had to, but because I sensed there were hidden treasures buried within the old king, even if his kingdom increasingly regarded his wisdom as irrelevant.

Everything has changed since those early days. Yet the king still looks at me like I am his own daughter. As if he does not notice that he can now gaze upon my entire face.

Maybe he always has.

Priam takes hold of my hand. The soft light in his eyes fades as he glances around the empty hall. Once again, he looks lost. Or maybe he is simply traveling to that place where old men like to dwell.

The past.

Where all his greatest deeds still lie ahead of him.

"Paris . . ." I begin, trying to call the king back.

Priam releases a sound like a wet cough crossed with a chuckle. "When Paris first returned to the city, he and Hector were inseparable. As inseparable as Antenor and I in our youth. As inseparable as Anchises and . . ." His shoulders slump forward, collapsing on whatever boyhood memory he was about to share.

"What changed?"

"Not what, who. *She* changed everything."

I assume he's speaking of Andromache, but then King Priam says, "He has the look of her. His mother."

I frown, confused. "Hecuba?"

There is no one in his family Paris resembles less. It is one of the few ways the gods have blessed him.

Priam shakes his head. "No. Derya. It's why their son always thought himself too big for his shield. Why Aeneas considers himself a Trojan . . . though I admit he has the look of one." A stark look of grief transforms the king's feeble face. The way the woman's name rolls around his mouth tells me that whoever she is, Derya once dwelled in Priam's chamber of secrets. The place I am sitting now.

"Anchises," the old king hisses, an ocean of regret filling his eyes. "He never understood her. He never tried."

Is this Derya, Aeneas's mother, the reason Priam and his cousin Anchises are no longer close? Enough of a reason for Anchises to betray his king's trust if given the chance?

"My cousin failed to see that even the strongest can drown when the waters rise too quickly."

And what I see is a flicker of the king, the *man*, Priam must have been. The man I believe he might still be. For even these fractured stories are not the self-absorbed ramblings of a delusional king. They have a grounded understanding that the vipers who gather around him surely twist to their own advantage.

Which raises the question: If the waters are rising once more, who is about to drown?

A throat clears behind us. "May I have a word, my king?"

I turn to find a man with deep-set eyes and heavy jowls standing before the throne. A large man, one I would not expect to be so light-footed.

"What is it, Tumaeus?" Priam waves his hand before releasing a yawn.

My ears tingle at the sight of Kalawashi's husband. His beady eyes rove over me as he licks his lips. He is no doubt greedy, but he seems like a man whose lusts are of the flesh, not power.

Even still, one vice tends to open the gates to others.

I listen carefully as the man speaks, straining to notice the distinctive lilt I once heard rising and falling in Paris's rooms through a layer of stone.

"It's the allies, my king. They continue making themselves known in Troy's Merchant and Artisan Quarters, and it's causing no shortage of discomfort among some of the Citadel Harssi who do their shopping there."

Priam nods, the king within him emerging. "Hector has taken to his foreign captains. As have the people in Troy's lower rings. After the role the allies played in containing the fire, I find it hard to blame them."

I hold my breath. And with it, all the things Priam is not willing to say to this man who speaks of Troy's fighting allies as if reporting an infestation of roaches.

Tumaeus bows with false sincerity. "True enough, my king. But is there nothing we can do to corral them back to residences more . . . suitable?"

"Tell Harsa Kalawashi that we will make sure our allies are preoccupied by other duties soon enough," replies the king.

I suspect Andromache will have a thing or two to say about that.

Tumaeus bows again and takes his leave. As I watch him go, I feel no more convinced that his was the voice I heard in Paris's rooms. Though I cannot rule it out either. I am about to make some excuse so I can trail the man when Hector and his cousin Polydamas stride into the throne room.

Normally, Priam's face would brighten at the sight of his vigorous heir, but today it cracks with what almost looks like sorrow. "I see that Troy's newest father wears his lack of sleep better than most."

"Playing parent to a thousand men has given me some practice," Hector says with a forced smile.

The exchange is courteous enough, but pulled with more tension than the thread of my loom. Hector eyes me wearily. Perhaps he wonders what I am doing here so close to Paris's haunts.

"You summoned me, Father?"

A *summons*? One Andromache cannot be aware of. I start to stand, but Priam holds up his hand.

"It's all right, Helen. You may stay."

I sit back down. It seems Priam wants me as a witness.

Hector clears his throat, continuing with all the hesitancy of a golden boy who has never once been sent to bed without supper. "Father, I know you think I acted rashly in riding out to rescue Aeneas, but it's time to correct past mistakes. It's time for us to do what we should have done long ago."

"What mistakes do you speak of?" asks the king dispassionately.

"The attack on the Lower City brought us close to ruin. We will not survive such an offensive twice." Hector tightens his grip on the horsehair helmet in his hands, avoiding my gaze. Most likely because we both know these words are not his own. I can hear Andromache in every echo. "Diomedes and his men were badly shaken by our deflection of their chariot attack, but we believe it was merely preparation for a siege. We should strike soon."

"The council will not move," Priam says, sounding more forceful and aware as the conversation goes on. "To break with the Five would undo centuries of customs put in place to protect Troy from internal strife and instability."

Hector nods; his expression is the opposite of surprise. "That leaves us one option, then: borrowing a strategy from our enemies. We must challenge one of their champions to a duel."

The king shakes his head. "We have tried that route before—"

"And it failed because we sent the wrong man," Polydamas cuts in before clearing his throat. "Forgive my impertinence, King Priam. I simply meant that if *Hector* had fought Menelaus instead of—"

"Then we would have no need for this audience," the king agrees. "My judgment that day may have been in error, but it makes me even less inclined to make the same mistake again. In ten years, Agamemnon has never attempted a siege. Coming so close to our walls would cost him dearly. In men. In supplies. What makes you think he is willing to do so now when it is precisely those resources, men, and supplies that are threatened by larger forces only the gods can control?"

It is a fair question. Hector's son is not even two months old. Aeneas, his right hand, is bedridden, trapped in some shadowy wood outside the Underworld. I shift my focus to Polydamas, Antenor's eldest son. His amicable voice has echoed through Paris's halls often enough. Might Polydamas encourage Hector to extend his own willing neck for other reasons?

Furthermore, has Hector told Andromache *any* of this?

No. She cannot possibly know. A duel is a strategy she would never encourage. Not when she knows as well as I that regardless of the outcome or what they promise, the Achaeans won't return to their crumbling king-doms without my buried dowry.

And no one knows where Paris has hidden it.

"That is not a chance I am willing to take. At this point, what else can Agamemnon do *but* siege?" Hector grinds his teeth, suggesting there's more he wants to say. Information whose true source can never be re-vealed. "This has always been my battle and my destiny, Father. As you said, I too have mistakes for which I must atone. It is why you called me here, is it not? So let *this* be my punishment."

The words are a trap so skillfully set, none in this throne room save Hector know it is there until it has fully sprung.

The king's eyes widen. He can hardly refuse Hector now.

Priam unclenches his trembling hands. During the long pause that de-scends, Hector glances my way. "How is Aeneas?" he asks, giving his father the time he needs.

"He remains with us," I say. "He has much in this world worth cling-ing to."

And so do you.

So why would Hector even consider this duel?

In the swallow that travels down his throat, it becomes clear that the near loss of Aeneas has shaken Hector's solid trunk. After all, if a warrior the people claim was birthed by a goddess—not this mortal woman Priam still grieves for—if even *he* can come close to death, then maybe Hector's own days are numbered. None of these warriors are as young as they were when this war began. Soon the old leaves will fall from the oak, making way for the new.

It's a slow realization that cannot be prepared for. A musing that at-tacks late in the night while a man rocks his newborn to sleep.

The faint whisper of mortality.

"What do you say, Father?" Hector repeats, his squared chest broad and firm. "Will you permit me to save our city from certain destruction and the house of Priam with it?"

"No." Something in Priam's voice alters. "We cannot risk losing you."

"*Yes*, we can. I can beat any man the Achaeans put forward. Because I must."

Tears spring to my eyes. Hector wants victory for the same reason Priam wants to deny it. To spare the son who would carry on his name.

"If you do this . . ." Priam extends his withered hand toward Hector. "Then you *must* win."

Hector exhales. Behind him, Polydamas glows with a triumph that leaves me uneasy. It is one thing to let Hector duel. It is another to *want* him to.

Yet it does not matter what I feel. King Priam has agreed that the prince of Troy will fight for the fate of his city, and it may well cost Hector his life. There is only one other person who deserves to know these plans she had no say in, and I will not let secrets divide us ever again. The resigned glance Hector casts my way before he turns to leave tells me he already knows it.

"Hector, before you issue the challenge, you must go and see your brother," the king insists. "If this is the will of the gods, then Helenus must confirm it."

Hector and Polydamas take their leave, and I murmur an excuse to Priam for my hasty departure. As soon as the throne room's smoke is behind me, I rush to Andromache's door. Telling her what I've learned while Andrius nurses sweetly at her breast is excruciating, but I do it.

I tell Andromache every word.

The clay cup on the table beside her shatters against the far wall. "*Why?* Why would Hector do this now? Without even talking to me first?"

Because he is a man.

"He knew you would try to stop him. I saw his face, Andromache." Just as I now see hers. There is something to be said for a woman who openly wears her anger like the brooch that holds up her robe. "Hector truly believes this is a way to end the war."

The hurt in Andromache's eyes assures me that this truth does not make his hidden actions sting any less.

She rises to her feet. The leveling look Andromache gives me is drained of all ire. Instead, it has a tinge of fear that leaves me wondering what she sees that I am missing.

"Oh, there is another way to end this war, Helen. And the council knows it well."

12

CASSANDRA

DRIP.

Drip.

Drip.

Drops of red trickle down the stone slab. Spatter, spatter on the floor.

The kill is fresh. Bright blood swelling the shallow tributaries carved into the offering table set between two large horns. Ruby rivers flowing toward images of thirsty gods holding up golden cups. Their goblets overflow onto the white tiles.

Drip.

 Drip.

  Drip.

Every drop echoes through the silent, empty temple. The priests and priestesses left after the noon sacrifice to cleanse their bodies in the antechamber. I watched them from the shadows. Only shadows wait with me now. And time. I can feel it. Wet. Slippery. Like blood from the stone, running viscous through my hands.

Not much longer, says the Crone.

I want to go. I don't like this place, whimpers the Child.

I do not like it either.

The High Temple is nothing like the modest shrine to the Mother goddess that serves the common people. No, this monstrosity sits directly next to my father's palace. Just like the palace, it is ostentation without substance.

Full of echoing cold.

It's the place where the Old Blood of Troy come to worship, which is a pretty way of saying it is where they come to bribe the gods for their favor.

A green prayer pool sits at the center of the temple, just beyond the offering slab with its gaudy horns of gold. Emerald water surrounded by white stones where the bones of offerings are thrown to honor the many deities of the Underworld. The ceiling is held up by heavy columns. Lining every wall are dozens of shrines. So many gods. So many forms of fear. Achaean and Hittite. Hattian and Hurrian. Phrygian and Thracian, and some older. Ancient as the mountains themselves.

It is the old gods that call to me.

At least they did, before I had the dream. The one of Apollo. The way he shone in the outline of my window. I had prayed and prayed, but if the true sun god heard my prayers, he did not answer them. Perhaps he even laughed as the truth of my dream was revealed to me.

Stupid, stupid girl, who thought she would be visited by a god. Let her be visited by misery instead.

I press my back to the cold stone pillar. I hate this temple. Hate everything it stands for. Old gods mixed with new. Novelty mixed with tradition until all the colors have run to a muddy brown.

It is a temple for people who have chosen to believe in everything, so their beliefs amount to nothing.

It is a temple for people who worship gods only as reflections of themselves.

She approaches the stone slab, a knife just like the one in my hand, hanging from the crimson belt of her robes.

The sight of her is enough to make me want to shed my own skin.

The Hawk explodes from my chest, screaming for the sky.

Steady. Hold steady now, whispers the Crone.

The Child whimpers.

The Fury hisses.

The Wraith rocks silently in the dark.

I grip my knife in my hand and step out of the shadows.

"Hello, Mother."

"Cassandra."

She stands before the huwasi-stone backlit by the fires of a hundred oil lamps that are never allowed to go out. To an observer's eye, Hecuba, Queen of Troy, appears impenetrable as the stone gods all around us, but I know better. I have surprised her.

Her fear is an incense perfuming the air. Sweet as honey on my tongue.

The Fury's laughter rings up the well. I bite my cheek to keep it from spilling from my lips.

My smile is a knife slash. "Have you come to pray for forgiveness?"

"Don't be so dramatic, Cassandra."

"Being locked away by your own mother will do that to a girl."

Painted lips lift like a curtain revealing the darkness she hides from the world. "The only regret I have in this life is that I did not drown you in the bathwater the day you were born."

The Child cries into the Crone's robes.

The Wraith rocks back and forth in the dirt at the bottom of the well.

The Fury inside me looses a scream loud enough to rock the very pillars of the earth.

"As you left Paris to die?" I ask.

My mother's face goes stark white. It is the secret we share. One not even my father knows. Like me, Hecuba believes in the truth of dreams. It was a dream that warned her Paris would bring ruin to Troy. Paris was meant to die of cold at the foot of the mountain. Only the mountain saved him instead.

A death sentence that was never carried out. A skeleton that did not stay buried.

When Paris returned to claim his birthright, our mother welcomed him home with a false smile and open arms. On the outside, she pretends to love him the same way she loves Hector and her other sons, but I have seen the truth.

So has he.

It is the one thing Paris and I share. We are both detested by the woman who bore us. But whereas my mother's hatred has imprisoned me, it has made Paris mean.

My smile stretches until it cracks. "Yes, Mother. I know your shadows. They whisper to me. *All* of them."

Hecuba snarls. "Do not presume to judge me. If I had succeeded in disposing of Paris back then, none of this would have happened!"

I take a step closer. Forcing myself to draw nearer to her darkness. It pulls at me. Beckoning. *Wanting*, always *wanting*.

"Or perhaps if you had kept him close, if you had loved him well, you would have raised a son who cared more for his city than himself. A son who would never bring ruin to her walls."

A son like Hector.

I do not say it. There is no need.

The shadows between us swirl. Hurt and Anger. Fear and Regret.

But none of these are the reason we have come here, chides the Crone.

"You are making an offering." My gaze drops to the knife in my mother's hand.

"For Astyanax." The way she speaks his name reeks of ownership. "Our little lord of the city." She lays her gifts upon the stone slab with a tenderness that squeezes something inside me. "His anointing ceremony is to take place on the new moon. All of the Citadel's women will lift his name to the gods."

The joy in her voice swells inside my breast. The very last thread binding us.

"He will need you. Before the end." I say the thing we came here to say. "When the time arrives, you must put aside your vanity and heed her call, for when she calls, there will be only one hope left." My words turn to glass. My throat stings with the effort of coughing up every jagged piece. "Listen. For once, Mother. You must *listen*."

"Stop it!" Venom spews from her mouth. "I will see your doors barred with heavy stones. I'll order the entire tower fired in clay if that's what it takes to be rid of your rambling."

"Then you have not heard?" I cast out her words and hear the pain echoing back to me.

"I have not heard *what*?"

"I do not live in the tower anymore."

"Cease with the nonsense, Cassandra. You are pitied in the palace and feared in every other circle of Troy. No one else would have you."

"He would."

The oil lamps around the altar flicker as a gust of wind rushes through the temple. A large form enters by way of the wide stone arches.

Hector! the Child cries out in delight.

The Fury lowers her sword.

Go! screeches the Crone. *Before it is too late.*

I run up to my brother as the Child urges me to, and I throw my arms around his neck. Even battle-weary and crushed by the weights he bears, Hector catches me and runs a hand over the back of my head the way he has since I was a girl. I press my nose into his neck and find it buried beneath the stench of death.

Sweat and hay. Horses and sandalwood.

Time crystallizes like honey until I am back in the stables with my brother when he wasn't so broad. When his face wasn't lined, and I hadn't yet found the well of shades inside me. My hands full of straw and my sandals covered in mud.

Back before the dream and the tower. When I was merely *strange.* Hector saw the way others looked at me. How they would pull their children close whenever I passed. And because he could not fight their fear, he sheltered me from it instead.

So many days spent in those stables. Horses and sun. Purple grapes, green olives, and blisters on my hands. Cyrrian of the Two Shadows, whom Hector brought along for reasons that were different but mostly the same. He didn't think I saw it. But I did.

"*It is good what you are doing for him,*" I told Hector one afternoon as we sat in a pile of straw eating olives with dirty fingers.

Hector had merely shrugged. "*It is not for his sake but for mine. I like his company.*"

I watched the sad, beautiful boy mucking out the stall nearby. "*When he is alone, he can hear her song too well. It saddens him,*" I said.

"*Whose song?*"

"*The Shade who walks behind him. Long veil and a twisted neck. Eyes of ocean tears.*"

Hector stilled. "*This woman? You see her now?*"

I glanced back at Cyrrian of the Two Shadows, and I nodded. "*I see many things, brother. Many, many things.*"

"*Things as they will happen?*" Hector asked quietly. Even then, he knew.

I nodded again.

And then he asked the question. The one I dreaded more than all others.

"What do you see when you gaze into my future, Cassandra?"

I looked up at my brother. My kind, brave, tenderhearted brother whose true strengths were those only a few would ever see.

Whose most important deeds would be those the world would never know.

Great Sorrow.

Even Greater Love.

I did not speak the words, but in my child's eyes, Hector saw the things I could not say.

Remorse flashed across his face. *"I'm sorry, little one. I won't ask you again."*

"There may come a time when you must."

He met my gaze. *"When that time comes, what if I trust you to tell me instead?"*

I nodded. The silence stretched between us, and then it was my turn to ask the thing we both dreaded. *"Am I very strange, Hector?"*

Hector's expression turned fierce. *"If you are, then so am I."*

At my frown, Hector's fierceness melted away. Laughing, he threw an olive at the back of Cyrrian's head. The beautiful boy turned and scowled at us, but I could see the smile in his eyes.

Hector met my gaze again, and I knew that my presence brought him joy, and that I loved him. In that moment, I loved my brother more than I had ever loved anyone before or since.

"You see things, but I hear them. Whispers." His voice was full of mysteries.

My mouth fell open as he held up his hand. One of the mares came trotting over to nuzzle his palm. Then she lowered her head and did the same to me.

Hector grinned at my awe. This was his secret, and he had shared it with me. Just as I had shared mine with him.

Of all our father's children, we seemed the least alike. But in the ways that mattered, we were the same.

Time flows again, and then I am in Hector's arms in this temple built of stone and lies.

My mother's leather boots echo against the tiles. "Hector, what are you doing here?" The concern in her voice sounds strange to my ears.

"Helenus sent me."

Just as quickly, concern turns to calculation. "Why?"

Hector does not answer, so I speak for him. "To ask the gods' favor. Hector will challenge a warrior of the Achaeans' choice to single combat to the death."

The blood drains from our mother's face. She does not ask me how I know. She does not look at me at all.

"Is this true?" she asks Hector.

"Yes."

Painted lips curl in a snarl. "The council is behind this. They will send my son to do what none of them would dare."

"It was not the council."

It takes her a moment, but finally, our mother hears the words he does not say. She rears back as if struck. "*Why?* Why would you risk yourself needlessly?"

"Perhaps because I think there is a need." Hector studies the altar. The ground around the base is still crowded with offerings of thanks for his son's birth.

Hecuba gnaws on her lip. "You seem certain of victory."

"The Achaeans aren't the only ones who can issue a challenge or set a trap," Hector says. "Diomedes won't be able to resist. He is young, foolish, and, thanks to my wife's men, newly injured. When I beat him, we will remove one of Agamemnon's greatest weapons."

"Agamemnon will never give up, no matter how many of his men you kill. This is not a trap," Hecuba spits. "It is folly."

"The council disagrees," Hector says simply.

"Or perhaps it is a trap," I add. "Just not one for Diomedes."

Hecuba meets my eyes. Knowledge stirs in their depths. Followed by a wash of hatred.

"Of course the council did not deny your request," she snaps. "You have delivered a gift right into their hands. If you lose, you will merely remove yourself from the path of your enemies. If you win, they look like paragons of wisdom for allowing it. Either way, this is what happens when women walk where only men should tread. If only your wife would—"

"Leave Andromache out of this," Hector says with more force than I've ever heard him use with our mother. When her lip begins to tremble, he

sighs. "I have a son now. And I would do whatever it takes to protect him."
His voice softens. "Just as you have always protected me."

When Hecuba doesn't speak, Hector takes her in his arms and rests his
chin on the top of her head. The sight of it sears me. "Helenus asks you to
make an offering of the most beautiful robe in the palace. Pray that your
cherished Athena gives me strength."

At the mention of the warrior goddess our mother has chosen as her
patron, the tears that threatened a moment ago evaporate like morning
dew. Hecuba steps back. "I will call up the women. It will be done as you
say." She gathers her robes to leave, but at the last moment, she turns. "Cassandra informs me that she is now staying at your house."

Though Hector's face hides it well, this has caught him off guard.

Please, my eyes beg him.

"Andromache is happy to have Cassandra's help with the baby."

My heart swells until I catch my mother's expression. Her secret wish.
To throw me from the tower with her own two hands.

Perhaps one day, we will let her.

She turns to go, and Hector leaves to follow. As he does, I glimpse it. A
black raptor sinking its poison talons deep into my brother's shoulders already bearing too much weight.

Rage fills me. Only this time, it does not come from the Fury. This time,
the rage is all mine.

Now! orders the Crone.

Run! cries the Child.

The Wraith points, but I am already moving.

I grab hold of Hector's arm. "Do you remember that day?" My words are
a fast-flowing river. "The question you asked me in the stables? All those
summers ago?"

He remembers.

I search the night pools of his irises and glimpse the stars as clearly as
I did that day when we were young and our city was at peace.

Love. Sorrow.

Life. Death.

Two roads draped in a shimmering mirage my sight can't pierce because the turns leading to either end have not yet been taken.

"It is not too late. You can still change it." I hold him fast.

"How?" One word. Lifetimes of weariness.

My fingers are claws on his arm as I pull him toward me. "If you follow this path you have chosen, it will lead to your death. We . . . I am asking you. *Please.* Don't do it."

The truth strangles the air between us.

Hector's gaze drifts through walls of stone toward the Scaean gate. "I have tried, Cassandra. But as hard as I have looked, I cannot see another way."

"That does not mean there isn't one." I take his hands in mine. "It will reveal itself in time."

"We can't afford to wait." Cords bulge at Hector's throat. "I won't risk it. I won't risk them. It comes down to me and Diomedes. I can beat him. Helenus has checked the signs, and Laocoon has confirmed them."

"Laocoon's head is stuck in the stars. Helenus is my pupil, and a sorry one at that. I am telling you, they are wrong."

"What would you have me do, Cassandra?"

"I would have you listen. To *me.*"

"It's too late." Hector's mouth sets in an obstinate line I have not seen since we were children and he first faced a horse no other man could break. "The duel has already been set in motion. The council and the Temple believe I can win, and so do I."

"*No.* They believe what they saw with their own eyes when your men pushed back the Achaeans to save Aeneas. They believe that if you are allowed to actually fight, you will *win,* securing your place as king. Think of it! There are those among them who fear a leader who can't be bought. One who can't be controlled and has the full backing of Troy's army and her allies. So they would seek to arrange a victory not on your terms, but theirs."

"Even if you're right, it changes nothing."

Duty. Honor.

Loyalty. Pride.

Life. Death.

Spinning, spinning on the loom.

My heart beats bloody against my ribs. "Even if following this course will mean your demise and the end of all you hold dear?"

Hector looks down into my face as he did that day in the stable. Years between that moment and now. Lifetimes.

Great Sorrow.

Even Greater Love.

"Those choices are made. Now I must do what soldiers do, Cassandra. And princes too. I must play the part the gods have written for me."

Gently, firmly, Hector loosens my grip on his arm.

No man will believe you, the god who was not a god told me that morning when I was nine years old. I knew it. Expected it even. But what I did not expect was that those who did believe would not be free to listen.

Hector turns to leave. This time, I let him go. But before his broad form disappears, I call out one last time. My warning was not enough to sway him, but there is someone who still might. I visited her before I visited him, knowing that it might come to this. More words. Useless things. The only things within my power.

"You will find her. On the wall," I tell him.

Hector leaves.

Even the Hawk cries.

13

ANDROMACHE

"WHERE IS HE? Can you see him?" I scan the plain from the rampart above the Scaean gate, searching for the outline of wide shoulders and a flash of bronze armor. The swish of horsehair and a gait I'd recognize no matter how many glittering helmets marched past these walls.

"Not yet." Rhea brushes back Andrius's copper curl as the babe wiggles in her arms. His dark eyes are bright with an alertness that seems unusual for his age. Six weeks that have passed like the blaze of a lightning bolt—overwhelmingly vivid, and gone in a blink.

Still, in the hushed sanctuary of those early days with my son, I finally understood. Why we continue creating life, even when the world seems always on the verge of ending.

Just as mine may end tomorrow.

The safe haven of our home has been breached. Hector has seen to that. My blood races like I'm there among the warriors milling outside the gate. Waiting to receive word that the Achaeans have accepted Hector's foolish challenge so they can begin preparations for the farce.

In all these years, each time he departed through this very gate, I clung to the belief that Hector would return home. But wanting it for the boy in Rhea's arms even more than for myself takes the anguish to new depths. *If Helen hadn't warned me . . . if Cassandra . . .*

The thought of her urgent words raises a lump in my throat.

"He must not face the Achaeans' champion. It will mean his death."

Even if Cassandra is right, Hector mustn't face Diomedes for other reasons—namely, because it is idiotic. Because this man-on-man combat the council enjoys watching from their positions of safety is costing us the war.

We finally have a chance to beat them. *Now.* While the army's morale is bolstered by the birth of Hector's son and the men have reason to hope for an actual future. Still, there is a truth I can't deny: what happens on the battlefield tomorrow happens not because of the council, but because it is the path Hector *chose.*

"There he is," Rhea says. She is looking not at the plain but behind us down into the city, along the road leading from the High Temple.

"What was he doing there?" I whisper, fear tickling my throat.

Hector walks the well-paved street toward the interior of the Scaean gate, his plumed helmet beneath his arm.

Perhaps it's the way the light lands on his face, but for an instant, I catch a glimpse of the younger warrior who first graced my father's hall. Confident yet humble, a few strands escaping the knot at the base of his neck, eyes dancing with a boyish mischief known only by me.

There is no mischief now. No youth. There is only grief. The anguish of a man who knows his fate—something he believes he can do nothing to alter.

Cassandra told him.

My feet fly down the rampart steps before my heart can descend my throat. "Hector!"

My husband looks up. And I know.

Before me stands a man who has seen his death.

Another cry, small but fierce, sails down the staircase behind me. Hector's face brightens, his sternness breaking into a hesitant smile. Rhea makes her way toward us, Andrius clutched to her breast like he is worth more than all the bronze that exists.

"What have you done?" I say, though I already know. There is only one reason Hector would visit Athena's shrine. And I've no doubt that's where he's been—I can smell the incense of Mycenae sticking to his skin like a cheap perfume.

"I've accepted the consequences of my choices," Hector says without emotion.

"And Priam agreed to this madness?"

When I said the Trojans should advance, we both know another point-less duel was never what I had in mind.

"He did."

Then some sinister demon on the council has taken hold of the king's tongue.

"You did not tell me."

"No, my *alev*. And why do you think that is?"

Because he is doing what he believes must be done. Because he remem-bers that in the past, I also kept things from him in the pursuit of victory. A triumph that means so much more than the two of us.

But not since Andrius.

In this world of three, there have been no secrets. Or so I thought. I glance at Rhea cradling my son, and the reason for my short-lived hope flees over walls that are high but scalable.

All we have worked for. All I've done to prevent this path. All undone by the very man I have fought so hard to protect.

"Why, Hector?" I say, voice trembling no matter how I try to prevent it. "Why must you be so reckless *now*?"

He'll say he has no other choice, but that *is* what this is. Recklessness. Pride. Some irrational death wish now that he has a child and knows a part of him will carry on.

The admission that there is no one else to blame makes the levee be-hind my eyes burst. Ten long years of silencing my worst fear. Pushing it deep so we can fight another day.

Hot tears stream down my cheeks. Rivers of grief and of fear.

But most of all, *rage*.

I let it all out, bolstered by this strange new heat that has flooded my body since Andrius's birth. One that can move me from elation to tears in a single breath.

"You know Diomedes has marked you, Hector. And you know your en-tire army would rise up to deflect his blows. But no, your pride will not permit it. So instead, you choose to face him on the banks of the Great River alone."

I follow Hector's silent gaze, fixed on our son, who stares up at his fa-ther like he is the only source of warmth and light in all the world. Another wail pushes its way up my throat. "Have you no pity for him? For *me*?"

A woman never more unready to be a widow.

Hector's eyes rise to hold mine, his own grief chased by a flash of frustration. It is true, something in me has changed, though we've both avoided speaking it out loud. The Harsa he meets before the Scaean gate is not the bold girl he married, the fearless Amazon who would have urged him to do his duty, all while seeking the glory that would be his eternal reward.

No, this frail, weeping woman is a mother.

Hector clenches his jaw. "Everything I do is for him. For both of you. *All* of you."

Rhea takes a step back, searching for a place she might disappear. I rest a firm hand on her shoulder.

Hector once told me he used to fear thunder as a little boy. Because he didn't want to imagine the gods might be upset with him. Just like he can't stand the thought that his father and the council are displeased with him now. "You would leave me and your son in the name of courage, when it is cowardice at what others will think. You would hide behind your honor, but what of your duty to us? Admit it, Hector. You fight this duel to save your pride. Even if your death will mean our doom."

Hector shakes his head, a gesture that almost resembles a sneer taking hold of his lips. "Your tongue is a lash, Andromache. I am not unfamiliar with its barbs, but this cut is deep. Even for you."

Still, it is necessary.

I open my arms wide. "Who else do I have, Hector? I've lost my father, my mother . . . all seven of my brothers to Achilles's spear. Will you not spare yourself even for your son? No. Instead, you rush headlong to meet Diomedes. A brute whose memory won't last an entire generation. So I'm asking you. *Please.* Pity us. Leave these prideful duels to childless men."

Hector's jaw clenches as he growls. "All this time, you've been pushing me out from behind the walls. And now, when the king would have me finish this, you ask me to hang back." He takes my tear-soaked face in his hands, his own voice cracking. "It is not like you, Andromache."

I shake my head. "You're right. This isn't me. It is the woman this war has made me."

Hector drops his hands back to his sides in defeat. My arms are suddenly desperate for Andrius, but he is content with Rhea, so I leave him.

Hector bites the inside of his cheek. "Do you think none of this weighs on my heart also? That I wouldn't rather remain here with you and our son? Since you are so fond of the truth, here it is: No matter his wealth, the prince of a prosperous city is never permitted the luxuries that matter. It has always been this way, and it will always be this way."

The strange and bitter resentment in his voice churns my stomach. "But it's foolishness! We went through it once when Paris faced Menelaus, and look where that got us. So again, I ask you, Hector. *Why?*"

"Because I am not Paris!" Hector roars. So loud it seems to shake the stones we are standing on. In the next breath, his voice grows so faint I can hardly hear it over the wind. "I gave you time to find another way, didn't I? We *tried*, Andromache. But sometimes the doors do not open. No matter how hard we pound. If this is my destiny, I will not run from it. My men respect me because I have always fought at the front. I would die of shame if I hid from fate now. Admit it, my *alev*. Deep down, you've always known this war could end no other way . . ."

No. Every muscle in my body screams this single word.

Eyes glistening, Hector wrenches his gaze from us to scan Troy's weather-battered ramparts. The blackened rooftops of the Lower City. "I have long felt there must come a day when even sacred Troy will die. That is the way of all kingdoms, no matter how thick our walls. Cities rise and cities fall. Soon my own father will perish. One by one, my brothers will follow." He looks at me again, so resigned it splinters my heart into shards. "It does not matter if I live to rule as king or not. In the end, Troy will be a ruin and the line of Priam will dry up."

"No!" This time, I let the scream fly.

I will not let it.

With great tenderness, Hector reaches for his son, taking the baby's tiny hand in his. "It isn't hopeless, Andromache. The end of the war doesn't have to be the end of *us*. Don't you see? Even if I die tomorrow, our efforts will be worth it so long as Andrius lives." Hector smiles, but there is sadness in it. "Better still if he is left with some semblance of a city."

"But how will that happen if you are not here to protect him?"

Grief lurks in the corners of Hector's grimaced mouth. His eyes flicker across Rhea, who weeps in silence, her face buried in Andrius's blanket. "I am not overly worried. You have your own army now."

My chest caves in on a long exhale. The gates have opened for Hector's departure. What enters on the wind is a swarm of greedy flies and the stench of death.

A warm hand wraps around my wrist. I turn toward it, and Hector is there, the distance between us closed. His hand slides up my arm until it grips my jawline in the tender space just below the ear.

His eyes are wet, but he does not let his tears fall. "Know this, my *alev*. There is nothing . . . *nothing* that can break me but the thought of them dragging you away in chains. It is the nightmare that keeps me awake through the third watch. The image of you weeping at another man's loom. A slave in some far-off land, forced to obey his young bride's commands. I've no doubt that every person who sees your widow's tears will say, 'There is the wife of Hector, who fought for Troy long ago.'"

"Stop it—"

"I can't! Don't you see?" Hector's head falls to his chest. "I would do anything for Troy. For my men and for Andrius. But the thought of you is what I cannot bear, and *this* is the only thing I can do to prevent it."

Hector's hand stiffens against my chin as a tremor runs up his golden arm. When he lets go, he places the plumed helmet firmly on his head. The mortal man who lives and breathes so much more than war is hidden beneath the convincing layer of bronze. "No, Andromache," he says through gritted teeth. "May the earth pile over my body before I hang back and let it happen. You have always asked me to let you do what you can. Now you must permit me to do the same."

Andrius releases a long mewl, and the wail puts out what remains of his father's rage. Hector removes the flashing helmet and takes his son in his arms, rocking him gently. "Shhh, there, there. I did not mean to frighten you." His eyes crinkle in a mournful smile. "You must know by now that your mother can light my temper faster than any pyre."

The glance Hector casts my way is a lance beneath the breastbone. He pushes the weapon all the way through when he lifts Andrius high in the air.

"All you immortals!" Hector calls out to the wind. "I pray this son of mine is like me in all ways but one. May he speak from his heart like the woman who bore him. And may his people one day say of him, 'Here is a far better man than his father.'"

Hector places Andrius in my arms, pressing his small body against my burning chest. In the space of a heartbeat, I tell myself every false comfort I can think of.

Hector is the better fighter. He has Athena on his side. And all the gods of Anatolia.

It has been years of the same farewell. Why do you fear for him now?

When my hot tears fall again with the lies, I try to smile through them. For him.

Hector strokes my cheek one more time. "Andromache, Andromache. Why so much weeping for me? Don't you know not even Achilles can hurl me to my death unless it be the will of the gods? It does not matter how bravely we battle nor how cleverly we scheme. In the end, no man escapes his fate." He kisses me gently on the lips. "And no woman either."

I moan against his salty mouth. "But what if we are *free*? What if there are only the choices that we make?"

And you are making the wrong one.

"Do not give in to fear, my *alev*." The next kiss he brushes across my lips is swift. Hector rests a hand on Andrius's silky head like he is afraid to let it go. "He is with you now. And so you can never be without me."

I sink to my knees as Hector turns to pass through the Scaean gate, joining his men who are making camp for a final night on the plains.

Another flash of bronze, and the breaker of horses is gone.

14

RHEA

ANDROMACHE ENTERS THE kitchen ahead of me.

Creusa stops shelling peas.

Bodecca's flour-coated arms go still as Andromache walks soundlessly toward her rooms.

Andrius cries against my shoulder as I trail behind. Bodecca catches my eye. I shake my head. The old woman's mouth goes slack as she stares through the empty doorway.

Creusa sets the clay pot of husks aside. "What happened?"

"Hector has challenged a warrior of the Achaeans' choice to single combat." My words are a chill wind in the warm kitchen. "Priam has permitted it. Helenus and Laocoon have sanctioned it. The Temple and the council are in agreement."

Bodecca is the first to find her voice. "This is how they would punish him for one moment of disobedience?" She lowers herself into the chair by the hearth, but not before I notice the way her legs tremble.

"Hector has many enemies on the council," Helen says, coming in behind us, her face flushed from the brisk walk down from the Citadel. "That is one thing I do not doubt. Helenus is not a true prophet so much as a puppet. Nothing he says can be trusted."

Creusa draws an audible breath. "Helenus is our brother and touched by the gods."

Cassandra makes a low sound in her throat that is somewhere between a laugh and a growl.

"The gods have nothing to do with this," Helen says with uncharacter-istic vehemence. "It is not gods who demanded Hector's punishment, but men who will never cease in their grasping for power."

"And what exactly does that change?" Bodecca finds her feet again. The fear she cannot show vents itself in frustration.

"I told him." Cassandra's jaw is a rusty hinge working back and forth. "I begged him to hear me. If Hector goes out to fight, he will die. I have seen it. Andromache knows."

The baby wails in my arms. I rock him even though I'm so wrung out, I can barely stand. "Andromache pleaded with him," I say. "He is trying to protect them the only way he knows how. Having set it in motion, he won't shirk his duty or go back on his word. Not even for her."

No one speaks. If Andromache couldn't sway Hector, then no one can.

"Maybe she should have tied him to a chair." Bodecca is deadly serious.

"Knowing Andromache, she considered it." A clear voice speaks be-hind us.

I turn to find Cyrrian standing in the kitchen doorway. Blood spatter and mud paint his face with savagery. He must have come here directly from the stables.

Cyrrian takes in my filthy tunic and red-rimmed eyes. "I'll find Hector. He'll have joined the men in the camp beyond the west wall while he waits for the Achaeans' response to his challenge. The duel will not be fought until tomorrow. Go get some sleep, Rhea. You look half-dead." His voice is neither warm nor cold. It is tepid, and that is somehow worse because it makes me feel like the argument between us never actually happened.

Cyrrian ducks outside. Clutching a fussing Andrius, I follow.

"Cyrrian, wait!"

He turns. The sun streams golden through the courtyard trees to dap-ple his face. My stomach does a sharp dip at his expression. For once there are no walls. Just an open window to the things he feels but never shows.

He is afraid.

"You believe Cassandra?" I forget sometimes that Cyrrian knows the princess better than almost anyone. Maybe even well enough to see her.

"I believe that this is idiocy. Then again, nothing about this war makes any sense to me."

Like all of Cyrrian's answers, it leaves much to interpretation.

"So you didn't know Hector would offer the challenge?"

"Of course I didn't know! I was expecting the council to make him grovel for defying them, but I never thought that he would—" He doesn't finish.

I clutch Andrius closer. "Will you try to talk him out of it?"

"If Andromache couldn't change his mind, it's done." Cyrrian rakes a hand through his sweaty curls, still half-flattened from his helmet. "Hector thinks he is doing the right thing, but it all feels like a game that someone is playing with us." A growl leaves his lips as he tosses his helmet against the wall.

The sound echoes sharply in the small space.

Andrius's cries fill the courtyard. The hard line of Cyrrian's mouth goes slack when he looks at the child. Gently, he runs a calloused fingertip down the copper streak in his hair. "Hector has given everything to this city, Rhea. He has stood like a wall between us and destruction, and I'm afraid the blow that finally kills him will be one that comes from behind his back." His arms drop to his sides. "I don't know how to protect him from it."

For once, I know exactly how he feels.

Words play through my head. The ones Bodecca said to me the day of the banquet when I first came to Troy. "Then it's up to us to protect him from all the threats he cannot see."

Something stirs in Cyrrian's gaze. Though I spoke in anger, everything I said to him the other night was true. After all these months of working together, I still can't claim to know him. Cyrrian of the Two Shadows is a beautiful maze of twisted corridors. Every time I think I'm drawing closer to the center, I run into another wall. But sometimes . . . like on the nights he walks me home in silence and we eat together in Bodecca's kitchen. Or when he plays his lyre for Andrius, and Cassandra goes still and peaceful in a way she never does . . . Times like these I feel like I understand him.

Cyrrian loves Hector and Andromache. It shows in every action he takes. Especially when he thinks no one is looking. They are his family every bit as much as they are mine. Our love for them binds us together, regardless of how little we care for each other's company.

His fear is my fear. Two fonts that spring from the same source.

Andrius continues to cry. Slowly, Cyrrian raises a bloodstained hand and runs it down Andrius's back. The child quiets between us.

"What will you do?" I ask, because this is Cyrrian. He will do something.

"Whatever Hector asks. But first, I think I'll find his useless brother." Cyrrian's lip curls. "Sometimes I wonder if it'd be better for everyone if I killed him myself."

"Not so loud!" I glance in the direction of the army's stables. Old Blood or not, one doesn't casually plot to kill a prince of Troy. He may drive me to distraction at times, but that doesn't mean I want to see Cyrrian run through with a spear.

"It might be worth the punishment." I've heard him use this tone before. Old hatred. The kind that can only come from old wounds.

"Why do you dislike him so much?" I ask. The other night Cyrrian said that I only needed to ask for his secrets. But even as I put his promise to the test, I do not expect him to keep it.

"'Dislike' is a generous choice of word. I'm sure you could find another more fitting in your extensive collection."

It is a careful deflection, which doesn't surprise me. The surprise is that he continues.

"Do you know there are dozens of Old Blood bastards walking the streets of this city? Unlike me, many can even claim Priam as a father, and yet I'm the only one who was invited to live within the palace."

"Your family?" I press gently.

"I had a grandfather who left Troy before I was born. I suppose he couldn't live with the shame." Cyrrian meets my eyes again. This time, they are swirling with anger. And so many shades.

"Why do they call you Cyrrian of the Two Shadows?" It is the one question that's been burning in my mind. The one I haven't dared to ask.

Cyrrian raises a dark brow. "All of Troy knows this story. If you wanted to hear it, why not pull any stranger off the street?"

"Because I wanted you to be the one to tell me."

"Why?"

"It's your business. If you don't want me to know, that's your right."

His expression turns inscrutable.

"My grandfather fought at King Priam's side and helped him wrest back control from the Hittite imposter. The king honored him by arranging a marriage between my mother and one of Priam's kinsmen. A man with a wife already but whose rise in influence more than made up for it." A sneer twists Cyrrian's lips. "My grandfather made his own fortune through trade. It was as good a match as he could've prayed for."

His tone sends dread curling in the pit of my stomach. "What happened?"

"My mother did the unforgivable. She fell in love with another man and became pregnant with his child right before she was meant to wed. Not just a man, but a Hittite prisoner—the son of a man who came to Troy to serve the Imposter King." He raises his hand again to stroke the soft hair at the back of Andrius's head. "My mother ruined the royal match and my grandfather hated her for it."

Bitterness swirls around my mouth. "And your father?"

"He vanished. Nobody saw or heard of him again. If my grandfather were still here I would ask him if he sold him back to the Hittites or had him killed or locked away . . ." His voice trails off. "Then at least I could stop wondering."

Sympathy washes through me; I understand all too well how he feels. "What did your mother do?"

Cyrrian's gaze drifts upward, over the walls to the palace. "She threw herself from Troy's tower a few weeks after I was born. I like to think that she did it out of love for the man she'd never see again, and not out of regret for my life, but there's no way to know."

Something sharp twists in my chest.

"I am so sorry, Cyrrian."

He shrugs. "My mother's choices have haunted me for most of my life. There were rumors about her shade. It made people afraid. Growing up in the palace there were no shortages of insults. No one relished them more than Paris." Cyrrian shakes his head. "Who knows how his twisted mind works."

Cyrrian may not see it, but I do. Paris revels in attention. Jewels, perfect curls, and artifice, and yet, next to Cyrrian's natural beauty, Paris would've washed out to a dull gray.

My throat tightens until it is hard to speak. "Did Hector know?"

"Paris was careful not to disparage me in front of him. And I didn't want Hector blaming himself for something that wasn't his fault."

It's exactly what Hector would've done.

"I don't live in the palace anymore," Cyrrian says. "But I haven't forgotten Paris's true face, and I never will." Cyrrian steps back from me. A retreat. "I should meet Hector."

"Will you drive his chariot tomorrow to face whoever the Achaeans choose?"

"I doubt it. Our drivers are more skilled and our horses superior. The Achaeans will choose to fight hand to hand." His expression is every bit as helpless as mine.

"It will be Diomedes," I say. "He'll insist on being the one to challenge Hector. I haven't seen him fight, but Aj—" I swallow. "I've heard the men talking. Hector is a better warrior."

Then why am I so afraid?

Cyrrian searches my face. The silence between us rings with the name I didn't say. "Diomedes doesn't scare me. There is only one Achaean that Hector can't beat."

"Achilles won't fight," I say hurriedly. "He's given his word, and his honor won't allow him to break it."

Cyrrian takes another step back. His face shutters until every bit of emotion is swallowed back into the depths of his eyes. "I am not talking about Achilles, Rhea."

HOURS PASS. ANDROMACHE doesn't emerge from her room. She also doesn't speak. Not even when I bring Andrius for his evening feeding and place him warm and sweet on her breast.

She lies on the bed, her eyes set on the balcony and the towering walls beyond. The windswept plain that gave her son his name. The one upon which Hector will fight. Tomorrow? The day after? There are no answers now. Only minutes trickling by.

Light bleeds out of the sky. Day fades into night.

Hundreds of campfires kindle to life across the Scamander plain. A constellation of men.

The Scaean gate remains closed. No heralds. No news from the front lines. After so many moons in the Achaean camps, I don't doubt they'll accept Hector's challenge. Their perverted sense of honor won't allow them to refuse.

The moon is at its apex when I set Andrius down to change his linen. He focuses in on me as if he is seeing all the things I'm trying to hide.

"Sweet boy." I pick him up and rock him. I can't even remember the last time I slept. My thoughts are an endless loop of images. The helplessness on Cyrrian's face when he left to find Hector. The way Bodecca's hands trembled on the scarred wooden table when Cassandra said that if Hector fought, he would die. The deadness in Andromache's eyes as she stared out the window into darkness. As if she would turn herself into stone.

Andrius roots into my neck. Reluctantly, I unwind him from my body and place him on his mother's chest. Her arms wrap around her son, folding him into her heat.

"He will stay with the men tonight. He will not come back until it is done."

They are the first words she's spoken since Hector left us at the Scaean gate.

I take in Andromache's profile. The smooth forehead. Straight nose and high cheekbones, and I'm suddenly choking with my own helplessness.

"He'll win, Andromache. I know the Achaeans. There's not a man among them who is Hector's match."

Andromache's hand clasps mine. I look down at our intertwined fingers. Hers long and smooth, but strong. Mine small and worn.

Andromache squeezes. "A man's destiny is not written by his worth. If it were, the world would be a very different place."

"I wish I could help you. Tell me how."

Fire flashes in her eyes. Less than a year ago, it would've sent me scurrying back into the shadows. Now that fire ignites an answering spark inside my chest.

"You have already done more than I could ever thank you for."

I shake my head, because what does it matter? What does any of it matter if it isn't enough to save them?

Andromache releases my hands. "Whatever tomorrow brings, know that you have been a blessing to Hector. And to me." She nestles Andrius into the covers and tucks herself around him. "Come," she says.

I lie down, facing her. Together we surround Andrius, two walls of flesh standing between him and a world that doesn't deserve him. His soft breaths are the only sound other than the wind, carrying to us brief snatches of song and raised voices from far across the plain.

Achaean? Trojan?

In the mouth of the wind every language sounds the same.

Andromache's breaths go deep and slow. I beg the gods for sleep, but it doesn't come.

Hector.

Andromache.

Andrius.

Bodecca.

Helen.

Larion.

Cassandra.

Every name is a brick in the life I've built here. I can't breathe with their weight upon my chest. But if I'm being honest with myself, ever since the night my farm burned, I haven't lived a single day outside death's shadow. It is the wondering that keeps me awake. The not knowing if I have done everything I can to stop it.

A piercing cry cuts through the night.

A bird's call.

Dropping a kiss on Andrius's head, I ease off the bed and out of the room. My sandaled feet tread soundlessly through the house and out into the streets. The temple of the Mother goddess waits, empty. I descend into the narrow tunnel.

All the nights before, the plain has felt like it belonged only to me. Tonight, it's alive with twinkling lights in the distance. It's not the first time Troy's armies have slept outside the walls, but it's the first time that they've made camp so far across the plain. An acknowledgment that tomorrow will change the tide of this war one way or another.

The bird cries out again, sending a spike of fear through me.

Scurry, scurry, little mouse.

The wind whips across my face as I make my way toward the bay, careful to keep my distance from the encamped armies and the worn paths of Odysseus's scouts. They will be out in numbers tonight. Expecting treachery.

My pace quickens. The wind eddies my hair. Tears obscure my vision as I run through a list of the Achaean kings one by one. All the things I've learned. All the pieces of information I've gathered.

Diomedes. Agamemnon. Menelaus. Idomeneus.

None of them are Hector's match, and still, fear claws at my breast-bone, infusing the air with a heaviness that makes me feel as if something is looming overhead, hidden by the darkness just as the clouds have hidden the stars.

The stench of the swamp drifts over me. My feet know the way without my eyes to guide them. They fly across the latticework and up into the grass that sits behind the latrine huts. Most other nights, I would make my way into the camp. Tonight, I walk along the swamp directly toward the circle of stones.

Please let him come.

I do not wait long.

My breath catches as the clouds part overhead, bathing Ajax in moon-light as he approaches the ancient shrine.

A dirty helmet lies in the crook of his arm. Bronze plates contour the hard ridges of his abdomen and chest. More armor spans the width of his shoulders and covers the powerful muscles of his forearms and calves. A war belt of dark purple sits snug around his narrow waist, and a massive shield is slung across his back, bound by a leather strap at his breast. It's as tall as he is and easily three paces wide. A tower of leather and bronze. One made for the only man on Sigeum Ridge with the strength to carry it. My throat goes tight.

A long sword rests in his grip. The sharp edge crusted black.

The joy slips from Ajax's face as he follows my gaze to the weapon in his hand. The splashes of blood across his arms and chest, staining the golden strands of his hair. Understanding lights his green eyes as they meet mine across the six feet of space between us.

Without breaking my gaze, he tosses his helmet to the ground beside the stones. His sword and armor follow next. Slowly, deliberately, his hands move to the clasp of his mighty war belt. And then he is standing in front of me in nothing but his tunic and shield. That he leaves slung across his back. As if he has forgotten it was there. As if the shield were not part of his armor at all, but rather a part of himself.

Without a word, his hands move to circle my waist. It is the same dance we do every night, but tonight, everything feels different. As if he senses the sudden hesitancy in me, Ajax's eyes lock on mine as he waits for our signal. At my nod he lifts me up onto the crumbling wall of the shrine.

A strange silence hangs between us. A silence I haven't felt since the earliest nights here. And it isn't all my doing. Ajax quickly occupies himself with resurrecting the dead fire. As much as I want to know what's bothering him, I didn't come here tonight for him or for myself.

I am here for Hector and Andromache.

Ajax will know Hector's chosen opponent. Including their weaknesses. If I can steer the conversation in that direction, maybe I can learn something useful. Something that could tip the scales of fate in Hector's favor. But first, I must violate the agreement we made to each other all those moons ago. I must break the magic of the stones.

I glance over at Ajax and it strikes me again that I'm not the only one struggling. He paces the small space, his half-bare body throwing off heat to rival the blazing fire.

"What is it?" A strange energy ripples through the stone circle.

Ajax faces me across the flames. "There will be a duel tomorrow. Single combat. Between Prince Hector and an Achaean champion to determine the outcome of the war."

I blink, and suddenly Ajax is standing right in front of me. His mouth breaks into a grin as he grabs me by the waist and lifts me up into the air. Stars spin above my head. When he sets me down again, I am breathless.

"It ends tomorrow, Rhea. No more pissing in a trench. No more breaking bread with men I'd rather kill than fight beside. No more slaying Trojan boys who can barely lift a sword. No more cursed wind and stinking sand."

No more nights with me, I realize with a dull ache.

Ajax's expression grows serious. "Tomorrow, we remove Hector. Without him, Troy will fall. Then we take the Citadel and sail home."

The lump in my throat makes it difficult to speak. "You seem certain of victory."

"I am." A calloused finger brushes a strand of hair behind my ear. "And I have you to thank for it."

I step back. "What?"

"When Hector first issued the challenge, we didn't know what to make of it. Then old Nestor gave us a thorough tongue-lashing, and suddenly, every king was clamoring for the honor."

I can picture it too easily. All of them posturing, squabbling among themselves for the chance at glory. As if there were any glory in death.

"I'm sure Diomedes's voice rose high above the rest," I say, my mind scrambling for a way to get at the information I need.

"It did." Ajax rubs the bridge of his nose. "He kept calling himself 'Killer of Trojans.' Demanding the honor as his right."

"So Diomedes will fight." It's almost a relief to know for certain.

Ajax's grin stretches wide. "Agamemnon isn't a fool. In single combat, Hector would slay him outright."

My heart is suddenly beating so hard, I can barely hear myself think. "Who did he choose instead?"

Ajax's eyes fly across my face. "He couldn't choose one without offending the others, so he had us draw lots. He had us make our marks on stones." He takes my hand in his rough palms. "For the first time in my life, I drew it right. I did it, Rhea. Because of you."

The world spins, and I sway on my feet. Ajax does not seem to notice.

"I did it just the way you taught me," Ajax explains in a rush. "Somehow, I knew it would be my mark even before I dropped my stone into Odysseus's helmet. It felt as if the gods had been leading me to that moment. As if they'd been leading me to . . ." Clearing his throat, he takes my chin in his calloused fingers. "Don't be afraid. Not for me."

My eyes fill with tears of horror and sadness, and, yes, *fear.*

Too much fear to hide.

Ajax tilts my chin toward him. "I swear to you, Rhea. I'll be back tomorrow and all of this will be over. And then I'll pay you back for what I owe."

I take a step backward. "What are you talking about?"

Ajax's hands drop to his sides. "I've been thinking about the things you said. About how my destiny was my own. My father has other sons to bring him glory. I've given enough of my life to fighting someone else's wars." His face sets in lines of determination as he reclaims the ground I've put between us. "Salamis isn't as sacred as Pylos or as rich as Mycenae, but it's home. With blue water and beaches of white rock that look like fallen stars."

I can see it so clearly through his eyes. "It sounds beautiful."

"It is. In its own unique way. Like most things dear to me." Ajax leans closer, his face alight with love of this distant land I'll never see. "When this war is over, I am going to find a bit of land by the sea where the timber is good. A place with enough grassy land for livestock. Or horses." His eyes dart back to mine. "I'll build a house, and I'll make things with my hands. And if I'm lucky enough for the gods to give me children, I'll teach my sons how to build cities instead of sack them."

I close my eyes, and I can see it. Ajax in a small house with a warm fire. Working the days with his strong body and the nights by the fire with his skilled hands.

Children with golden hair and green eyes running up and down beaches of fallen stars.

Laughter.

Joy.

Love.

All the things that he deserves, and yet the image of his future makes my heart ache with loss.

"I wish all those things for you, Ajax."

Truth.

His smile is so bright, it nearly blinds me. "One man, Rhea. One man is all that stands between us and the end of this war."

One man.

My legs give out. Ajax catches me before I hit the ground. Concern takes over his features as he sets me down by the fire.

My hands reach out to grasp his face. "Don't do this, Ajax. *Please.*"

Slowly his hands cover mine, holding them against the hard planes of his cheeks. His breath flutters across my wrist. "What is it, Rhea? Whatever it is, you can tell me."

Somewhere the gods are laughing at me.

"I am afraid."

Truth.

"There is no need." His expression grows stubborn, showing a glimpse of the boy he must have been. "I won't lose."

I search his face for a lie but find only conviction.

"Hector is the mightiest warrior in all of Anatolia."

Ajax nods. "But I am younger and stronger, and tomorrow, I prove it. I'll end this war that should never have started." Ajax brushes my tears away with the rough pad of his finger. "One more fight. One more, and then I'll never pick up another sword."

I meet his eyes. Overflowing with determination and so much *hope*. For a moment, he's so beautiful it squeezes the air from my lungs.

"Let it be someone else." The words spill from my mouth before I can stop them. "Where your kings fight for glory and treasure, Hector fights for love of his city. For his family. Can you really kill him? A good man who's done nothing to earn your hatred but fight for the people who depend on him?"

"You speak as if you know him well."

Warnings scream through my head, but I've gone too far. I have risked too much to stop now.

"He was a friend of my father's. I grew up with stories of his bravery and courage. Mostly of his kindness. When your boats came to our shores, my father left our farm to fight. Not for Troy, but for *Hector*. He loved him. He gave his life for him. My father picked his friends as carefully as he picked his horses. He wouldn't have left us unless the prince was worth it. Unless he was truly what they say he is."

"I've seen the way his men fight for him." Ajax shifts uneasily. "How they place their bodies between him and our spears. I've wondered about what kind of prince could inspire loyalty like that."

"A prince unlike any other." Conviction lends my words strength. "One who carries the love of a people. One I've heard has recently had a newborn son. Would you cut his life short? For no better reason than Agamemnon bids you to?"

Ajax leans back as if I slapped him. "I won't do it for Agamemnon. He and the rest of the kings can drown in the river Styx for all I care. I'd do it for myself. For *you*. Our past is one endless song of wars in which good men die. That isn't something I can change. But I can change the future. What else would you have me do, Rhea?"

I scramble to my feet. Across from me, Ajax rises too.

"I'd have you step aside," I say. "Let someone else do this."

"There *is* no one else." Ajax's voice dips low even as mine rises. All the joy seems to drain out of him at once. "Nobody else can beat him."

"Not even Achilles?" I hear myself ask.

Ajax merely threads his hands behind his head. "Achilles won't fight. And even if he did, I would still be the best man to stand against Hector."

"Are you saying that you're a greater fighter than Achilles? That if you fought your cousin today, you would win?" It's a challenge. Against him. Against myself and this impossible situation I've trapped us in.

Ajax's jaw goes rigid. "If I fought Achilles today, he would win, but not because I couldn't beat him." He meets my gaze and lets me see the truth he keeps hidden.

Everything inside me goes still. "You would let Achilles kill you just because he shares your blood? But you would murder Hector? A man who fights not for himself but for others?"

Ajax's face closes down. For the first time since I've known him, I can feel him draw away from me. "I'll fight him, and I'll kill him because I can't go on like this. Because you made me believe in a future I didn't think was possible."

His words break me apart and then send me soaring with the wind. "You may look like a god, Ajax, but you're still a man." My voice is a whisper. "All men have weaknesses."

"You think I look like a god?"

He's trying to make me smile, but I can't. Not even for him.

Some men are born cruel. Others good. Most are somewhere in between. But even good men can be made cruel with enough practice. The hardest armor is that forged by death and indifference. I look at Ajax and I know.

He feels everything.

The wind goes out of him all at once. "There's only one way that Hector might beat me."

Ajax pulls his shield from over his shoulder so that it lies between us. Its size is impressive, but upon closer inspection, it's the craftsmanship that is the true wonder. So many layers of leather carefully woven together to create a masterpiece of form and function.

"Fourteen layers of oxide and a fifteenth of bronze. It took a full year to make. I thought for sure I'd grow old before it was done."

"You made this yourself?"

Pink stains Ajax's cheeks, making him seem unbearably young. "I was fifteen. Not as skilled as I am now."

"What does that mean?"

Ajax smiles at the easy way I pick out meanings between his words. "Look here. Just in the upper-right corner of the center. Near the bird's wing. Do you see it?"

Bending down, I examine the shield. Just below his fingers. A gap between the layers. A slat just wide enough to fit a sword.

"A weak spot," I realize.

He nods. "I try to fight like I don't know it's there."

"Why not just fix it?" I ask.

He looks away from me. "I've killed many men. More than even you could count." He attempts a smile for my sake, but it falls flat. "I think . . . there's a part of me that is always hoping for the one thing I'm supposed to fear."

My chest aches for him. The greatest warrior of the Achaeans. A giant who would rather be killed than kill, not that he has ever been given that choice.

It's his secret. And he gave it to me.

My heart splinters in my chest.

In the east, the sky starts to lighten. "I should go." I force the words through my closing throat.

Ajax nods. "The men will be looking for me." He grimaces. "It'll be a long morning of boorish toasts to the gods."

Ajax lifts me up onto the stone, and I climb down the other side. We stand facing each other in the shadows, both knowing it's time for goodbye, but neither willing to say it.

"Will you wait for me here tomorrow? After?" he asks at last.

"I'll wait."

It's such a little thing, and yet it seems to mean so much to him.

Ajax bends down so that our faces are close together. Close enough that I can feel the heat of his breath. My body wants to fall up into him, but I force myself to stay exactly where I am.

Shadows dance across his face. "I've done terrible things. Things that once made me wish for death. But the way you spoke of Hector just now . . ." He swallows. "It makes me want to live long enough so that, some-day, I can become that sort of man in your eyes."

My mouth falls open.

Ajax walks away before I can say the truth trapped in my heart. The one truth that, until now, I've kept secret from us both.

You already are.

15

HELEN

KEEP HIM ALIVE, Helen ... Aeneas must live to see the light, or the sun will set in the west, never to rise again in the east.

The words Cassandra whispered by Aeneas's bedside refuse to leave me as I wipe the sweat from his brow. Drops of sunlight dance across the warrior's pale face through the open window, making him look slightly less like a corpse.

Given the time that has passed, even if Aeneas lives, I doubt he'll ever be the man he was before Diomedes's boulder. And will a broken Aeneas be enough for whatever destiny Cassandra claims to foresee? I wonder if she even knows.

Either way, there's a good chance I will not be there to witness it.

While Hector prepares to duel, I have my own battle to fight. A messenger arrived at Creusa's door with a summons from the council. It is precisely what Andromache has been hoping for, only it is on their terms, not ours.

Someone knows I went to see King Priam.

Paris has never once come after me since I fled his palace to attend Andrius's birth. He knows he is alone now. I've little doubt he continues his nighttime rides to the mouth of the Dardanelles, keeping council members' households well-stocked in silks and strong wine. The kinds of goods that buy favor and will at least make his fall from grace comfortable.

Yet if Hector loses ...

A thousand worries toil within me. When Aeneas makes a pained sound beneath my hands, I shove my feelings down to make room for his.

"Aeneas?"

There is no answer but for a slight fluttering. A flash of gray. For a brief moment, his eyes open, churning like the sea. And then, just as quickly as he arrived on our sunnier shores, Aeneas slips below the water's surface and returns to the shadowlands. His lucidity never lasts. Whatever dark realm he lives in now, whenever he returns to take a breath in this world, I always glimpse a man who has been tossed by merciless waves.

I push the herbal compress aside, and Aeneas's eyes snap open again, more urgent this time. His limp hand reaches for my chin, stopping just short of it. "I dreamed the goddess Aphrodite rescued me from the battlefield . . . but it was you."

He has said this all before.

"She isn't Aphrodite, husband," Creusa says softly at my back. "She is Helen. My brother's Harsa."

Creusa rises from her chair to join me by the bed. Her hand presses to her back as her growing stomach sways with each step. "You are safe, Aeneas. Prince Hector and his allies pulled you to the city gates."

This too she has explained before. Only before, Aeneas never seemed to hear her.

This time, he nods. He *speaks*. "How is he? My prince?"

Creusa and I catch each other's widening eyes.

"Hector is well," I say quickly. "He now has a son."

Aeneas's question is a hopeful sign, but there is no good answer to give him. Not when Hector will face a champion of Agamemnon's choosing. The last thing we want is to give Aeneas cause for further distress. His hand falls limply to his side as Aeneas's eyes travel down my face, then land on the bare wall closest to his bed. Suddenly, he jerks forward.

I reach for the basin, catching the slop of sickness in time. Another familiar routine whenever he wakes.

"*It is the swelling inside his head,*" I told Creusa when the pattern became undeniable. "*It may take months of rest before he recovers.*"

If he recovers.

He must.

Cassandra's desperate prophecy threatens the silence of the room. It almost felt like she was trying to say that if Aeneas does not make a full recovery, the rest of us will fare no better.

Aeneas wipes his mouth and starts to sit up, his swollen face turning away from mine. It cannot be easy for someone so proud to let himself be nursed. Especially not by me.

Creusa reaches for my hand. It's small gestures like these that reassure me she is grateful I am here. I'm grateful too. Ever since Cassandra brought me to Andromache, I've rediscovered so many things I thought banished to another life. Yet now there is this summons from the council . . .

What if it means these gifts are about to be stripped from me again? My pulse quickens and my face grows hot. I've no doubt there are council members who would eagerly support Paris if Hector falls in the duel and Paris is named the new heir. I have told Andromache as much.

"*But now there is Andrius,*" she'd said, confused.

"*Yes. Now there is Andrius.*"

The flash of dread in Andromache's stare assured me she'd understood. The birth of her son hasn't ended the threat to her household—it has merely added another target.

I carry the full basin from the bed to the room's door, where a servant waits to spirit it away. My feet hesitate on the threshold. This room has become both a battleground and a sanctuary, yet I'm struck by the fear that once I leave it, I may never return.

"Must you really go?" Creusa rubs her belly as though the motion might make the baby depart sooner. I can't blame her. The arrival of Andrius has made my own breasts ache for another child in a way I never expected.

"I've no choice." The words tremble in my throat despite my best efforts to remain calm.

Creusa is not one for politics, but her gaze reflects my own worries. The timing of this summons cannot be coincidental. If Paris wanted to punish me for leaving him, he could have acted as soon as I fled his palace. So why now, right before Hector's duel?

Oh, there is another way to end this war, Helen.

Gooseflesh travels up my arm as I stare at the closed door—as I have stared at so *many* closed doors—willing Andromache to walk through it. She can't possibly know about the council summons. If she did, she would be here already to try to stop it.

I take a deep breath and steady myself. Andromache cannot save me from this. There is no more time to delay.

"Wait, Helen. I'll send one of my girls to accompany you." The helplessness in Creusa's voice suggests my fears about a summons are warranted. "These are not days when any of us should walk alone. Most especially you."

And yet there are moments when we must.

"Do not worry yourself, Creusa. I have an escort."

THE MASTER OF Keys accompanies me to the High Temple. I walk straight to the council chamber and move to take a seat in the small section reserved for royal women of Troy, rarely if ever invited. The section sits empty except for Queen Hecuba. She gives me a cool glance as I enter, but she does not address me.

Priam sits in front of a green ceremonial pool, one of many throughout the High Temple. The king seemed frail in his own throne room, but here beneath the dead faces of so many deities, he looks like a pile of bones stacked on stone. Below the platform is a large and shallow basin of bronze glowing with fire. Flames that bathe an enormous statue of Apollo in copper light. My eyes land on Antenor, hovering behind his brother as usual. Dozens of other council members murmur in the chamber's wings. Though the king has the final say in all matters, he has never broken with the Five. It is a custom that often feels more like a law.

I study at least thirty members in total, nearly all of them gray-haired. Except for Polydamas, who earned his seat not because of his wisdom but because he is Antenor's son. Serving as the sole representative of the Trojan army, Polydamas sits in one of the chairs reserved for the Five. The priest Laocoon is beside him. On the other side of the king sits Anchises, Aeneas's father. The man I've recently learned the king secretly despises because of an old argument over a woman—an irony that is almost too painful.

The chair closest to Priam waits empty. For reasons I can't explain, the vacancy makes my skin itch like it has broken out in hives.

"Tumaeus has crossed over," whispers Hecuba, leaning my way as if commenting on the weather. "He took to his bed with a stomach ailment and never recovered."

What? I just saw the man yesterday in the throne room. He seemed in decent health then. "Why did no one send for me to help?"

"Tumaeus's sudden departure is a shock to us all. I feel for his poor widow. All those unmarried girls and not a merchant ship to support them now." Hecuba tsks and effortlessly changes the subject. "In any case, the king has called this council to appoint a new advisor to the Five."

My throat tightens. Then burns.

The queen turns to hold my gaze. "Let us speak plainly, Helen. I have never liked you, but I now see you harbor as little love for my second son as I do. Whatever your fate, I can guarantee you'll be far better off if it is Hector who sits on the throne of Troy once my husband is gone."

I don't even know what to say to that. Hecuba spears me with a pointed glance and presses on. "Don't you find it a bit unusual?"

"What do you mean, Mother?"

She flinches at the word like I've issued an insult. "I mean that a seat on the Five is vacated *now*. Right before Troy's heir apparent is poised to wrest control of this war from the soft hands of these lifelong politicians?"

"Not particularly." Whatever Hecuba is up to, I'm not sure I trust it.

She smiles. "Reticence suits you."

But then her thickly drawn eyebrows narrow. "There may be more going on beneath that crown of gold than I gave you credit for. I certainly hope so, for both our sakes. Because whoever they choose to fill this vacant seat may well decide what becomes of you. Along with what becomes of Hector's legacy."

I swallow a mouthful of temple dust, her meaning sinking in. Hector's fate and mine may be more intertwined than I ever realized.

"There is danger here," she continues. "Which means that, for tonight at least, our interests are aligned. When the danger shows itself, I will speak out as queen of Troy. And you will sit there silently, as you are accustomed. You must agree to whatever I say. Is that understood?"

"I—"

A gust of cool air passes through the temple as familiar footsteps echo down the central aisle. Paris enters the dank chamber. His eyes are no longer cast down in shame like they often were when I was a prisoner in his weaving hall. Now Paris walks like the conqueror of a kingdom. How fortunate that every man his own age who might stop this melee charge is spending the night on the battlefield.

Paris marches to the platform, giving Priam an elaborate bow. Without a word, he takes a seat in the empty chair beside Polydamas.

Hecuba releases a low hiss.

Laocoon begins intoning a lengthy prayer, his hands hovering over Paris's head as he utters words about service that ring hollow in this cavern of ambition. Throughout the entire display, Laocoon's head is lowered with a piety that could not feel more false. My skin prickles at the sacrilege, despite the sweat dripping down my back. I turn to find Hecuba watching me.

"*Now* do you see? Why they have chosen this of all nights to strike?"

They.

My eyes travel between Paris and his cousin. Polydamas has a more athletic frame compared to Paris's fluid grace, but both men seem too young and inexperienced to be given such a high appointment, one that lasts a lifetime.

Could they have seized it together? By bringing about Tumaeus's untimely death?

"Fools," Hecuba spits. I realize she's thinking only of Hector's welfare, but the future I see from this vantage point is somewhat different. Maybe because I also remember the past. And I know things about Paris that the mother who bore him and then left him for dead cannot begin to fathom.

This change in the Five is not only about Hector.

All the air flees my lungs as I double over, placing my head between my knees. I'd almost forgotten. This aroused state of constant fear, where my muscles go stiff with the need for flight and my blood is always humming. Waiting for the next knock, the next unwelcomed touch. And yet what is about to unfold in this temple has always been the ending to my song. I made peace with it long ago . . . only that was *before.*

Before my hands remembered what it was to heal.

Before I pulled another life into this burning world.

Before there were people who actually needed me.

Even more miraculous, they *want* my presence. An entire city that once loathed my very existence now begs for it.

Please. I do not want to go back.

Not only because I do not wish to die, but because, inexplicably, I want to *live.* To use my gifts to ease the bitter brokenness hiding in every crack

of every wall. I will never stop grieving for Hermione and all the years we
lost, but that old life is gone. Somehow, by a thousand invisible graces, I
have released it to the wind.

Troy is my home now.

A city filled with women who fight for what they love and who laugh
despite the tragedy that surrounds them daily. We may be trapped behind
these walls, and our stories will surely vanish when the last of us takes her
final breath. Yet neither war, nor sickness, nor enslavement can stop us
from weaving our lives together. As mothers and daughters and wives. As
friends.

For that is what women *do*.

It is what we have always done and will continue doing for as long as
there are sad songs and warm lips to sing them. No matter what sentence
Antenor is about to issue as he rises slowly from his chair.

"We are here to discuss the matter of Helen," the king's twin begins, his
voice booming to a crowd that isn't there. Although he speaks of me, Antenor does not look my way. Maybe he is ashamed of what he is about to
propose.

"A moment, uncle," Paris interjects. "I've got news that is relevant to the
council."

I can hear how Paris is trying to speak with the same reasoned detach-
ment the other advisors use. In reality, he must be all but trembling with
excitement.

Antenor glares at the interruption, yet he bows gracefully and gestures
for the prince to take the floor.

"I know who Hector will fight tomorrow," Paris announces. Gleefully.

"It doesn't take the gift of prophecy to see what's coming, cousin," says
Polydamas from his relaxed, almost reclined, position. "Diomedes has
been champing at the bit ever since we stole Aeneas out from under him."

"Only the champion the Achaeans have chosen isn't Diomedes." Even
from where I sit in the shadows, I can see Paris's eyes spark. "It is Ajax the
Great."

An explosion of murmurs. The hum sweeps through the temple, trans-
forming the council into an angry beehive. Beside me, Hecuba's skin pales
under her gaudy rouge.

"Where did you learn such a thing?" asks a balding man on the lower council I do not recognize.

"I have my sources." Paris shrugs. "And they are reliable. My connections with Troy's partners in commerce are the reason I was asked to join the Five, are they not? The sailors who cross paths with the Achaeans will gladly share what they hear for a few gold trinkets."

"Ajax is a large man," King Priam says abruptly, as if this is new information.

"The largest, brother," Antenor replies. "Which is why I'm disturbed that Prince Paris speaks as if this change in fortune is good news."

"Oh, it is, uncle. Ajax may be more giant than man, but giants are known to be slow. In their wits as much as their limbs. Hector is sure to be victorious."

"Can no one else hear how he spits curses instead of truth?" Hecuba clutches her white godstone, then drops it so her hand can snake out to grab my wrist. She knows what every man in this chamber pretends not to—that Ajax the Great is worthy of his name.

Which is, of course, what Paris is counting on.

As Hecuba's nails dig half moons into my skin, I see this moment for what it is. It is when Paris finally gets his way. And he will turn it into the performance of the century. Every effort we've made to thwart him may have been a play right into his hands.

I wait for the old helplessness to wash over me. The crippling sense that I am trapped in a web of someone else's making. One that has held me still and silent ever since I surrendered to that ship bound for Troy.

Yet the feeble feeling does not come.

In your weakness is your strength.

Reaching into the small altar on a nearby ledge, I brush my forehead with a scattering of ashes. Just like the cinder mark I used to make at my mother's hearth before chasing the call of the Unnamed One up a mountainside, my hair riding the wind.

Because ashes are what you are. But you are also more.

My feet move before my mind can change. A voice rings out, clear and true.

"And if he is?"

It's as if a bronze platter has clattered to the floor. A strong echo that moves through the stale temple among even staler gods.

The men gathered on the platform search the darkness right in front of them for its source. On my feet now, I pick up the single oil lamp providing the women's section with light.

All eyes are upon me. I do not flinch beneath their weight.

"If he is *what*, Harsa Helen?" Antenor is doing everything he can to maintain order. And yet he almost seems pleased. Maybe because my sudden appearance will make it easier to turn the council back to the subject of my fate.

I return the oil lamp to its place on the ledge. The council's initial shock dimming with it, the men stare into the black temple with blank expressions. As if there is not a real person behind the voice that cried out from the darkness. Regardless, they will hear what that voice has to say.

"If Hector is victorious and the Achaeans still refuse to leave . . ." I begin with a force I hardly recognize. "Will the King's Council finally allow him to advance his army forward?"

"Not only that, will they let him *lead*?"

The question from the shadows behind me is truly disembodied. Until Cassandra steps forward beside her mother. Queen Hecuba takes up the oil lamp I abandoned. That Cassandra is here in the temple, a place that terrifies her, is surprising enough. I'm even more shocked by how alike mother and daughter appear when standing side by side. Not in their bearing or style of dress or even in their coloring, but in their most basic of features. Broad foreheads. A birdlike nose. Keen eyes that long to see into other worlds.

A million thoughts race behind both pairs of eyes until the queen's lips curve into a slow smile.

"My daughters speak with a wisdom blessed by the gods." Hecuba's firm intonation makes it clear that she too has waited a lifetime to have a say in the running of this city. And her patience has run out. "If Hector wins this fight, you must leave him to command his army as he sees fit. Once and for all. What has the meddling of politicians ever done to hasten the end of this war? My son is a born soldier. He knows how to win."

Cassandra nods, though I can see her hands fidgeting at her sides. Not with anger, but with . . . fear? "If only you'd let him lead as he was always meant to."

With his wife beside him.

"That seems . . . reasonable," Antenor says.

"But what says our king?" asks Anchises, running his hands through his white hair.

King Priam bobs his head for a lengthy moment. "Perhaps it is time to set Troy's stallion loose. If Hector wins this duel, no one can deny he has the favor of the gods. If the Achaeans spit on honor and refuse to leave our shores, my son may do what he believes best."

"Very well," Antenor says in apparent relief. "The Five are in agreement."

The fire of victory burning through me is doused with his next words.

"But again, I must remind you that Helen is the reason we have gathered here. We've all witnessed the riots and unrest her sudden . . . er, *return* has caused. People flock to her with offerings that rightly belong with the sanctioned temple servants of the gods. I for one do not trust Agamemnon to simply pack up his ships and head home, even if Hector wins. Not unless we rectify the original cause of this conflict and meet the Achaeans halfway." The king's brother glares openly at Paris. "We must return Helen to Menelaus."

My insides twist as King Priam casts his gaze my way, a whirlpool of confusion.

Antenor does not give me more than an impassive glance. "It is well known throughout the city that she has left Paris's household for the bedchamber of Aeneas."

All gazes lock on me with the force of Cerberus's jaw. It isn't the untruth of this ridiculous slander that surprises me, but that I find I do not care.

What would you say to Hermione if she were here?

The soft whisper feels foreign in this lifeless temple, stained with the blood of innocent animals. A hollow place where men reach for the momentary favor of a god who does not reach back. I am more than familiar with the deep well of silence every person here either fills with distractions or pretends not to know.

I also know what it is like when that silence is finally broken.

A quiet prompting. A subtle intuition. Not to be found in the battlefield roar of a god who dons armor, or in the bedroom sigh of a goddess draped in luminous skin, but *here*—here in this single question that strips everything to its essence.

I would tell her she isn't powerless.

I would tell her knowing the outcome is not only impossible, it isn't even necessary. Because no matter what the three Moirai or the gods or any of the other forces beyond us decide, we *always* have a choice. A decision buried in the deepest chamber within us, the one that echoes with a suffering we all share simply by being mortal. For I have seen most of the prisons that exist in this world, and I can still remember who I am.

Whose I am.

The outbreak of debates across the council dissipates as Antenor raises his hand. Paris stands with haughty precision and takes a step toward me, as if he's been waiting for this moment.

In a sense, he has.

Hector's duel with Ajax is the perfect opportunity. While Hector chases after glory, Paris has a chance to redeem himself by playing Troy's sacrificial hero. The young, impulsive man who started this fight has matured, and he will now end the war by magnanimously giving up all that is precious to him. For the sake of his people.

When he looks at me, it's as if Paris's hand has reached across the temple's expanse, pushed through the flesh and bone of my chest, and wrapped its icy fingers around my heart.

"Members of the council," Antenor declares, "for the sake of Troy, we must cast our vote on the return of Helen to King Menelaus as a compromise that guarantees the Achaeans' departure. The Five will have their say and then it will be up to our king to make the final decision." Antenor casts his brother a deferential nod. "I, for one, humbly vote for Helen's return. For the good of Troy."

Queen Hecuba jumps up from her seat. "Helen has been a Harsa here for ten years! Is it too much to ask that you grant her a chance to speak in her own defense before you condemn her to certain death?"

Then the queen knows as well as I that Menelaus will not be forgiving.

Hecuba regards me evenly. There is no fondness in her expression, but neither is there outright loathing.

"I agree with my queen. We must let Helen speak," King Priam says with a tenderness more painful to me than any insult Paris might sling.

Hands trembling, I clear my throat.

Give me the courage.

"Despite my origins," I begin carefully, "I have long been loyal to Troy . . ."

But how to continue? What could I possibly say that would convince these men to keep me here? My words are the truth, but when has *truth* meant anything to those who judge me now?

It takes no lengthy pause for them to pounce.

"She should remain here. Submission now will only make us appear weak."

"Send her back! The woman has brought enough harm to this city."

"I agree. She must go."

"No, we keep her. Otherwise what have the past ten years been *for*?"

The members who make up the Five utter their verdicts one by one. My shoulders sag. There is only one man who hasn't cast his vote.

The slow smile of the snake who made himself my husband is the final squeeze. Despite the king's fondness for me, Paris's posture tells me he is confident his father will approve whatever he says next.

He will send me back. He will send me to my death.

And all of Troy will call him savior for it.

"It seems . . ." Paris says with excruciating slowness, ". . . that I've had a change of heart. True, my wife has often strayed, but I am not unaware of my own shortcomings. Perhaps I am to blame for our troubles as much as she."

Paris meets my gaze as if he has saved these words just for me. They feel like . . . an offering. For me to see him not as he is, but as he could be.

And that is when I know I will never understand the twisted nature of the man who has taken me as his captive. Paris's eyes pass to every member who makes up the Five, ending with Antenor. His lips twitch impatiently for a final verdict.

Another long moment of silence. Paris uses all of it to study me in the shadows, his expression a tangled ball of competing emotions I can't begin to unravel.

"Helen stays."

16

RHEA

I RACE THE dawn across the plain. Not toward the safety of Troy's walls. Instead, I cut across the open fields toward the Trojan army. Thousands of men holding spears, all of them searching for enemies in the slightest movement of the grass.

Odysseus's men are out here too.

My heart pounds in my ears as I draw closer. Somewhere among those hundreds of fires is Hector. I have to find him. Before the light breaks and I betray myself, implicating all the women who've risked their lives to help me. Before Odysseus's spies discover me or Hector leaves to meet Ajax, and I've lost my only chance.

Thoughts spin as I near the tall grasses at the edge of the Trojan camps.

Sounds to my left. Horses shifting in the dark. The burst of air through nostrils. The impatient strike of hooves against the earth.

Of course.

I may not know where Hector is in this churning sea of men, but I could find his horses blindfolded.

I close my eyes and call out to Lightfoot and Golden in whispers. Their answers are swift and strong. I follow their calls to the eastern edge of the Trojan camps, the cluster of tents closest to the front lines.

The wind sings through the grass. I crouch low and move forward.

A hand closes over my mouth. My body is wrenched against someone hard and unyielding. I struggle against the arms holding me, stopping only when I catch the familiar scent of citrus. He seems to recognize me in the same instant.

"Rhea?" Cyrrian lets me go. The fury on his face sends me back a step.

"Are you *mad*?" he hisses. "The plain is crawling with warriors. You can't be here." He pulls me away from the Trojan line toward the city walls.

I wrench free of his grip. "I have to speak with Hector."

"Coming out here now was reckless. Even for you. You can't keep doing this, Rhea."

The dark is still heavy, and yet I've never seen his anger more clearly.

"What I have to say can't wait."

"Hector is sleeping."

"Then wake him up."

Cyrrian opens his mouth, but whatever he sees on my face has him swallowing his tongue. "Stay here," he grinds out. "Or I swear to every god from east to west that I will smack you like a child and drag you back to the city myself."

Minutes pass before Cyrrian returns. This time, Hector is with him.

Hector looks as if he hasn't slept in days. Dark shadows fill his face, and still, his primary concern is for me. "Rhea, are you all right?"

"The Achaeans' chosen champion isn't Diomedes." The words tumble out as the dawn breaks in the east. We are running out of time. "It's Ajax the Great, and he is too strong."

"You came all the way out here to tell the man he is doomed?"

Hector raises his hand, and Cyrrian falls silent. I look up into Hector's warm eyes, and I make myself say the words that will break me. "There's a way that you can fight him. Maybe even beat him."

"What are you talking about?" Cyrrian demands.

"His shield." The words are burs sticking in my throat. "It has a weakness." I tell them the secret Ajax revealed to me in confidence. Because he trusted me.

Because he thought I was his friend.

"How do you know this?" Hector asks when I've finished.

"I couldn't sleep so I went back into the camps. I heard . . . I heard one of the Achaean kings speak of it."

It isn't a lie. But neither is it the truth.

Cyrrian's gaze bores a hole into my profile.

Hector embraces me. I lean into the familiar scent of horses and hay, and I tell myself that I'm doing the right thing. But knowing does not make it any easier. It doesn't stop the pain.

"Thank you, Rhea." Hector holds me at arm's length. "This will do more good than you know. I've had word from my father. The council called a session in my absence."

I stiffen. Whoever called the meeting of the council knowing Hector was gone wouldn't have his best interests at heart.

Hector squeezes my shoulders. "The king and the Five agreed. If I win tomorrow and the Achaeans still refuse to leave, I'll be granted the freedom to use the full power of our armies as I see fit. Then we can finally end this."

It is right there in front of me. The determination. The desire to stop the bloodshed once and for all. The same hope that lit Ajax's face when he left me in the shrine.

Hector steps back, his posture straight. His gait sure as he leaves me in the shadows to attend whatever preparation he deems fit.

All around me, horses cry out in the dark as he goes. Animals Hector broke with his own hands. Like the horses, I can't bear the thought of something happening to him, but I also can't picture a world without Ajax's smile.

Impossible.

Dangerous.

Stupid. Stupid, stupid girl.

Tears stream down my face.

"Are you crying for Hector? Or are your tears for *him*?" It isn't until Cyrrian speaks that I realize he is still here.

I straighten, but I don't hide my face. I don't deny it either, even though I could. For some reason I can't explain, I can't lie to Cyrrian. Not again.

He steps closer, all the while studying me as if I am something strange, someone he doesn't know.

"I knew it! You're still meeting him. Ajax the Great. Murderer of Troy's sons. Defiler of women." His eyes flash blue fire in the dark. "I told myself you couldn't be that stupid. That you weren't a traitor, or a liar. But it seems you had me fooled."

At the word *traitor* my grief hardens into fury. "Ajax is not a defiler." My voice trembles at the memory of the first time we met. The careful, respectful way he has always touched me. Spoken to me. "If he kills, it's because that's what he is forced to do." My hands fist at my sides. "He is a good man."

"He is an *Achaean*, Rhea. The men who want to kill our sons and enslave our women."

"He is my friend."

He jerks back as if I slapped him.

"How can you say that?" His voice lashes hard as the wind. "When you know what he and his kind have done? What they plan to do to the people you claim to care about? The ones who care about you? How could you have let this happen?"

He is furious. At himself. At me.

But as angry as he is, I am angrier.

"I don't know! I didn't plan for this. I didn't think—"

"That earning people's trust would be complicated? That war would be ugly and your choices might have consequences for those who—"

"I didn't think that I would care for him!"

My words tear through the plain until there is only wind and silence.

Horror crashes over Cyrrian's face. Betrayal. And then there's nothing. Just painful beauty and the half smile I hate because I know it is a lie. "I thought you could be trusted." He shrugs as if it means nothing to him. As if *I* mean nothing. "Where is your dignity? Your loyalty? Hector and Andromache gave you everything. They love you, and this is how you repay them."

"Don't speak to me of love!" I seethe. "You pretend not to care about anyone. Not even yourself. As for loyalty, I've proven mine a thousand times over. Every time I went through that wall." My voice is grated to shreds. "Every time I came *back*."

I walk toward Cyrrian until nothing but the truth separates us. "I owe Hector and Andromache my life, and that's exactly what I'll give them. But I won't pretend that Ajax is the monster you claim. He is good, and he is kind, and he is a thousand other words I don't owe you. He is my friend, and in giving Hector what he needs, I may have killed him." My voice breaks. "Isn't that enough?"

I don't wait for him to answer. I turn and walk away.

I CROUCH IN the grass between the ancient shrine and the swamp and listen to the sounds of the camp coming alive. Weapons being sharpened. Bronze plates hammered back into shape. Horses strapped into their chariots.

Hundreds of men visiting the latrines before leaving for the plain one last time.

In the full light of morning, Ajax's and my meeting place feels exposed in a way that the dark has always hidden.

The sun rises higher.

Voices dance on the wind. Orders and calls to arms. They are greeted with unusual silence from the men. Their normal clamor dimmed by the weight of this day and all it holds.

Wheels lurch. Thousands of feet pound as the Achaean armies march for the Kesik Cut. The wind whips over Cape Sigeum as I crouch in the weeds and count the separate armies.

Ajax and his men from Salamis aren't in their usual place next to Idomeneus and the Cretans. Agamemnon must've placed them farther up the line in the spot of honor next to his Mycenaeans. My heart aches to have lost this chance at one last sight of him, but a deeper part of me is relieved to remember Ajax not as a warrior bedecked in armor but the way he has always appeared to me.

A young man with dimples and soft eyes who loved nothing more than carving treasures out of tiny bits of wood.

So I sit and I wait, and when I can't stand it anymore, I pass the hot hours of afternoon attempting to climb over the shrine wall I've always needed Ajax's help to mount.

I fall again and again, scraping my skin raw. The pain is a welcome distraction from the thoughts that circle like distant birds over the battlefield, where the two men I care about most in the world are facing off against each other.

Hector. Ajax.

Ajax. Hector.

I whisper their names over and over again as I climb. By the time I finally make it over the lowest wall, their names have run together into a single prayer. My feet hit the ground inside the shrine of the old gods as the sun rises and then sinks again into the western horizon. Every part of me that wasn't aching before is now scratched and sore.

I fall to the grass beside the dead fire. The hollow in the stones seems to whisper with all the words Ajax and I have spoken here. I close my eyes, and I can see him. Laughing at something I've said. Watching me in that way of his that always makes me feel, if not beautiful, then special.

The waiting starts again. It goes on so long that I think I'll burst through my skin.

How does Andromache stand it?

Andromache. If she knew where I was, she'd feel betrayed. Though I console myself that Andromache isn't alone. She has Bodecca, Helen, Cassandra, and Creusa to bear these hours with her. She has Andrius and an entire city of people waiting for Hector. Saying prayers for his return.

Ajax has nobody. Nobody but me.

So I wait, and I wait, and finally, night falls.

I hear the distant sound of the army moving back across the Kesik Cut. Men call out to each other. Cries of victory or defeat. It's impossible to tell.

Hector or Ajax.

Ajax or Hector.

One way or another, it's already done.

Ajax will appear atop these stones, or he won't.

Hector's shadow will fall across Andromache's door, or it won't.

Either way I lose.

My heart has started beating sideways when a shadow falls over me.

I look up and Ajax is there. My pulse soars at the sight of him even as my stomach is pitched off a cliff.

He is wearing full armor, covered in so much blood and dirt it's hard to tell one part of him from another. His green eyes glow through the slats of his helmet. Wild. Like I've never seen them before. And his hand . . . in his hand he carries a sword.

The sight of it rips the world out from under me.

How many times have I seen that edge carefully sharpened by the glow of a hearth fire?

How many prayers have I heard lovingly sung over that blade in Andromache's voice in the still hours before dawn?

I try to stand, but my legs refuse to support my weight.

Ajax lands in a crouch inside the circle. He walks forward until he is standing over me. His helmet hits the ground. His breastplates. His shield. And then his knees are in the dirt, and his head is in my lap.

My arms move without a thought to send them. I hold him to me, rocking his face against my stomach as Andromache must be rocking Andrius now.

Ajax's shoulders shake under my hands, and even though a part of me is quietly dying, I know that this day has taken something from him too.

I cry for Ajax. I cry for Hector, whose face I'll never see again. For Andromache staring down the rest of her years alone. For Andrius, who will never know his father, and for myself. I cry for myself and the part I've played in all of it.

Time passes. I don't know how much before Ajax lifts his head.

I look into his red-rimmed eyes and make myself ask. "Was it a good death?"

Ajax studies me like he studied his mark the night we met. As if he could brand it into his memory. "No, Rhea. Hector is very much alive."

His words are a gale, scattering my thoughts.

"But . . ." Hector's sword.

Ajax follows my gaze to the weapon and lifts it between us. "He gave this to me. A gift of friendship."

"Friendship?" It's as if all the words I know have lost their meanings. Hector is alive, and Ajax is here, and for this one moment, I want for *nothing*.

Ajax's fingers close around mine. He studies our clasped hands as if they are a miracle. Or maybe it isn't our hands he sees at all, but something else. "We fought for hours. Until we couldn't hold up our swords. We skipped over spears and hurled rocks at one another like boys. Until there was nothing left." Awe fills his expression. "I've never seen anyone fight like that. It was as if . . . as if he was fighting with a strength that wasn't his alone."

I force myself to speak. "What happened?"

Ajax's gaze refocuses on me. "I had him pinned on the ground, but then he thrust up his sword." Ajax runs his hand across his neck, and I see the shallow cut at the juncture of his collarbone.

Had the blow been even a half inch lower, Ajax would not be standing here.

The knowledge breaks something inside me.

"He found it. The weak spot in my shield."

The air leaves my lips in a rush.

"He knew, Rhea. He knew about my shield."

Everything inside me goes still as I wait for the accusations that will surely come. For the betrayal to break across his face, but it doesn't. Instead, Ajax's expression fills with wonder.

"The gods guided his sword. I don't think I really believed such things were possible until I saw it for myself." His eyes go distant as the stars above us. "They were punishing me. For the things I've done. For all the times I've wished I were . . ." He swallows. "You were right. I'm on the wrong side of this war, and when the muses sing my name, there'll be no honor in their songs. Only blood and shame."

My heart aches at his grief even as guilt twists my stomach.

"Yet here you are." I reach for him like I've never allowed myself to do. The way I've been afraid to imagine, even in my dreams.

My fingers trail across his jaw, running over the sharp edges of his stubble. I feel the sharp intake of breath across my wrist.

Ajax stays perfectly still as I touch him. I don't know if it's something he wants. If I'm stepping across the bounds of our friendship, and he's too kind and honorable to tell me to stop. Suddenly self-conscious, I pull back. Ajax catches my hand, denying my retreat.

"There's more." I feel his words against my palms. "Even with the help of the gods, the last time he fell, he didn't get up. He reached for his shield, but I kicked it away." Ajax swallows. "I don't even remember picking up the rock."

My fingers twitch against his cheek.

"I could've killed him, Rhea."

"But you didn't." The words are a whisper.

Ajax's eyes go glassy. "I kept hearing your voice in my head, telling me about the kind of man he was. About all the women who offered their finest robes and last cuts of meat to the gods to pray for his safety. All the old men who left their homes and their daughters to fight for him. Not because he promised them gold or because they feared him, but because they loved him. And I couldn't do it."

Ajax sits backward so that the stones bear the brunt of his weight. He takes his head in his hands. "How many brave Achaeans will die because of it?"

How many Trojans will live?

Ajax's strength fails him, but mine rises up, enough for the both of us. For once, my thoughts are silent. The only thing I can hear is the thundering of my pulse as I scramble into Ajax's lap. I wrap my arms around his neck and place my head on his chest directly over his beating heart.

His breath hitches, and then Ajax is holding me. His big hands run over my back. Up and down my spine. He touches me like I didn't know one person could touch another. Not skin to skin, but deeper. And though I'm small and frail next to his strength, I've never felt less like a child.

Our breaths mingle. Our heartbeats race each other through our chests.

I lean back, reclaiming some of the space between us. "Tell me the rest."

It takes his eyes a moment to focus. "Nobody watching could've known that my throw had missed on purpose, but somehow, Hector knew." Ajax's body goes taut against mine. "The fight was over. He had nothing left, and he knew it. So he climbed to his feet and walked toward me. No weapons. No shield. I met him there, and for a moment, I saw in him all the things that you told me. I knew there was only one way we could both leave that plain alive." Ajax leans his cheek into my palm. "I held out my hand, and he clasped it. Then I heard myself say that I wished we could part as friends. If only for the day. He agreed."

My love for Ajax is a river, flowing swift and strong.

"I gave him my war belt, and he gave me this." Ajax reaches for Hector's sword. A pang issues inside me at the sight of it in Ajax's hand. "When I finally leave this place behind, this sword will be one of the two things I take with me."

"What will the other be?" I want to save each and every one of his words like the treasures they are so that I can hold them even when he's long gone. I want to sink into his thoughts until there is no separation between us.

"Your horse," Ajax says, his voice rough. "Do you still have it?"

Confused by the sudden change in subject, I reach into my satchel and hold up the figure he whittled for me after our first meeting.

He smiles at the sight of it in my hand. One flash of those dimples, and the river inside me becomes an ocean.

Ajax takes the horse with one hand and his knife in the other. I scoot backward to give him room, but quick as lightning, his arm comes down, holding my legs fast.

I sit there, studying him as he works. Mesmerized by his movements and the strong lines of his face as he focuses all his attention on the small piece of wood. I'm not sure how much time passes before he places the figurine in my hand.

I flip it over on my palm. Three lines now run across the horse's stomach in a pattern of graceful swirls.

"What is it?" I ask.

"Your mark," Ajax says.

"My mark?"

He nods. "It is the wind. That's how I think of you. Everywhere all at once. Changing things without anyone even knowing you're there."

The world fades in and out of focus as Ajax reaches into the war belt lying beside us. He places something else in my hand. A second figurine just like mine, only bigger.

A stallion.

On its belly is another mark. His.

"They are a pair," Ajax says, drawing my gaze back to his face.

Blood pounds in my ears. "I don't understand."

He takes my hand and studies every scar and callus. "When this war is over, I am going to bring you back to Salamis. I'll build you a home and a pasture for your horses. *Real* ones." His gaze meets mine. Steady. Sure. "If you want, I'll build you a tomb of stones just like this one. And I'll make you talk to me every night until we are toothless and old and there's nothing left to say."

My vision narrows until his face is all I see. I open my mouth to speak, but for once, there are no words.

Ajax doesn't need them.

Slowly, surely, he pulls me forward onto his lap. "Today when I stood across the plain from Hector, I glimpsed a world where my mark didn't mean death. I saw a life with you that makes everything I've seen, everything I've done, worth it because it's led me to this place." His hands on me tighten as his forehead drops down to mine. "Tell me, Rhea. Tell me you see the same thing, because if you don't, I swear to the gods, I'll gladly let the next Trojan boy kill me."

His words are a spark, kindling me to flame. My mouth has stopped working. So I let my body speak instead.

I wind my hands through his mane, pulling him in. His lips are there to meet me. Blood on his tongue. His or mine. I don't know anything except that I want this. *Him.* More than I have ever wanted anything.

Ajax smiles against my mouth. "I take it you aren't opposed to the idea."

My laugh rings out as Ajax lifts me with one hand, flipping us over in one quick movement. My back hits the ground, and then he is hovering over me, blocking out the stars with his broad shoulders. With a groan, Ajax pulls his mouth from mine and kisses my ear. His lips brand a path down my neck to my collarbones. The scruff on his beard abrades my skin. The most wonderful sting I've ever felt.

Every kiss he rains upon me falls with another word. "I've imagined kissing you so many times." His body lowers over mine, but as suddenly as I feel his weight, it lifts again.

This time, it's me who holds him fast.

"Where are you going?"

He smiles at my eagerness, but there's more tenderness in it than humor. "I don't want to hurt you."

"Because I'm small?"

Carefully, he lowers more of his weight on top of me. "I've always had a fondness for little things." Those dimples flash, and I feel myself falling through the very center of the earth.

The dimples disappear. "You are perfect, Rhea."

I think of all the women I know. Not girls. *Women.*

Andromache. Briseis. Lissia. *Helen.*

"No. I'm not."

It may be the first lie he has ever told me.

"You are beautiful," he says. "In your own way."

My smile warbles. "That's just another way of calling me plain."

"No. It's my way of calling you *mine.*"

My heart stops at the look on his face. And then his full weight is pinning me to the ground. I feel every ridge. Every ounce of his size and his strength, but I am not afraid.

He covers my mouth with his mouth. He blankets my body with his hands.

Above our heads, the wind screams.

The stars burn.

But we burn hotter.

17

ANDROMACHE

"ON THIS DAWNING of the seventh day, in the home of Troy's heir, I make a libation and invoke the ancient gods of Anatolia. In Luwian, I pronounce these words: for the horses of the stable; for Troy's future king; for the son and seed of Prince Hector . . ."

I pour the cup of honeyed wine three times, each splash spreading across the bronze plate that sits on the small altar beside my bed.

"May all go well."

May all *continue* to go well.

It is hard to believe it has been seven days since Hector made his peace with Ajax the Great. Seven days since we were spared.

My eyes drift to the cradle where Andrius sleeps soundly.

Seven days of bottomless gratitude.

I turn back to the curved plate Hector gifted me on our wedding night, the golden shapes of a sun and moon inlaid in its blue-green patina. Adding a handful of dust from the Ilium plain to its shallow basin, I run my hand in a circle three times, in the direction of the east wind, until the earth has mixed with the fruit of the vine.

Every movement has sacred significance. Every item on the altar I touch has a history that extends as far back as my earliest ancestors' memories.

Memories I alone must carry forward.

"What are you doing?" Helen asks from her place at my loom. She has not left our house since the council issued its verdict to keep her in Troy . . . at Paris's request.

"Preparing Andrius's birth rite."

Helen's hands pause. "I thought the dedication ceremony for the heir was to take place in the High Temple."

"So it will," I reply. "But *this* ceremony is older than Hecuba's gods. Older even than the first men who built Troy upon the plateau."

I gather sprigs of lavender, mint, and rose petals, along with an acorn from the massive oak that grows just beyond Troy's gates. I lay the items on a large blanket spread across my bed, a gift from my mother. Before she died in this very room after Achilles's raid on Thebe, she'd urged me to remember Kamrusepa, goddess of mother and child, patroness of a good birth and protector of the home. I take nine sacred combs carved from ivory and place them carefully beside the other items. Nine combs for nine illnesses that will be brushed away as I run them through Andrius's hair.

"This rite was a long-held custom in the land of my birth, as it is among many Anatolians who follow the old ways."

Helen arches a perfect brow. "In other words, what the queen does not know will not hurt her?"

My lips quirk. "Essentially."

"I have always thought your Luwian customs beautiful," Helen says, coming to stand beside me. "The practice of the *atamanui* especially." Her fingers touch a drop of wine on the bowl's edge. "A symbol of a life, carried into death. I find great comfort in it."

I've pressed hundreds of *atamanui* into the hands of dead Trojans while their mothers wailed beside me, so comfort is not my immediate association. Still, I find that Helen is right. The custom is beautiful.

Before I can say so, Bodecca enters the bedchamber with a harried look.

"Is it Rhea?" I ask. "Has she returned?"

"Not yet." Bodecca's eyes rove cautiously over Helen.

"She is usually back by morning," I murmur, knowing Rhea has been venturing out almost every night since the duel. It's as if the crucial information she gained that helped spare Hector's life has driven her mad with the desire to collect more. Especially as the Trojan army prepares for its offensive. The sawing of wood and smelting of metal behind the walls of Odysseus's settlement has a firm hold on Rhea's thoughts.

I suppress a stab of concern as the sun rises over my balcony.

"The duel would have caused upheaval in the Achaean camps. Maybe she is simply being cautious," Helen offers.

I shrug off my fear and turn to Bodecca. "What is it, then?"

"The Trojan captains. They have arrived."

"Already?" I drop the last of the nine combs to the bed. "They weren't meant to be here until midday."

"It seems the invitation you extended has left them anxious."

I should have expected as much of Trojan-born soldiers unfamiliar with my requests. Smoothing my robes, I turn to the door. Andrius has yet to stir from his morning nap, so his blessing will have to wait.

"I will watch over him," Helen offers.

I nod and follow Bodecca downstairs. "And Hector?"

"With them. In the kitchen."

"The kitchen," I murmur. "Why must everyone always gather in the kitchen?"

"Because the dining hall hasn't been properly cleaned since your Spartan friend turned it into an apothecary. I told them if they wanted food, the kitchen was the only place I'd serve it," Bodecca says in exasperation.

The silence that greets me before the hearth is as thick as the sage Bodecca is fond of burning. As if divided by an invisible wall, my allied captains sit on one side of the room while Polydamas and his Trojan captains sit on the other. Bowls of olives, goat cheese, and the last of our figs rest untouched on the table between them.

Sarpedon is the first to stand when I enter. The other allied captains follow suit, though the Trojan leaders show greater hesitation. They have not been part of our training. They are as unaccustomed to being in a woman's world as they are unaccustomed to a woman trespassing into theirs.

My gaze fastens on Hector. "It seems everyone is eager to send the Achaeans on their way."

"You make it sound as simple as rocking a baby to sleep."

Every muscle from my upper back to my neck stiffens at the voice. A voice I have not heard in my home since the last time he dragged his wife from this very kitchen. Slowly, I turn toward the seat in the far corner, where Paris's body speaks the language of a petulant child. He is the leader of Troy's deadliest archers. There was no way Hector could not include him.

Still, the thought of Helen upstairs, so close to his clutches, has me on guard.

I clear my throat. "It could be that simple. So long as we are clever about it. If we use all of our talents in a way the Achaeans cannot counter."

"Talents?" Paris's brow arches as he regards the allied captains.

"Things a person is good at," Glaucus offers helpfully.

Sarpedon smirks, and Akamas outright guffaws.

"What exactly are you proposing?" Polydamas directs the question to Hector, ignoring the rest of us.

My husband offers me a nod. It is an act of confidence. Of faith. The fact that he is still here to give it overwhelms me with gratitude all over again.

When I'm done explaining the careful strategy Hector and I have been building in our bed for months, Polydamas's gaze darts between us, aghast. "You wish to attack their camp? At night?"

"We propose to send our fastest and most stealthy men forward before the day's battle. They will lie in wait and ambush the Achaean army as they return at sunset to cross the Kesik Cut, where they will be trapped by its narrow gates. The rest of our troops will then turn around and pin them to their own wall."

"But how will we fight if we cannot see?" asks an allied captain.

"We have done it before," Glaucus says, referring to the night we thwarted Odysseus's raid on our cattle—a battle none of the Trojan captains know anything about. At my warning glare, Glaucus quickly adds, "During training, of course."

"When is this nighttime escapade to occur?" Paris asks drolly.

Hector answers. "Tonight."

Paris's face pales. "Tonight . . . I fear my archers will not be ready so soon."

"Have they run out of arrowheads?" asks Pyraechmes. "If so, my men will be happy to lend you some. Though ours are undoubtedly longer than those your men are used to."

Muffled laughter clumsily disguised as coughing.

"We have plenty of arrows," Paris sneers. "But it is foolishness to charge in unprepared."

He is afraid, I realize. And perhaps for good reason. This strategy is one that will take him and his archers farther from the walls of Troy than they have ever been. Than any of them have been.

"My Lycians volunteer to fight at the front," Sarpedon says. "Simple men as we are, we've no need for elaborate preparations."

"My Thracians will feign the retreat and then ride hard to swarm the Achaeans at their gates," Akamas adds. "Not to worry, Prince Paris. It will be better for all of us if your archers remain in the back."

Paris's glower is a poison that spreads through the kitchen. Hector and I share a glance. This is not going well.

"This attack will be made by the Trojan army," Polydamas says. "So it should be Trojans at the front."

"Wouldn't that be a welcomed change," Sarpedon mutters.

"Enough pissing on each other's legs." Hippothous takes a deep pull from his wineskin. "Let us conclude our business and each go prepare as we see fit."

"This is your chance," I say, meeting the stares of the Trojan captains. "Now that the Citadel has removed your restraints, it is time to hit the Achaeans where it hurts."

"And if we fail, you will have made us all look like fools," Paris says.

"Looking foolish is not our greatest risk! Can't you see this is bigger than the reputation of any one of us? It is about the freedom of the Troad from both Mycenaean conquest and Hittite influence. If you think the Achaeans will stop coveting the untold riches of our homelands, that they will stop seeking the minerals they *need* to forge bronze, then you are more naïve than my infant son."

A dozen chins lift in unison. At the mention of the young prince, something in the room shifts.

"We will discuss the best means of attack for each battalion with our men," says Sarpedon.

Glaucus nods. "And we will share that strategy with the Trojan captains once we decide."

"Then you are dismissed," says Hector.

I rise from the table with him as he stands, but not before I catch Polydamas's glare and Paris rolling his eyes. Still, I am confident neither will disobey Hector's orders. Not now.

The Trojan captains must accept our allies as equals. They must learn to get along.

What other choice do they have?

~⁓~

WHEN I LEAVE the kitchen and return to the stairs, I am surprised to find Helen standing at the bottom. She cradles Andrius tenderly. Naturally. As if he is as precious to her as he is to me.

"How long have you been standing there?"

"Long enough." Helen smiles. "You were most fierce. The men admire you. I'd say they even respect you."

I shrug off her compliments. "If only it were so easy with some women."

Helen smiles again. On that point, at least, we have shared experience.

"Can I help with the birth rite?" Helen asks. When I hesitate, she adds, "The admiration of women is hard-won, but maybe we are too often the ones standing in each other's way."

It is an observation that shines a light on all that has changed between us since her early days in Troy. Never in a thousand years would I have imagined that Helen of Sparta would be living in my home, an Achaean woman asking to assist with an ancient Luwian ceremony.

"Come," I say with a nod.

Back upstairs, I return to the dish of hammered bronze. Licking a finger, I draw one vertical and one horizontal line in the dampened dust, dividing the dish into four identical quadrants.

"Spring is followed by summer, and summer by autumn." Straining to remember the words my mother spoke when she led this rite, I sprinkle the lavender, mint, and rose petals into the first three quadrants. Then I take a piece of charred wood and shave off a sprinkle of ash into the final section. "Winter is the turning we most fear, the season we try to resist, and yet it eventually arrives. In a life, it means old age. In a civilization, it may well be the death of an entire people." I gesture for Helen to bring me Andrius. Then I reach for the nine combs before speaking an old magic. The same words recited over me and all seven of my brothers. Over my father and mother and their father and mother before them.

All of them dust.

"Time does not move in a straight line. Though we cannot know when the seasons will change, this cycle is one we can count on. But the cleansing fire of its final turning is not to be feared. Not when the ashes of a long winter enrich the soil that leads to the buds of spring."

I lift the small acorn and press it to Andrius's forehead. To his petal-soft lips. And then to his heart. His curious eyes follow the oak seed like it is my own face.

The acorn is the last item added to the bronze dish. Helen watches my every movement as intently as the babe does. "So it is with the lives of mortals. The wind scatters one life as another takes root."

Gripping the dish with both hands, I move it slowly in a circular motion until the acorn has moved through all four quadrants, blurring every line. There is no need to explain to Helen. As a healer, she will understand that the ways of nature and the ways of men follow but one pattern. No matter how much we'd like to believe that human beings aren't subject to the coming catastrophes the sky serpents point to.

"As with the pulling of tides and the phases of the moon, the circle of time shifts without our consent. Changes in seasons and in fortune. Our task is to live with as much courage as we can, in whatever season we find ourselves in."

A gust of drought-ridden air blows in from the balcony. Helen holds my gaze, her eyes filling with tears.

We both know what season our world is in.

But is there still a chance my son and Helen's daughter will live long enough to inhale the sweetness of another summer? For that possibility, I would sacrifice a hundred ewes. A thousand rams.

Andrius reaches for my face. I clutch him even closer, breathing in his spring. Trailing my hand through the charcoal-streaked dirt, I rub a thumb across Andrius's forehead. Leaving behind a thin line of ash.

Helen and I share another pained look, one that assures me she is whispering the same silent prayer for her child.

Let them live. Even more, let them thrive.

If tonight's attack on the Achaean camp fails, this ancient blessing may be the only legacy of my Thebean family that I can leave Andrius.

For if my gamble is misplaced, our forces will be greatly weakened and the Achaeans must respond with siege.

It is a near certainty. One that leaves me cold with dread despite Andrius's body heat.

After the baby's hair is combed and the birth rite is finished, Cyrrian knocks on the door. He was there in the kitchen with the captains, though he did not speak a word.

"Has Rhea come back?" he asks softly.

"She has not."

"Then she won't know the attack is coming."

"She will be back in time. She always is. What reason would she have to linger?"

Cyrrian's expression hardens as we both look out across my balcony toward the fading light. At a setting sun and a sky streaked not with serpents but with flame.

18

RHEA

THE SUNBAKED STONE warms my back, but the heat does not penetrate the chill that has settled deep in my bones.

Our spot. Tomorrow, Ajax said to me as he traced the line of my collarbone with the pad of a finger. We've not missed a night in the stones since he returned from the duel with Hector seven days ago. Any semblance of control I'd been clinging to was sucked out to sea the first time our lips touched. Which is how I find myself here in the full glare of the sun.

In the hour before the sun is highest. On the tide. Don't be late.

When I pressed him on why, he'd simply asked me to trust him.

I should be back in Troy by now. All the Achaeans left hours ago to meet the Trojans on the plain. Ajax would've been with them. I assumed he'd left something here for me to find, but when I searched the tomb, there was nothing. So here I sit in broad daylight.

A seagull dives low over the stones, cutting through the crash of the waves on the west side of Sigeum Ridge. The sound is louder with the tide coming in, the birds an erratic cloud of feathers darting over the marsh. In the harsh sunlight, our meeting place seems closer to the camp than it ever has at night. Even the air feels different. Charged, as if something is blowing toward us.

A shadow falls over me.

I blink against the sun. The black spots of my vision clear to reveal Ajax's face.

I drink in the sight of him even as alarm brings me to my feet.

Ajax stands completely still, his eyes fixed on me with an intensity to rival the sun beating down on our backs. Every moment of silence that lingers only adds to my dread.

"What are you doing here?" I ask.

He clears his throat. "Last week's duel took a toll. Agamemnon has graciously given me and my men some time for rest."

"You're hurt? Where?" My eyes rake the tall, broad length of him, searching for some hurt that I might fix.

Ajax's smile is amused. "My wrist. I'm no good to anyone if I can't grip my sword."

"Let me see." I reach for his right hand, but he lifts it high out of my reach. "Ajax," I say, striving for calm. "Let me see."

His expression turns thoughtful. "What will you give me if I do?"

"This is not the moment for jests."

"You're right." His good hand comes around me, and his fingers drag down the length of my spine. "I can think of better uses for our time."

Ignoring the way my belly tightens, I step out of his grip. "Charm doesn't suit you."

Laughing out loud, he lowers his giant hand so I can take it in both of mine. "Is it painful?" I turn it over. "Where does it hurt? Perhaps Machaon can—"

Quick as lightning, Ajax's hand slips through mine to grip my chin in a firm but gentle hold.

It takes me a moment to understand. "There is nothing wrong with you."

"I'm not sure that is entirely true," he says jovially. "But if you're suggesting that I lied to buy myself and my men a day of much-needed rest, then I freely admit it. The plain will still be there tomorrow." A shadow flits across his face. Just as quickly as it comes, it goes.

"Agamemnon will be furious if he finds out." More importantly, someone could see us. My gaze darts to the marsh, but the area between the latrines and the swamp is as empty now as it is during the dead of night. "You risk too much, Ajax."

"Only because it's worth it." His fingers dig into my hips, sending a shiver through me. "Besides." He rubs his nose against my ear like a giant cat. Though I would never tell him, that is how I've begun to think of him:

a golden lion with a fierce roar and no teeth. "Agamemnon has bigger worries at the moment."

I draw back, ready to ask him what he means, but his expression stops me.

"Just once." His voice is gentle.

"Just once what?" I ask.

"Just once I wanted to look upon your face in the light."

The cries of the birds. The howl of the sea. They all recede into the distance.

"Are you disappointed?" I ask quietly.

Golden hair rains down around my shoulders as Ajax presses his forehead to mine. "You could never disappoint me, Rhea." His hungry mouth fastens on mine, and every thought is swept from my head in a rush of blood.

"So this is the secret you've been keeping."

Before I can utter a sound, Ajax has spun us both so that his body is a shield between me and the disembodied voice.

"No need to go reaching for that sword, brother," the voice continues. "My mother prefers my head where it is."

Brother?

The tense muscles in Ajax's back relax. "What are you doing here?"

"I followed you. A body like yours can't exactly go missing without somebody the wiser."

"Has anybody else made such careful note of my comings and goings?"

"The men assume you spend your time with one of the women in the weaving tent. They don't know you like I do."

"Go back, Teucer. This doesn't concern you."

"The more you try to get rid of me, the less inclined I am to leave. You know how persistent I can be when there's a problem that needs solving."

"I am telling you to walk away."

"Since when have I taken orders from you? Come on, little brother. How bad can it be? Are you whittling again? Or has your rebellion taken on a more sinister form? Basket weaving, perhaps?"

There is no cruelty in Teucer's tone. Just taunting and clear affection.

A sigh echoes toward me. "I am in danger of growing old, Ajax. Are you going to step aside and let me see what you're guarding so carefully, or must I hold your head under the surf until you submit like I did when we were children?"

Ajax hesitates for a moment. "It will be all right," he says for my ears alone.

I shake my head and try to pull away. His grip assures me there is no way out of this. Not anymore.

My knees tremble as the worlds I have kept doggedly separate collide beneath my feet. I've allowed myself to believe that my meetings with Ajax were different from my work in the camps. That they were something just for me. Safe. But all this time, it was a lie. Just as Ven warned, the very worst kind. The kind I told myself.

Ajax angles his shoulders sideways, revealing a man one or two summers older than he is whom I've seen with him often. His half brother. The archer Teucer.

Ajax squeezes my hand. *Trust me*, his eyes beg. But the truth is that I made that choice already, and there is no going back.

I take a breath and move out from behind Ajax.

Loud silence. "Are you going to introduce me?" the young man asks, smiling broadly to cover his surprise. Though he is two heads shorter than his brother, the gods have blessed him with proportions that are every bit as pleasing. His features are sharper than Ajax's, and though they share the same green eyes, Teucer's hair is a darker amber.

With an audible groan, Ajax sweeps his hand in a grand gesture of presentation. "Rhea, this is Teucer. My insufferable big brother who is incapable of minding his own business. Teucer, this is Rhea."

Drawing a deep breath, I step forward at the sound of my name.

"My girl," Ajax adds, and my steps falter.

This time, Teucer isn't quite as accomplished at schooling his features. His eyes narrow on me, and I can feel them taking me apart piece by piece.

"Well," he says, folding his arms across his thick chest and leaning back against the stones the exact same way Ajax did the first time we met. "I can't say I saw this coming."

"She belongs to Odysseus." The quiet way Ajax speaks only underscores his words. "Nobody can know."

"Odysseus is not a man I'd choose for an enemy." Teucer rubs the back of his neck. Another trait he and Ajax seem to share. "This is a dangerous game you are playing, brother."

"It is not a game." Ajax's arm comes around my waist. "Not for her and not for me."

Teucer's eyes drag between us. "I see."

"You can't tell anyone." I find my voice at last.

"What do you take me for? Agamemnon's loudmouthed herald?" Teucer pulls a disgusted face before he approaches us casually. "What were you two up to before I intruded? Or would I rather not know?"

My cheeks burn, but Ajax just says, "As it happens, I had something planned."

I can feel Teucer watching us, measuring our gestures and actions. The way we have learned to communicate, both with and without words. Deliberately, Ajax winds his fingers through mine. "Come on."

Ignoring Teucer, who needs no invitation to fall into step behind us, Ajax leads me by the hand toward the swamp.

My heart is racing by the time we draw up to the edge. "What are we doing here?"

"Don't be afraid. You won't fall in. See?" Ajax steps out onto the lattice-work, which is still mostly hidden by the grasses. The boards don't even groan under his weight—a testament to the skillful hands that made the ingenious system that allows the Achaeans to make full use of the swamp. "There is a path here. We built it when we first arrived so that we could fish the marshes at night."

"You built it?"

"Teucer did the design and the calculations. Unlike me, he is good with figures. I merely did the grunt work."

I study the beams as if I have never seen them before. "The craftsmanship is every bit as clever as the design," I say, earning another glance from Teucer. This one tinged with approval.

Ajax shrugs off the compliment. "The men from Salamis are fishermen and builders by trade."

"We are also the best looking," Teucer chimes in, clearly lacking his brother's modesty. "Though I don't need to tell you that, do I, Rhea?" He moves past us, stepping easily over the latticework to the far side of the swamp.

Ajax leads me by the hand, staying close as if he is afraid I might fall in without his help. Every step increases the sick feeling in my stomach as we make our way across the swamp to the open mouth of the Scamander, where it pours into the bay. My feet turn leaden when we step onto the old dock that Hector and Cyrrian built when they were young. Not ten paces away, my dinghy lies hidden in the tall grass.

"Beautiful, isn't it?"

I jerk my eyes away from the hidden boat. The sun rides high on Ajax's cheekbones, turning his hair to liquid gold.

"Wh . . . what?" I stutter.

"The sea. The river. If I lived here, I would come to this spot every day. It can almost make you forget what goes on beyond the swelling of the plain."

I survey the open mouth of the river and the bay in the full light, and I have to admit it is beautiful. Something I can't say I ever noticed. From here, one can stare right into the open mouth of the Dardanelles, where the water is so blue it looks like another sky. Or a mirror for the gods, framed in yellow-green bands of earth.

For a few moments, the three of us sit side by side on the dock. Where my feet barely skim the water, Ajax's legs are submerged past the calf.

Teucer's tunic hits Ajax in the face a moment before the *splash*.

"The water is perfect," he calls to us. The current eddies around him in circles. "Come on. I'll race you across. Since your girl is watching, I might even let you win."

Longing fills Ajax's face, but he shakes his head and tosses his brother's tunic to the dock behind us. "I'll stay with Rhea."

"Go on." I nudge his shoulder.

"What about you?"

"I'll watch." I shrug. "It's what I love to do."

The smile on Ajax's face rivals the sun for brightness. In one fluid motion, he stands and pulls his tunic over his head. In the daylight, the crests and valleys of his chest and abdomen make him look like the young god I mistook him for the first time we met. He catches me looking. The satisfied curve of his lips is the last thing I see before he dives into the water.

I count to forty-three before his golden head resurfaces. Water flies through the air as Ajax whips his long hair back, smoothing it down with his hands. Then, pushing Teucer under with one hand, he breaks hard for the opposite shore. Teucer gives chase. They move like seals even as they laugh like boys, their strokes cutting through the water with impossible grace.

One race turns into two. Then some sport that involves depriving your opponent of air until death is imminent. Clumsily, I weave strands of long grass together while I watch them play with a deep contentment I can't ever remember feeling. Like the light of the setting sun, it is golden. So precious because I know it can't last. I give myself over to it, and for the first time in months, I lose track of the hours. The sun is low in the swirling Aegean when the men finally crawl out of water to lie down on either side of me. Ajax puts his head in my lap, the heat of his body is a sharp contrast to the chill of the water that still clings to it. I set aside my poor excuse for a basket and play with the ends of his hair, now coarse from the sea.

The sun sets fully, and darkness falls. None of us move. The stars have begun to salt the sky when my stomach growls against Ajax's head.

"You're hungry." He sits up.

"I'm fine."

"I stole some bread and figs from Idomeneus's kitchens. While the rest of us eat slop, that sneaky bastard always manages to have fresh fruit. I left it in a basket back at the stones."

Before I can stop him, he presses a wet kiss to my lips and sets off for the shadowy swamp. Night falls, ushering with it a cool wind. I close my eyes and absorb the heat still trapped in the boards. Like this day, I cling to it, wishing it might last forever.

"Ajax has never been overly at ease around women." Teucer's eyes are closed, and still I can feel him observing me. "Not that he didn't have ample opportunity. By the time he was sixteen, our father had paraded every eligible girl in Salamis before his eyes."

I finger a strand of grass while I run over all the things that Ajax has told me. And the things he has left unspoken.

Teucer slings an arm over his face. "He was raised by a hard man. We both were. Nothing soft was allowed near us. Not even our mothers. But as hard as our father can be, he is also fair."

I want Teucer to like me. At the very least, I *need* him to keep my secret, and still I cannot stop myself. "Is it fair to take a child's dreams and crush them in your hands?"

"He told you that." Teucer props himself up with one arm.

"You sound surprised."

Teucer shrugs. "It isn't like him. We were taught that to share our weakness was to paint a target on our backs." He flops back down to the boards. "Ajax understands, though he pretends not to. Our father protected us the best way he knew how. This world isn't gentle. Or fair. He wanted to make his sons strong so that we would survive it. Is that so wrong?"

I pull another blade of grass. It is long and pliable, but woven together with many others, it would bear more weight than bronze. "Not all strength looks the same."

"Perhaps you're right." Teucer lies back down. "He is different since he met you."

"How so?" I ask quickly. Too quickly.

"When we were young, Ajax was all laughter and quiet kindness that had no place in our father's hall." Teucer considers his words. "Until today, I had almost forgotten the sound of his laugh."

I frown. "You make it seem like a bad thing."

He sits up so that we are facing each other. "There is no place out there for softness." He jerks his chin toward the plain. "Or mercy. It is kill or be killed. That is . . . harder for Ajax than most." His expression grows fierce. "Which is exactly why Ajax has to survive. He is the best of us."

Before I can come up with a response, Ajax returns. I know that something is wrong before he reaches down to lift me to my feet.

One glance at his brother's face in the starlight and Teucer rises. "What is it?"

"Trojans," Ajax says through gritted teeth.

The breath freezes in my lungs. "What? Where?"

Ajax tucks me into his side. Tension runs down the length of his body. "Lying in wait just beyond the swell of the plain."

Teucer yanks the tunic over his head and refits the war belt around his waist. "Agamemnon and the other kings?"

"Coming back to camp now. Half of the army is inside for the night. The rest are waiting in a line at the Cut."

"If the Trojans are camped at the Cut, what are they waiting—?"

A cry tears through the night. The thrum of a bow. Screams echo across the marsh along with the clash of swords.

"How many?" Teucer asks as we make our way back toward the swamp. Ajax's hand is a steel clamp around my wrist.

"Enough." Ajax guides me over the hidden latticework, using his body to shield mine even though no bow made by mortal hands could ever cross the distance. Ajax and Teucer set a blistering pace. My legs are burning by the time we pass the latrines and step out onto open ground.

All around us, scenes of chaos.

To the south, the gates at the Cut lie open, letting in a stream of men and chariots at dangerous speed. The song of battle pours in around them. Everywhere, half-dressed Achaeans are rushing to the ramshackle barrier across the Kesik Cut. Even with Odysseus's extra fortifications, it is barely higher than a grown man. Compared to Troy's ramparts, these are a sorry excuse for walls. More important, they are walls that have never been tested.

Arrows rain down on the gates from the hills to either side. Hector must have divided his forces and sent some of them to lie in wait. Pressed as they are to their own defenses, the Achaeans have nowhere to run. It is brutal. Utterly efficient.

Andromache.

I watch it all happen as if in slow motion.

"If they breach that wall, they'll be within range of our ships," Teucer says grimly.

Without their ships, the Achaeans will be trapped here in a hell of their own making.

Ajax's hand tightens around my wrist. "I'll bring Rhea to the infirmary and then meet you at the gates. You'll be safe with Machaon," he tells me.

"I'm sure Rhea can find her own way. We need to gather our men and reinforce that wall right now."

Soldiers rush past us, heading for the Cut. One of them clips my elbow with the blunt edge of his spear as he goes. Ajax shoves him back and tucks me into his side. "I am not leaving her alone in this."

Teucer nods tersely. "We'd better hurry."

We fight the grain of men on the way back to the infirmary. Without Ajax and Teucer to carve a path, it would've taken me twice as long.

Inside, the tent is already filling with bodies, dragged back from the gates. My eyes find Isola where she is bent over a young warrior with a gash across his chest.

"Machaon? What are you doing?"

At the sound of Ajax's voice, I turn to find the old healer standing in front of the curtain that leads to his rooms. Gone are his stained tunic and worn pouch full of surgical tools. In their place he wears a plate of battle armor every bit as old and scarred as he is. His gaze sweeps the rapidly filling beds with what looks like pain.

"Agamemnon has called every man to fight." Machaon tightens the bands at his wrists. "Isola will need your help, Rhea. Follow her lead, and you will both do well."

I swallow the lump that threatens to choke me.

"This is lunacy," Ajax growls.

Teucer ducks into the infirmary. "Unless the gods are up to one of their tricks, I just saw old Nestor parading around in full armor. Antichilus almost broke his back trying to lift him up into a chariot."

Ajax looks as furious as I have ever seen him. "Nestor is worth a hundred soldiers like us. You are worth even more, Machaon. You've both earned your honored places at the back of the lines."

So why would Agamemnon order it?

Ajax seems to reach the same conclusion I do. "He wants my cousin to know that even the oldest among us would fight before he does. He thinks he can shame Achilles into battle."

More screams drift toward us. Closer than before.

Machaon pulls the helmet over his balding head. "For all our sakes, let us pray that he is right."

Ajax grabs my hand. He must read all the things I am trying to hide because despite the room full of men watching he bends down low. "Don't be afraid," he says. "I won't let anyone hurt you."

He ducks out into the night before I can tell him.

It is not myself I fear for.

THE SOLDIER GRUNTS as I lift him onto his side. Blood drips to the dirt floor. Isola packs the stomach wound with a poultice, just as Machaon taught us. At Isola's nod, I release the soldier's weight. He hits the cot with a groan.

I look up to meet Isola's red-rimmed gaze. We've been working for hours that feel like days, tending men pulled directly from the battlefield, which now consists of the narrow strip of ground in front of the Kesik Cut. A trench filled with broken chariots and more bodies than I have the heart to count.

When the wind blows toward us, I can hear them.

Screaming, fighting, *dying*.

Isola looks up desperately from the side of another boy barely older than we are. When she lets go of his hand, it falls limp onto the earth.

"We need help," she says.

A blast of heat and noise heralds a new group of men entering the infirmary. They are arriving quicker than we can clear them.

"Ven will know what to do." I stand. "Will you be all right?"

Isola wipes the sweat from her brow with a look of grim determination. "Just go quickly."

I step out of the infirmary into a burning world. Streaks of fire sail over the wall, setting the Achaeans' huts aflame, filling the air with the smell of smoke and retribution.

Memories rise with the scent of fire. My body turns to stone even as my mind hurtles backward through time until I am crouched in a burning barn, holding my sister's hand. Then running through streets echoing with screams, frantically searching for Andromache though the burning maze of the Lower City.

An arrow whistles close overhead, bringing me back to myself. Forcing my limbs to move, I make my way to the bathhouse, the inside of which has been converted into a secondary infirmary for those whose injuries are too grave to be taken far. I look around at the haphazard rows of dying men, and a sense of hopelessness fills me.

Muffled curses draw my gaze to a girl emptying a basin of filthy water into one of the large soaking pools now stained the color of wine.

"Salama!" I have never been so glad to see her. "Where's Ven?"

"How would I know?" she snaps, resting the basin on her hip.

Someone calls for fresh water. A desperate plea. Salama lazily scoops some up from the clean pool but makes no move to deliver it.

"Isola and I need help in the infirmary. Is there anyone you could send?"

"Look around you," Salama says.

"We can't treat all these men," I whisper. "What are we supposed to do?"

A small smile twists the blade of her mouth. "Let the invaders die."

The sun is threatening to rise again when I begin the lonely walk back toward the infirmary without help. A hoarse yell draws my gaze toward the Kesik Cut.

Movement at the gate. The crack of wood and the bowing of the doors as something smashes them hard from the other side.

Before I can question it, I am taking the lattice over the swamp to the hill directly across from the Cut. From up here, I have a clear view across the trench to the meager wall and the armies that occupy both sides.

The small stretch of earth between the trench and the gate contains thirty Achaeans packed shoulder to shoulder, shields held high. Trojans swarm the footbridge, fighting to reach the gates. Arrows rain down from both sides. Paris and his archers work from a spot of relative safety high on the ridge to the west. A group of Andromache's allies with longbows take up the ground to the east. Their arrows find cracks in the Achaean shield wall. As quickly as bodies fall, they are rolled down into the trench, making room for more men to slip through a crack in the gate and take their places at the front.

Two burly Mycenaeans stand on top of the wall, clad in armor and wielding weapons in both hands. The last line of Achaean defense.

The Trojan army is a spear pointed directly at the Achaean gates. The two men who form the tip of that spear are both instantly distinguishable by their armor.

Hector and Polydamas, who now fights in Aeneas's place at Hector's side.

I have never seen Hector fight. Not even on the training grounds. Watching him now, I can't understand how any man on earth might claim to be greater.

It isn't Hector's size. It isn't even his strength or his speed, both of which are formidable. It is the way he changes the nature of the space around him. Drawing men in and then sending them forth to the beat of the song that comes from somewhere deep inside him. Like the horses' whispers, it is something that is felt rather than heard.

He fights like the entire world is at stake.

Hector and Polydamas batter the Achaeans, but as many warriors fall, more slip through the gate to take their place. Arrows rain from the other direction, causing heavy Trojan casualties.

A spear sails toward Polydamas's head. He knocks it aside with his shield and then uses his own spear to skewer the charging Achaean. Polydamas stumbles, pushing the men behind him a few steps back across the bridge. He calls to Hector, his body language screaming retreat. Men bearing the black horse of Troy stationed around Polydamas start inching their way back across the bridge.

Another warrior pushes his way through the Trojan soldiers to Hector's side. Though his face is covered with bronze, I recognize Sarpedon of Lycia by the flame emblazoned across his shield. Andromache's Alev. Something passes between them before Hector and Sarpedon melt into the mass of Trojans still crowding the narrow bridge.

A silent command ripples through the Trojan ranks. As one, they split into two lines, making room in the center for a small group of men to sprint through, their bodies bent low to the ground. Nhorcys the Strong leads the Phrygians, his massive shoulders bulging from the weight of the heavy board resting on his back. Achaean arrows bounce uselessly off the wood.

With a roar, Nhorcys and his Phrygians hurl the board onto the wall, creating a precarious path to the top. In their wake, a single man sprints full tilt across the makeshift bridge.

Sarpedon is naked to the waist. Without his armor to slow him down, he flies at desperate speed. A thick hail of Paeonian arrows drop over his head, catching the Achaeans off guard. In the half second this buys, Sarpedon sprints up the ramp Nhorcys and his men provided, toward the two giants standing guard at the top of the Achaeans' wall. His shoulder slams into the first, while his knife makes short work of the second. Before they have even hit the ground, Hector and his men are breaking toward the gates.

They slam into the battered doors. Once. Twice. On the third strike, the gates break open. Hector is the first one through. The entirety of the Achaean army waits for him on the other side. My heart leaps into my throat when I lose sight of him in the fray.

Fear churns in my gut as I sprint back over the swamp and into the camp. Every Achaean who can wield a spear is making his way toward the gates. Almost every Achaean . . . I turn back toward Cape Sigeum and the Myrmidons' settlement. A hundred warriors stand there, watching. Some are stone-faced. Others seem to vibrate with the desire to do . . . something. Most are wearing armor, prepared to defend themselves if it should come to that. Their leader, Achilles, is nowhere to be seen.

I dodge a group of Cretans rushing toward the fighting. One of them stumbles. His shield slams into me.

Pain explodes in my shoulder. I hit the ground on my side. The Cretan falls to his knees beside me, a gaping wound in his forehead.

The second hangs frozen. Then time starts again, moving too fast. Something whizzes past my ear. I turn to see one of Andromache's mounted Thracians charging toward me. Hooves sail over my head.

I scramble to my feet and sprint hard up the cape.

Smoke thickens the air. The scent of melting copper. The outline of the infirmary is just visible in front of me when a roar cuts through the camp. The sound stops me cold.

On Sigeum Ridge to my west, the long line of Achaean ships sit tied together with their gangway of wooden planks. The Trojans have reached the first of the ships. Tongues of flame lap the hulls.

Without those ships, the Achaeans will be trapped here with no way home and no means to supply themselves. A small host of Achaeans stand bravely against the bulk of the Trojan attack, but slowly, they retreat against overwhelming force.

More ships catch fire in the dark.

In the flickering light, a single Achaean runs toward the burning ships while everyone else breaks the other way. A lone figure moving against the tide.

My heart seizes in my chest as I recognize that golden mane of hair.

Ajax moves faster than any man his size has a right to. He leaps onto the gangplank between the ships, a spear in one hand and a sword in the other.

The Trojans outnumber him a hundred to one. The only thing that keeps them from swarming him is the gangplank that provides the only access to the ships. At its thickest point it is only wide enough to accommodate three men. Or a single giant.

Ajax kills the first three who approach him so quickly I can't track the movements. The same is true of the second wave. And the third. Torches and bodies fall into the waves crashing below as Ajax fights with a fury that I have never seen.

The Trojans stop to regroup. In the pause, Ajax turns back toward the infirmary. Despite the distance, his eyes find mine.

I will not let anyone hurt you.

The Trojans charge forward again, this time in organized groups of two so as to give each other room to wield their weapons. With a scream of rage, Ajax faces them down, and in the light of flickering flames he becomes more than a man. More than a giant. He becomes the god I sometimes mistake him for. So large and powerful that to watch him makes me feel as if I had glimpsed a world beyond this one. A world in which impossible things suddenly become possible.

Down on the beaches, the fleeing Achaeans halt at the sight of the giant fighting off the Trojan army alone.

"Ajax!"

Another warrior sprints toward him, holding a towering shield. Teucer tosses the shield to his brother. Ajax drops his spear and catches the shield in midair before slamming it into the face of the oncoming wave.

The Achaeans start to run again, only this time, they run back toward their ships, not away.

A war cry rises from the center of the camp. Agamemnon fights his way to the ships with his brother Menelaus at his side. This is not the same man I saw in Machaon's rooms with his sumptuous purple robes and pompous manner. This Agamemnon has guts on his sword and blood in his eyes. The Achaean king joins Ajax and Menelaus, and step by step, they drive the Trojans back behind the gates.

I search for Ajax in the mass of men. When I find him, he is holding someone in his arms. My heart squeezes when I recognize Machaon.

Nestor limps at Ajax's side. Another man walks with them. One I recognize from my first visit to the bathhouse all those moons ago.

Achilles's second. Patroclus.

For once, Nestor isn't calm. He gestures widely at Patroclus, who listens intently. They are too far away for me to hear, but I resolve to ask Ajax later. For now, I must get back. I've already left Isola much too long.

My gaze sweeps Sigeum Ridge one last time. The dozen ships closest to the Kesik Cut are lit like oil lamps in the night.

A strange sensation grips my heart. It is what we have been working for all these many months, but I watch the flames devour that row of ships and I can't decide if the thing I feel is joy or sorrow.

19

CASSANDRA

MY TOWER SITS empty. Cold.

Wind howls from the open balcony, circling the room before rushing past me down the stairs.

It hears everything, the wind. Sees everything.

I let the wind whisper its secrets into my ear, and then I cross the threshold into the circular chamber. Everything is exactly as I left it.

Chair chained to the floor.

Bed pressed up against the wall marked by the Wraith's broken fingernails.

Bits of bone and twine adorning the Hawk's roost.

I stare at the walls that hold my past and find in them nothing worth taking. When we left this room for my brother's house, I thought it would be for the last time. Yet here we are again.

Here we are, the Crone sighs. *It can't be helped.*

Quickly, begs the Child as she cowers behind the Fury's red cloak. *I want to go home. I want to hold the baby!*

The Wraith's jawbones work soundlessly in her rotted mouth. She hates this place. Even more than I do. But just like me, some dark, twisted part of her is secretly glad to be here.

We both have our reasons.

I walk out onto the balcony. The sun has started its rise over Mount Ida in the southeast. Its rays skim the palisades. Smooth stone like glinting opals. Setting the bronze roof of the High Temple aflame. I have seen that temple burning before.

In my dreams.

When the wind blows my way, I can smell it.

Incense and bribery. Blood and vainglory.

I blink the visions from my eyes and focus our attention southwest, where the Lower City wakes. Children running to the well with stirrup jars. Women hanging out washing. The smell of bread baking in clay ovens and the sound of tired men tending to their spears and helmets. The ones who can afford them.

Thousands of threads in as many colors.

Shifting, stitching, rearranging.

My tower rises above them all. The world spreads out from Tenedos in the west all the way to the Dardanelles in the east. Not even my father can claim a better view.

You've paid dearly for it, cackles the Crone. Her words sting, though she doesn't mean to hurt me. She can feel it too. They all can.

Shifting sands and changing tides.

Tapestries unwound and then wound again, their writhing images moving too quickly to grasp.

The wind screams, and I blink into the rising sun.

The Ilium and Scamander plains are laid bare all the way to the sea. Behind the swelling of the plain, hidden from sight, the ships. Black monsters with twisted beaks. The view is the same as it has always been, and yet today everything is different.

How much can change in a matter of weeks.

How much can change in a single moment? asks the Crone.

Men move far across the plain, drawing my gaze. Achaean or Trojan. From this distance there is no way to tell, but the Hawk's eyes are better than mine.

I throw out my arms and call him to me. His cry rends the air as he flies through the clear sky. Over the plains now dried and growing. Every inch sown with toil. Watered with sweat and blood.

The Hawk glides over the distant ridge, swooping over the hidden beaches. The Fury screams out her satisfaction at what we see through his eyes.

Funeral pyres run the length of Sigeum Ridge. Overflowing infirmary tents. Stacks of shields and weapons with no more hands to wield them. But that is not all.

A massive structure now runs along the line of the Kesik Cut. A hideous construction of stone, mud, and mismatched timber. The wall is surrounded by a freshly dug trench. Even now, they scurry around it. Adding to their feeble defenses. Tending their wounded and piling the bodies on mounds of stinking ash.

So it has been since the council took the restraints off Troy's armies. Since the day Hector, prince of Troy, fought Ajax the Great, and lived.

But how? wheezes the Crone. *How?*

"I don't know," I whisper to the wind. It flies against my face, sending my hair twisting in dark coils. Something kindles deep within my chest. The thing that brought me here. So bright and sharp, I can't take a deep breath for fear that it will cut me.

With a shuddering sigh, I set the Hawk free until my eyes are my own, and it is just the five of us on this balcony overlooking a city that would appear unchanged to anyone gazing upon it. But not to *me*.

The city that fills with light below is one I have never seen.

Gone are the raptors. Ugly, black monstrosities with twisted talons dripping death from daggered beaks.

Gone are the billows of smoke hanging over the houses, turned to layers of rubble and brittle bones churned up by metal teeth on grinding wheels.

Gone are the rivers of blood running through the cracks of limestone.

Gone are the nightmares I see whenever I close my eyes. Visions of a future that have haunted me since before I was old enough to understand them.

In their place now lies a heavy mist. A curtain of white that circles and shifts. The pictures veiled behind it not yet fully formed. Their lines shifting even now.

Waiting.

Waiting.

For the choices that will make them.

Hope flares to life inside me. So sharp it draws a gasp from my lips that is carried off by the wind.

The Crone prays. The Child falls quiet with awe. The Wraith smiles with rotted teeth. Even the Fury has stopped her raging. Because the truth is right there in front of us. Bright and blazing as the rising sun.

The future that was written has now been unwritten.

A fray in the tapestry, now come undone.

Stitches.

Moments.

Choices.

Unraveling the nightmares of the past, leaving a tapestry blank.

A tapestry that can be *changed*.

That day in the temple when I held my brother, I saw him die at a giant's hands. Even as Hector stood there, holding me in his arms, I saw the rock that would smash his skull through the bronze plate of his helmet. It was clear. As clear to me as the plain below with its copse of trees and winding rivers.

Hector was meant to die, but he didn't. He *didn't*.

And now anything is possible, says the Crone.

Who was it that pulled the thread? asks the Child.

Who indeed?

Was it the Weaver?

The Spindle?

The Mouse?

We must know. Without the truth, we are wandering in the dark, sighs the Crone.

Yes. It is why we have come.

Hurry! screams the Fury.

No time to waste, agrees the Crone.

I walk back into the room. The raptor still hangs over Andrius's cradle every night in Hector's house. Even though the war has shifted in Troy's favor, and the city no longer burns in my dreams, death still hovers over my nephew. We have guarded him to the best of our ability. Every minute of every hour. We have waited for the danger to make itself known, but *this*. This could not wait.

For the first time since this war started, I am as unprepared as I was that morning when the false god came to me and took what was not his. But as hard as I have tried to glimpse what lies ahead, no new visions have come.

Your greatest pain was here, says the Crone. *So was your greatest sight. The blood of stolen innocence has much power.*

Yes. It was that blood and pain that brought the Crone and the others to me, after all. Dark power. It lingers here still.

I return to the balcony, waiting for some hint of the future. Nothing but empty wind and cold stone.

Disappointment is thick as incense. I turn to leave and catch a glint of metal on the bed. A ring. Bronze band. Purple stone.

I know this ring. The cold sting of it against my cheek. The bitter taste of metal in my mouth all those times I tried to scream.

He has been here, and he left his ring as a reminder.

That my visit to the council meeting with Helen has not gone unnoticed.

That he hasn't forgotten me. Just as I will never forget him.

Bile burns up my throat. I recoil from the bed. My back smashes into the wall.

The vision comes to me as they always do. As the false god with the purple ring came to me in the Light. Not gently, but by *force.*

The room fades away. The tower. Even the well inside of me disappears under the flood of images that slam into me like the tide.

A new future sprawls out before me—different than those I've seen before. A future in which Troy's sons prosper, her walls and her men stand tall, and her women sing songs of joy, not of sorrow.

In the center of it all is a dawn just like this one. *This* dawn. And Hector. All his glory lit in the blazing sun, his sword thrust through the faceplate of a warrior whose armor is unmistakable. For it is said to be the armor of a god.

Achilles.

The hero falls to his knees before my brother. His life's blood watering the plain. Behind him, the Achaeans run back to their burning ships.

The vision leaves me shaking against the wall.

You have your answer, whispers the Crone.

Get up! orders the Child. *Run hard and you can still catch him!*

The Fury screams her impatience as I force my trembling legs into a run.

Time slips. The future wavers with every inch that the sun rises.

SWEAT DRIPS DOWN my chest as I crouch in the shadows of the stable and watch Bodecca lovingly polish Hector's armor.

The old woman's back is stiff. Her hands tremble in the way she takes pains to hide. I've seen the death bird lurking over her shoulder. Her time is coming soon, and she worries how the rest of them will get on without her.

Like all gifts from the gods, old age comes at a price, sighs the Crone.

But I am not listening. I am too busy watching the door.

Bodecca leaves.

Seconds fall.

Sands and chances. Sifting, sifting through my fingers.

And then he is there, ducking his broad shoulders through the entryway.

I step out of the shadows and into the light.

"Hector."

He turns at the sound of my voice. I was sleeping next to Andrius's cradle when Hector returned from making his report in the Citadel to wake Andromache. She peeled the armor from my brother's bruised body, but no amount of scrubbing could erase the damage the smoke of burning Achaean ships had wrought. It is as if all the blood that has been spilled has flooded his eyes.

"Cassandra? What are you doing here?"

"The future, Hector. I have come to place it in your hands." My fingers reach out to clasp his tunic to prove to myself that he is real. That I am not too late.

"I don't understand." There is weariness in his voice. Resignation. Though he doesn't have my sight, it's possible my brother has glimpsed the future in his own way.

"He will come," I say. "You have left him no choice. He will appear on the battlefield to turn the tide."

"Who?"

"Achilles. He will charge across the plain in golden armor, and behind him will run the full strength of Achaea's forces. You've done too much damage, and now the Achaeans have their back feet in the Aegean. Even Achilles knows how this will end if he does not rouse himself to fight."

Hector's calloused hands are gentle as they cover mine. "If Achilles planned to rejoin the fighting, Rhea would know."

Frustration bubbles up the well inside of me.

"He will break that vow. Today. You must believe me."

He does. I can see it in his eyes. As he believed me that morning in the High Temple, and still, he left to fight Ajax the Great, knowing what it might cost.

"A death raptor sits over Andrius's cradle," I say the only words that might get through to him. "It stalks your sleeping son even as your wife holds him to her breast. Will it be your seed or that of Achilles that takes root?"

My brother studies me in the shadows. "I believe you see things, Cassandra, but that doesn't mean you can't be wrong. You said that if I fought the duel with Ajax, I would die."

My fingers claw at the front of his tunic. "The future isn't static. It can be changed. By us. The choices we make. Here and now. Something changed the tapestry of fate before you fought Ajax. Whatever it was, it spared your life."

Hector's brow furrows before realization washes over his face. "Ajax's shield."

"What?" I demand.

He shakes his head. "It doesn't matter." Hector looks down at me, and all at once, it isn't the man he is that I see, but the boy he once was. The boy who brought me to this stable, and made me laugh, and offered me olives with glistening fingers.

"We have carved out a chance to change the future that was sung. But it will pass us by unless we *take* it." My throat aches with every word I have been holding back for all these years. "I have seen it. I've seen this city burn a thousand times in my dreams. I have watched the streets run with blood and all the people that you love endure nightmares you can't imagine. Over and Over and Over. But everything is different now. *Everything.* You can change it all. You *must.*"

Hector squeezes my hands. "Tell me what to do."

Relief weakens my knees as I sag against the stable door. Behind me the

Fire Horse rears in his stable. A threat and a promise. Boards crack under the might of his hooves.

Hector's gaze moves to the unrideable beast for a moment before they return to me.

"He will come with the sun and charge the west walls three times," I say. "After the third attempt, you will be there to meet him. And then you will kill him."

Hector loosens his grip and I back away. All the words that need to be said have already been spoken between us.

I watch my brother put on his armor and mount his horse.

Only when he leaves the courtyard at a trot do I run out of the stables. Across the winding streets of the Lower City to the walls. Stairs blur under my feet. Wind drives hard against my face. I spill out onto the battlements. Just as a lone rider charges out of the Scaean gates.

Hector's bronze helmet flashes in the light of the rising sun.

Directly in front of him, another warrior charges toward him on foot with the Myrmidons at his back.

It unfolds before my eyes. Exactly as it did in my vision. Both fast and slow so I do not know if it is minutes or hours that pass.

The Myrmidons shred through our troops like silk. The tip of their spear, Achilles, charges the weakened west walls. Once. Twice. Three times.

Hector dismounts his horse and cuts his way through the ring of Achaeans until he has reached the warrior in golden armor. Achilles watches him come. He turns his back on our walls.

The flutter of hope inside of me soars through my chest, and for once, I do not need the Hawk's wings to fly.

The space between the two warriors dwindles with every stride.

I lean forward over the ballast to get a better view. A high-pitched keening starts in my ears. The ground and sky switch places as the world spins round me. Gasping, I dig my fingers into the stone to keep from falling over.

The vision hits me hard and fast.

Every detail. Every moment unfolding exactly how it did before. Only this time, the vision does not stop. It keeps playing to the end.

The hope that had sent me soaring toward the stars now brings me crashing back down to earth.

Colors between the spaces stretch and yawn, creating flickering images.

Hector's sword plunges through Achilles's helmet, and the great warrior falls to the ground. In the swimming hues, my brother pulls his sword free. He leans down to remove the champion's helmet, revealing the face beneath. A face that does not belong to Achilles.

I stagger back from the ledge. My body trembles the way it hasn't since I was nine years old.

And I know. Just as I knew that morning when the false god stepped out of my dreams and into the reality of my bedroom. I know that I have seen not what was, but what I *wanted* to see, and in so doing, I have sealed all our fates.

The vision leaves me gasping against the wall. I lift my head to see the two warriors running toward one another on the plain below me.

A choice made that can never be undone.

The Hawk soars through the sky as I scream into the wind.

THE SHADE

It rides the gale,
a tortured moan.
Of choices made
rend flesh from bone.

A Serpent's tail
a long cold trail
answers buried deep
within graves of stone.

Shade guards the babe.
Horse dreams of running.
Both bear the weight
of what is coming.

Another horse,
one of ash
not fire,
moves in the shadows
of a pyre.

Race to be run
song to be sung,
from the lowest tunnel
to the highest spire.

The ramparts ring
with twist of fate.
Most painful truth,
one known too late.

BOOK
III

20

RHEA

ADRESTUS. CEBRIONES. HELICON.

I kneel at the side of a pale-faced warrior and wrap the stump of his arm.

Menstius. Menion. Sergentus.

Names and faces blur together. A never-ending parade of vacant gazes; lips twisted in agony. They shouldn't be here. None of them should be here.

Please, please go home.

Death surrounds me. After Hector broke through the gates last night to set fire to the ships, his Trojans were pushed back across the Kesik Cut by Ajax and the Achaean charge. Now the Trojans have their enemies pinned to the swell of the plain. Even with Odysseus's fortifications, the Achaeans' defenses won't hold much longer. For the first time since they came to these shores, the Achaeans are the ones fighting with their backs pressed to a wall. It's hopeless, but they refuse to retreat. It goes against everything they believe about themselves.

The line of wounded outside the infirmary stretches all the way down the ridge. Salama is outside, directing the more serious injuries toward us. Mostly, I suspect she's enjoying watching them suffer.

Ven signals for me across the room. Sweat beads on her brow. Her movements are brisk as she hands me a stack of cloth strips, but it's plain in her gaze when it passes over the scene around us.

Triumph.

The linens grow heavy in my arms as I walk back to the workstation.

On my way, I pass fifty men, some of them no older than Larion. I wish I could see these men as nameless, faceless enemies. The way Salama and Ven do. I wish I had their sense of justice to shield myself from the part I've played in this, but I feel no triumph. No satisfaction. All I feel is sorrow.

The scent of blood and waste mixes with the bitter tang of parsley from the drying racks. Stomach acid rises into my throat. I place the rags down onto the table and grip the edge for balance.

A gentle hand comes to rest on my back. I turn to find Isola standing over me, her expression so unlike that of the timid girl from all those moons ago. As if she, like me, has found more in these camps than she ever expected.

"Are you all right?" she asks.

No. No, I'm not all right.

Whenever I close my eyes, I see the future Ajax offered me. The little house on a beach of fallen stars. A garden and a pasture. Horses running wild with children through fields of green.

I open my eyes, and Isola is there. Isola, whose brother fought and died for Troy and who still looks at the Achaeans as if they are not just enemies, but men. If I told her about Ajax, maybe she'd understand. Maybe she could help me figure a way out of this that doesn't end in despair.

All the words I've been holding inside bubble up my throat, but she speaks before I can.

"You should get some rest."

"I'm fine." I straighten. "I just need a moment."

Isola wipes the back of her hand across her cheek, leaving a streak of blood.

"Go," says a gruff voice.

Machaon lies on a cot, his shoulder heavily bandaged.

"Be still." Gently, Isola places a pillow behind his back with hands that betray a slight tremor. "You'll only aggravate the bad humors."

"Have you forgotten who taught you about humors in the first place?" Machaon asks with a quiet kindness.

Isola offers the healer a soft smile. "I didn't forget. Just as I haven't forgotten when you told me that a dead healer was a useless one."

The man waves off her fussing. "I put Isola in charge. She told you to rest, Rhea. So, go. Rest."

"Isola has been here even longer than I have," I say.

Machaon sits back and closes his eyes. "That can't be helped."

With Machaon injured, Isola is the best chance many of these men have at survival. Men who no longer include only foot soldiers.

Agamemnon. Odysseus. Menelaus. All of them have visited the infirmary since Hector and Sarpedon's charge through the gates last night. The fighting has moved back beyond the swell of the plain, just out of sight of the Cut, but is still close enough to hear the wet work of war.

How much longer can they go on like this? The Trojans will soon be banging on the gates at the Kesik Cut yet again. The next time Hector breaks through, he'll set the entire camp ablaze.

It's the very thing we've been hoping for, working for, so why does the thought make it hard to breathe?

More warriors enter the infirmary, two carrying the third, much larger Achaean between them. I release a long breath when I see that the man in their arms isn't the one I dread seeing here.

Since the day Ajax and Hector dueled, we've spent every stolen moment together. In the stone circle, it's just the two of us. No armies. No war. But in the darkest hours, when our words have run dry and Ajax's strong, steady heart beats against my cheek, I've wondered if he regrets letting Hector live. If he'd go back now and change that small act of mercy if he could.

When he wakes, I never ask him.

Isola gives me a gentle push, and I walk out of the infirmary into the open air. Daylight is bleeding out of the sky, the nearby battle slowly growing less intense. I walk toward the bathhouse and the Kesik Cut, where the Achaeans' hastily erected wall stands as their last defense. I'm nearing the bathhouse when there are shouts from up ahead. On tired legs, I stumble forward just in time to see a group of warriors cross the bridge spanning the Cut.

The black panther on their shields proclaims they are Myrmidons, but how can that be? Achilles expressly forbade his men from joining the battle.

Questions swell in my head when I spot Agamemnon and Nestor among the men. Behind them, drawn on Nestor's chariot, lies the body of a warrior.

The chariot rolls to a stop outside the bathhouse, just a few feet away from where I stand. All across the camp, people watch four Myrmidons lift the warrior out and place his body high on their shoulders. They carry him not toward the infirmary but toward their settlement at the far end of the ridge. The one belonging to Achilles.

The warriors draw even with me, and I glimpse the face of the naked man they carry. An image rises in my mind. The same face smiling at me that very first day in the bathhouse. The same young man listening earnestly to Nestor only yesterday after Sarpedon's charge.

A hush runs through the camp. There is grief in this silence. And something more. It skates across my skin like the charge before a storm.

I give the slain man's name to the steadily building wind.

"Patroclus."

"Stop!" Agamemnon's order rings out. The sun begins a slow set behind him as he stalks to where the Myrmidons stand.

There's a hitch in Agamemnon's stride from the thigh wound Isola stitched just hours ago. He tries to hide it as he approaches the Myrmidons. "Where are you taking him?"

"To Achilles," answers a grizzled soldier of middle years with long black hair to match his black gaze.

"Not yet. Wash the dirt from your face, Menesthius. Drink a cup of wine, and then go when night falls."

"I will take Patroclus to my king without delay." Menesthius doesn't raise his voice, and yet there's a force to his words that is absent in Agamemnon's. As if the soldier's power is drawn from within himself, and not merely from the authority he wields over others.

"I am ordering you to wait," Agamemnon says coldly.

"The only orders I follow are those that come from my king."

"I am your king." Agamemnon reaches for his sword.

Bronze whistles as every Myrmidon in the camp suddenly has his spear in hand.

The crowd of men breaks apart, and then Ajax is there, stepping into the space between Agamemnon and the Myrmidons. "Easy, Menesthius," Ajax says. "No one here would prevent you from telling your king what he needs to hear."

"Then why is he still in my way?" Menesthius asks.

When Ajax's eyes cut to Agamemnon, they silently ask the same question.

"We don't wish to stop you from doing your duty," Nestor begins calmly. "We are merely asking you to go about it with a little less haste. If you reach Achilles before dark, what's to stop him from charging onto the battlefield and throwing away his life in some foolish bid for vengeance? The Trojans have stripped Patroclus of Achilles's armor. Would you have him face Hector with nothing but bare skin? Can you live with his blood on your hands?"

It's hard to fault Nestor's reasoning. None of the men try.

"Go back to Achilles." Gently, Nestor pats Menesthius's shoulder. "But walk slowly, so as not to beat the dark. You'll be giving him the gift of a few more minutes of peace before this storm."

"I'll come with you." Ajax places his hand on Menesthius's other shoulder. "Achilles is kin. It should be me that tells him."

Menesthius makes room, and Ajax takes his place under the body. He must crouch low to maintain the same line as the other men. The Myrmidons and Ajax set out on foot, slower than before. As they pass, Ajax's eyes find mine. Grief glistens in their depths.

Without a word, Agamemnon breaks for his settlement, which lies just across from the bathhouse. Nestor follows on his heels. Another warrior quietly joins them. The blood rushes through my head when I recognize that prowl and wild mane of hair.

Odysseus.

While he fights on the plain like every other man, he and his Ithacans continue to lock themselves away behind their gates. Whatever they are doing behind those walls, it only seems to be escalating.

Straightening my shoulders, I follow the Achaean kings toward Agamemnon's compound. The soldiers at the front don't stop me. They've seen me come and go enough times that I'm just another part of the scenery. The hallway inside Agamemnon's house is crowded with men, heads pressed together. They are speaking in hushed tones, Patroclus's name on their lips. I keep to the edge of the room, farthest from the hearth, and slowly make my way toward the hallway that leads toward Agamemnon's private chambers. I stop short at the sight of three guards.

Whatever is happening in that room, Agamemnon does not want an audience.

I crouch in the corner and force my mind to recall everything I know about the layout of this house. There was a window. In Agamemnon's private bedchamber. I remember the way the light shone through it over the heaps of plunder the day I met Briseis. It was small, but not so small that it would keep me out. I could use it to slip in behind the guards without anyone the wiser. But if I try it and someone sees, no excuse on earth will save me.

I've almost talked myself out of it when Ven's scarred face flashes through my mind. Then Isola's and Salama's. Zeyra's and Lissia's. Briseis's. A dozen other faces. More and more every day. All of them daughters of Anatolia who are taking greater risks than this every day to save a city many of them have never even seen.

Because they can.

Because it is right.

Because they wish someone had done it for them.

The dark is falling fast when I step outside King Agamemnon's house. I wait for the guards outside to face the other way, and then I duck into the shadows clumped at the corner of the building.

The wind rushes over the sea, hitting me with a blast of sand and brine. In the weakening light, the waves are tussling shadows, crashing upon the breaks. Crouching low, I move around the side of the building toward the back, where Agamemnon's bedchamber boasts a view overlooking the beach. I'm just turning the last corner when I hear voices on the wind.

Warriors have gathered on the shore nearby. Dozens of men with long, loose hair. Myrmidons, judging by the black panther stamped on their shields. It is a standard I've not seen among the ranks of soldiers leaving the Cut to fight in all the months I've spent in these camps. Now the shields with that symbol are covered in dust, streaked with mud and blood.

The Myrmidons do not often stray outside their settlement. It seems strange that they would choose to do so now. It is almost as if, like me, they are hiding from something.

I watch them from my crouch in the shadows. Their faces are hard to read in the fading light, but the hunched shoulders . . . the anxiously darting gazes. They scream not just of grief but also of . . . fear.

Something is coming.

They walk farther up the beach and disappear out of sight around the hill said to be the tomb of the hero Herakles. The muscles in my legs tremble as I stand back up against the wall. A hide flap hangs down over the narrow opening above me. The rough outline of a window. Every one of my senses focuses on dim and silent space beyond as I wedge myself through.

Something sharp pricks my throat.

Blood roars in my ears. Slowly, I turn toward the beautiful woman holding the knife.

"Briseis."

The dagger falls from my throat, but Briseis doesn't drop it. Instead, she grips it in her fist.

"Something is happening," I tell her.

"Something has already happened." Emotions flicker across her face in rapid succession. Sadness. Confusion. Fear like that of the warriors outside.

"Patroclus is dead," she says.

"I saw him. The Myrmidons were carrying him back to their camp." Before a large number of them took to the beach for some unknown purpose.

Briseis stares through the walls and up Cape Sigeum as if she could gaze right into Achilles's compound. "They've done it, then."

"Done what?" I don't like the way her shoulders round. It makes me feel like everyone on this ridge knows something I don't. "Who has done what, Briseis?"

"The old man and the farmer from Ithaca," she says.

Nestor and Odysseus.

"They've found a way to win this war despite Agamemnon's best efforts to lose it. They could not move Achilles, so they approached Patroclus instead. I heard it from the old man's lips as he stood boasting to Agamemnon. Last night, he begged Patroclus to take Achilles's armor and fight in his place. He said it would inspire the men to make up the ground they'd lost."

"Is Patroclus such a great warrior?" I ask.

Briseis laughs. An aching sound. "No. He was always a much better leader. He was kind to me," she says quietly. "When I was taken to Achilles's camp."

Her grief shines stark on her face. She meets my eyes and raises her chin, daring me to judge her. But I don't. I can't. Not when I am guilty of far worse.

"He was a more decent man than he was a warrior," Briseis says. "Which is exactly why Nestor and Odysseus knew he'd do whatever they asked. Just as they knew Hector would kill him. In the end, they've gotten exactly what they wanted."

"I don't understand."

Briseis's eyes flash. "Tonight they'll be celebrating in Troy, but their time would be better spent preparing. Patroclus will prove much more dangerous to Troy dead than he ever was alive."

"You think Achilles will fight to avenge him."

Her nostrils flare. "You saw how Achilles behaved when Agamemnon took me from him. That was a matter of pride. This . . ." She wraps her arms around herself as if to fight off a sudden chill. "This is something else."

"He is one man," I say, suppressing a shiver of premonition. "How dangerous can he be?"

Briseis raises a dark brow. "You are only a girl, Rhea. A little slip of a thing. How much damage have you done? How many Achaeans have died because of the words that have crossed your lips?"

The blood drains from my face. I turn to go. Briseis stops me with a gentle hand. "I've been trying to reach you. I went to the women's tents. The washing house, where I finally found Lissia to send you a message."

The urgency in her voice has all of my hackles rising. "What is it?"

"There may be an even more immediate danger facing Troy." She casts another glance over her shoulder. "Hector and Andromache's son."

My veins run to ice. "What about him?"

Silence.

My hands find hers and squeeze. "Briseis. What about Hector's son?"

She meets my gaze, unflinching. "Agamemnon knew the challenge for the duel would come before Priam's heralds ever arrived. Someone in your city's Citadel is plotting with the Achaeans. I've watched them come and go, though I've never glimpsed his face."

A howling starts somewhere in the back of my head.

But how? How could this person get out of the city and approach the Achaean camp without being seen? Without being seen by me? "What are they planning?"

"I've only heard bits and pieces. There is no way to know for—"

"What are they planning, Briseis?"

"They intend to hurt Hector through his son."

Her words are a noose slipping around my neck. "When?"

"I don't know." Briseis says. "I tried to find you as soon as they left, but now . . ."

Now the traitor has returned to Troy and there might not be time to stop him.

My hand reaches out for the wall. I picture Andrius, his sleeping face pressed against Andromache's chest. The soft weight of him in my arms. The feel of his hair against my nose and the sweet scent of his breath. The way he sleeps in his cradle with his hand gently pressed against the horse's head, as if he is already determined to follow in his father's footsteps.

My heart bucks in my chest. Whatever he is building, Odysseus has no need to break through Troy's walls. No need to stalk our gates. Not when he has someone on the inside to do his dirty work for him.

Outside, the sun is nearly drowned in the sea. My mind flies over my last conversations with Andromache, focusing on any mention of Andrius. When I left them last, they were preparing for a ceremony in his honor. One that is to be held at the High Temple.

In the Citadel.

I start for the window.

Briseis's fingers dig into my arm. "Odysseus's men will be out on the plain tonight. I heard him say so. If you leave for the city now, they'll find you and they will kill you."

"If I don't, they'll kill him."

I pull free of Briseis's grasp and climb through. Wind lashes my face as I make my way through the camp and toward the swamp. I don't stop until I'm past the latrines. Up ahead, the ancient monolith looms. I'm a few feet from the shrine when I see the figure standing high on the crumbling wall.

My heart cries out at the sight of Ajax, but I can't let myself be seen. Not tonight. The figure on the stones turns, and I dive down into the shadow and pull my knees close to my chest.

That isn't Ajax.

His body is too lean. His hair white, blond instead of dusky gold. And his face . . .

Fury twists his features. Hatred the likes of which I've seen only once. On the face of a girl in a slave market. Right before she handed me a sharp stone and pressed it to her own cheek.

Achilles throws his head back and unleashes a roar. His cry rings across the plain.

The son of Peleus roars again and again.

The sound rends the night. I press myself to the stone, trembling at the naked fury in that cry. The promise it holds. I am filled with a sense of foreboding I have not felt since the night I saw the snake of fire eat its way through the stars.

Minutes pass with agonizing slowness.

I pull my basket to my chest and rock back and forth as tears of help-lessness stream down my face. Every passing moment could bring danger closer to Andrius. I have to get back. I have to beat the sunrise to Troy's walls, or I'll have to risk traveling in the day. Something I've never done before because it would leave me completely exposed.

I picture the little red face I love above all others. His chubby hands and dark lashes. The way he fought his way into the world.

Astyanax.

Scamandrius.

Our Andrius.

I say his name over and over. Until the dawn begins to break, and I've forgotten every other word.

21

ANDROMACHE

FOR A SECOND time, I hear it. The heart-stopping roar replaces the gale that usually greets me during the third watch. Chills race down my back. Then up again. I pull my robe tighter as I peer over the edge of the balcony, tucking Andrius's body into the linen shield. It does no good. The agonized echo coming from the plain—more animal than man—invites every creature who hears it to make good use of his lungs. My son is no exception.

When Andrius wails, his face turns as red as my father's used to when he was furious. The memory brings a smile to my lips. Though he has my husband's eyes, Andrius looks more like King Eetion every day. A secret comfort I keep to myself.

"Hush. I'm here." I bounce Andrius and pace the balcony, searching for the source of the unearthly sound. Was it close to the walls or from somewhere far beyond? On the ramparts I've heard the cries of men who are angry or dying or both. But this . . .

This was something different.

Andrius will not settle, so I open my robe. His cries fade to whimpers as the warm relief spreads through me. Most Harssi in my position would hand over their child to a wet nurse as soon as possible, but when the moment arrived, I couldn't go through with it.

There isn't much time.

The wretched thought is what keeps me from giving up these sleepless nights. A gnawing fear that hasn't lifted with Hector's storming of the

Achaean camp like I thought it would. No matter the advancements we make on the battlefield, I can't shake the sense that I may not have such moments with my son for long. It is a foreboding that keeps on twirling, reeling like a spindle wound tight.

And now, this roar . . .

What does it mean? The lack of a breeze only adds to the feeling that the stars have shifted. Or maybe I'm worrying myself without cause, something I am more prone to lately. I take a deep breath and smile at the sweet sight of Andrius nursing. Perhaps I've been spending too much time with Cassandra and now read annihilation into every shadow. The faint scent of jasmine fills my nose as the tingling heat of Andrius drinking down life radiates through me. He clutches my garments with relentless hands, his heart-shaped mouth making small, piglike noises.

And I wonder. How has such a thing come to pass? How was this little being ever made by my hard, aching body—a physique trained to destroy more than it was ever taught to nourish?

Queen Penthesilea's face flashes before me, her wide nostrils flaring. "*What are you made for, daughter of Eetion?*"

"*To wage war on our enemies.*"

Once, on a visit to Thebe, the Amazon queen had staged a mock battle with all the youth of my father's household, boys and girls alike. I'd raced to the front of the line . . . alone. Penthesilea intercepted my solo charge, catching the shaft of my spear midair.

"*Wrong. You are made to protect,*" she'd barked before breaking the spear over her muscular thigh. "*The vulnerable do not care about your vainglory.*"

I take a seat. My eyes drift to my own leg, soft and round beneath my thin nightdress, connected to a body that has grown softer and rounder still.

The seventeen-year-old girl I was then knew nothing of motherhood. It was not her fault. It makes no difference how many times she watched her own mother succumb to the pains of childbirth and the endless labor of caring for an infant. There is nothing that can prepare you. No experience that might convince you that while your body, in its youth, may mimic the sharp angles of a man, there is a reason it bends into a stubborn curve.

Both a cup to be filled and the wine poured out for others to drink.

Andrius stirs against me, a silvery line of milk dribbling down his full cheek. Blinking, he glances up briefly before reattaching to my breast. Only now his suckling is more for comfort than anything. Soon, he begins to doze.

My chest swells, but not from the blood flow that stimulates my milk. This surge is different. More pleasurable and more painful still. None of this has been anything like falling in love with a man. For that sensation is truly a *fall*, which means that at some point, you must rise from the ground and run out to meet him—an act of the will. No, the love of a mother is more like lying lame before a stampede of charging horses.

There is nothing to be done.

And after everything you *were* has been pounded into the scorched earth, a battered heart is all that survives. Only now it is wrapped in another's flesh. Soon, that heart will crawl, then walk, then run about you, vulnerable to the slings and spears of an indifferent world.

I brush back the copper curl from Andrius's sticky forehead. His face puckers and his mouth tightens greedily in protest.

A throat clears behind us. I glance up to find Hector standing in the doorway of our bedchamber, his eyes heavy even as his mouth teases a gentle smile.

"What?" I ask, smiling back.

Every time Hector has left for battle since his duel with Ajax the Great, it has been nearly as unbearable as that first farewell by the Scaean gate. But I doubt we shall ever repeat our good-byes. All words between us have been spoken, every tear shed. Now that Hector has the freedom to lead the army as he must, each parting is potentially our last.

Still, it is done. Our choices made. Saving the city for Andrius is all that matters now.

"This." Hector lifts a hand toward the chair where I am nursing his son. The sky glowing beyond the balcony catches fire as Tiwad's chariot drags forth another day. "Everything."

His impenetrable look tells me it will do no good to ask what he means. The mystery slips back into the mist of his eyes as quickly as it came. Something darker takes its place.

"What is it, Hector?" I rise from my seat.

For a moment, he doesn't seem to hear me. I rest a hand on Hector's bare arm. He shudders at the touch.

"Yesterday, I killed a man." Hector speaks as if this duty that occupies him daily is somehow new. "His movements, his armor. I . . . I swore it was Achilles."

My throat tightens. "Rhea says Achilles refuses to lift a sword for Agamemnon ever again."

"I don't doubt she's right." When Hector meets my gaze, I glimpse a fear I've never seen. Not just the fear of a good man with much to lose. This is something more primal.

Hector looks at his son sleeping against my chest. He runs a rigid hand down Andrius's back. "Cassandra . . ." He swallows hard. "I worry I've done the one thing that might bring Achilles back into this war."

My mind sifts through the fog of sleepless nights for what he could possibly mean.

"Patroclus." The name is a whisper. And so much more.

We've all heard the stories. Two men united since boyhood. One the white panther leading the charge, the other his shadow. Prowling together when large cats typically hunt alone. There are some earthly attachments that defy explanation. Some bonds that cannot be housed in a single jar of clay.

Still, even shadows sometimes wish to step into the sunlight.

"You killed him. You killed Patroclus."

Hector hangs his head as the roar I heard from the balcony reverberates through me all over again.

"We were winning!" I explode across the bedroom. "We *are* winning."

"I know," Hector says softly. "But this changes things. I've ordered some of our men back to the Lower City ramparts. If Achilles advances, *when* he advances, we must be ready. But we also can't afford to lose the ground we've gained."

What Hector doesn't say is what he fears most. If Achilles is back in this fight, it is only a matter of time before he comes for Hector. Only moments before their swords clash and the war songs sung by poets receive their long-awaited ending.

"So which is it? Who sees the truth? Does Achilles fall in this war? Or do I?"

Dread prickles the skin down my arms. Andrius suddenly feels too heavy, so I approach the cradle carved by Hector's hand. When I reach the dimly lit corner where it sits beside our bed, a sharp breath escapes my lips.

"Cassandra!"

Except it isn't. It's a creature we've not seen for some time, a face I prayed was gone for good. Knees huddled to her chest, Cassandra rocks back and forth like a lost child, her eyes two pools mirroring the same hopelessness I witnessed in Hector a moment ago.

"What have we done?" she mutters again and again in a high-pitched voice. The Cassandra who'd returned to us before Andrius's birth, the young woman who'd cradled her nephew with such loving care, is lost inside herself again.

No, *lost* isn't the right word. Perhaps she is merely hiding.

But from what?

Slowly, I approach her. Cassandra slinks farther into the corner, like she doesn't know who I am. A knock at the door stops me before I can reach her. Hector permits Bodecca and Faria into the bedchamber.

"Is my little prince ready for his big ceremony?" Bodecca says with an exuberance reserved for Andrius alone. She fails to see Cassandra in the corner, and I'm grateful for it.

What I regret is failing to give the dedication rite much thought until this moment. A public spectacle at the High Temple to be witnessed by highborn women of the Citadel, a ceremony whose solar brightness the queen intends not for Andrius, but for her own prestige.

There will be no getting out of it.

"Please dress the prince and deliver him to Queen Hecuba. I will meet you at the temple." I hand off Andrius to the old woman who once cradled Hector in much the same way. "And, Bodecca . . . be vigilant."

Just the thought of my son entering that den of deceit is enough to make my skin crawl.

"When am I not?" Bodecca grunts, then returns to making ridiculous faces at the child, who is wide awake now. "But don't *you* be late. The queen will waste no chance to make a scene."

"My mother will find something to be displeased about regardless," Hector murmurs with an aloofness that isn't like him.

Still, Hector isn't the child of Hecuba who most concerns me. I turn to Cassandra, utterly catatonic. Hector leaves the room with Bodecca and Andrius so I can run his sister a bath. I pray the heat will give her the strength to climb out of whatever mental well she's fallen back into. She allows me to guide her into the tub, where she sits limp as I wash the grease from her hair.

"Are you still with us, dear one?"

Cassandra's hand shoots out, grabbing my wrist with a firmness that doesn't match her birdlike bone structure. When she meets my gaze, there's a fury in her eyes that sends another bolt of trepidation through me. Even worse than when I heard that low roar across the plain.

"He is coming, Andromache. He is coming for Hector, and the panther will not back down until he has tasted blood."

MINDFUL OF BODECCA'S warning, I head to the High Temple early. Inside its courtyard, I make my way toward the imposing doors, until the *crack* of something underfoot stops me. Beneath my sandal, I find the crushed cap of an acorn. It lies in the middle of a round paving stone, slightly larger than those around it. The design of the faded carving at its center is unmistakably Anatolian.

It is also one I've seen before, if only in my imagination while an old woman shared nearly forgotten memories.

Blame the serpents.

I crouch down to run my fingers across stone at least as old as the cantankerous cook who told me of its existence.

The design of the serpent stone isn't detailed, but it *moves*, capturing the essence of the creature it is meant to convey. I've some time to kill before the start of the ceremony, so I continue walking around the courtyard, counting seven serpent stones in all. Equally spaced in a large circle around the temple.

Reaching for the dagger at my belt, I kneel down to dig into the cracks around one of the stones. The mortar is loose in places, but my fingers aren't small enough to get a good grip.

If only Rhea were here . . .

After a few more breaths of determined prying that leaves my ceremonial robes stained with sweat, the stone pops free. I slide it aside, searching the empty streets. Finding I am still alone, I look down.

Down, down, *down.*

For the black well is bottomless, the locked-away air that blasts my face ice cold. I inhale its coolness, not minding the stale smell after so many months spent living inside an inferno.

But what exactly am I looking at?

I toss a few bits of mortar down into the hole, but not a sound echoes back to me. The fall must be far, then. Bodecca thought these stones might cover a cistern dug below the Citadel. In that case, I should have heard a *plop* when the debris hit water.

Something to ask Laocoon about.

When I enter the High Temple, I'm greeted with the musky scent of burning animal fat. Deities sourced from all ends of the earth look down on me as I make my way to the ceremonial pool. Hecuba's favorite pantheon from across the Aegean is housed nearby in the most prominent position, but everywhere I look, there are gods carved from rock or molded in gold. Many are Luwian. Some Hittite. A few are even Assyrian.

All incessant in their competing demands. All jealous for our loyalty.

Will any of them hear Troy now that the favored Achilles has returned?

Some say he is part god, born of an immortal mother. He isn't the only warrior to claim such origins. It has long made sense to me that the stories we humans tell overlap and even borrow from one another. All peoples spin similar tales to capture the same essence. The truth whispered in the many echoes. A story of mothers who grieve for slain sons. Of divine fathers who grant the world light, only to have darkness thrown back in their faces. Of heroes born to the heavens who descend into the mire of mortals, on a quest to restore their birthright. To remind us of who we might become, if only we could be bothered to lift our faces to the stars.

That is where my eyes focus now, searching for yet another serpent, though the sky before me is crafted from human tools. A massive limestone pillar sits in the oldest part of the High Temple, but its weathered surface is not so worn that I can't make out the carved image taking center stage. Not a snake, but a hound. And not just any dog, the *Great* Dog.

Sopdet. At least that's what my father said the Egyptians called the brightest star. Their pharaohs had good reason to pay it close attention— the rising of Sopdet meant the flooding of the Nile, signifying the end of summer.

The end of summer?

Or the end of everything?

Only this Great Dog is not alone in his limestone sky.

Ah . . . there they are.

Faded carvings of serpents with gaping jaws emanate from the constellation like waves. A chill follows the hot wind up my skirts as doors open behind me.

"Andromache."

A woman's ethereal form moves through the hazy space. Not Helen. The scent of lily oil, which the woman bathes in daily, leaves no doubt.

Queen Hecuba materializes. Holding my son like a prize.

The queen dons a heavy veil embroidered with thread of gold, and Andrius wears a starched gown that matches it precisely. Hecuba's eyes rake up my superior height, judging like she is one of the gods she believes she is so close to. But would any one of those deities feel even a twinge of sympathy for a young soldier who takes a sharp spear in the side?

Because a trail of corpses is how Achilles will mark his path to Troy's gates.

"I didn't expect to see you so early." Hecuba speaks without emotion as she pulls back her head covering. She props Andrius high on her hip like some overdressed doll.

"I did not expect to see you here." I gesture to the older Luwian gods that surround us. Their faces are less refined than the recent rendering of Athena that the queen adores, which stands watch in the temple courtyard.

"The Anatolian gods are weak." Hecuba's hair, dyed a deep red with henna, glows like a wildfire. "They abandoned Troy long ago. I honor the children of Zeus and Hera because I care for this city's future, and it is *they* who will decide the fate of this war."

Hecuba's eyes find an altar shelf that holds a sculpture of Hannahanna, a matron with swollen breasts meant to feed the entire world.

"Though there is something to be said for the simpler faith of one's childhood," she murmurs. "I will make an offering to the old Mother on Scamandrius's behalf. If it pleases you."

Hecuba does not wait for my response before reaching for an incense brick. Still, she will have it. "Then say a prayer for Hector as well. Achilles has returned to the battle."

I don't give Hecuba this information to ruffle her feathers. I say it because there is no one else in this city who understands what the words truly mean.

The queen does not speak. She simply hands me Andrius so she can kneel to light her incense, thin hands trembling. Closing her eyes, she whispers desperate words etched on her heart from deep memory.

It isn't her sincerity I doubt. Queen Hecuba loves Hector with a fierceness I understand too well. It is her pride—the unwavering belief that *she* will be heard when the petitions of so many others go unanswered—that rubs me like coarse salt. Perhaps because that particular vice feels regrettably familiar.

The pride of a mother who believes she is her child's only hope.

When the queen finishes her ritual and again rises to her feet, Hecuba's handsome face regains its former severity. Cunning but controlling. It is like standing before a polished plate of bronze that reflects a future self.

Unless I decide once and for all to take a vastly different route.

"The women are gathering." Before Hecuba turns toward the ceremonial pool, her eyes graze the megalith behind me. The corners of her mouth pinch tightly. I want to ask if she knows about the pillar's origins, along with the serpent stones that surround the temple. The pit they conceal and what it is used for. But ever-grasping Hecuba takes Andrius from my arms, turns her back on the gods of her youth, and marches to the platform above the waters where Laocoon waits.

It is an impressive structure, this ceremonial pool. At one end, a waterfall the height of a man cascades from a shelf in the temple's wall, where clay pipes pump out water from a spring deep below ground.

Laocoon begins the ceremony, and the dedication rite is as tedious and impersonal as I imagined it would be. Thankfully, it is also brief. Helen and Creusa attend with the other Harssi of the Citadel who wish to remain in the good graces of their queen. No one seems to notice Cassandra's absence, but I do. Just like I noticed the absence of Cassandra's true self as she sat in my tub, staring at a blank wall.

My gaze lands on Laocoon, the only man here.

It is an opportunity I will not waste. When the rite is complete and the

Citadel women descend on Hecuba to fawn over my son, I corner the old priest as he disposes of extra entrails he did not use in his offering.

"The serpent stones in the courtyard," I say without pretense. "I never noticed them before. "

The cloth Laocoon is using to clean his knife stops moving.

"It is easy to overlook that which we look down on."

I ignore the slight. "Do they block air vents, these stones? Some kind of ventilation for an underground chamber?"

Because these stones were the only mystery that occupied me while Laocoon recited stiff words over my son. With Achilles back in the battle, not only Hector but everything Hector stands for and shields is once again at risk.

I lick my lips, feeling parched all of a sudden. If the Citadel sits upon some hidden chamber that might be used to shelter Troy's people, then I must know about it. Even if it is a long-buried secret, it's potentially one that could save countless lives if the Lower City burns again.

My gaze travels across the sanctuary until it finds Andrius.

Motionless now, the priest stands in silence with his back to me. This temple is his domain. A place with many rooms I am not permitted to enter. He has the higher ground here, and when he turns to face me, it is obvious we both know it.

"An astute observation, Harsa. The ducts do feed air into a small chamber buried beneath the temple, a private refuge for the king and queen should the Citadel come under attack."

I frown. "The spacing of the seven stones suggests a room much larger than that."

Laocoon smiles, revealing a row of reddish-black teeth, stained from a rare nut that temple priests like to chew to keep them awake during late-night rituals. "Regardless of the stories the people of the Lower City like to tell, I assure you the shelter is small. It is a last resort should our rulers find themselves in mortal danger, but it is no great secret. Ask your husband; I'm sure he knows all about it."

"Andromache, we're ready to—"

I lift a hand as Helen approaches with the recent widow Kalawashi. The sense that Laocoon is hiding something grows with every inch of raised hair along my skin.

I take a step closer to Laocoon just as he takes a step back. "Hector tells me everything he knows. He has never said a word about this."

Which means Laocoon is lying. Achilles's return will bolster the Achaeans to a bloody frenzy. Doesn't this priest see that if the city has an underground chamber with access to a central spring, we may need it sooner than he can imagine? The heavily fortified Citadel is too narrow to hold all the people who will rush its gates if the weakened walls of the Lower City are breached.

Thousands would be slaughtered. And if Laocoon knows something that might save them, it will be more than the blood of goats and pigeons that stains his hands.

"I'm told the serpent had special significance to the men who first built Troy." I soften my tone, suspecting the best way to lower the priest's guard is to let him play the sage he believes himself to be. "As one not born to this city, I've long wondered about their meaning. You are descended from one of these founding families, is that right?"

Laocoon's eyes spark. With the queen's ardent overhaul of Troy's older gods, the priest has had little opportunity to share the story of his illustrious pedigree with eager ears.

"That is correct, Harsa. The carvings you noticed are sky snakes. The same falling stars we saw over Mount Ida when the war resumed after the winter rains. Generations ago, when my forefathers and the first people of the Troad made this plateau their home, they too saw serpents in the sky." Any wistful nostalgia in Laocoon's voice vanishes. "Serpents that warned of a coming disaster. A thousand years of ice and the downfall of many kingdoms. Few survived." The priest pulls his shoulders back with pride. "My ancestors were among those who did."

"How fortunate," I say dryly.

"And how did they manage such a feat when so many other civilizations were lost?" Helen asks.

The priest's brows narrow. "Superior stock."

I meet his hardened gaze head-on. "No doubt. Or perhaps the serpents sent them fleeing to the safety of some den."

Laocoon laughs, covering the row of gold rings lining his right hand with the bare knuckles of his left. "Again, Harsa, I know of no such lair. Though I wish such a place existed." The priest waves a heavily robed arm at Helen. "Between Hector's baiting of Achilles and your friend here with her bag of sorceress tricks, the only miracle on display in Troy is that the gods have spared us their wrath."

My hands ball into tight fists. "Ten years. That's how long Troy's sons have painted the Ilium plain red. What could possibly be a greater sign of the gods' disfavor?"

Laocoon closes the gap between us. "That's what you and your upstart allies fail to understand. I have no doubt you *believe* you are helping Troy by introducing all manner of novelties, but how will you protect this city when you despise everything she was built on?" The priest takes another step closer, until I can smell the wine and charred offerings on his breath. "The Old Blood are Troy's guardians. There is no one who cherishes her legacy more. You would do well to remember that."

"And you would do well to remember *whom* you are charged to guard. Or did your forefathers not warn that those who labor to save bygone stones at the expense of breathing people have a tendency to lose both?"

Laocoon's lips spread into a red-stained smile. For a moment, he resembles the snakes that adorn his precious sanctuary. "Perhaps you are right, Harsa Andromache. Perhaps you are right."

22

HELEN

"HARSA HELEN, HARSA Andromache. I must speak with you."

Kalawashi corners us in the temple as soon as Laocoon manages to flee Andromache's interrogation. I study the widow. The change in her is profound. The deep lines of her face seem less like sorrow and more like the consequence of worries with no place to go.

Kalawashi pulls her shawl around broad shoulders and even broader hips. "Harssi, won't you join me for a toast to the good health of your son and the future heir of Troy?"

Andromache looks like she wants to make an excuse, but I rest a hand on her arm. Something about the way Kalawashi watched Laocoon—her expression a potent blend of contempt and distrust—makes me think she is eager to speak with us alone for a reason.

"Bodecca can take Andrius home for his nap, can't she?" I give Andromache a pointed look. "You deserve a few moments to yourself."

Andromache frowns. We both know if she was granted a free moment, she would spend it not drinking wine on a plush sofa but planning the next attack on the Achaean camp.

"I suppose Andrius won't miss me for an hour or so."

We step into the morning light and join Kalawashi on the short walk from the High Temple to her house. It is the one Citadel home I have tried and failed to gain an invitation to. Though now that Tumaeus has crossed over, I suppose we can safely eliminate him from the short list of council members who might have colluded with Paris.

Once we enter the silent home, Kalawashi pours wine from a simple pitcher while Andromache stares at the abandoned loom near the hearth. Head tilted like she is listening for footsteps. For any sign of life at all. "Your daughters. The last time I was here, they graced us with their lively presence."

Kalawashi flushes. "I've sent them to the palace to serve the king and queen. It will teach them how to better manage a home."

The woman strives to keep her chin high, but I can see her loss of pride plainly, if not her downright humiliation. Yet there is also a keen intelligence in Kalawashi's gaze that seems to grow stronger every time we cross paths. Along with a pointed resentment.

"We are sorry for your loss, Kalawashi," I say as Andromache begins pacing the room, searching for what I can't imagine.

Kalawashi wrings her hands. "Tumaeus was in excellent health. One of the best-fed men in Troy." Andromache stiffens at that. "He was even beginning to see the merits of your cause."

Heavy footsteps go silent.

"What are you saying?" Andromache asks, joining us on the sofa.

The widow leans forward, as if she is afraid to speak the words even in her own home. "I'm saying I do not believe Tumaeus's death was accidental."

Andromache reaches for one of Kalawashi's hands, which seems to surprise her. "If that is the case, we will seek justice on his behalf. On your behalf. But in order to do that, you must tell us what you know."

"The priest Laocoon," I add, sensing what Andromache is after. "You did not seem to care for him."

"They are all deceivers," Kalawashi spits. She stands and beckons for us to follow her.

The woman's kitchen is larger than even Andromache's. Nothing appears out of the ordinary. Bundles of herbs hang from the ceiling and six large amphorae, presumably filled with oil and wine, sit in the far corner.

That Kalawashi still has this much to store is the only detail that stands out.

"Over here," she grunts as she struggles to move one of the heavy amphorae aside. We join her in rolling the clay containers away from the wall. On the ground where the amphorae sat is a circular floor stone, one much larger than those around it.

A stone stamped with a faded serpent.

Andromache drops to her knees, brushing off the dust that has settled into the grooves of the carving. The snake is so small it would be easy to miss. She feels around the stone's edges, but the seal must be tight because she gives up quickly, smoothing her skirts as she rises from the floor.

"Can it be opened?" I ask Kalawashi.

"I imagine, though I've never tried," she replies. "Many of the Citadel's oldest homes have stones like this in their kitchens. I always assumed they were decorative. But when you asked Laocoon about the air ducts around the temple, it made me wonder . . . why would the builders place ventilation shafts inside kitchens? They are the smokiest rooms in any home."

Andromache regards the widow contemplatively for a long moment. "Then if these are not air ducts, perhaps they are entrances."

I nod. Only entrances to what?

"Based on that temple rat's caginess when you pressed him, I would not be surprised if they were," Kalawashi says.

Her response is unexpected. For years, Kalawashi's husband served alongside Laocoon as one of the Five, and Paris always talked as if the two men were thick as thieves. Yet when Kalawashi speaks of Laocoon now, her mouth sags in disgust.

Andromache catches it too. "I take it you are not a friend of our esteemed high priest?"

"My late husband didn't just flap his lips in the face of good food," the widow offers coyly. "He had leverage on every member of the council, and he was not above using it."

Andromache crosses her arms. "What do you mean?"

Kalawashi shrugs. "What good does it do to bring you into the only source of power I now possess?"

"We know all about securing influence in difficult circumstances. Which is why you want us on your side."

"Even when you thought yourself so much better that you chose to live beyond our gates?"

Andromache balks, as if this is the first time she has fully understood how her and Hector's distance from the Citadel has been viewed by those who cannot escape it. Not as a show of solidarity with the Lower City, but as a sign of their disdain for the higher rungs.

"It might surprise you to know that we women of the Citadel do more than wait on our husbands and stand at our looms," Kalawashi continues. "We hear things. Know things. *Because* we are overlooked."

Serving as ornamentation is something I am familiar with. "There is nothing wrong with working the loom. This city would not function without—"

"Yes, yes, without the women who clothe its warriors' naked backsides." Kalawashi all but rolls her eyes. "I've heard it before. Most often from equally pampered Harssi who believe they're the only ones who wish to be recognized for their minds in addition to their nimble fingers."

Andromache grunts with begrudging respect. "Then tell us what such recognition would look like."

Kalawashi crosses her arms and nods at the stone we stand over. "There is little a woman in my position can do to aid her city, but that doesn't mean I can't work to see my own children spared. Let me do some digging of my own. I will go through Tumaeus's possessions. Ask the other wives of council members if they've heard of these serpent stones and what they might conceal."

"You would do that?" I ask, suspicious of the sudden change in her.

"Yes, but my motives are not so pure." Kalawashi's scowl deepens. "Those vipers killed my husband, leaving me nothing but debts and three daughters who lack dowries. Who will protect us when the Achaeans come? Should they break into the Citadel, my girls would be taken as whores."

Like every other woman in this city, I think but do not say.

"If Troy is besieged, we would defend you," Andromache says.

Kalawashi's laugh is more of a bark. "Not every woman requires a bow to protect the ones she loves."

The Harsa turns back to the serpent stone as if it holds the answers to all that ails her.

"We must find a way to open it."

ANDROMACHE MARCHES FROM the Citadel like she wants no part in its sanctuary, hidden or otherwise.

"I know it is frustrating," I say, struggling to stay on her heels. "But if Hector continues pressing the line, the Achaeans will soon flee to their ships and we may not need to—"

Andromache whirls around with a wild sneer.

"Achilles is back."

The vivid colors of the Citadel bleed together before fading entirely. "That is impossible."

"And yet it has happened."

"How?"

"Patroclus." Andromache spits the name like a curse before adding, "He fell by Hector's hand."

The low buzzing that has been building between my ears at the first mention of Achilles grows to a dull roar. I have sat with Achilles and Patroclus for many meals in Menelaus's hall, and I have seen their bond firsthand.

Only the mutual love and respect of Hector and Andromache might hope to rival it.

"When?" I ask.

"Yesterday," Andromache says, eyes searching the Merchant Quarter. "We are running out of time."

With a roar of frustration, Andromache knocks a row of clay flowerpots from the wall they sit on.

"I wanted to despise Kalawashi for what she said. About her main concern being not the city but the fate of her own children." Andromache's chest rises and falls rapidly. "And yet I find myself consumed by the same thoughts. Achilles is coming, Helen. If he breaks past these walls, it won't only be Hector he targets with his spear but his entire line."

Her desperate eyes scan the empty streets.

I know the wild fear she speaks of—the desire to sacrifice all others for the sake of *one*—and I do not judge her for it. Yet there is something else I know, and I trust Andromache will see it for herself in time.

A mother's instinct to protect is a mantle that will gather in many others when it counts, whether they are her children by blood or not.

"We are winning now, but if the tide of battle turns again, I will not be caught unprepared." Andromache's urgency fills me with deep foreboding.

"What are you thinking?"

"I don't know yet," Andromache says, hands clenching. "But I sense our new friend Kalawashi will play a part."

I nod, the threads of possibility spinning as the wind ruffles my skirts.

Gate of Ghosts . . . hidden dens.

What if one secret leads to another?

23

RHEA

FARIA YELPS WHEN I stagger into the kitchen. The piece of pottery in her hand crashes to the floor.

Bodecca stands over a boiling pot.

Cassandra stops rocking in the corner, her hands hugging her knees.

Larion pauses with his midmorning meal halfway to his mouth.

Bodecca's words are lost to the wind tunnel inside my head. There is only room inside me for one thought. His name is a chant as I climb the stairs and stagger down the hall to Hector and Andromache's rooms.

My eyes fly first to the cradle, which is missing from its usual place. Frantically, I spin toward the bed.

Something moves in the corner of my vision. I turn, and there they are. In a chair out on the balcony, Andromache sits with Andrius sleeping soundly in her arms, the cradle at her feet.

The windstorm goes still.

Beams of morning light spear the air between us as I move closer. I don't trust my eyes. I don't trust my heart not to lie and show me these things I want most to see.

Slowly, my hand reaches out to touch Andrius's back. His skin is warm, rising and falling under my palm with his rapid baby breaths. He moves in his sleep. His soft cheek rubs against my fingers, and something cracks inside me.

My knees fold and then I am sliding down to the floor.

The sun is rising higher over the balcony when I feel two palms on my shoulders. Andromache kneels in front of me, her arms empty. She lifts me to my feet and presses my cheek against her breast, still warm from Andrius's sleeping body. She holds me as I've watched her hold him so many times. As if every line of the world were drawn from the point of connection between us.

And then I'm clinging to her like the child I haven't allowed myself to be since I ran away from a burning stable.

"Andrius . . ." His name is a gasp for air.

Andromache's palm cups the back of my head. "Is sleeping after the ceremony." When I start to shake, Andromache pulls back to study me. "What is it?"

I squeeze her arms with all the strength I have left and tell her. About Briseis's warning. The traitor. I give her all my words until there are only these left: "I thought I was too late."

Andromache's face blurs in my vision. She wipes the tears from my cheeks. "You are here now. Exactly when I need you. As you always are."

I sag but her arms hold me fast.

"Nobody will hurt him." The softness flees Andromache's face to be replaced by a darkness deeper than any I've met upon the plain.

I pull free of her grip. "We have to warn the council. When they learn there is a traitor, it will force them to act. Hector will—"

"Hector will do nothing. Neither will the council."

I run over her words again and again, willing them to make sense. "How can you say that?"

"Because we aren't going to tell them."

"Andromache—"

"This morning I've learned the treachery in that den of vipers goes deeper than we ever imagined. Besides, what proof do I have to offer the council?"

My stomach sinks when I catch her meaning. "You can't tell them what I heard in the camp without admitting that I was there in the first place." It is an impossible situation. "What do we do?"

Andromache nods, and I realize with a jolt that it is her trust I crave as much as her love. Secrets are eating away at me slowly. With every moment that passes, my lies of omission feel more and more like a betrayal. Of her. Of Ajax.

"The council acts only in their own interests. I am done seeking their approval or their aid. And Hector . . . Hector has Achilles to contend with." Andromache's eyes narrow. "We will deal with this on our own."

"He won't thank you for keeping this from him."

Andromache's smile is serrated. "He will be furious, but there are threats everywhere. Pointed at us from every angle. I'd bear his anger a thousand times to protect them." Her gaze drifts from Andrius in his cradle over the ramparts of Troy. "That is what love does. It makes walls of us. Only we never really know if we are standing strong between danger and that which we cherish, or if we are the ones hiding."

Her words are lights, shining in the darkest corners of my mind.

Andromache's gaze stays fixed somewhere beyond the distant mountains. I know her expressions like I know her moods. The way I know her heart even when she doesn't allow herself to show it.

For the very first time, she is *afraid*.

I walk over to the cradle and place a blanket over Andrius while I wait for Andromache to return from wherever her thoughts have taken her. When she does, I'll follow her example. I will stop hiding behind the walls I have built between all the people I love. I will face my fears and tell her everything. She'll understand. She *has* to. Once I explain about Ajax. His laugh. His kindness. The beautiful things he makes.

The way he spared Hector's life.

I rub Andrius's back, my resolve strengthening. Not just to tell the truth, but to *live* it.

We will beat the Achaeans. Even if Achilles has rejoined the battle, we will win because any gods of justice will be on our side. We'll drive these invaders back to their shores, and when they go, I'll go with them. To start the life Ajax has spent all these nights painting inside my dreams.

I could do it. I could go. Nobody would ever have to know the role I played. Not even Ajax. We could start again on the other side of the sea, and in time, when anger fades and wounds heal, we could return to this city on the plateau. Not as enemies. But as friends.

The decision winds through my chest on a wave of joy. A rush so strong and fast, it leaves me dizzy. I can't remember the last time I slept, and yet I'm suddenly bursting with eagerness to run back to the camp. To throw my arms around Ajax and tell him that I'll follow him wherever he goes.

My hand trembles as I reach for the wall to steady myself. My body feels weak with the weight of the decision I've made. Every corner of me resonates with the rightness of it.

"Andromache, there is something I have to tell you."

She looks at me, and I know she hasn't heard. That her thoughts are too far away for any words of mine to reach.

It's as if a fog has lifted. Suddenly, every ounce of her strength and intensity is focused squarely on me. "I have a favor to ask you."

"Anything."

Always the same word between us. The first time, her demand sent me cowering in a stable. This time, whatever the question, I will not run from it.

Her eyes soften. She remembers too.

"We will do everything we can to protect Troy from our enemies, but one day, even our best defenses might break. Hector will fight for this city until there is nothing left of him and I . . ." Her throat spasms. "If the time comes that I must fight beside him, it is you who will take Andrius. And it is you who must keep him if . . . if we fall." Her face fills my vision. "Promise to do this for me."

A cold shadow kisses the back of my neck. "You are his mother. He belongs with you."

"He belongs with whoever can protect him if I no longer can. You are the only one among us who can hope to move unnoticed." Tears shine in her eyes that she will never let fall. It's not in her. Just as it isn't in her to ask for something unless there is no other option.

But none of this changes that I can't do this.

"I won't take him from you, Andromache. Never. Don't ask it of me."

"I already did." The words drown in her throat as she grips both my hands. "You have no family here. No ties but us. We *are* your family. You are the only one I would trust with my son's life, if I am gone. The only one."

No family.

No ties.

I close my eyes. My mind spins in circles, desperately seeking a solution. "It will not come to that."

"Cassandra said . . ." Andromache does not finish that thought and I do not ask it of her. She leans against the wall. Agony sings in every line of her body. "I can't let Hector face his enemies alone. I pray that we send the Achaeans bleeding into the sea, but if Tarhunt and Runtiya abandon us, I need to know. Will you do this, Rhea? For Hector? For me?"

I close my eyes again, and I see Ajax's face.

A house by the sea and a corral full of horses.

A little boy with golden hair and green eyes riding high on a pair of wide shoulders.

A little girl with dark curls and dimples mounted on a pony under my hands.

Ajax. Sitting in the light of a hearth fire while he carves a child's toy in his hands.

Dreams that are not dreams, but wishes.

When I open my eyes, there is only Andromache. Her heart in her eyes. *Courage* because I know that she would do this. She'd cut her heart out of her chest and give it to me if only it would keep her son safe.

Andrius in his cradle. Sleeping softly. The sweet, warm weight of him in my arms. The pressure of his hand as it grasped my finger.

Not dreams. Not wishes. Gifts I have been given.

My heart breaks even as I say the word.

"Yes."

24

HELEN

"ACHILLES IS ONLY one man." I struggle to convince even myself of these words.

"He is." Andromache moves through her kitchen like it is a cage. "But he represents an ideal. And ideals are more dangerous than the men who try them on. The Achaeans will follow Achilles into battle with a ferocity we haven't yet seen."

"We should go to the king. We'll tell him there is a traitor on the council, that Laocoon knows something—"

"No."

Andromache and I turn to the young woman in the corner, a fractured version of the Cassandra who has lately dwelled in these rooms.

"What other choice do we have?" I say. "Priam listens to me. More than some."

"My father has great affection for you, yes. But he would have handed you over to Menelaus if the council had voted to do so." Cassandra shakes her head, seemingly herself again. "He will never believe you. Just as he never believed me."

"What do you mean?" Andromache brings her son to her breast. It is more of a comfort to her than to him.

Cassandra shrinks into the chair. We can do nothing but watch as her body contorts wildly, each expression a different face. It's like they are each fighting for center stage, and she has yet to choose who will take it. Or if *she* will take it.

"You can tell us," I say gently when the woman we know and love resurfaces.

Cassandra's throat bobs like it is painful to swallow. She then speaks of horrors every woman has feared and too few have escaped.

A false god who was not even a man but a monster.

A childhood that was stolen. Innocence lost.

She relates her story of sorrow in a steady voice that must take all the strength of her will. "After it happened, I told my parents. Priam and Hecuba both."

"And what did they do?" The tremble in Andromache's voice leaves no doubt as to what *she'd* do if her child came to her with such a confession.

Cassandra's laugh cuts like broken glass. "It is the story you know well. They locked me away. Their own daughter. Said I was mad, that I was telling lies and defaming the gods." Her gaze bounces between us. "Imagine how they will respond if you tell them things they do not wish to hear. Things about those they have already decided to trust. A disciple of Amazons and a foreign queen who shares the blood of our enemies."

"I am sorry, Cassandra." I can't help but picture Hermione's sweet face at that same age, along with the fate I fought so hard to save her from. Who wouldn't long to retreat inside themself? Flee not only from abuse but from betrayal? It is an unfathomable cruelty. Committed by her own parents, her own *mother*. My arms reach for Cassandra, but she shrinks away, a woman who has lived ten lifetimes without the consolation of touch that gives.

She has known only touch that *takes*.

"Who?" Andromache's voice is deadly quiet as she asks the one question left unanswered.

Cassandra's entire body trembles as the entities inside her fly across her face at speeds too rapid to see clearly. When they stop at last, she collapses against the wall, spent. "I . . . I can't."

"Why not?" Andromache wields the question like a hurled spear.

"It would unravel too many threads . . . I can't see what the picture would look like after."

I don't know what she means, but I do know threads. What happens when you pull on one that is central to your tapestry.

Cassandra's teeth begin to chatter, filling the room with the unbearable sound. "Patroclus. I didn't see it. Not all of it. I saw only what I *wanted* to see. It . . . it is my fault."

"None of this is your fault, Cassandra." The words are dust in my mouth.

Andromache does not bother with platitudes. I watch as the resolution of a thousand questions etches new lines in her forehead. She has no idea how to respond to something this raw.

Cassandra holds Andromache's gaze. "Placing the truth in hands that can do nothing only makes matters worse. It also unleashes forces that are not easily controlled."

"We are in agreement there." Andromache stands with Andrius as he begins to fuss. "There must be a way to smoke out this traitor . . ."

"Do you think it could be Laocoon?" I ask.

"Possibly, though he'd probably send one of his hooded acolytes to do his dirty work. No matter who it is, that traitor spoke my son's name in the presence of our enemies. I will not sleep soundly until I hunt him down."

"This isn't something we can resolve ourselves." And yet, despite the hard truths that have been shared here tonight, I can't help but smile at the sight of Andromache stroking the feathery down of Andrius's hair.

"It is strange, isn't it?"

"What is?"

"The lengths a mother will go to defend her child."

When Andromache glances sideways, I wince and regret my words. I'm grateful Cassandra has retreated inside herself again, blank-eyed and motionless in her chair.

"Most mothers." Andromache's hand goes still on her son's head. "Hector would do the same. If only he was able to see the full nature of the danger."

"That may be the difference, then. A father will run into a burning house without a second thought, whereas a mother will do everything she can to prevent that house from catching fire in the first place."

Andromache studies me closely. "What are you saying?"

"She is saying the city will fall!" Cassandra's voice rears its head as viciously as before. With the hiss of a whisper and the strength of a scream. "Don't you see? Troy will burn! All the paths you are paving will turn to ash. There is only one thing we can do to save Hector's son."

"And what is that?" Andromache demands.

Cassandra stands to her full height. All the other faces within her flee into the shadows. "You must look to the west. When the gates open and the race begins, you will know that it is time."

"Time for what?" Andromache snaps.

Cassandra looks at her with mournful eyes. "To save him, you must let him go."

I watch warily as Andromache's entire body stiffens.

"No." Andromache shakes her head like a horse shakes its mane. "It is impossible. There is nowhere for him to go that would be safe. We'd be hunted at every turn."

"Then the prey must become the predator. It is the only way," Cassandra says, her words heavy with sadness. "When the time comes to choose between the Serpent and the Horse. You must get Andrius out."

~⁓~

"WILL YOU HELP us?"

The Master of Keys is as surprised to see me as I am to see him here, though I knew of nowhere else he might be. This small alcove in Cassandra's tower is the soldier's only home when he isn't guarding me on my errands within the Citadel. The pallet sitting in the corner is still sparse, but the expanse of chalk sketches on the walls has only grown.

The old warrior does not hesitate when I explain why Andromache and I have come. If there is anyone in this city who knows about underground dens and secret passageways, it is him. Andromache will not simply send her child out into danger, but she is eager to find a way to keep Andrius hidden *within*. The Master of Keys grabs an oil lamp and leads us to his map of the city. He has added much to it since my last visit. The sketch no longer depicts the peaceful Troy of his youth.

Instead, it is a city engulfed in flame.

Four freshly sketched figures, all women, stand at different points of the city, both within and without her walls. One at each strategic position.

The plain, the ramparts, the Citadel, and the tower.

Rings upon rings, layers upon layers, songs within one song.

"You have seen much in your dreams, old friend."

The Master of Keys shrugs, almost as if to say he doesn't see much difference between drawings and the dreams that make them.

"And what about a hidden lair below the city?" Andromache asks with a force that is startling, even for her. As soon as Cassandra gave her prophecy, I watched Andromache's conviction harden like pine pitch. Her need for there to be some shelter beneath the Citadel. Some way to protect her son, under her watch and on her terms. "Do you know of such a place?"

The Master of Keys looks confused. He points to a spot on his map, the gesture itself a question.

"Yes, the stones in the temple courtyard may point to its location. But we need to access it. It is a secret known by only a precious few in the Citadel . . . perhaps you are one of them?" Andromache gestures to the key ring at the old man's belt.

Regret paints his face, and the Master of Keys shakes his head.

I point to another spot on the map. Not a hidden den, but a harrowing cliff. "What about here? Do you know how to get us to a rampart near this wall?"

Something sparks in his eyes. The Master of Keys nods and beckons us toward the staircase. Once we descend the tower, Andromache and I follow the bowlegged man along a series of connected corridors that lead us through the Citadel. We pass the High Temple and the bathing house, exiting onto a narrow rampart directly beneath Priam's palaces. One that is impossible to see from above. I look up the steep wall behind us and glimpse the edge of my old balcony.

Yes. This is the spot.

"What are we looking at?" Andromache turns away from the Citadel, staring down the cliff face of the plateau before lifting her eyes to the strip of plain and the moonlit bay beyond.

"We must wait." I gulp down the thick night air. To my left, the Master of Keys peers through an archer's slit, studying the Kesik Cut in the west where the distant embers of the Achaean camp glow like fallen stars.

I don't know if Paris will ride out to meet his spies among the Sea Peoples tonight. I only know that the winds are favorable and the evening is both clearer and cooler than it has been in weeks.

Yet I would be lying if I denied the intuition that led me here. Just as the quiet promptings of the Unnamed One on the wind are what have led me to so many moments. A deeper knowing that is a threat to those who wield the scepter because it is a knowing that cannot be controlled. And because gaining power for itself has never been its final aim.

The tingling certainty grows stronger the longer I stand here, the sea breeze tousling the jagged ends of my hair.

Andromache must feel it too. Because for a series of breaths, she is quiet. Still. She does not demand explanations or an immediate plan of action, the things that normally soothe the fears that plague her.

So we wait. And before the moon starts to set, we have our answer.

A lone chariot appears on the horizon, its horses riding hard from the bay and the narrow straight of the Dardanelles just beyond.

There is no need to see the driver's face.

I peer over the edge of the wall as the Gate of Ghosts parts and the cloaked driver slips silently into the city. Whoever has been guarding this gate all night, waiting for the prince's return, Paris must have paid them well.

"A hidden gate built into the side of the plateau?" Andromache is a huntress who has caught the scent of first blood. "Where does it lead? How is it accessed from inside the city?"

"That I do not know."

The Master of Keys presses a finger to lips. He beckons us back into the streets of the Citadel. We follow him to the main entrance of the High Temple, positioning ourselves behind the pillars in the courtyard. Before long, the massive bronze doors of the temple open.

Paris steps into the moonlight, flanked not by horses but by two hooded figures in scarlet robes. Robes of the cult of Apollo.

"The hidden gate leads to the High Temple?" Andromache whispers, the Master of Keys nodding vigorously beside her. "But how? And why?"

"Paris has been using the Gate of Ghosts to meet his trading partners. It gives him a direct route to the Dardanelles without having to ride around the entire city," I explain. "I thought it was simply a shortcut."

Andromache gnaws on her lower lip. "The serpents . . . It cannot be a coincidence."

"But what does it mean?"

Andromache does not speak as she puts together the many tiles of this mosaic. When she turns to us, there is fire in her eyes. "What if the serpents don't just lead to a den beneath the city? What if they are also connected to this very gate?"

Cassandra's words echo through me.

When the time comes to choose between the Serpent and the Horse . . .

"Andromache," I say as the wind picks up. "What if this is a way out?"

25

ANDROMACHE

WE MAKE THE short walk home from the temple, each of us lost in our own thoughts. A Gate of Ghosts. Serpent stones. The tangled web of secrets I'm trying to unweave only seems to grow more knotted.

"What Cassandra said," Helen begins. "About finding a way out."

"Cassandra's words always have more than one meaning. She knows there is nowhere for us to go." More importantly, she knows I could never abandon Hector. My allies. Troy's people.

"I don't think she meant . . ." One look from me, and Helen swallows her tongue.

Silence closes in around us. I can feel all the things Helen wants to say. Things I do not wish to hear.

We've reached the cobbled path leading to my front door when a deep blow cuts through the air. A sound we've not heard since the day the Lower City fell.

Helen's gait falters. "That is Aeneas's horn."

I break for the alley that connects to the stables. Skirts tangle around my legs as I cut through the courtyard, past the stables to the stairs set into the wall beside the Scaean gate. The steps spill out onto the battlements overlooking the Scamander plain.

It takes me a moment to understand what I am seeing.

"They've crossed the Scamander," Helen says breathlessly, coming up behind me.

Beyond the river, the camp Hector and his men had made before the swelling of the plain is a smoking ruin. They must have been taken by surprise. It is the only thing that could explain how we've lost so much ground.

Even as we stand here, the Trojan line is falling back. Each one of their retreating steps bringing our enemies closer.

A tremor runs through me. The memory of a roar.

"How?" Helen asks.

"Achilles."

One man. And yet he has always been so much more. Not only because he leads the most fearsome fighting force in the west but because of the thing he represents to those who follow him. A deal made with the gods who rule our fates despite our attempts to change them.

So which is it? Who sees the truth? Does Achilles fall in this . . . or do I?

"Look!" Helen points to where a lone horse separates from the distant Trojan line.

A chariot follows on Hector's heels as he gallops hard for the Scaean gate. The doors open for the prince of Troy.

"Andromache!" Helen calls out behind me.

The stairs blur under my feet as I run back the way I came.

Bodecca is waiting in the kitchen. She sits motionless in her chair by the hearth. Her bloodless face lifts to mine. Hector's helmet is tossed haphazardly on the table. Next, I find his breastplate, discarded on the stairs. When I reach the doorway to our chamber, he is yanking his greaves free and hurling them at the small table beside our bed.

A clay vase rocks sideways.

"Hector."

He spins on me, his eyes as wild as I've ever seen them. In that moment, I glimpse the man our enemies do in the instant before they die.

Concern swells inside me as I slowly approach.

"I did not expect to find you here," I say.

"He pulled me back."

I do not ask who. Only one person on earth has the power to command my husband, and to my endless frustration, it isn't me.

"Priam—" I begin, but Hector cuts me off.

"Achilles has turned the tide against us," he says in a tone I can't decipher. "His Myrmidons are rested, where our men are bone weary. And they fight with fire in their hearts for Patroclus."

A vanity screen crashes to the ground. A bowl that was a gift from Hecuba falls next, exploding against the wall. Each sound echoes with the blame he places upon himself for something that is not his fault.

"If Priam called you back from the front, it is because he wishes to protect you."

"I won't do it, Andromache! I refuse to hang back while dozens of my men meet the tip of a spear meant for me."

I watch patiently as he wreaks more havoc on our chamber. Only when his wrath is spent do I walk toward him, cupping his face in my hands. His forehead drops to my shoulder as my fingers weave through his sweat-dampened hair.

"I have done everything, everything my father has ever asked of me. But this . . . I don't understand it."

I cradle his face against my breast. "You are what Achilles wants."

"Then let him have me! Let us finally see who is the better warrior. Before more good men have to die."

"*No.*" Our faces are inches apart. "Achilles is fueled by a rage that must burn itself out. If you meet him now and fall, Agamemnon wins. Every Achaean will have blood in their eyes. Every Trojan, fear. Priam is seeing clearly for once, thank the gods. Do the same thing you have asked of me for all these years. Allow your men to do the jobs for which you have trained them. Be patient. When you meet Achilles, let it be on our terms, not his."

Wind stirs the tapestries over the windows. It howls with all the things we will not say.

Slowly, Hector retrieves his greaves from the floor and fits them back over his shins. He slips past me, picking up the discarded pieces of his armor as he descends the stairs. By the time we reach the kitchen where a flushed Helen waits with Bodecca, Hector has become Troy's steady prince once more.

We trail after him, watching as he mounts his horse so he might rejoin the battle his father has forbidden him to fight without restraint.

Hector has just placed his helmet on his head when a scream sails over the walls.

"Hector!"

It is a cyclone of rage and fury set loose.

Bodecca stiffens. Helen glances at me. They know who calls my husband. Just as they know one day he must answer.

Achilles roars his name again.

Dust swirls under Goldenfoot's hooves as Hector urges his mount forward. We watch him ride toward the Scaean gate, and I put words to the thing I most fear. The thing I have felt since I first heard that distant roar.

"We are running out of time."

"HECTOR!"

Again, the cry forces its way into our room, carried by a chill wind from the plain. No matter where I go, the cry follows. Churning stomachs. Raising hair on end.

Hector!

It hounds me now, even in my dreams.

Only a few days have passed since Achilles rejoined the fighting. Already we live in a different world.

All the ground Troy and her allies have gained.

Lost.

Too many of the men who poured libations to the gods while Achaean ships burned have now themselves become smoke on the wind.

At Priam's command, Hector remains behind the lines, though how much longer he will stay there is anyone's guess. Each day, the Achaeans are emboldened by their success. Each hour, they press closer to our walls. The sounds of the battle can be heard from the Lower City all the way to the Citadel. The screams of the dying are the nightly lullaby sending every Trojan child to sleep.

You must get Andrius out.

Cassandra's warning echoes in the wake of Achilles's roars.

My knuckles turn white around the edges of Andrius's cradle. Behind me, someone bursts into the room in a whirl of silk.

"Aeneas is awake! This time, I believe he may stay that way."

I join Helen, who is already reaching for my cloak. "Then let us return to Creusa's to welcome him back to the land of the living."

"Aeneas isn't at their home," Helen says

My hands pause on the cloak's clasp. "Then where is he?"

Helen's lips purse. "The training yard."

I take a steadying breath. "Pigheaded man."

"It seems to be a common malady."

Helen falls into step beside me, her normally graceful gait punctuated by the rhythmic slap of her sandals.

As promised, we find Aeneas in the training yard. A group of our allies surrounds him. The sorry state of their armor suggests they've come directly from the stand Troy's forces have made to protect the last bit of ground before our walls.

They gather around Aeneas, wielding insults in a host of languages, all expressions of relief. Aeneas takes the ribbing good-naturedly. But at the first sight of him up close, my steps falter. His hair, normally tied back in a tight tail, hangs loosely around his shoulders. Even Aeneas's posture is more . . . relaxed.

"Is he quite himself?" I ask Helen.

She crosses her arms over her chest. "He was a much better patient when he was unconscious."

I do not doubt it.

"Aeneas," I call out.

He turns. "Hello, Alev."

It is the first time he has used the title the allies bestowed on me. And it throws me more off balance than if he had sent a spear sailing for my head.

"It's good to see you on your feet again. Though I can't say this is where I hoped to find you. You should be in bed."

"Yes," Helen adds firmly. "You should be."

The yard echoes with the hush of men who are never quiet. The last time my allies glimpsed Helen, her hair was shorn and her face was a patchwork of cuts and colors. I'd almost forgotten the power that face can wield.

Helen does not shrink under their stares. That's when I realize that in our long, complicated history, it was her timidity that bothered me more than her perfect face.

Helen is not timid now.

As she approaches Aeneas to examine his head, Sarpedon elbows Glaucus in the ribs. Both men drop their eyes with obvious effort.

"I've rested long enough," Aeneas insists, though he stands still so Helen can inspect his bandages. "It seems the Achaeans have grown too comfortable in my absence."

Hippothous claps Aeneas on the back with the same enthusiasm he applies to his wineskin. Helen releases a disapproving sound.

And then Aeneas does the unthinkable. He clasps Hippothous's filthy forearm, pulls the bare-chested Pelasgian into that awkward half-embrace so unique to men. And he grins.

"Helen?" I whisper as she rejoins me.

She sighs. "I assure you; he has full use of his faculties."

I watch Aeneas repeat the same greeting with Glaucus, Sarpedon, Akamas, and Nhorcys the Strong.

For as long as I've known him, Aeneas has carried the burden of expectation. And as is the case with Hector, what has his faithfulness ever gotten him? While Troy's armies and her Old Blood sat back and watched Diomedes hunt him down, *these* men risked their lives to save him. The strange new intensity in Aeneas's eyes when they land on me says he won't soon forget it.

"Listen, Alev. If Achilles and his Myrmidons have rejoined this fight, you need every man at your disposal," he says. "No matter how reckless or badly damaged."

It is as close to an apology as has ever crossed his lips. And he's offered it to me with all the allies as witnesses. It will be weeks before Aeneas regains his full strength, but with Achilles bearing down, we don't have that kind of time.

"You do not seem overly damaged to me."

Aeneas's smile widens.

Helen just shakes her head. "You're as hopeless as they are," she says before walking back the way we came.

The men watch her go in reverent silence.

"It seems I've missed a great deal," Aeneas says, studying me openly once Helen has disappeared through the courtyard.

"Achilles is killing Trojans by the scores," Akamas reports. "Priam has ordered Hector to stay behind the lines, but sooner or later, the Citadel will run out of men to throw in Achilles's path."

"What do you make of it all?" Aeneas asks me.

I release the breath that I've been holding since Achilles first screamed Hector's name, and I let these men I've come to trust see my uncertainty. "Something must give. Hector cannot ignore him forever."

And he won't.

"We may soon find ourselves backed against our own walls," I add.

"Then it may be time to try some other tactic." Aeneas studies each allied captain with an openness he has never before displayed. "That is what we are about, is it not?"

His enthusiasm is catching. One by one, the men around us nod. I study this new Aeneas, and I pray the plan he is concocting has been gifted to him by whatever gods remain on our side.

"What do you suggest?" I ask.

The intensity in Aeneas's smile is almost unnerving. "We throw at Achilles the one thing he won't know how to kill."

He recounts his strategy, which is both risky and extreme. It's as if the act of defiance that brought about Aeneas's injuries has snapped the binds he's always placed around himself. It makes me wonder if this is who he has always been. He just needed to travel to the edge of the Underworld to free it.

"What do you say, Alev?" Aeneas's gray eyes seek more than agreement. They seek acceptance. Maybe even forgiveness.

"I say we would have to be truly desperate to resort to such a measure. But if all else fails, we should be ready." And still, it only addresses one of the threats facing us.

I motion for the captains to follow me back to the kitchen. There a flustered Bodecca thrusts Andrius onto my hip before returning to her post by the hearth, where she can listen to every word we utter.

The allied captains gather at the table. "Nothing I am about to say can leave this room," I say.

Nhorcys the Strong's neck goes red. "My men have proven themselves trustworthy."

"It is not *our* men that worry me."

I tell them of the Trojan traitor in the Achaean camps.

Not even Tarhunt could stop the collective storm that gathers at my announcement.

"Do you know who the traitor is?" Akamas's lips curl back in a sneer.

"So far, all roads lead to the High Temple." That Laocoon has become impossible to find does not feel like an accident.

"What about Paris?" Sarpedon asks.

I nod. "Worth considering, but what would Paris stand to gain by such a betrayal? Troy is his city to rule. He does not want it to burn. He *wants* it to endure, if only so he can claim it. Though he undoubtedly wishes Hector would fall in the process."

Laocoon is surely moved by simpler motives.

Status.

Gold.

Survival.

"I will kill Paris," Aeneas says calmly.

"If that time comes, the honor will be mine." I let myself speak truth to the darkness that has been gathering since the first day Paris looked at me with a smile on his lips and malice in his heart. A hundred veiled slights since then. A thousand silent daggers launched at those I love. I sigh. "Paris is part of the Five now. We can't wield wild accusations against him without bringing the council down upon our heads, putting those who have helped us at risk."

"Your shadows." Sarpedon does not ask for confirmation he knows I can never give. "That puts you in a very difficult position."

Every man at the table nods in silent agreement. They know. Perhaps they have always known. Still, they have guarded my secrets. It gives me faith. And hope that Rhea will remain safe, so long as we all do our part within these walls.

"Paris is dangerous, but he lacks the strategic mind to pull off anything so complex," I say. "The high priest, on the other hand, knows more than he is willing to share. He also has an odd habit of going missing whenever I am trying to find him."

"You want him followed." Sarpedon catches on quickly.

"We will watch his every step. If that old priest breaks wind, I want to know about it." I resist the urge to sigh again. This next part will not be easy. "It is not only Laocoon I want shadowed. We cannot afford to narrow our field of vision when the possibilities for treachery on the council are endless. Not until we are certain we have the right snake gripped firmly by the head. Which means we need someone who can be granted full access to the Citadel while I am occupied by other matters."

The only man at this table who can boast such standing sits upright.

"I am done with the council," Aeneas says. "I will not enter its chambers again."

I am familiar with his frustration. "But you are the only one with the access we require."

"There is another option." Aeneas sits back in his seat, his expression one of ruthless amusement I've never seen him wear. "As a sitting member of the lower council, I can temporarily assign someone my place. Since I am not yet well enough to attend my duties, I nominate my friend here." He slaps Hippothous on the shoulder.

A cup of wine pauses halfway to the Pelasgian's open mouth.

I study Hippothous's filthy face. There is a distinct possibility the man has not bathed since Bodecca forced him into a tub many moons ago. In all that time, he still has not managed to find a shirt.

"Hippothous is well suited for the task," Aeneas says, capitalizing on my silence. "He enjoys the sound of his own voice, and he isn't overly wedded to reason."

"How generous." Hippothous places his cup down with more force than necessary. "A chance to see the many scented corners where Troy's chosen take a shit."

"Listen to me, Andromache." Aeneas leans forward, ignoring the disgruntled soldier beside him. "Hippothous will be an amusement to the council. Men with power talk loosely around those they deem themselves above."

Yes. Something else I am familiar with.

"So be it," I say, knowing I must trust those whose trust I have asked in turn. "As long as Hippothous agrees."

A pause hangs over the table.

"One question," says the Pelasgian, scratching the dusting of hair on his chest.

I rub my throbbing temples. "Yes?"

He grins. "Will there be wine?"

ONCE AENEAS AND Hippothous have left for the Citadel, and the other captains have rejoined their men, I pace the worn earth of our kitchen and lament my inability to be ten different places at once. A challenge that has only intensified with the arrival of Andrius.

I have no choice but to trust others to do their part. Hippothous will trail Laocoon. Kalawashi will labor to uncover the secret her serpent stone conceals. We are running out of time to unravel the many mysteries this city has on offer. We must act on the knowledge that we actually have.

Achilles is coming. Coming for Troy. For Hector.

Raising a hand, I trace the smooth leaves of the lemon tree that has grown here since Hector and I were married. I breathe in the musk of the stables and the once-jarring scents of a city crammed with people. All around me, horse pellets litter the ground along with the footprints of a hundred soldiers coming and going. Earthy sights and smells that used to drive me mad but that I would give anything to preserve now.

Cassandra has seen many things, but her most recent warning cannot be true. She thought Patroclus was Achilles, meaning even she can make mistakes. I can't risk my son's life on a harebrained scheme that isn't likely to succeed. I won't. Not when keeping Andrius among those who would die for him without hesitation is the far safer path.

And yet . . .

I pluck a lemon and put the rind to my nose, trying to recapture the tranquility this courtyard once brought me.

Hector!

The wind carries Achilles's scream over the walls. Even closer now.

How close? How much more ground have we lost this day alone?

The citrus falls from my hand. I close my eyes and draw a shallow breath before turning for the kitchen.

"Bodecca."

"What is it?" The woman moves toward the doorway where I stand, trapped on a threshold of impossible choices I don't want to make. Her limp is more exaggerated than ever. It strikes me that Bodecca is getting old.

"I need you to prepare provisions."

She does not hesitate. "What kind of provisions and for how many?"

"Provisions for one adult and one infant." It hurts to swallow. "Enough for a two- or three-day journey. They must be compact and easily carried."

Bodecca's hand shoots out to grip the table. Painstakingly, she lowers herself into a chair. Her eyes peer into mine, and I'm offered a mirror of my own pain.

Bodecca has heard Achilles calling. Like me, she knows it won't be long until Hector must answer.

"You can't," she says hoarsely.

"And I'll do everything in my power to avoid it." A tremor runs through me. "But I will not fail to prepare for the future simply because it is the one I most fear."

Bodecca seems to age another decade right in front of me. But after a moment, she pulls herself back to her feet. "I will see it done." She starts to leave, but at the last moment, she reaches for my hand and squeezes. I squeeze hers back for all I am worth.

"Harsa?" A young voice speaks up behind me. "Captain Sarpedon said you wished to see me."

I allow myself to bend under the weight of what I am considering, and then I straighten my spine like Bodecca did moments ago and turn to the stable boy.

"You are Rhea's friend. Larion?"

He nods.

"Then you know the two horses she spoils. The Phrygian mares."

"Ishtar and Carris," Larion supplies enthusiastically. "I've been taking care of them for her."

I find a smile within myself to offer him. "Do you remember my horse as well?"

"I . . . I think so, Harsa." His slow smile reveals the gap in his front teeth. "Kasirga?"

I nod. "See that the horses are fed well and watered. Stash a good blanket in the stall and enough feed in a bag for several days." I take a step closer to the boy, and he flinches at what he sees on my face. "Can you do this without raising any questions?"

He lifts his chin and nods.

"Then go."

He runs back the way he came.

As soon as Larion leaves, I sink to the ground beside the hearth. My face finds my palms. I can hardly bear the preparations. How will I survive if I'm forced to put them into effect? My hands fall back into my lap.

I can't let that happen.

Resolve floods me as Hector enters the kitchen.

"The Achaeans have fallen back for the day," he says. "They seemed strangely subdued for all the ground they've gained." He rubs his hands over his jaw. "Perhaps they're having second thoughts about the losses that come with a siege."

"Perhaps." We both recognize the lie for what it is. If Agamemnon's armies are growing quiet, it can only be for one reason.

They are making preparations too.

Hector and I stare at one another across a kitchen table carved with memories.

A ragged breath escapes me. My allies will have to take care of the traitor on the council. Helen and Kalawashi are actively hunting for a sanctuary within the Citadel. But if everything else fails and this last resort becomes necessary, I will need Hector's blessing.

I rise to my feet and walk toward him.

It's as if all the parts of Hector are stretched to breaking. How can I ask this of him now? No matter what I say, he will only hear that I believe he has failed in protecting us. That I don't think he can face Achilles and win.

I open my mouth, but I can't force out the words.

"Come," I say instead. "Rest."

I lead him to our bed, where I remove his armor and rub his sore muscles before curling up beside him. It feels like I only close my eyes for a moment, but when I open them again, the night is gone. My aching breasts scream that hours have passed. I'm gently shaking Hector's shoulder when Rhea bursts into the room.

"You need to come with me," she says.

26

RHEA

DAWN HAS NOT yet fully broken across the plain when I spill out on the battlements overlooking the Scaean gate. It sits empty now. A narrow walkway reserved for the grinding wind and the Shade they say haunts these ramparts. Dimly, I hear footsteps ascend the stairs behind me.

My knuckles glow white against the stone partition, but I don't feel it. Everything within me is fixed on the horizon to the west.

"Rhea, what is it?"

It is the third time Andromache has asked. I did not have an answer for her the first time, and I don't have one now. Every word that might serve me was lost somewhere between the Lisgar Swamp and the plateau beneath us.

Hector places his hand on my shoulder. Not a demand. Reassurance, I barely register. A storm of whispers sails toward me in more directions than even the wind knows. Beside me, Hector stiffens. He hears it too.

The anxious tapping of hooves in the stables behind us.

The desperate cries of carrion birds over the plain.

The fire horse pacing his stall. His every muscle coiled. A squall of helpless fury rattling the walls of his cage as he senses what sails toward us on the wind.

A flash of gold on the horizon to the west. Not the sun. A man.

His armor-clad body emerges, reflecting the rays of the rising sun as if channeling the full power of the dawn.

They say he is the fastest man alive. The fiercest. They say his aim is without fail. That he is the son of a goddess.

The scent of cloves as my father knelt down to place us eye to eye. *He may be all those things, but they do not make him great.*

"Achilles."

I do not know which of us utters his name, but the wind picks up the sound only to send it hurtling back against Troy's walls.

He walks across the plain. A figure carved of bronze and fire. Unhurried as the dawn that slowly makes its way toward us. Hundreds of men stand shoulder to shoulder behind him. A wall of flesh and bone and bronze. An unbroken line of shields that stretches as wide as the plain.

I've never seen the Myrmidons fully assembled. Not even during the duel between Paris and Menelaus. To see them now is to know that every rumored whisper about the men from Phthia is true. It is not their number or their size, though these things alone would be enough to strike fear into any enemy. It is the way they move. Fully in step. All passion bridled. All fury tightly coiled for the moment it might be unleashed. They move like men who know they will win before they ever take the field. Because their fate rests not in the hands of fickle gods but in the power honed and the skill wrought by their own hands.

"They will try for the walls today," Andromache says. Her fingers twitch at her sides. I can almost hear her counting numbers and measuring strengths. Theirs. Ours.

She doesn't understand yet. I search for the words to tell her. A sharp intake of breath beside me, and I know I will not have to.

Behind Achilles and his Myrmidons, a hundred more men emerge bearing strange wooden constructions on their shoulders. Four-sided pillars of wood bound with rope, easily as tall as ten men.

Towers.

"How?" The word is a whisper as Andromache watches Death dawn in the west.

"He made his move at the end of the second watch," I say, finding my voice at last.

I had been walking toward the ancient shrine to meet Ajax when the gates of Odysseus's settlement flew open. Gates that were barely wide enough to accommodate the towers carried through them high on the

Ithacans' shoulders. The battering rams came next. Crude, heavy objects that took even more men to lift them. I counted them as they emerged.

One for every gate.

All this time Odysseus has kept us running in circles. He let us think that we were avoiding his own spies, but he was planning this *right under our noses.*

Hacking, hammering, sawing in the dark.

Now we all know why.

I should have seen this coming. I should have found some way to slip past Odysseus's gates. Instead, I let his hunt for us distract me from my hunt for him.

That was not the only distraction.

"They will press those towers to the walls," I say. "The Ithacans have been working on them secretly for weeks." They were not alone in their efforts. A crowd of Achaeans had gathered with me as I watched those towers leave Odysseus's settlement in a bizarre procession. The crowd parted and more men joined the march to the Kesik Cut. Nestor's son, Telemachus, led the men from Pylos, each holding bows and wearing quills of arrows dipped in pine resin.

By the time Agamemnon appeared in full armor, the moon was rising behind the clouds, and every man and woman on Sigeum Ridge knew exactly what was coming.

When I reached the stones Ajax was already there, waiting for me.

"*It's happening, Rhea.*" He'd pulled me into his chest. "*We'll camp out on the plain until we take the Lower City. Odysseus, Nestor, and Agamemnon planned it all without telling us. Soon this will be over.*"

His words set off a drumming in my head.

"*When?*" My voice quavered. Ajax wrapped me in his arms.

"*Now. But I couldn't leave without seeing you first.*" He kissed me fiercely. His lips sealed mine with a promise, though there was no time just then to think of what it might mean.

As soon as Ajax left to rouse his men, I ran.

"He knew that we were watching," Andromache says hollowly, bringing me back to myself. "And he made sure that we would not be ready."

"Look." It is one word, and yet the weight it carries in Hector's voice is enough to sink entire fleets.

The line approaching us cuts to the south. More men move to join it.

Agamemnon and Menelaus.

Idomeneus and Ajax the Lesser.

Menestheus and Thaos and Agapenor.

Nestor and Eurypulus and Prothous of Magnesia.

Every Achaean king stands to be counted. They move as one. No longer fighting in factions but bound to a single purpose. I search the many companies of their warriors for Ajax's towering shield, but it is part of the solid wall of men next to the Myrmidons.

Their lines continue to move. Not directly toward us but in an arc. At once, their intentions become utterly clear.

Shouts of warning rise from the ramparts to our left and right as Paris's archers spot the danger. Having seen enough, Andromache and Hector make their way back down the stairs. I follow in their wake.

The cries of alarm have now moved from the exterior walls and are making ripples across Troy's rings. Oil lamps light in the early morning as people pour out of their homes onto the streets. Their screams move faster than we do. By the time we cut through the alleyway beside Hector's house, the small courtyard is already filled with captains both allied and Trojan.

"It is happening," Andromache announces. "Agamemnon and Odysseus have emptied out the Achaean camps and will soon throw every man they have at our walls."

I slip around the edge of the courtyard and take shelter in the shadow of the fountain. The skin on the back of my neck prickles. I glance up to find the Lycian captain Sarpedon tracking my movements. He is not the only one.

The towering marble fountain is suddenly not thick enough to block me from the collective stares of Andromache's allied captains.

"How long will it take them to reach us?" Cyrrian asks, fastening his war belt as he moves to block the men's view of me. At Cyrrian's attempt to shield me, Sarpedon's eyes narrow. "Not long enough," Andromache says, bringing their attention firmly back to her. "They will have us surrounded before day breaks."

"They outnumber us ten to one." Aeneas's mouth hardens as he seems to make a series of rapid calculations. "If they manage to surround us, they will be extending their forces to a degree we lack the manpower to match.

Not with every body in Troy." A stable boy hands him his spear, and he grips it tightly. "We must stop them on the plain before they can fully encircle us."

Or we will not be able to keep those siege towers off our walls.

Every man present hears the words he does not say.

"The trenches you had us build will slow them down, Alev," Peirous says.

Sarpedon nods. "It won't be easy for them to get the towers over them. That might buy us a little more time."

"We will need every moment of it." Andromache shares a wordless look with Hector. The prince nods once.

"Polydamas," Hector orders. "Raise all the men off duty in the Lower City."

"Go with him, Peirous. You too, Akamas," Andromache adds. "Try the winehouses and the brothels first. Every shield and sword in Troy to the Scaean gate."

The Trojan and allied captains leave side by side. For once, not wasting time on arguments. If Andromache notes the small victory, it is not one she has the time to savor.

She shifts her gaze to Sarpedon. "Take your fastest runners and go door to door. We need every man and boy who can lift a sickle standing outside the walls when the Achaeans come. If they succeed in pushing us behind the gates, we will not open them again on our own terms. We must make full use of this short warning we have been given. Cyrrian, take more men and go with them. Tell Madam Morgestia to mobilize the women. She will know what to do. *Go.*"

Cyrrian is moving before Andromache has finished speaking. Sarpedon starts to follow, but before he ducks outside, he turns to me where I still cower in the shadow of the fountain. The Lycian captain inclines his head. He's gone before I can fully grasp what the gesture means.

Already, men are running through the alleyway toward the stables. Some are carrying weapons. Others seem to have come directly from their beds. We follow them toward the training yard where the piles of armor Andromache has collected from Troy's dead are quickly dwindling as hands dip into its offerings.

The training grounds are chaos. The stables too. The panic of the men is a bitter tang in the air. The horses cannot help but react to it. Every-where, they fight their leads and resist any efforts to harness them. I grip the lead of an angry gray as it trots past, running my hands over its flank in reassurance. A young stable boy comes to a breathless stop next to me, and I hand him the rope. In every corral, Troy's army of stable boys are busy coaxing the frightened horses into the chariot yard, where their driv-ers wait.

More and more men flood the grounds. They are quickly ushered to the Scaean gate by Hector's captains. They make for the Scamander plain in a haphazard stream that looks nothing like the neatly regimented rows for which Troy is known. They pass me on their way. Some of them smell like wine. More of sweat. All of them stink of fear, and yet their faces are sober, their jaws locked in determination not to shame themselves as they make their way past their prince.

Movement at the stable doors catches my eye. Larion is helping another figure, equally familiar, into armor that is easily the most pristine thing in this training ground.

"Polydorus." Hector's voice cuts through the clamor of men and horses.

Hector's youngest brother looks up as Larion fits the breastplate across his chest. Polydorus does not ask his brother for permission. He does not beg and plead to join the fight he has been, until now, so carefully pro-tected from. Instead, he meets Hector's gaze squarely, and he lifts his shield.

Andromache comes to stand at my side. She grips my arm.

A flash of sorrow. Of pride. And then Hector nods once. He mounts his horse Lightfoot without looking back and follows his men toward the Scaean gate. He does not see how Polydorus's shoulders sag as the boy re-leases the long breath he has been holding.

Larion grins at his friend as he fits the war belt around Polydorus's waist. Glaucus claps the young prince once on the back on his way out of the stable, leading Akamas's horse. Nhorcys the Strong grabs the young prince's oversized shield and thrusts it back to Larion.

"Take this," he says, handing Polydorus a beautiful Phrygian shield in-stead. "It is lighter and stronger. No Achaean blade will touch you with this on your arm."

Polydorus nods his thanks, and the stocky Phrygian follows Hector and the other men to the gates.

By now, most of the horses have been cleared out of the stables. Still, figures stir in the shadowy stalls behind Polydorus. One by one, Troy's stable boys approach the small pile of discarded armor.

"Larion." I grab his tunic. "What are you doing?"

He lifts Polydorus's old shield in one hand and a warped spear in the other. "You heard Prince Hector. Troy needs all her sons to fight for her."

"No!" I tell him furiously. "The Achaeans are raised with spears in their hands. You don't even know how to fight."

Andromache squeezes my shoulder again, halting any other words I might say.

Behind Larion, Nekku rifles through the rubble until he finds a rusted sword. All around us, a dozen other boys trade their brushes and lead ropes for broken pieces of armor that are older than they are.

The youngest among them is a boy scarcely ten summers old. He selects a knife—the only weapon he looks capable of lifting. He fits the knife in the frayed loop of his belt with trembling hands.

Andromache watches the boy search the pile for anything he might use as a shield. Her eyes glisten with tears, but she blinks them fiercely out of existence as she approaches him.

"Thank you," she tells the boy. "For making swords out of sticks and slings out of cloth stolen from your mothers' looms. The blade in your belt is steady. It will serve you well."

She offers the words like an invocation. The skin of my forehead burns as I remember a night in a cold stone temple where she pressed a similar prayer into my skin before sending three girls through a wall made of stone.

She takes a step to the left so that she is face-to-face with Larion. "Thank you for wrangling Hector's horses. For rolling in the mud and tracking it into my kitchen even when it drove Bodecca mad." This earns her a flash of gap teeth. She returns the smile before she moves on to Nekku.

"Thank you for stealing lemons from my tree and using them to break my flowerpots." The boy looks down at the ground, but Andromache lifts his chin. "You did not think I noticed, but I did. That skilled arm of yours is needed now on behalf of these, your brothers."

Then there is only one left. Stone-faced, Hector's youngest brother stands steady as Andromache inspects his armor.

"And you, Polydorus. Thank you for roughhousing with your hounds. For venturing where you were not wanted and getting underfoot to remind us all of what we once were." Andromache takes a step back, surveying yet another army made of small bodies but great hearts. "Thank you for taking hold of your childhood, even as the world was burning. For being boys who will now become men when men are needed."

I watch them go, and it overwhelms me all at once. The knowledge that everything I've done may not spare them. That every risk I've taken and lie I've told has been in vain.

And then it is just me and Andromache left in an empty stable.

"Let's go," she says. There is no question about where she means. Together we cut through the courtyard and the alleyway into the wide streets of the Merchant Quarter, where we make our way through Troy's inner gates.

Crowds stream past us in the opposite direction. People moving toward the training yard and the Scaean gate. Not soldiers, but regular men who have been spared from conscription into Troy's service because of their age or because the skills they possessed were deemed too valuable to squander.

I recognize the owner of the Fair Winds among them. A portly man with a loud laugh whose girth has shriveled along with the city's food stores. There is also the ancient baker who runs the shop directly next to the southern gate. More and more stream past us. Blacksmiths with wide shoulders and strong arms, stained black from smelting. Tradesmen whose hands are as soft as the wares they peddle. Old men with bent backs, quietly leading wide-eyed boys who've seen too few summers.

When we reach the south wall, not a single man remains in the Lower City, but that is not to say that the streets are empty. Everywhere I look, women and children are quietly working, fighting a battle that is theirs alone.

Lines are strung between windows up and down the streets to our left and our right. Wide, tightly woven baskets reinforced with fired clay hang suspended from the taut ropes, forming a system designed to move water wherever it is needed. Every third home we pass bears a newly constructed ladder, providing easy access to the flat roofs where nimble-footed children are busily drenching fronds. If these homes burn again, it will be despite these people's best efforts to save them.

Down below, small groups of women work together to empty Troy's many vendor carts. Still more women reach up to cover the carts with thick tarps of carefully sewn ox hide, providing safe spaces for people to hide from arrows while moving up and down the Lower City's narrow lanes.

Andromache takes in these preparations without a word as we cut toward the Lower City's primary well, which sits close to the south wall. Spotting our approach, a lone figure breaks away from the children laboring to fill as many of the waiting baskets as they can.

Dark rouge runs with the sweat down the madam's face, giving her the appearance of one of the painted warriors I've heard live in lands far to the north. Time and again, the proprietress of Troy's most infamous brothel has proven herself one of Andromache's most capable allies.

"The preparations are in place," Madam Morgestia says. "If they come close enough to use their arrows, they will find a city that is much harder to burn."

"You've done well," Andromache says, but the pinch between her brows tells me our thoughts are running in the same direction.

Baskets of water won't help us if those towers are pressed to our walls.

Andromache rolls up the sleeves of her robes and reaches for one of the empty baskets. "Leave this to us," she tells Madam Morgestia. "Here." Andromache holds out a basket for me to take.

I back away from her on unsteady feet. "I can't. I . . . Ven and Isola will worry if I . . . I should get back." I stagger down the wall in the direction of the Mother temple.

"Rhea."

When I turn, my legs are already shaking. The men leaving the Scaean gate. The women and children busy all around me. All pieces of a shattered urn slowly coming together in my mind. It's as if my body has accepted the thing my heart still refuses to acknowledge.

"It is over, Rhea."

Darkness floods my vision until there is only a narrow swatch of light. Andromache's face fills it.

"What do you mean?" My voice is small. Lost like it hasn't been since I first entered through Troy's golden gates as a different girl.

"By tonight, we will either have thwarted the Achaeans or be under a full siege. Either way, there is nothing more you can do."

Her words echo toward me from somewhere in the distance. The ground and the sky swim together. I reach out to steady myself against the wall.

Andromache brushes a hand across my cheek. "My brave girl." She looks at me as if she wishes to say something more, but whatever she sees on my face causes her to bite her tongue. "You haven't slept," she says gently. "Rest here while you can. I'll help the madam and then find you after."

She leaves me in the shadow of the south wall.

I sink to the ground. All the tears I've been holding back flood my cheeks as I reach for the wooden horse and wrap my hands around it.

Memories wash over me. Ajax's voice, speaking in the dark. The brush of his lips over my skin. The way he smoothed my hair when he thought that I was sleeping.

I'd been so frightened. So desperate to get back to Troy, I never paused to recognize the moment for what it truly was.

Good-bye.

Pain claws at my chest. So many words. So many phrases in every language under the Anatolian sun, and I'd trade them all for the chance to go back and say the only ones that truly matter.

27

ANDROMACHE

THE SUN SETS blood red across the plain.

I find Rhea in the lengthening shadow of the south wall, exactly where I left her. Exhaustion and grief are a shroud hanging over her young face. It is the same aura slowly donned by every woman in the Lower City as the long hours of the day passed. With every turn of Tiwad's crown, the cries of dying men have come closer and closer, until the crash of bronze is a hum felt deep within every chest.

We leave the Lower City women to their preparations and silently make our way through Troy's rings. I remember a time when these streets were unknown to me. Now they feel even more precious than the hills I roamed as a girl who knew nothing of the world beyond her own desires. Rhea and I pass through the gate into the Artisan Quarter with its tightly packed rows of shops and stalls, and though a part of me begs to soak up every detail, I cannot make myself look. Instead, I focus on the ground beneath my feet. One step after another until I enter the second-to-last ring of Troy and cross the threshold of the home Hector and I have shared.

Bodecca is waiting in the kitchen with Andrius sleeping soundly against her shoulder.

"He's gone through the milk," she tells me. "He doesn't like it, but he'll take it." Bodecca made no secret of her disapproval when I'd thrust the skin into her hands and left to aid the efforts in the Lower City. I didn't have the heart to tell her why I deemed it necessary.

"Rhea. Stay here and rest while you can." I struggle over how much to tell her. How much I am willing to admit myself.

I kiss my son's soft head before I tear myself away. The sounds of the raging battle echo off the walls as I make my way to the Scaean gate. There, I'm met with screams and groans.

The thing no one tells you is that there is a moment in every battle. An instant in which the scales cease their swaying and fall weighted to one side or the other. It is something that cannot be explained, only sensed. Though I am not on that plain fighting at Hector's side as I've imagined so many times, the warrior inside me can feel it now. The turning of the tide. The tipping of the scales.

I do not need to climb the steps to the parapets to know exactly what I would see.

The Achaeans closing in around us, driving us back with numbers we cannot match. Men fighting, suffering, dying for everything they love as inch by inch they are pushed back to our gates.

When those gates finally open, I am there to meet them.

Hector's brother Deiphobus and his cousin Polydamas are the first through. Deiphobus's thick neck is streaked with blood, his wide chest struggling for each breath. Polydamas helps support his cousin. Troy's regular troops stream through the open gate behind them. Far fewer than left by those gates this morning. I search the crowds of blood-spattered, exhausted faces. All of them tell the same story.

My stomach sinks when I spot Sarpedon and Akamas limping through the gate. Sarpedon braces Akamas under one shoulder.

"What happened?" I duck under Akamas's other arm, helping to bear him to the closest wall.

Akamas leans against the stone, his weight firmly planted on his right leg. "The bastards got my horse."

"A spear took the poor beast in full stride," Sarpedon says. "Our Thracian friend here did his best impression of a bird, though his flight was painfully short lived." Sarpedon tosses his shield aside and kneels to examine Akamas's thigh, already all the colors of spoiled fruit. "If it is a break, it is a clean one."

Akamas grits his teeth. "I can still fight with one leg."

"Our men?" I ask.

"The Achaeans fought in tightly ordered ranks," Akamas says grimly. "No matter what we tried, we couldn't coax them out of their lines." Sarpedon pokes at his thigh again and Akamas hisses. "We lost many."

A steadying breath before I ask. "Any of the captains?"

Akamas goes still as he studies Sarpedon, kneeling before him.

"Glaucus." Sarpedon offers his cousin's name as he slowly stands.

The wind screams over the wall. A howl of pain unspoken. The stark image of a warrior who once offered me a clean cloth to wipe my face, and with it, his trust.

I do not tell Sarpedon I am sorry. I don't offer platitudes because the only language left to us now is one made of actions, not words.

"How?" I ask instead.

"Ajax the Great." Sarpedon's eyes shine with a deadly promise.

Nhorcys, Pyraechmes, and Peirous join us at our post against the interior wall. Behind them, my allies mix with Hector's soldiers as they make their way back to the training yards, dragging the injured between them.

Hippothous is next through the gate. One of Aeneas's fine tunics, the only sign of Hippothous's short-lived visit to the council, hangs in tatters under his armor. The Pelasgian steers two smaller figures in front of him. The grip on my throat loosens when I make out Polydorus and Larion. Behind them, Aeneas and Hector are the last men through.

The gates are quickly barred shut in their wake.

The boys make their way over to us while Hector and Aeneas stop to ensure that the gates are firmly secured. Hippothous grips Polydorus's shoulder. "He fought well," the Pelasgian says. "A prince to make his city proud."

There is no pride on Polydorus's face. Only sweat and blood and knowledge that the glory he has always craved does not taste as sweet as he thought it would.

Not because you are weak, I want to tell him. *Because you are good.*

Larion bends over, hand pressed to the mudbrick. The stable boy's narrow frame shakes as the battle rush leaves his system. His eyes are a glassy ocean full of horrors. They seem to surge all at once. He turns his bloody face to the side and vomits against the wall.

I search the nearby ranks, but I do not see the boy. The one with the knife for a sword.

Hector joins our group. I wait until the other men are preoccupied examining Akamas's leg before I ask, "How many did we lose?"

"A third of our regular forces." He closes his eyes briefly.

So many.

"We sent them to their deaths," I say.

Hector cups my cheeks in his bloodstained hands and for one moment, it is an old man peering at me through my husband's eyes. "It is what leaders do, my *alev.*"

Later. Later we will sit together with the meaning of this day and all the horrors that it holds, but not now. Now we have a city to defend.

Hector's hands fall from my face. "Every archer to the walls!" he shouts to a group of his captains gathered nearby. "Pitch and torches at every access and parapet. Shoot anything that comes close. Burn their towers." They move at once to follow his orders.

"Will it stop them?" I ask.

"No," Aeneas says, joining us. "There are too many of them, and too much wall to spread our numbers thin. Even with Paris's archers, their towers will eventually meet our walls." A muscle tics in his jaw. "We need a smaller area to defend."

Truth echoes in the silence.

We must give up the Lower City.

A cry catches in my lungs, only this cry is not my own.

It is the grunt of a hundred women carrying baskets of water from the well.

The desperate wail of a mother lifting her baby high over a burning wall.

"They may take the Lower City." Hector bares his teeth. "But we do not have to make it easy for them."

I meet my husband's eyes, now the charcoal of scorched earth. For a moment, he lets me see it. The savagery he fights so hard to tame.

It sings to me.

Rage and vengeance flow molten in my blood.

Every step. *Every* inch. We will make them *pay.* I swear to every god of war in every spoken tongue. For each tower they raise we will bleed a hundred of their men.

"How long can we hold the exterior walls?" I ask.

"That depends," Hector says. "How long do we need them to hold?"

"Let me try, Alev," Aeneas says.

I meet his gaze. When Aeneas proposed his plan, it seemed like a last resort that would never come into play. Now it is the only play we have left to make. If it doesn't work . . .

"When can you be ready?" I ask him.

"Dawn tomorrow," Aeneas says. "I will need some light to work by. The Myrmidons will be the first ones to try the city walls. Achilles would have it no other way."

"How many men do you need?" I ask.

"No more than a dozen if Nhorcys would be so kind as to lend me his strength and that of his warriors."

"Even in the dark with a small number, it will be a risk to leave by way of one of the gates," I tell Aeneas.

He shrugs. "It is one we will have to take in order to reach the olive grove."

"I know a way through shrub grass from the west gate." Someone speaks up. It is Larion. "I can show you the best path." He wipes the sickness from his chin.

Aeneas nods.

"Be ready to move on the third watch," I tell them both.

Metal flashes in the corner of my vision—the needle point of Cassandra's tower glinting in the dying light.

There is only one thing we can do to save Hector's son.

The wind assaults me with the memory of Cassandra's words.

If we ever hope to use the Gate of Ghosts to get Andrius out of the city, the time is now. A small number might make it through those gates before the hand around us fully closes. This may be my last and only opportunity to send him to safety. If only I knew where and how to access the temple passage leading to the gate.

But even if I did . . .

I study the battered faces all around me. Not a man here, allied or Trojan, would abandon the battle now. Whom does that leave to send with Andrius? Who would protect him as well as *us*?

A groan draws my gaze to where Peirous is bandaging Akamas's leg while Sarpedon holds the Thracian steady. Beside them, Hippothous hands a white-faced Polydorus his wineskin and then guides it to the prince's cracked lips.

These men—my men—are here because I asked them to stay. I cannot leave them now any more than I can leave Hector to Achilles.

No, if worse comes to worst, the Citadel is still Andrius's best defense. We have enough numbers to guard them day and night. With the Achaeans concentrating their full force on a siege, they will have no means to raid or provide for themselves. We will last longer than they can. In the end, it will be the Citadel walls that save us.

A bitter irony.

"This can work, Alev."

Startled, I meet Aeneas's gaze.

"It had better."

I am betting my son's life on it.

Aeneas gestures to Larion. They walk off without a word.

"We can hold the Lower City walls until dawn," Hector says. "But it will be a near thing. Will it give you enough time?" he asks, reading me perfectly.

We both know what must be done and how dangerous it will be.

Love for Hector burns within me, hot as any flame.

"We will manage," I say. "But I will need . . ." My brow furrows. "Where is Cyrrian?" I ask, suddenly aware of who is missing.

"Right here." Cyrrian steps out from behind the Thracians' horses. One side of his face is covered in blood. "What can I do?"

"Go to the brothel and fetch Madam Morgestia," I say, ignoring the fact that he needs a healer. "Tell her to meet me at the Dardanian gate as quickly as she can."

Cyrrian wipes the blood from his eyes and does as I ask.

And then it's just my allies left.

"Don't," Hippothous says fiercely.

"Don't what?" I ask.

"Don't tell us that if we want to leave, now is the time," he answers calmly.

I shut my mouth. That is exactly what I was going to say.

"Everything has changed," Peirous says, his wizened face dotted with blood that dyes his white beard red. "All of us have felt it. One way or an-other, the world will not look the same when this is over. If Troy falls, there is nothing to stop this wave of chaos from flooding our lands too."

"We stop them here, together, or there'll be nothing left to save. For any of us." Quiet Pyraechmes uses his voice for the very first time unprompted.

"We made the choice to stay." Sarpedon is the last to speak. "And we would make it again."

I swallow around a closing throat, and I nod.

When I reach the Dardanian gate minutes later, Madam Morgestia is already waiting for me. Her silks are rumpled and the paint that once brushed her lips is now an angry smear across her cheek. She does not look happy to be summoned. She will like it far less when she hears the reason for it.

"I need your help," I tell her.

"By all means." Bangles clink as she broadly waves her hand. "It is not as if there are other pressing matters that require my attention."

"We are surrounded, Morgestia." I do not waste time putting it delicately. Our previous dealings have left me with the distinct impression that she would not thank me for it. "Despite our best efforts, the Lower City will fall. It is not a matter of if, but when."

Heavily lashed eyes blink as she takes in what I've just told her. Every sacrifice she has ever made. Every abuse suffered and cost paid to build a life that is about to be taken from her. From all of us.

"Are you breaking the news to all your lowly subjects personally?" she asks bitterly. "Is that how you plan to assuage your guilt when you leave us to burn while you and your Old Bloods hide behind the Citadel walls?"

She wants to fight me. It is an impulse I understand. But rising to her bait will serve neither of us. More importantly, we do not have time for it.

"I intend to bring the people into the Citadel. They are the thickest, highest walls in Troy, and we should still have more than enough men to defend them."

I have surprised her. Something, I'd venture, that is not easily done.

"The Citadel gates have never been opened to the people of the lower rings," she says, as if this well-known fact has somehow escaped me.

"They will open today," I say. One way or another. No matter what it takes.

"What does your precious council have to say about this plan?" the madam asks.

"I don't know because I did not ask them." I stand over her, using my height and my strength only because I know she will respect them. "The Citadel is a safe haven meant to protect life. If the Old Bloods want grain to fill their bellies, they will have to take the people that grind it."

Morgestia's expression turns speculative as she studies the guards at the Dardanian gate, whose numbers have doubled since the Achaeans began pressing Troy's walls. A dozen armed men stand before those reinforced doors.

"I will spread the word," she says at last.

"Have the women prepare their children and supplies. No valuables. Only food. We can take stock of what we have once everyone is safely inside."

"We can use the carts that were intended as temporary shelters," Morgestia says, proving I have chosen my allies well. "But we will not be able to carry all of this on our own."

"My men will help." I nod to the allies where they stand across the street, unsure of what is happening but still ready for my command. Morgestia nods, and my men join her on the trek back to the Lower City. It is not long before the first wave of people arrives. They are but a small fraction of the full number who live in Troy's lower rings, and already the street before the Dardanian gate has grown crowded.

There isn't enough room to house all of Troy in the Citadel. Not by half, and not for long. Even if I can get them through those gates, Mother help me find a place to put them.

I approach the soldiers standing guard over the Dardanian gate.

"These people are seeking shelter. Let them through."

When the guards make no move to carry out my request, Sarpedon unburdens himself of a large sack of grain and moves to stand off my right shoulder.

"You heard her," he says simply. "Move or be moved."

"None are permitted through these gates."

Peirous takes the space to my left. The wizened warrior meets my gaze for a moment. White teeth flash in his ebony face. A reminder that this is not the first time we have stood before one of Troy's inner gates and demanded access.

I face down the last doors in this city that have remained barred to us.

"I am Troy's future queen and mother to her heir. You will step aside now and you will help these people through."

"I am sorry, Harsa." The guard does not sound sorry. "We answer to the king and to the council. None but the Old Blood are permitted through."

I take a step toward the gates. The guards do not stop me. After all, it is not me those gates are meant to keep out.

My captains fall in behind me, and at once, the guards form a wall of shields blocking their path.

The gate is so close to me now, I could reach out and touch the heavy wooden doors. I have never spent much time studying Troy's inner gate, but I do it now. At close proximity, the horse heads carved into the guard tower base are more ominous than welcoming. At the top of the tower that overlooks the Dardanian gate, three archers train their arrows on the allied soldiers facing off with the guards below.

No. Only two of the men are holding bows. The third has no weapon at all. So why . . . ?

My gaze snags on the lever beside him. A thick cord of rope runs from that lever to a beam held high behind the door. Once that bar drops into place, these gates will be impossible to force open, no matter how many men we throw at them.

We cannot let that happen.

I turn back toward my men just as Hippothous forces his way to the front. Cords of sinewy muscle glide under bronzed skin when Hippothous places his sack on the ground beside the gate. Battle blood streaks his chest. One of his men tosses him a spear, which he catches neatly. The guards' hands move to their swords as they watch him approach.

Behind my allies, the streets ring with the voices of women gripping frightened children's hands. Old men dragging bags of grain they could never hope to carry. These people have fought and bled for Troy even when Troy had all but forgotten them.

I will burn the Citadel to the ground myself if that is what it takes to ensure that never happens again.

I open my mouth, but someone speaks before I can.

"These are your families," Hippothous says with surprising gentleness. "Do you think the Old Bloods care if your wives and children burn so long as their own remain safe?" His eyes shine with the conviction of a man who speaks from experience. "Think carefully about where your loyalties should lie."

A few shields lower. The line wavers but does not break.

"Attempt to push your way through, and these people will die," says the guard who spoke earlier.

"These people will die if we leave them here," I say as I search the faces of my men. Sarpedon plays with the daggers in his hands. Peirous and Nhorcys bare their teeth. Hippothous just shrugs at me, as if to say *I tried*.

All of them wait for my signal.

The wind steals the cry from my lips. Hippothous tosses his spear high over the line of guards between us. The shaft drops into my open palm. Twirling it in my hands, I let it fly again. The blunt end strikes the unarmed man in the tower above as he reaches for the lever that will lock the gate in place. He falls with a grunt.

My men swarm the guards, but I am the only one close enough to those doors to do what must be done.

The remaining archers in the tower above train their arrows on me. I meet their eyes and push with all my might. If they want to stop me now, they will have to kill me.

They do not fire.

Gritting my teeth, I throw my weight against the doors and wedge them open. The rest does not take long.

A sea of anxious, desperate people floods through the Dardanian gates to fill the Citadel streets. Cries of alarm ring off the high walls as well-dressed Harssi retreat inside their stately homes and slam the doors shut behind them.

So much for a warm welcome.

"Andromache!"

Two familiar faces make their way toward us.

"It is dangerous to cram so many people into such a confined space," Helen says as we watch the steady flow pass through the gates and into the Citadel. Mothers carrying crying infants in their arms. Grandmothers leading children by the hands, their backs bent by years and the loads they carry. "This siege won't be over in a night or two. Where will they all stay?"

"I don't know yet," I say, cursing Laocoon under my breath. Access underground is what we need.

And we need it soon.

"I take it your serpent stone was a dead end?" I ask Kalawashi, who is watching the Citadel streets fill with an unreadable expression.

"Other women on my street have the same in their kitchens, but no one knows how to open them." Kalawashi's tone suggests she is as unhappy to deliver this news as I am to hear it. "So that is it, then?" she says. "Prayer and a slow starvation is all that is left to us?"

"We still have one arrow in our quiver." I send a silent plea to the Mother to speed Aeneas on his way. "If that fails it will be a test of their resolve against ours."

Every woman gathered shares a look of grim determination.

A figure huffs toward us from the Dardanian gate. Madam Morgestia's gaudy silks look hideously out of place in the stately Citadel. "Your men are emptying the granary and the shops," she tells me gruffly. "They'll need a cool place to store the goods and strong backs to help unload." Morgestia spares Kalawashi's fine robes a critical glance.

"Kalawashi, can I borrow your daughters?" Helen asks. "We need to mine the gardens for every herb that we might use without stripping them bare."

"Take some of my girls too," Madam Morgestia offers. "We have a garden in our courtyard that we use to make our own medicines."

"Are you a healer?" Kalawashi asks in a weak attempt at politeness.

Morgestia offers her a grin full of golden teeth. "Healing is one of the many skills required of the women in my line of work, Harsa."

Kalawashi's daughters approach wearing confused faces. Their mother's lips pinch. Still, she sends them with Helen.

Morgestia's sharp gaze passes over the anxious crowd, and I know we are all thinking the same thing.

"These people will not survive without roofs over their heads," she says. "They need protection from the smoke and the elements."

"We must find more room," I agree, searching the crowded streets for space that is not there.

Kalawashi lifts her chin. "If we cannot find shelter, we will have to make it." She starts to walk toward her home. "Follow me."

28

RHEA

THE HEARTH FIRE has burned down to embers when Aeneas re-enters Andromache's kitchen.

"Andromache?"

"Still not back." My words echo through the hollow of my chest.

"Where did she go?"

"I don't know." I haven't seen her since we came back from the Lower City.

Gingerly, Aeneas rubs the back of his head. "I need two horses," he says at last. "Small, strong, and preferably darker in color so as not to stick out among the olive groves. Are there any such to be found?"

There are.

"You are going to break the levee," I say. It is the only thing near the olive grove that would hold any interest for him. How many times did he visit it during the months of rain to reinforce its construction?

Aeneas studies me for a long moment. As with Captain Sarpedon, he is looking at me as if he has never seen me before, even though I've passed him almost daily on my journeys back and forth from Andromache's hall. It is an odd sensation. To be seen.

I cannot yet tell if I like it.

"Few realize it, but the true might of Troy is not in her walls or her tow-ers but buried deep under her grounds," Aeneas says. "The people who built the very first city on this plateau possessed old knowledge. The lands around Troy are marked by a series of canals and underground springs.

They feed her drainage and water pipes and irrigate our fields. But as impressive as this system is, it was not built to handle the rains of last winter. The rivers had to be dammed to keep our catches from overflowing, and so every stream from here to Ida is bloated. If we time it right, we can use the overflow to flood the plain, wiping out Achilles and the Achaeans' towers in one fell swoop. It is the final option to prevent a siege."

My heart seizes before I remember that Ajax and Teucer were born swimming in the sea of Salamis. Even if the water caught him, it would not keep him.

But that is not the case for so many others.

"The grove is very close to where the Achaeans will approach the walls with their towers." After all these nights, I know the earth surrounding Troy as surely as I once did the pastures of our family farm.

Aeneas shrugs. "We'll be careful."

I bite my lip. Andromache was clear in her order not to wander, but I can't just sit here. She wouldn't. "I know the horses for the task. I'll help you get them ready."

Aeneas nods. "Collect them and meet me in the allied training yard."

THE STABLES ARE a whirlwind of animals and men. Everywhere I look, weapons are being sharpened, arrows tipped with resin. It's no different than the preparations I've witnessed a hundred times before, and yet nothing feels the same.

I grab Astra and Selene, two ponies with strong bodies and good natures. When I find Aeneas, he is surrounded by a small group of men. I recognize Nhorcys the Strong among a few others, all of them Phrygian. They watch me approach with the horses, and I am instantly aware of their stares.

One by one, they bow their heads.

A lump forms in my throat. Maybe once I would have welcomed their respect. Craved it, even. But now the one thing I want lies outside anyone's power to give me.

A few offer blessings in Phrygian that I have no heart to return. Especially when I spot one of the stable boys gathered with them.

Larion's cheeks are hollow, his skin pale as death. The unfailingly cheerful line of his mouth is set in a grimace. I try to catch his eye, but he avoids my gaze.

When Aeneas reaches for the leads, I pull them back. "I'll come with you."

"I don't think—"

"I can keep the horses calm," I say, unwilling to be brushed aside. If Larion goes, then so do I. "It won't be them that gives you away."

"It will be dangerous," Aeneas warns.

"More dangerous without me. And I have faced worse."

Not a single man speaks. But they know. The silence echoes loudly in the training yard with the knowledge of all the things I don't say. All the dangers I have courted and all the places I have gone when no one else was watching.

They are watching now.

Aeneas clears his throat. "All right, then. We had best be quick about it."

I HUDDLE AT the top of the hill above the olive grove, keeping the horses quiet while Aeneas and the Phrygians work to dismantle a section of levee just beyond the trees.

Larion wiggles restlessly beside me. After we used the ponies to pull the first few logs loose, there's been little for us to do but wait and watch. They are things Larion isn't accustomed to but at which I've had much practice. There is a darkness in his eyes that doesn't belong there. After all these nights with Ajax, I know it is not one that I can force him to share. So I wait and offer him what comfort I can through silence.

A hint of light colors the eastern sky. For some reason, it reminds me of Ajax's laugh. How it always brought out a flush in his cheeks—proof to anyone who cared to look that he was not a giant carved of stone or bronze, but a young man made of flesh and bone like the one crouched here beside me. I wonder what he is doing now. If his men will line up next to Achilles and the Myrmidons when the attack against Troy's walls finally comes.

"The stables aren't the same without you."

Pulled out of my own thoughts, I study Larion's profile in the soft dawn light. The line of his jaw is more pronounced than I remember it. As if the man he will someday become is slowly making himself known to anyone who cares to notice. How long has it been since I really stopped to look?

"I've missed you too," I say thickly. "Thank you for taking care of Ishtar and Carris while I've been—" I don't finish. I don't know *how*. To Larion, it must have seemed like I abandoned the stables almost as abruptly as I entered them. Whatever he thinks about my long absence, he has never asked.

Perhaps because he has always known.

Birdsongs fill the olive grove, announcing this new day and whatever it will bring.

"My father was Trojan born," Larion says in the silence between us. "He met my mother during a visit south to Caria and brought her back to Troy." He reaches for the leather belt around his waist. One that has been wrapped more than once to fit his narrow frame. "He died in the fifth year of the war. My mother could have left Troy to return to her people, but she stayed. Troy had become home."

"I understand."

"I used to want to be a warrior. Like my father," Larion says as he watches the Phrygians quietly work on the levee under Aeneas's direction. "I thought he was the second bravest man in the world after Prince Hector."

"I'm sure he was a great warrior," I say.

"He was." Larion swallows. "I don't want to be like him anymore." He meets my gaze. "You've shown me there are other ways to fight."

The trembling smile he offers me breaks my heart in ways I didn't know it could still break. Like Andromache's allies, I do not feel worthy of the respect it holds. This longing for Ajax feels disloyal to everyone I love. But so does the thought of all the Achaean men who will die today if Aeneas's plan works. I don't know what to feel anymore. I only know that I am not the hero Larion would make me out to be.

Words tangle on my tongue. Before I can sort them, the ponies fidget in the olive grove below. Their whispers turn my head.

Two men creep toward us through the trees.

Astra's nostrils flare. I place a calming hand over her flank as I watch the men approach from the south.

Achaeans are the only ones who would approach Troy from that direction.

A sharp intake of breath beside me. Larion sees them too.

One of the two men raises his head. I recognize him straightaway—a young Ithacan I've seen on the plain. One of the ones Odysseus sent to hunt me.

He doesn't see us. He is much too focused on Aeneas and the men working on the levee between us.

A shiver runs through me as the Ithacan gestures to his man. Slowly, quietly the second warrior retreats back the way he came.

Larion's face is pale as he scans the distance to the levee. I grab a fistful of his tunic and shake my head.

"We have to warn them," Larion hisses. "Before more of them come."

"They'll come," I hiss back. There's no stopping that now.

Fear flashes across Larion's young face. The same fear I am trying to hide.

My gaze sweeps the olive grove before coming to rest on the horses lying down beside me. I take a long breath and then I reach out to Astra in the language of the whispers. One quick slap to her rump, and the old pony breaks down the hill toward Odysseus's spy.

Aeneas looks up from his work just as Astra reaches the hidden Achaean.

Aeneas pulls his spear. With a barked command to Nhorcys, he leaps off the levee wall.

The Ithacan climbs to his feet, his own weapon at the ready. Aeneas does not hesitate. The spear sails out of his hand, skewering the Ithacan to the tree before he can lift his blade.

Unhurried, Aeneas approaches the tree where the dead man hangs. He is yanking the spear free when another man appears at the bottom of the grove. A warrior clad in golden armor so new I can almost smell the oil used to buff its shining plates. A warrior whose hair burns like white fire in the dawn.

Achilles.

My skin prickles with the memory of his grief and his rage. The way it had split the night like one of Tarhunt's bolts.

Larion grips my arm hard enough to bruise. A few paces away, Nhorcys the Strong and his men are working furiously to free the last logs from the levee wall. The work is coming faster now, but it is not done yet. They need more time.

Aeneas twirls his spear. Blood flies from the tip to spatter his face. There is no fear. No hesitation. Instead, something wild and eager lurks in his eyes. The bared fangs of a beast long caged.

He and Achilles approach one another, unhurried. Theirs is a dance of predators. It's only when they meet at the edge of the grove that they explode into movement. Their blades move so quickly, I seem to see each strike half a breath before I hear the clash of bronze.

Achilles knocks Aeneas's second spear aside, and then the Dardanian is down to a single knife. With a snarl, he lunges. Achilles flinches back. Not quickly enough. The blade opens up a shallow wound across the Achaean's cheek.

Blood stains Achilles's teeth when he smiles. The shaft of his spear drives into Aeneas's nose. Bones crunch.

Aeneas hits the ground on his hands and knees. With a roar, Achilles charges. He stops over Aeneas, but the roar carries on without him. It grows and grows until it seems to have gained a life of its own.

"Rhea!"

At Larion's cry, I look back at the levee, only to find that it's no longer there. Instead, a wall of water crashes down the hillside below, drowning the grove in a churning mass of white. Neither Achilles nor Aeneas has time to run. One moment they're there. The next, they're swept away.

Cracks and groans echo through the grove as the water meets the trees. It takes less than a breath for the brown wave to reach the plain, hitting Troy's east walls before parting around them in the direction of the Achaean horde.

Cheers rise from the walls while screams echo from the plains just beyond.

I tear my eyes away from the plain and search the grove below me for any sign of Aeneas. There! Halfway down the hill. He is pressed against a tree, holding on for dear life.

Before I have formulated a plan, my hands are already moving, yanking the lead rope free from the pony's head and letting it out to give myself as much length as possible to work with.

"Aeneas!"

He looks up and chokes on a mouthful of water. For the very first time, I see genuine fear.

With a grunt of effort, I throw the end of the rope. It falls pitifully short, but the Mother must hear my prayer, because the current answers my call, carrying it down the hill.

Aeneas catches it with one hand.

"Come on, Selene," I say to the stout little pony. "You have to pull."

Though it pains her old bones, she does as I ask. When Larion and I finally drag Aeneas out of the water, Selene is covered in a lather of sweat.

"Can you walk?" I ask Aeneas, who is worshipping the ground on his hands and knees.

With great effort he staggers to his feet. "Yes. But I could use a shoulder if you have one to spare."

Larion takes one arm while I take the other. With Aeneas between us, we make our way to the walls. I don't know where the Phrygians are: if they were swept away by the water or if they fled while they had the chance. The sound of distant fighting reaches me on the wind. I grit my teeth and force my legs to move faster.

We've made it most of the way back to the east gate when Aeneas stops suddenly. I turn and get my first look at the plain.

At first, all I see is a muddy lake where the plain once stood, punctured by lost spears and shields, eddying in the water. My heart leaps at the sight of the siege towers, shattered in pieces farther than my sight can reach.

Aeneas stiffens beside me. I follow his gaze to the land beyond Troy's defensive trenches. The water is already receding. Men rising to their feet. Thousands of Achaeans re-form into their groups, all of them ragged but still very much alive.

One of them stands taller than the others.

Larion is the first to say his name.

"Achilles."

29

ANDROMACHE

AFTER THE WATERS on the plain receded, the enemy came at night when the moon was brightest. It didn't take long for clouds of smoke to snuff out the stars, thanks to the pyres the Achaeans built along the walls of the Lower City—fires fueled by pig lard and goats' blood. From there, the Achaean archers lit their arrows, one after another, shooting high over the walls, just as they had the night I rallied Troy's allies. Only this time, the flaming arrows came not from Odysseus's elite forces.

They came from Agamemnon's entire army.

What they want is the Citadel. They will not leave without it.

And there is no place left to go.

Kalawashi's home is packed as tightly as the amphorae in her pantry. Looms and furniture have been pushed to the walls. At least twenty women, children, and old men sit near the central hearth on the floor of the main room. Even more wait in the bedchambers of Kalawashi's daughters upstairs.

I look down at the room's plush rug, its elaborate, colorful pattern woven by a skilled hand. Mud and ash streak the tight designs, and bread crumbs have been ground into its fine fabric.

The women of the house do not notice.

Kalawashi and her girls move swiftly among the ranks, handing out blankets and cups of thin broth.

Andrius snores against my shoulder when I approach her. "What can I do to help?"

"You can sit back down and let Prince Astyanax sleep." Kalawashi wipes the sweat from her face with the end of a linen rag she wears around her waist like a belt. It's hard to say how many tears it has dried, but every person in this room has cried them.

I nod and obey. Kalawashi and her daughters are more than capable. The woman galvanized many of the Citadel Harssi, who opened their homes to those in need of shelter, even as the doors to the palace remain locked. Without these women, many more from the Lower City would have met their end choking on smoke.

Still, these refugees haven't even been here a full night and already the home is cramped and the people within it impatient. The stench of human excrement from overflowing bed pots has overtaken any oil of lily perfume. Those who sit on top of each other are beginning to bicker, and I have no doubt tempers will only run higher as the food stores run low.

These people cannot remain here forever. They won't even last more than a few days.

I kiss the top of Andrius's silky head, a stab of regret lancing my chest. The time for finding an open door and a way out has closed. I made my choice.

All of our earlier victories are ashes. The efforts the Lower City's women made to protect their homes are a part of the rubble. Meanwhile, Laocoon and the rest of the council bar themselves behind the temple and palace gates.

We are left with only our walls and the men who fight for them. Men that Achilles is slaying by the hundreds. His bloodlust won't be satisfied until he faces Hector on the Ilium plain.

Hector's troops have made their stand at the stone walls of Troy's secondmost ring. The one that protects our stables and our home. It's a small triumph I can feel in my bones with every shrill cry from the children in this makeshift shelter. People whose world has shrunk to the size of this room, an echo chamber of babies mourning in step with the grandparents who cuddle them close. The elders who can remember this city *before*. As I sit here with them, I come face-to-face with the reality I cannot outrun or outthink. No matter how hard I have tried.

We are trapped.

"Do you have another infant cloth?" asks the young woman beside me.

White ash streaks her dark hair, and the baby she bounces on her lap is covered in soot.

"Here. Take this." I hand the young mother one of Andrius's extra linens.

The girl does not seem to recognize me. Or perhaps she is too tired to care. I don't blame her. No one expects me to seek shelter in this place where every sign that might distinguish lowborn from high has burned to cinders.

I should be out there fighting . . . with them.

An accusation that will not leave me. Our men are battling to hold the Merchant Quarter, but they'll soon be forced to abandon even that. And still, whenever Andrius releases a frightened mewl, I know I could never leave him.

I hug him to my chest now, craving his warmth despite the room's stifling heat.

There are few I'd trust to defend him if the Achaeans break into the Citadel. Not Cassandra with her moods, not even Helen, though I trust both more than anyone else.

Anyone else but Rhea . . . and Rhea is not herself.

Helen and Bodecca have been moving between the Citadel homes all day, tending to the needs of Troy's people. I assume Rhea is with them, but when she stopped by Kalawashi's house earlier, she looked like a woman in full mourning. I can't understand it. We all fear for Troy and grieve for the Lower City. But fear and loss have never left Rhea paralyzed.

"The Pergamos will hold, Harsa."

I look up from where Andrius is nursing and meet the gaze of an old man, his face etched with confidence and crow's feet.

He nods at Andrius. "It has stood solid since the days of my father's father. And his father before him."

Only these fathers never had to defend their city from Achilles. It kills me that his smug, hateful face is the last thing so many Trojans have seen.

Drypos.

Laogonu.

Dardanus.

Deucalion.

Tros, a pitiful sop who wrapped his arms around Achilles's knees, begging for mercy.

He found none.

Still, no matter how many men Achilles slays, it is not enough. It will never be enough until Hector answers his call.

I grit my teeth.

"Ouch." I jerk back as Andrius nips me. He sits up from the breast, a drizzle of milk running down his chin. The baby girl beside us giggles with a delight that is jarring. She can't be much older than my son, and both have identical heads of dark curls. Throughout the hours we've sat here, the two babes have watched each other with curiosity while we, their mothers, stare vacantly into an endless night. All while the grinding of metal and the sound of Achilles screaming Hector's name grows strong enough to shake stars from the sky.

A sky that tried in vain to prepare us for what was coming. Tried to warn us that every monument of triumph built by the hands of men will one day reach its end.

"Andromache!" Helen pushes her way through the crowded room. The people on the floor look at her uncovered face with dulled awe, but they do not move to approach her. It is then that an even deeper defeat seeps into me.

"What is it?" I rise from the floor. Rhea follows on Helen's heels, looking dazed.

"The Achaeans are shooting arrows into the Citadel," Helen pants. "If we don't get more people inside, there will be no cover for them."

I follow Rhea's vacant stare across a room packed with sweaty, unwashed bodies.

"There is no room." I offer the words Rhea can't seem to manage herself.

"I tried the gates to the temple and palace before coming to find you. They remain shut," Helen seethes. She is angrier than I've ever seen her, which only adds to my restless unease.

Rhea comes out of her trance. "Where will they go?"

I think of all the times she's taken the Mother's pass. Felt the rough walls of the plateau press in on her until she feared her next breath would be her last.

I picture Paris, lounging on his sofa, drinking his finest wine to the dregs before heading to the High Temple. Perhaps he meets Laocoon in its shadow, the pair of them descending to some hidden crypt that leads to the

Gate of Ghosts. While the city at their back goes up in smoke, Paris's chariot races to meet a ship with hired sailors ready to take them far from here.

The scenario is not such a stretch, and it makes the fire within me glow white-hot.

"You," I say to the old man who spoke with unfathomable faith in the Pergamos that may soon be his pyre. "I need your help. Bring your friend."

That friend is even older and needs a crutch to walk. Still, my request rouses both men to their feet. I hand off Andrius to Helen, who scoops him up gladly.

"I'll need you too, Rhea," I say, hoping I'll soon have work for her that is honed to her talents.

As we move toward the kitchen at the back of Kalawashi's home, I grab a sharp poker and iron shovel from the hearth, handing one to each of the old men.

"Come."

Kalawashi's daughter, the one with dead eyes, mixes water and wine in a bronze pitcher. The last of the amphorae lie empty on the floor behind her.

"What's your name?" I ask her. She isn't a small girl, with large hands that must be strong, given what it takes to pour an amphora on one's own.

"Marassa." The girl's heavy-lidded gaze passes from me to the elders before landing on Rhea.

"This stone." I push the empty containers to the wall. "We must break it."

"Yes, Harsa," say the two men without hesitation.

The one holding the iron shovel wields it with surprising strength. It comes crashing down on the serpent, creating a deep crack in the center of the stone. After a few more swings that leave him breathless, the stone breaks apart into large chunks. His friend plunges the fire poker between the fissures, his ardent prying doing more damage than his frail appearance would suggest.

Once the largest piece of limestone is freed, Rhea and Marassa scramble to pull it off to the side. More debris breaks away and flying hands follow.

I hold my breath. With the four of them working furiously in such a small space, I can't see much of the floor.

"Andromache! Look!"

The Rhea who speaks now is the girl I know.

I join them over a hole in the floor, large enough for one person to pass through at a time. The man with the crutch uses his good foot to kick broken bits of limestone into the cavern. We hear them land in a fraction of a heartbeat.

Not too deep.

"I'll go first." Rhea is already sliding to the floor, seemingly eager to return to the dark.

"Here, we'll need oil lamps." Marassa rifles through the cluttered shelves behind us.

"You'll have to lower me," says the elderly man with the crutch.

"I don't think that's neces—"

"Please, Harsa." The man turns to me with a weathered face that has seen kingdoms rise and then crumble. "It is."

I nod. "Your name, elder of Troy?"

"Yarra."

"And I am Santazitti," says his friend, "son of Halpazitti and Pihazitti before him."

"We need to determine how large this sanctuary really is, Yarra and Santazitti. How many people it might hold." I take the lamps Marassa has lit and hand one to Rhea.

"When you enter this den, there could be many passages. Tunnels that connect to multiple chambers. We need to know where they all lead as well as any dangers within. But we don't have much time. Not if we are to move the people taking enemy fire into this shelter . . ." I turn to the two girls. "You may need to split up. One elder with one youth."

Rhea and Marassa nod, eyes alight with new purpose.

They descend without a word, leaving me to do the one thing I fear above all others.

Wait.

───⁙───

THE HOURS PASS painfully back by Kalawashi's hearth. Still, the time Rhea and the others have been gone tells me one thing—this serpent's den is large, which may mean it has room to hide Troy's people.

I look down at my dozing son.

To hide Andrius.

I stroke his fire curl, aware of how nature is both cruel and just at the same time. No matter how loving a father may be, a mother harbors the burdens of carrying a child and feeding it after. Our bodies are their home. Our voices the song they hear while floating in the warm dark. There is nothing fair about the labor involved. And yet it is mostly boys and young men we send in droves to meet an early death. Perhaps the scales do even out then, in some sense.

Though it remains to be seen if survival is itself a reward.

"You are Prince Hector's wife." The same young mother I sat beside earlier states it like a plain fact.

"Yes."

"I saw him at the brothel once." The girl blushes. "Not that. I only meant . . . He was looking for someone, one of his men. The prince—"

"I know."

She sits up straight. "Hector will not let his city fall."

Three weeks ago, three *days* ago, I might have said the same. But now . . .

While my faith in Hector will never falter, I wonder if there are some evils too great, some forces too dark, to be overcome by even the best of men.

Still, it is the best of men who will be sacrificed upon the altar of trying.

"Alev!" I turn and see Sarpedon at Kalawashi's door. He lowers the damp cloth tied around his neck to shield his face from smoke. The Lycian moves through the throng of women like he feels at home among them. I've never seen such a serious expression on Sarpedon's normally languid face. His mouth sags with the cares of a man once accustomed to freedom who now finds himself backed against a wall.

Cradling Andrius, I start to stand. "What is it, Sarpedon?"

The captain grasps my forearm as he helps me to my feet. "Hector. He is asking for you."

I glance around this sea of a hundred strangers. "There is no one I can leave Andrius with."

"Bring him. Hector said so. The Achaeans have slowed their assault on the Merchant Quarter for the night. We will keep far from those walls. It won't get any safer than this, I fear."

I grip Sarpedon's arm guard. I want to tell him about the den. Let him know there might be this one last path to safety. But the young mother is watching us, and I can't risk rumors of sanctuary until we find out what Rhea and the others have discovered down below.

Meaning I should be here when they return.

"Tell Hector I need some time—"

"You must come *now*, Andromache."

The way he says my real name, not *Alev*, lodges itself in my chest like an arrow.

Sarpedon raises a hand covered in dried blood and strokes the back of Andrius's head. As if the child might break beneath the weight of his fingertips. "My son was about this age . . ."

He stops, choked up. I wait for him to finish the thought, even though I fear it.

". . . when I first sailed for Troy."

Then the child he'd meet upon his return would be unrecognizable to him now. "Troy is in your debt, Sarpedon. *We* are in your debt."

The Lycian captain doesn't seem to hear me. He is too mesmerized by the small life beneath his hand.

"It is something no one can tell you." Sarpedon lifts his bloodshot eyes to mine. Shining with the glass shards of a hundred memories that were stolen. "At the time, you never realize that the sweetest moments of your life will be utterly ordinary. So mundane and fleeting, you only recognize them for what they were when looking back."

I turn away, the sight of his longing too much. Because if what he says is true, then all my sweetest moments are behind me. Just as Sarpedon's are.

Our eyes meet again, knowing.

"Come. I will bring you to him."

I nod. When Rhea returns, she'll know what is needed. Troy's underground has always been her realm to rule.

With Andrius pressed to my chest as we take to the streets, I cling to Sarpedon without shame. The place that awaits us outside is no longer the Troy I know. It is a strange, foreign land of red dust and black shadows.

The sky above the Citadel glows orange from the fires still burning in the Lower City. Rooftops that were once homes, the hearths where the million small moments Sarpedon spoke of were made.

Close as it is to Troy's second ring of walls, our own home could easily be among them.

Angry shouts and curses have replaced the chattering of women as they fetch water from the city's wells. The former laughter of children overtaken by the groans of wounded soldiers staggering in search of help. Sarpedon steers us clear of the Citadel's outer walls, but when we come to a curve that provides a lookout over Troy's lower rings, I pause, panting hard.

"Please. I want to see."

Sarpedon's eyes shift from Andrius to the stone fortress that is my face. "There isn't much left to look at."

I peer over the edge of the wall, the maze of the market streets that once made up the Lower City demolished. The weight of responsibility hangs heavy around my neck. Even if there is a place to hide beneath this ruin, will it be enough to save anyone? Or is it merely a delay of the inevitable?

The destruction before me screams the truth I never wanted to entertain: we have reached the fatal point in a battle when all strategy breaks down. When every soldier fights for one thing and one thing only.

The glimpse of another sunrise.

Sarpedon looks to the horizon. "Hurry, Alev. We don't have much time."

The Lycian leads us to the last place I'd expect to find Hector—a leader who has always walked among the lowest of his men rather than look down from where they could not follow.

We stand before the entrance to Cassandra's tower.

"What is this?" I ask Sarpedon as he leads me up the circular staircase. At the top, the Master of Keys is already unlocking the chamber's door.

Sarpedon places his hands over mine, which press Andrius against my body to shield him from the smoke.

"This is good-bye."

It takes a moment for me to realize what he is saying.

"Don't talk like—"

The captain presses a finger to my lips. "If, by some miracle, we manage to push back the Achaeans, I can promise you I will be on a boat to Lycia before the victory celebrations can even commence."

I squeeze the hand of this ally who has become an unexpected friend. "As you should be, Sarpedon."

"Take care, Alev." He nods toward the door. "And take care of him."

Before Sarpedon disappears back down the stairs, he glances over his shoulder. The bronze shield that bears my symbol, my flame, flickers in the torchlight emanating from the sconce above his head. "You remind me of her, you know."

"Who?"

"My mother. She had the heart of ten men." One more flash of the wry smile I've come to love. "Your boy is fortunate to have you."

I don't let the single tear I've reserved for Sarpedon fall until he is gone. The Master of Keys pushes against the door, guiding me into a chamber filled with amber light.

In the center of the room, a blanket covers the floor, surrounded by a dozen glowing oil lamps. A clay pot, a basket of flat bread, and a jug of wine sit in the middle of the cloth, two small cups placed with care to the left and the right.

The rind of ripe lemons, the aroma of a Mount Placos summer, washes over me.

As the door closes, a man steps out from the shadows behind me. Not a hair rises in fear; I'd know him even if the light never reached the bronze undertones of his skin.

"Hector," I say as Andrius looks around the room in wonder. "What is this?"

Dressed in a fresh tunic and far cleaner than he should be, Hector takes a cross-legged seat on the woven blanket. He extends an arm, inviting us to join him. "When I was lying beside my men in a mosquito-ridden aqueduct the other night, I couldn't stop thinking."

My heart pounds against my chest. "About what?"

He smiles gently. Sadly. "I couldn't shake my regret. That when we held the feast honoring our allied captains' origins last spring, we did not ask Bodecca to include a meal from your homeland."

I would laugh in disbelief if I weren't so distraught. Babbling happily, Andrius reaches for his father with chubby arms. Still, my feet won't leave this threshold. "*Kekikal?* Hector, there is no need, we shouldn't—"

"We should." Hector beckons me forward. "How many moments have we had to ourselves in all these years? *After the war*, we always said."

He doesn't finish the thought. It is too excruciating to acknowledge.

"How are you even here?" I ask, my throat painfully tight.

"I am here because I trust the men I lead. The battle will still be there when I join them in the morning."

But this . . . this may not be.

The words he doesn't say are forgotten when Hector removes the lid from the clay pot, filling the room with the savory scents of lamb, olives, and fresh thyme, all braised in lemon juice. It is the dish my parents served at our betrothal feast in Thebe under Mount Placos. What the people huddled in Kalawashi's house would give for one bite . . .

"We can't, Hector." The guilt is too much.

"Berating yourself for tasting goodness does nothing to relieve their suffering, Andromache. Nor does it honor it."

Perhaps he's right. Perhaps we must all be grateful for whatever crumbs we are given.

"Bodecca is a witch," I say with a small laugh. "How did she manage this?"

I take a seat on the floor beside my husband, laying Andrius between us. The boy grabs hold of his toes, rocking back and forth as he casts Hector a drooly grin.

The echoes from the battle raging beyond this tower fade slightly.

"I didn't ask too many questions. I'm not sure I want to know." Hector pours us wine before reaching across the modest feast for my hand. There is a lightness in his eyes that should not be there. Not with everything that has happened, that *is* happening, as Troy collapses around us.

All at once, when his eyes pass from me to his son and back again, I *know.*

"Hector—"

"Please, Andromache. We can leave it for just one moment."

But I can't. Not when I know Hector will fully claim this fleeting victory, one no Achaean can ever strip from him. Everything inside this chamber that isn't Hector's face fades to black.

This is his good-bye.

Now the scent of the food turns my stomach sour.

"I do not tell you this enough, Andromache, but you have been my greatest ally." Hector's grip around my hand tightens, his glistening eyes holding the promise of a thousand days we *should* have had.

A rush of heat and I rise from the blanket, storming to the tower's balcony for air. Beyond the shadowy plains, the sea shines under the moon as it always has. Calm. At peace. Knowing its waters will be there tomorrow.

With Andrius in one arm, Hector's hard chest finds my back, his free arm encircling my waist. He rests his chin in the crevice between my neck and shoulder, then whispers, "There are a thousand islands in the Aegean. A hundred lands beyond those. After this is over, there is nothing to keep you and Andrius from making a home in any one of them."

After? As if there will *be* an after once he is gone. The hope in his voice turns his arm into a snake, squeezing all air from my chest.

"There's nothing to stop me except everything *I am*." I whirl around to face him. "I won't be hunted like an animal, Hector. I am known by every Achaean king who stands between these walls and that shoreline."

What's worse, we missed our opportunity. There may still be a chance to hide within the city's depths, but there is no way anyone can leave Troy now. We are surrounded. Every way out shut.

And that is my fault alone.

I shouldn't have hesitated.

I didn't try hard enough.

I should have *believed* her.

Unable to look at Hector, I turn back toward the balcony. He returns his head to my shoulder, but I can't tear my eyes from the silent moon. From the motionless sea begging for the fresh salt of my tears.

"You should eat something, Andromache. Please." Hector pulls me back toward the blanket. His voice stiffens even as it softens. "Achilles is calling for me a hundred times a day, and I will not hide any longer. I cannot delay meeting him. This night may be all that we have."

My entire body seizes up. I inhale deeply. Then I turn to my husband, my son, my *life*, hands clutching only a shield of air.

"Yes." I force a smile as the rivers stream down my face. "Then let us feast."

And we do, savoring every drop of oil as we reminisce. Sharing memories of the years that have shaped a union we do not need to be told is rare. Relishing it all. Reliving *us*.

By the time our plates are empty and all the wine is gone, Andrius is fast asleep on the blanket between us.

Hector nods toward the tower's bed. "Should I move him?"

I turn and see Andrius's cradle, the one Hector carved from oak when our son was but a wish. Of course Hector would have it brought here instead of leaving it to burn.

Tears prick my eyes as I watch Hector lower Andrius into the cradle with a gentleness that takes my breath away. He stands, extending a hand to me. "Come to bed, my *alev*."

Hector's voice is raw now. Not with passion or longing, but with a sadness that somehow tastes sweet. I fall into him. My lips cover his neck and face, committing every inch of him to memory. His hands do the same, running through my hair, traveling the full length with me, following a long trail of silent tears.

His and mine.

When we finally come together, Hector holds back nothing. He consumes me—first with tenderness, then with desperation that borders on pain. As the room spins and I rise out of myself, the faded sounds of the battle return with a low roar.

Anguish and joy.

Rage and love.

I savor all of it.

After we return to our frail bodies, Hector buries his wet face against my chest. He shakes like he is cold. "I don't want to *go*, Andromache."

He is afraid. And the way his voice breaks with this admission is what finally cracks me open. I press him hard to me, stroking his hair, saying nothing while losing everything.

I hold Hector tight and I let him mourn, until neither of us has anything left.

MY EYES SNAP open to the sight of Cassandra's face, peering out from the wall of her thick black hair. I sit up with a start, reaching for blankets to cover our nakedness. Hector is still sleeping, but the baby between us stirs at my sudden movement.

"Cassandra? What's wrong?"

"It must be now."

The sound of another's voice in this tower is enough to rouse Hector. "What must be now?" he demands groggily, sitting up.

Only Cassandra would not be embarrassed by the intimacy of her bare-chested brother in bed with his wife and child. "Your son's escape," she says in a straightforward way that suggests this is a matter Hector and I have discussed at length.

Hector turns to me. "What is she talking about?"

"It's impossible, Cassandra," I say, ignoring his question for now. "But there is still hope for Andrius. We've gained access to a shelter—"

"There is no shelter that can keep the Achaeans out," she whispers, and it is somehow louder than if she'd screamed in the Fury's voice. "Not with the horse they have."

I meet Cassandra's gaze, wondering what it is that she knows.

"But we have horses of our own," she continues, amber eyes swirling with broken promises and ageless knowing.

For a moment Hector sits in silence, staring at the first hints of light that have broken into this chamber of stone. Our last refuge as a family.

I rest my hand on his tense arm, absorbing Cassandra's words. "Hector, you know what the Achaeans do to the male children of their enemies. No matter how young."

"Yes," Hector says softly. "The same thing we would do to their sons."

I swallow hard. "I have agonized over this, and I thought we'd missed our opportunity. But if Cassandra thinks there is still time to make it right. Some way out . . ." I steel myself for Hector's protests. For his insistence that I go with Andrius, thus endangering us both. "It may be the only way we can guarantee our son has a chance, a mere *chance*, at survival if this city falls."

"When it falls," Cassandra clarifies.

Hector lifts his eyes to mine. "Then a part of Troy, a part of us, must survive too."

Relief flutters in my chest as I turn back to Cassandra. A part of me resists trusting her—the part that wants to keep Andrius as close as possible even as I let Hector go. Still, I can't shake the burning sense that she is right. That I've been deluding myself with the grasping hope that I might be able to keep him with us and keep him safe.

There is no guarantee Andrius would be safe even in the serpent's den. Not if our enemy believes Hector's son still lives. If the Achaeans take the Citadel, they will tear the walls apart looking for him and then the sanctuary would become the tomb.

"Do you believe me?" Cassandra asks.

I read the unspoken question on her face. *Do you believe me when no man ever has?*

I think of Patroclus's death, the one time she didn't see clearly. As well as all the other times she did.

Clarity, not certainty.

Then Sarpedon's voice, flying on the wind.

Love demands risk.

"Yes," I tell her after some time. "I do."

The words are the leap I failed to make before. An error I will not make twice.

"What is your plan for getting him out? The city is under siege at every turn. I will not risk my son being captured."

"You are mistaken, sister. The Achaeans no longer surround the entire city." Cassandra's eyes land on her brother. "Achilles is calling for you, Hector. And this time he will not take no as an answer. He has the entire Achaean army stationed at the Scaean gate."

Leaving other gates unguarded.

Hector shakes his head. "He wants to put on a show."

"It is worse than that," Cassandra continues. "Last night, Aeneas deployed scouts to gather any remaining supplies cached in the Lower City. They were intercepted by the Myrmidons, and now Achilles has them lined up outside the gate. If you will not fight him today, Achilles is threatening to slit the throat of each Trojan at sunrise before tossing their bodies into the sea."

The breath I expel is almost a groan. Achilles would give these captives not only a coward's death but an eternity of unrest in the realm of shadows.

"The scouts were young boys, Hector." Cassandra's voice cracks. "Polydorus is among them."

At the mention of his brother's name, Hector is already sliding the tunic back over his head.

"Who will take him?" I ask, voice trembling.

Cassandra looks at me with a new heaviness. "You *know* who. In your heart, you have always known. There is only one who can ride fast enough."

"But I've sent her on another errand. I don't know if she is back—"

"She is on her way here," Cassandra says. "She'll need to ride out of the east gate, the farthest from the plain where Hector will meet Achilles and every warrior will watch. It is their only chance to escape unnoticed."

"How long must I last?" Hector asks quietly.

Cassandra swallows hard. "As long as it takes to circle the city three times."

My heart sinks deep into my stomach.

Hector nods. It seems to dawn on Cassandra that he is waiting for her to leave so he can finish getting dressed. But instead of departing, she throws her arms around his broad shoulders. He staggers backward but holds her fast.

At last, Cassandra pulls away and clears her throat. "I will tell the Master of Keys to unlock the east gate for Rhea. Farewell, brother." She looks past the tower balcony and toward Mount Ida beyond, her tears belonging to no one but her. "Run as you were always meant to."

Cassandra pauses to place a hand on the baby's head, and then she walks away.

The moment she's gone, I bring a mewling Andrius to my breast and watch Hector put on each piece of armor. First the bronze greaves for his shins and forearms, then the gleaming breastplate. Finally his plumed helmet, which he does not wear near Andrius since the child fears it so, but instead places it under his arm.

How many times have I watched this ritual? How many times have I wondered if it will be the last?

I do not wonder now.

Once he is no longer my husband but Troy's commander, Hector walks to my side of the bed. His hand reaches for the curls at the base of my neck.

"You will do everything in your power to protect him? To get him out and to safety?" he asks distantly, as if he's making a request to one of his men.

"With all the fire that burns within me," I say, eyes fixed ahead.

He nods and turns to depart, still unable to glance down.

"Hector, wait."

"What is it?" he whispers. A plea for me to not drag out this moment any longer than necessary.

"Achilles is best known not for his skill but for his speed. You must buy them time."

The light of what I am asking him to do arrives with the dawn.

He does not respond, but he will do it. I know he will. No matter what it costs him.

With the rawness of a soldier charging the line, Hector marches across the room and kisses me fiercely on the lips.

One more exhale, and Hector is gone.

As the door slams in his wake, Andrius responds with the piercing wail I long to release. But I can't. Not if I am to find my resolve for what must come next.

Helen arrives a moment later. "Cassandra told me. I thought . . . I thought it might be easier if I take him now," she says quietly as I dress Andrius, hands trembling in a way they never would brandishing a spear. "Rhea will be here soon."

All of her words seep into a dense fog.

"We can wrap him in this." Helen unfolds the woven textile that rests in her arms. Even though my charred heart is bleeding out and I struggle to stand, I can't help but notice the masterpiece Helen spreads across the bed. Every stitch, every pattern of the blanket is its own work of art.

A hawk.

A spindle.

A weaver.

A mouse.

And at the center of the design, a horse of fire and flame.

"Here," Helen says, showing me the small pocket she has sewn on the inside of the blanket. "For his *atamanui*."

My eyes well as they search the barren room. Andrius has no *atamanui*. I've not had a spare moment to even think what it might be. Nor have I known this child long enough to see the many different shades of his character.

And now I may never.

A gentle breeze sails into the chamber through the open window. Cassandra has turned its wide sill into a miniature garden, lined with small clay pots of dirt. Only these pots do not contain any plants, living or dead.

Resting on the topsoil of each container is a small acorn.

"I tried telling her they must be buried *in* the soil," Helen says, smiling sadly. "Even then, it takes a thousand acorns in the ground for every oak that sprouts."

A thousand acorns. One oak.

I remove one of the large seeds and tuck it into the *atamanui* pouch. My eyes linger on each image Helen has woven as I wrap my son in their colorful embrace. Still, my feet refuse to take the final step.

Helen gently pries Andrius from my arms, her gaze filled with the painful knowledge of all I am giving up. Tremors rack me as she cradles my child as if he were her own. She grants me another pained smile, one she has earned with every unwiped tear she's ever shed.

"Now, no matter where Andrius goes, we will go with him."

30

RHEA

WHEN AT LAST I emerge from the serpent's lair beneath the Citadel, it is Cassandra, not Andromache, who waits for me.

"It is no den," I say, pulling myself out of the rough hole in the floor. "It is a twisted maze of tunnels and small chambers carved out of the rock. Some may be able to find shelter there for a time, but not for long." Hours of searching have yielded one dead end after another. In the cool shadows of the tunnels, it was easy to pretend that I was making my way through the wall.

To Ajax.

"Where is Andromache?" I ask, searching the rows of tightly packed, sleeping bodies for her familiar form.

"Come" is the only answer she gives me.

Cassandra melts into the shadows that run across the walls of Kala-washi's kitchen. For a moment, I consider leaving Cassandra alone to run whatever mad errand she is on, but then I hoist myself to my feet and follow the princess onto the Citadel streets.

The shadows part for Cassandra as she leads me down a twisted pathway that hugs the inner wall of the Citadel. We pause in a darkened corner by a crumbling fountain. Bronze grates against stone. A door opens in front of us.

I stare down the narrow passage.

One city. So many secrets. How many of them are trapped inside Cassandra's haunted mind?

I glance sideways to find Cassandra watching me with an expression that is equal parts amusement and sorrow. "So many questions, little mouse."

"How—?"

"No answers. No time." Cassandra jerks her chin. "Come."

She says it again, and again, I follow. One narrow corridor after another until we've arrived at the last place in Troy I expected to be taken.

Cassandra stands framed in the center of the arched doorway. Beyond her shoulder, steps wind a twisting path upward. There's only one place those stairs could go.

She reaches for my hand. I pull it back.

"No more riddles, Cassandra. It's nearly dawn, and I'm tired." The very act of breathing in this smoke feels like a chore. Everything has since I crawled in through the wall for the last time, leaving half of myself behind.

Cassandra's eyes find mine in the lightening dark. She is watching me with an expression that is strange, even for her. Resignation and desperation, mixed with pity.

"Speak, Cassandra. Tell me what we're doing at your tower, or I'm walking back."

Cassandra cocks her head. Listening to something only she can hear. "It is time."

"Time for what?" An edge enters my voice despite my best attempts to soften it. Every second that I am awake grinds me between mortar and pestle. All I want is to go to sleep, where the only things that can touch me are dreams.

Dreams that are not dreams.

Another pang issues through my chest.

"Time for the mouse to become the lion. Time for promises kept."

Cassandra takes a step toward me. Until now, I've always thought of her as little more than a girl, but it is a woman's eyes that meet mine now. Not just any woman. A Harsa of Troy.

"Time is the needle, and you are the thread. A thousand choices. One moment."

"You aren't making any sense."

Irritation flashes across her face. She jerks her hands through her hair and holds tight to the ends. "Words are just sounds. Nonsense. It is people who give them meaning. The same is true of prophecies."

A sound reaches us from the tower above. Cries.

Andrius.

My stomach tightens. "Where is Andromache?"

I search Cassandra's eerie yellow eyes. They are as clear and as sad as I have ever seen them.

"Saying good-bye."

I take a shallow breath. "I don't understand."

Her hands twist the fabric of her robes. "The Achaeans are knocking on Troy's gates. This is a city full of the dead, though they do not know it yet. The fist around us is closing fast, little mouse. Prince Andrius must slip through its fingers before it is too late." Her shoulders straighten, her voice going deeper. "And you are his way out."

The meaning of her words creeps in, bringing with it a wash of dread. "The city is surrounded. The Achaeans have companies blocking every gate. I'm not a warrior, or a sorceress, or a worker of miracles, as you seem to believe. I am not the way. There is no way." If there were, Andromache would have found it.

"But she did." Cassandra answers the words I did not say.

"*No.*" I back away from the stairs.

With an animal grunt, Cassandra pushes me up against the wall. Pain echoes in my head.

Her breath is hot and angry on my face. "If you can't hear the truth, then look upon it." Nostrils flare as she grabs my chin and jerks my head sideways so that I am gazing out of the narrow slit in the stone, out onto the streets of Troy. "*Look.*"

I take in the city below. The trenches full of broken chariots. The mud walls of the Lower City studded with spears and toppled over in places. Roofs still dancing with small fires and streets cluttered with bodies.

"The Citadel will fall." Cassandra's nails bite into my jaw. "I have seen it in my nightmares. I have watched it happen every time I closed my eyes for twelve years. They will burn our homes. Rape us. They will kill every man and boy who breathes within these walls. Except for one. They can't have him. I won't *allow* it."

I stare into the shrinking black of her pupils and the horrors painted there. And I know in that part of me that hears the horses whisper that she is telling the truth.

My shoulders slump even as her grip on me loosens.

"Steady now, little mouse." Cassandra takes a step backward, giving us both room to breathe. "Call on the shadows, your friends. But the time is coming when the shadows can't hide you anymore. When that moment arrives, you must find your claws."

Footsteps echo above us. Helen's graceful form descends the steps with a bundle clutched in her arms. She comes nearer, and I see Andrius, wrapped in a blanket and sleeping soundly against her shoulder.

Helen's steps falter at the bottom of the staircase. "He's fed and changed." Sadness and determination line her face as she shifts Andrius in her arms and holds out a satchel. When I don't move, Cassandra takes it and places the strap across my chest. She pulls the hood of my cloak up over my head and adjusts a pack onto my back. I watch it all as if it were happening to someone else.

"The skin contains goat's milk. Enough for two days," Helen tells me. "I gave him some herbs to help him sleep. They will wear off soon. Ride hard for Ida. There is an old temple at the top of the mountain. Gargaron. A place of healing. They have a signal fire. Light it when you get there so we know that you are safe." She holds out something else. A bag. "Andromache packed it with food and su—"

Andromache.

"Where is she?" My eyes fly up the stairs. Expecting her imposing form to appear at any moment. It doesn't.

Helen's hair is lank. Her skin and clothes caked with dirt and blood. "In the tower." She rocks Andrius. "I thought it better to take him from her there. Some wounds are better inflicted quick—"

I push past Helen. My vision narrows to the light coming from the chamber at the top of this twisting tunnel. It drifts in from a balcony facing the plain. Just out of reach of the light, with her back pressed against the wall, sits Andromache.

She has collapsed in on herself, her cheek resting on her knees as she gazes up at the light breaking across the sky. She doesn't move, but I know that she can sense me there.

I walk across the room and fall to my knees in front of her.

She doesn't look at me. "Go, Rhea. Please."

My heart breaks under the weight of her sorrow. At the wrongness of seeing the strongest person I have ever known bent and broken on the floor.

"I can't do this. Please. Don't ask it of me."

"I already have." She lifts her face, revealing the wetness on her cheeks. My heart pounds against my ribs. "They'll catch us."

"They won't." Her hand snakes out to grab hold of mine. "At first light, Hector will answer Achilles's call. The men will gather to watch them fight. Hector will draw it out as long as he can. The east gate will be unlocked. You will ride for the foothills of Mount Ida. You will ride as you have never ridden, Rhea, and nobody will catch you."

"What if they leave men to guard the gate?" They would see me coming as soon as the doors open. "This will never work."

"It will."

"How can you know that?"

"Because it has to." Love burns in her eyes. So fierce it sinks beneath my skin, branding me.

"I am afraid."

"Good." Andromache's chin thrusts upward. As I've seen it do so many times. "Fear will keep you alive."

As hard as she is squeezing my hand, I squeeze hers back. "I am afraid that I can't be what he needs. I'm afraid I can't be you."

Every line of her face sags. "You will be you, Rhea. That is enough."

Tears stream down my face. Tears for Ajax and Helen and Cassandra. For Hector and Andromache, and for Andrius, who will never know who his parents were or how many people sacrificed to give him this one chance.

Yes, he will. He will, because I will tell him.

Andromache's hands move to cup my cheeks. "When my son speaks his first words, they will be for your ears. When he takes his first steps, they will be into your arms. It is your hand he will hold as he discovers this world, and that is how it must be. I give you my heart, Rhea. So that when you love him now, it will be for both of us." Her voice breaks.

"I promise." A ragged blast of air. "I will tell him who his mother was. His father. I will give him every memory I have so that he will know you both the same way I do."

Andromache's lips wobble. "Memories fade."

"Not *mine*."

I throw myself into her arms.

"Go." Andromache's voice is hoarse against my cheek. "Go and don't look back."

A sob rises in my throat. I swallow it as I stand. And then I do the thing she's asked of me. The one thing I promised myself I'd never do again.

I run.

BITS OF FLOATING ash drift over the walls to the empty streets of Troy's Merchant Quarter. I pull my headscarf over my mouth and run with Andrius clutched against my breast.

Soldiers line the walls separating the second ring of Troy from the parts of her that have already fallen. Some are crowded down below, waiting for their turns to go up to watch what is about to unfold. None of them notice me as I take the turn that leads toward the stables. Just as I come around the corner, a shade steps out from the shadow of a nearby building, blocking my path. My arms wrap around Andrius where he lies in a cloth sling against my chest as the cloaked form steps forward.

Light shines on the hooded face. Two thin, white hands push back the cowl.

"Why are you following me?" I ask, my hands dropping back to my sides.

Cassandra meets me in the center of the abandoned street. "Because there is one more thing you must know."

"What?" I don't know if I can bear any more of Cassandra's help.

She answers my question with one of her own. "Which horse will you take?"

"Carris. She is brave and steady enough for whatever comes." I say the words even though I haven't allowed my mind to move beyond this moment to what lies ahead. My thoughts are too consumed by everything I'm leaving behind.

A sound echoes from outside. The blast of a horn.

A call to arms.

The deafening roar of Achaea's armies rises up over the walls to wake the sleeping city. No longer a distant threat. Their cries are now close enough to raise the hairs at the nape of my neck.

The streets come alive. Doors and windows fly open in the Citadel above as people pour out of the homes where they are sheltered in answer to the call. The names of Hector and Achilles are whispers running wild on the wind.

My throat goes hot and tight. "Say what you have to say, Cassandra."

She moves like the Wraith that lives within her, light as smoke. "There are men on the other side of the gate. Hunters. They ride Aeneas's stolen stallions. You know the ones." Her eyes burn into mine. "Brave and steady will not suffice."

"I know horses, Cassandra." Every fraying nerve is laid bare in my voice.

"I know things too." She steps in close. "I know there is only one horse capable of taking you where you need to go." Her finger jabs my breast directly beside Andrius's sleeping face. "You know it too. You saw it. The day you brought him here. Do you think it was an accident? A coincidence? Do you really believe there are any such things?"

Her words bathe me in ice. "He can't be tamed. Even Hector couldn't break him."

"The horse will run for you. If you ask him, he will run for you, Rhea." She backs away, her lips trembling. "But what I know doesn't matter, does it? The truth never does. Not unless you *live* it."

Cassandra steps aside. I push past her and down the street to the courtyard behind Hector and Andromache's house. I don't stop until I reach the stables. Cassandra's words haunt me every step of the way.

If Storm and Wrath, Aeneas's stallions, are waiting for me outside the gates, Carris could run until her heart bursts and still never beat them. There is only one animal capable of outlasting those horses across open ground.

The musk of hay and manure greets me inside the darkened building. The stables lie abandoned. Every man, woman, and child left in Troy has moved to the walls to watch the duel between Hector and Achilles. A duel Hector can't win quickly. Not without sentencing his son to death.

I saw the truth in Andromache's eyes. The thing she couldn't bring herself to admit, not even to me. Hector may be stronger, but Achilles is younger. Faster. His body hasn't been worn down by months of combat. Hector's best chance of winning is to overwhelm Achilles with force when the duel begins, but that is the one thing he can't do. Not without cutting the battle short and dooming our only chance of escape.

It's a chance Hector won't take.

Andromache knew it, and so do I.

All around me, the horses are restless in their stalls. As if they too can sense what is coming.

My feet take me down the long row. Old friends poke out their heads to say hello. Ishtar and Carris wait for me. I run my hands over their velvet muzzles, letting them speak for me. My touch holds all the years and the memories. All the moments and the words I can't bring myself to say, because to do so would break me. And I have Andrius to worry about now.

Be brave now, my friends. Good-bye.

I force myself to let go and make my way to the stall at the very end of the row. One separated from the rest by two layers of reinforced wood.

He dances on his feet as he watches me come.

Defiant. Proud.

Beautiful and powerful and full of rage. So much rage.

Atesh. Prince of Horses.

I face him across a distance of several paces. His back hooves lash out to strike the stable wall.

Wood splits. A warning I do not heed. I swallow my fear and close the distance.

I have come to set you free.

My heart sings out in the language of my blood. The Prince of Horses stills.

But first you must do something for me.

Atesh's outrage dances through my veins. His neighs shatter the stillness of the empty stable. He tosses his head, his nostrils flaring with disdain as he regards the helpless child in my arms.

Love and desperate courage flare inside me as I take that last step forward.

He is a prince. Same as you. And just like you, he cannot stay here.

I place my hand within reach of the beast's teeth.

Run for me, Atesh. Run for us, and I'll see to it that all the ages sing the glory of your name.

The animal approaches until he is close enough to hurt me if he wishes. His massive head bends low. My heart lodges into my throat, but I raise my fingers to the hinge on the stable door.

A hand closes around my shoulder, spinning me around. A gasp escapes my lips as I look up into eyes the color of the sea.

"Cyrrian?" My gaze flies over his face. The deep cut above his brow and the bruises on his cheeks, matched by two pairs of battered knuckles.

I haven't seen Cyrrian much since the night on the plain before Hector and Ajax dueled.

"What happened to you?" I reach for the tender flesh across his cheekbone.

He stills.

I pull it back but he captures my wrist before I can. "I called Hector a fool. Along with a dozen other names I'll never forgive myself for. I told him I'd rather watch the Citadel burn than stand by while he killed himself for nothing."

"So he *hit* you?"

Cyrrian shakes his head. "No. Aeneas did the honors." His broken lips bend in a grimace. "It seems he has recovered his strength."

"And Hector—?"

Cyrrian squeezes my wrist. "He left a few minutes ago to answer the challenge."

I stare at Atesh where he waits, watching. Every second now feels like sand, slipping through my fingers.

"What are you doing here?" I force my focus back to Cyrrian. I have to make him leave. I have to get this horse out of the stables and down to the east gate before the battle starts, or we'll never make it.

"I came here to breathe. I was afraid if I went to the plain too early, I might do something stupid. I refuse to dishonor Hector when . . ." Cyrrian catches his breath. "He is walking to the slaughter." Tears spill out of Cyrrian's eyes. "And for the life of me I can't understand why."

It takes all my remaining strength to speak. "It is his choice."

Cyrrian rears back. "No. Hector would never agree to face Achilles on a field that plays to every one of Achilles's strengths. To save the city, yes. But not like this. Not when waiting costs him nothing. Not when losing costs us *everything* and winning makes no difference for Troy."

I swallow a mouthful of spit that tastes like blood.

"What if winning is not his object?" I ask quietly.

Cyrrian's gaze moves to the sleeping child in my arms. It slides to the fire horse waiting with preternatural stillness in the stall behind me.

The truth registers in a single moment. "No." He steps forward to grip my arm, yanking me toward him. "Rhea, *no*."

I pull back, but it's useless.

So I meet his eyes with a matching fire, and I let him see it on my face. Every thought. Every feeling and intention. It's past the point of hiding now. Cyrrian will either help me, or he will stop me.

And I won't let him stop me.

"Andrius can't stay here. The city will fall. What happens to Hector's son when it does?"

It's a question that every soul in Troy already knows the answer to.

"You can't know that Troy will fall," Cyrrian says, more to argue with me than because he really believes it.

"I know it because Cassandra told me. I know because I have eyes." He shakes his head, but I press on. "Do you think Andromache would have placed her son in my arms if it weren't true? Do you really think she would've sent Hector to face Achilles or that he would have gone willingly if it wasn't the only way?"

He knows I'm right. I can see it. Just as I can see how badly he wants not to believe it.

"I can't—" His voice breaks. "I can't just stand there and watch him die. And he will. If he faces Achilles like this, Hector will die."

"But his son will live." The only thing that matters now. "Help him, Cyrrian. Help him and Andromache by helping *me*. Please."

His eyes close, but I've already seen it. The desperation. The helplessness.

The love.

And then every emotion is thrust firmly behind that wall of stubbornness.

Oh, Cyrrian.

"You can't take that horse," he says. "He'll toss you before you make it out of the gates."

Warmth winds through my chest at his words even as I lift my chin the way Andromache taught me. "It's this horse or none."

"Is that your way of telling me that I should stick to worrying about my chariot and leave you to the horses?" Our exchange from the day of Paris's duel with Menelaus feels like a lifetime ago. Cyrrian smiles sadly. "My memory isn't as good as yours, but it holds on to the things that matter."

His eyes search my face. Every thought leaves my head but that this will be the last time I ever see him. Cyrrian will fight even if Hector loses. Until his last breath. And when Troy falls, so will he.

Everything inside me rages at the unfairness of it. The waste. How many friends? How many brothers and fathers and sons will be lost before this is over? And for what? When does it *end*?

An urge rises up inside me, compelling as the tide. To throw my arms around Cyrrian's neck and bring him close. But my arms stay locked at my sides.

What little hope there was left bleeds out of Cyrrian's eyes. "What gate will you take?"

"The east," I offer quickly. "Helen sent someone to open the way."

He nods. "Let's go. It won't be long now."

We walk down to the gate in silence. The morning is somber despite the rising sun. Even Atesh must sense it for he comes willingly, walking between us like a child keeping the peace between quarreling parents.

When at last we reach the gate, Cyrrian turns to me. "You are either uncommonly brave or uncommonly stupid." More words from our past.

Does he doubt that I can do this?

Does it matter?

The horse will run for you. If you ask him, he will run for you, Rhea.

I straighten my spine. "They won't hurt him. Not while I'm alive."

His eyes melt in the morning light. "I believe you."

On the far side of the city, a sound builds slowly. Like a wave. The clash of a thousand spears hitting a thousand shields in a rhythmic beat.

"It is starting." Cyrrian stares through the walls toward the Ilium plain where Hector is preparing to fight. When he turns back to me, his eyes no longer remind me of the ocean. Instead, they make me think of the hottest part of a flame.

With a single step, he backs me up against Atesh. His body presses mine until the child in my arms is the only thing separating us.

"Ride, Rhea. Ride like the wind is chasing you."

Every word on my tongue dries up under the heat of Cyrrian's gaze. He starts to back away, but then something in his expression hardens.

Alarm flares through me.

Mouth set in determination, he raises both of his hands to my cheeks, cupping my face in palms calloused from gripping leather reins. Hot breath fans my cheeks as he leans forward, dropping one of his hands to raise mine between us. He presses his lips to the inside of my wrist.

His gaze pierces me. "For good fortune," he says.

From outside the walls, the clash of swords and shields goes still, and it's as if all of the world has stopped to hold its breath.

In the quiet of the moment, Cyrrian takes a sleeping Andrius from my arms. My hands shake as I find the fire horse's mane and climb up onto his back. Atesh stands steady. Strangely calm since we left the stable, as if he knows that his time has nearly come. When I look down again, Cyrrian is right below me.

"For Hector." His voice catches as he raises the prince of Troy. "Breaker of horses."

"For Hector." Tears burn as I clutch Andrius to my chest. "Tamer of men."

Cyrrian smiles that rare smile. The one that is *real*. Then he throws open the city gates. The wind rushes through them from far across the plain.

I gaze out between the reinforced doors. Miles of open space that lead to the foot of the mountains.

We must run them all.

Go, Rhea. Go and don't look back.

I start to whisper the command to Atesh, but he is already moving. Out of the gates and onto the open plain.

His mane turns to flame under my hands. We run.

Not even the wind runs faster.

31

CASSANDRA

MY HANDS FLAIL to grip the wall.

A flood rages.

Not in this tower. Inside me.

Dark water. Rising, churning from down below. Drowning out the voices.

Don't, gasps the Crone. *Not like this.*

Stop it, please! The Child's strangled cries echo up the stone walls.

The Fury rages as the darkness pools around her legs. Her anger as powerless as her sword to stem the rising tide.

In the shadows, the Wraith leans against the wall, red tears diving off the sharp ridges of her cheeks.

I push myself from the wall and climb the last few steps. The door to my tower lies open. The room beyond it, empty. Wind blows in through the balcony, sending ripples through the wine pooling on the floor from a toppled cup.

Andromache's grief hangs in the air, seeping into the walls. I taste its serrated edge with my tongue. Hidden bitterness.

Betrayal.

The kind for which there can be no forgiveness.

The water inside me swells until it brushes the Crone's stooped shoulders. *You had no choice,* she says, her lips trembling with cold.

Don't be sad, begs the Child.

The Fury sags, all her rage spent.

We did what was necessary. What had to be done.

Your fault. All your fault.

The voice rises up from the dark water at the bottom of the well, making all the others go still.

What is that? cries the Child, holding tight to the Wraith's robes.

The Hawk screams, climbing high into the clouds above the tower.

The Fury spins in a circle, her blade a whirl of steel.

Beast from the deep. The Crone shakes her head in sadness. Long ago, she fought at my side to lock it away. We thought it was dead, but it seems it was merely waiting for the moment when we would have no more strength to stop it.

End this. You know how.

The beast's voice echoes in my head when I close my eyes. Blindness that brings no peace. Only visions. Playing, playing in the dark.

The city burning.

Andromache's dead eyes staring through toppled walls. Over the plain, scattered with a thousand shields.

My father's mouth gaping open. Silent scream. Blood on the floor. Insides where outsides should be.

The face of a young man. Savage. Chasing me up an altar to pin me down on the offering stone with his unyielding weight.

Taste of ash mixed with fear. Stench of copper and smoke. A baby ripped from sheltering arms. Bundle of soft blankets, stitched with loving hands, thrown over the edge. The sound that comes at the end of a fall.

Over and over. The same visions.

Over and over. Torture chamber inside my head.

I thought I could change them. I thought I could remold their shapes with my hands, but all I've done is breathe life into their still forms. Because of my pride.

No. Because of your hope.

Broken.

Cursed.

Liar.

Yes, all those things and more the world will never know.

I am tired of holding it in. Tired of knowing. I want to forget.

You know the way. You have always known it.

How many times have I walked it with my eyes closed? How many times have I counted out the steps in my dreams?

Five paces past the bed to the open door.

Two across the balcony.

One step over and then . . .

No! screams the Crone, her voice wet. *Oblivion is not peace. Just ask the Wrai . . .* Her words end in a gurgle.

My eyes open, and then I am here. On the balcony. The one my mother left open even when all other doors were barred closed. Escape offered but never taken. White knuckles grip the ledge. Below me, the city swarms with death birds. So many raptors that the buildings are hidden under their black, bloated bodies.

One of the raptors breaks away from a nearby rooftop. Dark wings billow wide. Twisted beak. Black eyes. Flint yet to be struck. It lands on my shoulder. Talons dig into flesh, tightening like a noose. I do not push the creature away.

Yes. Surrender to the things you see. You are but one broken woman. You cannot alter the course of the ages. You cannot change the will of the gods.

Tears drip down my face. *What gods?* Why give me these visions if there is no way to change them? I have tried. Tried so hard to use the things I saw for good.

And look what it has gotten you.

The dark water surges to the top of the well as I tilt my weight forward.

Not all changes can be seen, child. The Crone's voice finds me through oceans. Through lakes and rivers. So thin I can hardly make it out. *Who knows how far a single ripple can travel across a still pond.*

Memories rise out of the darkness. Helen's face, covered in sweat and beaming with joy as she placed Andrius's glistening body into Andromache's arms. Bodecca and Creusa shelling peas side by side in the kitchen. The scent of spices and baking bread. The feel of warmth and companionship and the sound of laughter.

Andromache's groans through gritted teeth. Rhea's small hand clutching hers. The way her other hand had reached for mine, connecting us. Bound together. Stitch by stitch.

What good has it done me?

I blink, and Troy is spread out below me. My home and my prison. But when I look now, it isn't the shadows I see, but the thing they cannot fully hide. It is there. Just below the surface. Just as it always was.

A chance.

A hope.

Glittering in the dark.

We fought to change the fate of Troy, and that fate has not changed. But everything is not the same. *We* are not the same.

A hundred stones dropped into still waters sending ripples far and wide. How far will they go? What distant shores will they reach?

I step back from the ledge. The dark water is receding, seeping slowly back into the place where it lives. The Child gasps for air, her head held above the surface by the Fury's scarred hands. Beside them, the Wraith steadies the Crone with an arm locked around her waist.

The Wraith holds out her free hand to me.

I stagger back from the ledge and blink into the rising sun. The beast groans its retreat into the darkness as light floods my vision, cutting the scene below me in gem tones.

The Ilium plain choked with men. A ring of Achaean warriors a hundred deep. Their forces centered on the Scaean gate and the small group of Trojan soldiers who stand on the wrong side of our defenses. Four men against all of Achaea's armies.

From the ramparts above, Troy's Old Blood and her squabbling council look on. Their anger and confusion light a spark of satisfaction deep within me. They don't know what to do. The men outside the gates are acting on their own. Their defiance is a sharp kick to the vipers' nest that has sent them slithering around the feet of my father's chair.

The air is alive with hissing. With a strength I do not recognize, the old man at the center rises up from his seat to approach the city walls. His voice shakes as the king begs his son to retreat to safety. Beside him, the queen echoes his pleas. Their voices scatter like dust upon the howling wind.

Hector's shoulders stiffen. He hears them. He hears them even when they are not there. Voices of duty in his head every bit as real as the ones inside mine. He has always sought to make them proud, to honor them even when they did not deserve it. The best of men. The picture of duty. The perfect son.

Until now.

My brother doesn't look up as he walks toward the enemy. Back straight. Helmet flashing. Hector walks for a young girl on a Horse made of Fire. For the sleeping infant in her arms. He walks for an old woman with a hard tongue and a soft heart, staring into a hearth full of memories. And another woman standing high on the ramparts, jagged ends of her golden hair dancing in the wind.

Hector walks for the one he loves above all others. Standing at a loom in the wreckage of the home they shared because she has laid down every weapon.

And me. Hector walks for me.

Because I asked him to.

Every step brings Hector farther from the walls. Toward a future I could not protect him from no matter how hard I tried. My failure is a shriek that pierces the dawn as my brother walks away to face the Achaean army alone.

No. Not alone.

I throw up my hands and call the Hawk to me. His scream rends the sky as he soars over my tower. Above the ramparts and the den of snakes, spitting venom from the walls.

Orders ring from the ramparts. Inside the city walls, a company of Trojan soldiers approaches the gates. The doors inch open, but Andromache's men are there to hold them back. Shoulder to shoulder they press against the wood. Sweat runs down their backs. Feet drag inch by inch through the dirt as they press the gates closed from the outside.

Sing to me, cries the Hawk as the men below fight to buy Hector time.

So I sing to him their names.

Sarpedon of Lycia.

Akamas, son of Theseus.

Aeneas of Dardania.

Cyrrian of the Two Shadows.

On the other side of the city, a single rider screams across the plain on a Horse made of flame. The beast's hooves spark a trail of dust in the direction of the mountains.

The Hawk's eyes move farther east along the Horse's path. Movement on the foothills. A hidden danger. The rider doesn't see it yet. None of them see yet. But they will.

The final lie.

One more to fix all that is broken.

The girl spots the danger in the distance. She pulls up on the reins. The fire Horse dances beneath her as her mind measures the outcomes. The angles. All her thoughts. Spinning, spinning on the loom. Every thread of the tapestry, resting with the reins in the palms of her hands.

Turn back or run?

Death or life?

A thousand decisions. A single moment.

The Mouse makes her choice.

I call the Hawk back to me. He soars over the tower banking westward toward the sea. Circling lower and lower over my brother walking slowly forward while his thoughts run with the girl riding hard the other way.

The Hawk cries in my voice, and in that moment, the part of Hector that has always seen me glimpses me there.

Seconds and years. Thens and nows all stitched together.

Sticky fingers and secret smiles.

The smell of hay and the sweetness of sweat.

Trips to the stables riding high on wide shoulders.

Hector smiles for me. Forgiveness and love and a thousand things the world will never know, because we are the same. In the ways that matter, we have always been the same.

I back away from the ledge.

Hector reaches Achilles and dismounts onto the plain. My brother strikes the chestplate of the armor he wears. An insult to both men who wore it before he claimed it. Not because he wants to, but because he *must*.

Achilles lunges with a cry of rage that has the Fury inside me beating her breast. Inside the Achaean warrior, a Fury of his own.

Spears fly. The clash of bronze.

Dust and sweat and the beating sun glinting against bronze helmets.

Strikes and blows. I do not count them, but the men watching do. Step by step they record them in their hearts so that, one day, all the ages will remember. A dance of heroes. A battle for all time. But the things they see are just another vision. The songs they sing are truth stacked on truth in the tower of a lie.

For that is the nature of visions. Songs too. They tell us less of truth than they do about those who sing them.

Two armies watch Achilles's feet blur across the dirt. His blade a lightning strike. Hector deflects the blows. Every step Achilles takes forward is one that Hector takes back. Not weakness. A wiser warrior biding his time.

The Hawk dives low just as Hector's opportunity comes. An elbow raised too high above a drooping shield. An open doorway to a different future. A different song for the ages to sing.

It hangs suspended in front of my brother, glittering like gold against the light of the rising sun. And though I know what it will cost, I silently beg him to reach for it. To claim the glory that was always meant to be his.

Sing to me, the Hawk begs, and I do.

I sing over and over again.

Hector turns away from the door he could have taken, and he does the one thing that every man on this field will remember. Because it was the one thing they could *see*.

Hector runs.

And Rhea rides.

Gasps from the ramparts as he flees around the walls. Jeers from the gathered Achaean army. Slurs of cowardice. Of confusion. Of shame. Hector hears them all.

With a howl of rage, Achilles sets off after him. Every step Achilles takes, he gains.

Once around the wall. They fly past the golden gates.

Minutes like sand, slipping through my fingers.

Twice.

Past the fig and oak trees and the ramparts and the springs where the women of Troy do their washing. Where Hector splashed as a boy, clinging to Bodecca's skirts.

Three times.

The sun rises in the sky. Hot sweat pours like rain. Trails of dust and salt as Achilles bears down, every moment drawing closer. But Hector never slows. Not even when the armor on his body begins to drag him down. Not when long lines of enemies hurl rocks at his feet and insults at his back. Not when the people of Troy pour their shame and their sadness upon him from the walls above.

Hector runs until his strength is gone. And then he keeps running. Until there is nowhere left to go but back to the beginning. Every man watching records it. Both the truth and the lie.

Two names for all the ages. But it was never the fight between them that mattered.

It was the run.

Every voice inside me cries as Achilles draws his sword. My brother casts up his eyes. His gaze pierces through the past and walls of stone. Across wide streets and houses until it finds a woman with strong arms and a straight back cradling a missing infant to her heart. *Great Sorrow.*

Even Greater Love.

A desperate block. A cry of rage. The thrust of a sword through golden armor.

Even the wind goes silent as he falls.

Hector. Breaker of horses.

Song forever left unsung.

THE SHADE

Nails break and claw
through walls of clay,
up twisting darkness
where ghosts hold sway.

Work of ancient hands,
passed through sifting sands,
a thousand Serpents
that point the way.

A silent witness
to her son's sorrow,
where he must go
Shade cannot follow.

Escape once taken
now holds her bound,
chains of blood once spilled
upon the ground.

They wait with her,
companions in grief,
deep in that Well
no Light can reach.

Gates thrown wide open,
now the race begins.
One Horse goes out
the other, in.

BOOK
IV

32

RHEA

THE PRINCE OF Horses does not run. He flies.

Wind lashes my face as we gallop across the plain. His mane is a living flame, dancing against my cheek.

The ground gives way beneath us. So fast the colors run. Even the sky. Blue streaks above our heads.

Atesh's gallop is a thunder in my ears. I bend forward, cradling Andrius's body against my chest.

The rope jerks in my hands. I draw it in, but it's like trying to hold back the tide. Atesh wants his head. My palms are raw with the effort of checking his gallop. I say a soft thanks to the Mother for the cloth wrap Helen secured across my chest. If both my hands weren't free to grasp his mane I would be thrown in an instant.

He tosses his head, jerking my arms in their sockets. His stride lengthens.

Everything about Atesh is built for speed. The angle of his head. The power of his stride. It eats up the ground and spits it out behind us in a cloud of grit and dust.

His power steals my breath. A fall at this speed would kill us, but that isn't the only reason to check his pace. At this rate, we won't see any danger up ahead until we are running right—

A trench appears in front of us. Ten feet across. The stallion's muscles bunch beneath me. One of my arms closes around Andrius while the other grabs a fistful of black mane.

The horse's front hooves hit the dirt on the far side of the trench, then his back legs. The impact jolts my bones. Despite Helen's sleeping draught, Andrius makes a startled sound against my neck.

Atesh doesn't slow. Instead, he races past fields of charred earth. Past the ford and the Hill of Kallikolone. All the while, he fights my feeble attempts to slow him. Just as he fights the laws of the gods. The ones that separate the creatures of land from those of the sky.

Mountains solidify in the distance. Mount Ida stands stark against the sun, a day's hard ride away. Another few hours to get to the top, where I'm to light the signal fire so that Andromache . . .

Andromache.

I clench my teeth and pull on the reins. Tears sting my eyes as I fix them forward. That's when I see it. Movement among the swells of low hills up ahead.

Muscles scream as I rear back, lying down until my back is pressed flat against Atesh's rump. With a cry of indignation, he dances to a stop. He bucks and circles under me, but I hold him fast. Finally, he relents, giving me a clear view of what awaits us.

In the distance, a line of men stretches across the foothills between the open plains and the mountains. A wall of swords, cutting off our path.

My eyes take in the scene in rapid blinks. Ten chariots. Seven wagons, loaded down with cargo.

They are Achaean. I can tell by the outline of their chariots—bulky, artless things they brought over from their distant isles. They must've seen me breaking toward them from the moment we left Troy's gates and have been lying in wait for us since.

A quick glance at their wagons tells me what they're doing so far from camp. The wheels creak under the heavy burden of wood. Fresh timber. These men must've been dispatched to Ida to gather fuel.

My heart sinks when I see the black panther stamped across their shields. If these are Achilles's Myrmidons, they are the best Achaean fighters and among their better charioteers. Dread pools in my stomach when a chariot breaks free from the others. It stops in the open space between us.

The men's faces are hidden by their boar's tusk helmets, but I would know those horses anywhere. Storm and Wrath. Aeneas's stolen stallions. They stand alone, pawing the ground.

Atesh tosses his head, feet dancing sideways. His body is coiled tight. Ready to spring with or without my command.

A hawk screams overhead as I take in the scene before me. The Semiosis River is a barrier of water to the north, blocking any escape. The Trojan Bay glitters to the west, another dead end.

My mind flies over all the things I know and all the things I don't. Returning to Troy is not an option. The gates will be barred behind us. We'd be trapped outside the city walls with nothing but the Achaean army for company. There is only forward now. I have to get across the open plain or we will be too easy to follow. By now, Hector has engaged Achilles outside the city walls to buy us time to get to those distant hills—time that is slipping away every second that we stand here.

But the party of Myrmidons in front of us will never let us pass, and I can't fight my way through them.

I have to find a way around them. Somehow, I must make it to those foothills before the armies behind us disengage, or the Myrmidons sound an alarm, and we are trapped between two closing battalions of our enemies.

The fire horse bucks beneath me, his mane flashing in the sun.

Let me go. Let me run, his demand screams through my blood.

The lone hawk in the sky issues a shrill cry. The sound lifts the hairs at the back of my neck.

The chariots break toward us. As I watch, they split into two groups. The first, led by Storm and Wrath, heads right for us. The second breaks for the hills leading toward Ida, cutting off our only escape.

My gaze travels backward across the plain to the burning ruin of the Lower City. Smoke rises over the white Citadel walls, still standing high and proud upon the charcoal-streaked plateau. The wind shifts around me, whipping across the plain from the direction of Troy, bringing with it the music of men screaming, jeering, cheering.

The sounds wash over me. I tighten my arms around Andrius. The wind howls again, scattering every choice. Every thought and notion until all that remains is Andrius's weight against my chest, that mountain in the distance, and the miles standing between us.

He is yours now, Rhea.

The hawk cries again.

The chariots blaze across the plain, the sound of their approach a reverberation in my chest. Fifty paces narrow to forty. Then thirty. The Achaeans are twenty paces away when I drop the reins. With one smooth motion, I yank the lead rope free from around Atesh's head. His nostrils flare as it lands in the dust at his feet.

Fly for me, Prince of Horses.

My heart sings the plea even as I fill both hands with his mane.

The fire horse hears my challenge.

He explodes beneath me. Atesh turns on his heels, a blur of smoke and fire as he sets off at a gallop, not for the mountains or for the city at our backs, but toward the glinting patch of sea at the mouth of the bay.

Wind whips hair against my face. I shake it loose and dare a glance over my shoulder. The chariots fan out behind us as they give chase. They are close. Close enough to—

Something whizzes past my head. Pain stabs at my ear as a long spear strikes the ground ahead of us. Atesh veers around it as hot wetness drips down the side of my face.

Copper fills my mouth. I whip my head forward and curl my body around Andrius, making myself a smaller target. My heart races to keep pace with the beat of Atesh's hooves. They drum faster and faster until there's no longer any doubt. I was wrong. Up until now, the Prince of Horses has been checking his speed.

He isn't checking it anymore.

The stallion runs as if his tail is on fire. His stride lengthens until his hooves barely touch the ground.

It feels like falling.

It feels like flying.

Despite the danger, a cry of unbridled joy rises in my throat as we streak across the plain, a burning star in the bright light of day.

Behind us, angry shouts. They fade along with the sound of pursuit. It grows fainter and fainter as we put distance between us and the men at our heels. And still, Atesh runs. He runs through the hills, across open ground all the way to the sea. We hit the beach in a blast of sand and salt.

The men behind us are too far back to see. Still, our tracks on the beach will be easy to follow.

As if reading my mind, Atesh charges straight into the sea. Stinging cold slaps my feet, drenching the bottom of my tunic. Drops of water fly around us, glinting in the sun as we race along the swirling surf, using the water to hide our path as we scream down the beach. And still, Atesh runs. He runs until I can't think. Until I can't even breathe. Which is why I don't see where he is taking us until it's already too late.

Cape Sigeum and the Kesik Cut solidify in the distance. The Achaean camp lies exposed upon the high ground, vacant and ugly in the harsh sun. I reach for the lead to pull the horse back before I realize the rope is lying in the dust somewhere back on the plain.

We pass the mouth where the Scamander meets the sea. He charges through the water, past the reeds where Hector and Cyrrian's fishing dinghy lies hidden next to the dock where I lay in the fading light and watched Ajax and Teucer swim. Within moments we are blazing toward the swamp. Atesh finds one last burst of speed.

A cry leaves my mouth as we sail over latticework and steps I've carefully counted in the dark. I close my eyes, and then we are crashing into the high grasses on the other side of the swamp.

The Prince of Horses walks through the grasses until he finds the old shrine I never thought I'd see again. He stops beside the crumbling wall and looks back at me, as if accusing my traitorous heart of leading him right here.

Beyond the tall grasses, the chariots emerge on the empty beach. They circle the sand, searching for our tracks.

Legs shaking, I slide off Atesh's back and pull him behind the high stone wall. My arms wrap around Andrius, feeling the rise and fall of his sleeping breath as I watch the Myrmidon riders circle the beach in confusion. To them it must look as if we rode right into the sea. When they find no tracks, they divide again. Half drive up the beach to the west while the remaining chariots retreat back to the foothills.

The Prince of Horses nips my shoulder.

His coat is wet, covered in foam. Even so, I can feel the latent power within him. Speed and strength and heart.

Those men won't have seen my face. They won't know who I am or what precious cargo I carry. But they'll know the Prince of Horses when they see him again.

Run, I tell him. *Run far from here. Take the riders with you, but don't let them catch you.*

Atesh tosses his head. His breath blasts from his nostrils, and I feel his thoughts as clearly as if he had spoken them.

As if they could.

He tosses his head one last time before he runs straight through the enemy camp, leaving a path of destruction in his wake. People scream. Carts upturn and dash against the ground just like they did the first day I saw him in that market back in Cyzicus. I track him with my eyes as he glides over the Achaeans' trench, his hooves hammering the dirt on the other side of the Kesik Cut. His coat gleams in the sun as he blazes across the plain, and when he goes, he takes a small part of me with him.

The ache is quickly drowned out by something even more insistent. It rises fast as I spin around to face the one place I never expected to find myself again.

The last place on earth Andrius, the prince of Troy, should be.

The Achaean camp.

33

ANDROMACHE

FROM THE TOWER, my eyes follow the trail of blood up the Ilium plain. Every twist and turn is a dagger ripping through me. Until there is nothing left to feel and no part capable of feeling it.

Achilles dragged him.

Sickness. War. Betrayal. We think we are well acquainted with darkness, when really we are dancing in the twilight before the sun dips. Still, the long night is coming.

For me, it is already here. A total eclipse of the sun.

While all of Troy watched Hector and Achilles race around the city, I made my way through abandoned streets until I reached our home. On the edge of a burning world. The door stood open for me, waiting. I climbed to our bedchamber and stood by the loom I rarely used, in a house that should have been on fire but wasn't somehow. Staring at a red robe I'd worked on in the weeks after Andrius's birth, one Hector would never wear. Waiting for the fearful sound I could already feel welling up inside my own chest, ready to fly.

I see now why Helen did it. Wove her grief until her hands bled from the pain that is always part of creation.

Perhaps at the end of all things, the spindle outwields the sword. But for me, there was nothing left to create. When the city's rising lament told me it was done, *finished*, I left.

The walking shell of what was once a woman, a mother, a wife. I made my way back to this tower, arriving in time to see Achilles drive a lance through Hector's ankles. That tender place I sometimes held while he slept. I watched as the beast tied my love, my life, to the back of his chariot and dragged his body through the dirt.

Hecuba's screams and Priam's groans filled the chasm left by my silence. I could see their crumpled forms and torn garments in the unraveling sound, one that ignited wails in every corner of the Citadel. The people of Troy had witnessed not only a death but a humiliation. The desecration of a treasured son Achilles had treated worse than a stray dog.

And still . . . I could not cry out.

Even when Achilles stripped the armor from Hector's body and every Achaean between Troy and the river welcomed the opportunity to plunge a spear into his still-warm flesh, I could not moan or find it in me to plead with the gods.

I could do nothing but sink. Deeper and deeper into darkness.

Achilles's horses dragged Hector, *my* Hector, back to the Achaean ships. There, Achilles will leave him to rot beneath a swarm of flies and a relentless sun. Until the corpse is torn apart by wild animals—a guarantee that Hector's noble soul will never find rest in the afterlife.

By that point, my eyes shed no more tears for my beloved. They were too busy searching the outline of the purple mountain glowing beyond.

A mountain I continue to watch even now. Waiting as only a woman knows how.

The bed behind me is cold. The nest where Hector and I found shelter during our final night as a single beating heart. Embers in the hearth turned to ash. There is no escaping it. We have reached the twilight of Troy and though I wait for a flash of light in a bleak, black sky, it does not come.

It will not come.

It *never* comes.

Hector. His name is my every exhale. *Hector, what have we done?*

Even if Andrius and Rhea make it past the Achaean army, what meager existence have I sentenced them to in my effort to be the hands of the gods? Hunger and hard labor will follow them the rest of their days, this boy the people lovingly called Astyanax, little lord of the city. A lord destined to wander and beg for his bread, the foster mother burdened with his care hardly more than a child herself.

What hope can exist for two exiles cast beyond Troy's walls? Orphans of a desecrated corpse, the only man with the strength to shield these city gates.

And it was you who banished them.

The black tar within me stirs, bubbling like the water I once warmed for Hector's baths. It gurgles up my throat with more rage than the rushing Scamander. My lips are forced open, acidic bile burning. The violent scream comes not from me, but from somewhere deeper. A secret chamber of shared grief known only by those who have felt the sting of a death that comes too soon.

The guttural wail leaves my body like a thousand blackbirds bursting from a cage.

Below, the mourning city takes a collective inhale. For a moment, Troy is still. But as soon as the last blackbird flies from my mouth toward a dark and silent mountain, the groaning of an entire people without hope resumes, their lament rising even higher than before.

"It is early yet. Give them time," says a voice behind me. Soft but sharp like shaved iron. "The sky must grow completely dark if we are to have any chance of seeing so small a light."

Slowly, I turn to her. "I will watch with you." Helen eases herself into the creaky chair Cassandra has spent half of her life in. She watches me like I am the city's madwoman now.

Perhaps she is right.

I turn back to Mount Ida, desiring nothing but this new, tingling darkness. A darkness I have invited into whatever shambles are left of me.

Hours pass. I hardly register the sun's slow movement across the sky. The mourning wails in the streets below us do not cease. All that remains for us is a slow surrender to an endless night.

Soon, my milk comes in.

I feel the seeping dampness first, then the ache in my breasts as it joins with the pulsing pain that has become my entire existence.

I look down at the two wet circles.

He does not like to feed lying on his back, Rhea. He likes to sit up big and tall. Only I forgot to tell her. *How* could I forget to tell her?

It is enough to drive my gaze past leaking nipples to the stones below—stones that have glistened with a woman's blood before. The Shade who ended her earthly life from this very balcony, only to be trapped here forever in death.

All these years, and Cassandra never jumped . . .

"Andromache." Helen's voice has an even sharper edge to it now. "I know it is difficult, but we need to talk. What do we do about the traitor on the council?"

I shrug. "They've won."

And we delivered their victory on Hector's shield. Still, any triumph the council celebrates will be short-lived.

"Only, what might they do to *you* now that Hector . . ." Tears choke Helen's words. "You aren't safe, Andromache. You no longer have a standing that will protect you should they decide to blame—"

"It doesn't matter what they do to me," I say, though my voice sounds worlds and lifetimes away. "What they do to you. Our ending was written long ago. You know this better than anyone."

Helen does not speak for a long time. "I used to think that was how it was . . ."

Another eternal pause.

"But then why are we permitted to endure if our lifeblood is already spent? If we have been granted this time, even if it is short, there must be some greater purpose in it."

"Do not speak to me of signs from the gods!" I turn on her, angry saliva flying from my mouth. "They do not hear us."

"I do not speak of *them*," Helen says softly. "Yet I do know this. Andrius's life is woven together by many threads of sacrifice. Hector's, Rhea's, yours . . ."

She does not list her own name, but I hear the echo of it all the same.

"The cost paid by so many cannot be in vain," Helen insists. "Andrius will live. I can feel it."

Then why don't I? I am his *mother*.

I search Mount Ida's peak again, painted by long shadows of the setting sun. Rhea rode out at dawn. They should be there by now.

And still the sky grows darker.

Helen is wrong. Nothing comes of unseen sacrifice that does not grasp for glory. There is no god who honors suffering because none of our gods have tasted death after drinking life's bitter cup.

There is only the clash of metal on metal. The crunch of earth beneath a hollow corpse as it falls to the dust it will become. Inflaming the rage of yet another warrior to seek revenge.

This. *This* never-ending cycle of blood and bone is the reason we endure.

I take a step back from the balcony and the sliver of horizon beyond.

Hector has my heart. He always will. But he has taken the woman I was with him to whatever lies between this realm of shadows and the river beyond.

Now it is Achilles who knows me best.

Achilles who understands the ways of this world and the ways of men. He helped invent their language, after all—the tongue the mighty will continue to speak until the end of time.

Glory. Revenge. Death.

And above all else . . .

Rage.

I whirl around to face Helen again, seeking to banish her humility and her faith before they threaten the only action I have left to take. Like she said, if I survive the rape of Troy and my own body with it, there must be some higher purpose.

There must be an enemy's head still in need of a spike.

"Where is Cassandra?" I ask as the sky above Mount Ida goes black.

"I . . ." Helen hesitates, her face reflecting back the wrath I am about to unleash across the ages. "Why?"

"There is no signal fire. If my husband gave up his honor along with his life, I want an explanation. If I have sent my infant son and a girl I consider a daughter to their deaths, then I demand to know why she insisted *this* was the only way."

I rush past Helen on the wings of furies, but she remains as poised as the statue she resembles. "Andromache, wait."

"I will not! Cassandra must give an answer for the careless words she speaks." When I fling open the tower chamber's door, the prophetess meets me on the other side.

She waits to receive my rage like an empty tomb.

34

CASSANDRA

"WHERE IS MY son?" Andromache wastes no breath on things that do not matter.

I push past her and into the tower room where Helen is standing against the wall, her arms folded across her breast.

Andromache follows close behind. "They should have made it by now. They should have lit the signal fire."

I move toward the balcony. Open sky. Naked stars. Wind beckoning from across the plain. Andromache's fingers close around my arm.

"Answer me, Cassandra." Her tone is as unyielding as her grip. In her eyes, a roiling anger has risen up to replace the emptiness.

No, not anger.

Rage.

Sing to me, screams the Hawk in his circling flight high above the city walls.

Careful, girl, the Crone cautions. *She is a bow drawn taut.*

The Child whimpers. The Fury grips her sword in her long-fingered hands. They all sense the threat. Danger born of too much grief and too little hope.

I push their echoes down to the bottom of the well. Andromache will hurt me if I don't guard my words. So why not let them run? A roiling river from my mouth. As terrible as Andromache's wrath is sure to be, it is no less than I deserve.

Andromache's gaze sweeps my face as if she can hear the discussion taking place within me. "No!" The word is a blade, wrenched sideways. "You will not retreat inside yourself. You will not hide from this as you hide from everything else." Her nails cut into skin, but my shame cuts deeper. "There has been no signal fire. Rhea hasn't reached Mount Ida."

"No," I say. "She hasn't."

Andromache's hands fall to her sides. The Fury tracks their every twitch with rapt attention.

"How can you be sure?" Helen speaks up from the shadows.

"The ride has failed. A party of warriors intercepted them. Rhea and Andrius were forced to seek shelter."

"But if they sought shelter, that means they are alive." Helen moves to Andromache's side, drawn in by the other woman's pain.

"For now," I say. "But they will not stay that way. Not without help."

"Where are they?" Andromache's voice is flat, lifeless. Wrong. All wrong.

I meet her eyes. "The Achaean camp."

Andromache's stillness fills the room, pushing on the walls of this tower until I fear it will break apart around us. I almost wish that it would. To spare us all from what is coming.

Heedless of the danger, Helen places her hand on Andromache's shoulder. "How can you know for certain?"

"I saw it." My gaze is riveted to the spot where Helen's palm rests against Andromache's bare skin. Wonder that it does not catch flame.

"Another vision, I imagine?" The corner of Andromache's mouth twists. The only part of her that moves.

"No. With my own eyes." I nod toward the Hawk's nest in front of a missing stone in the wall facing east, and I remember another night in this tower. Andromache bending forward to press her eyes against that gap. The fear on her face when I placed my hand across her rounded belly. Swell of hope. Love that felt like pain.

Andromache's hand moves over her flat stomach. Her face hardens, and her arms drop back down to her sides. "Why should we trust your eyes when your visions have utterly failed?"

The bond between us lies burned to ash, just like the Lower City.

And she doesn't even know the truth.

Don't do it, groans the Crone.

Please, begs the Child. *Think of us.*

The Wraith just shakes her head because she knows. We are all far past the hour of saving.

My fingernails dig into the flesh of my palms. "My visions did not fail."

"We have all made errors in judgment." Helen offers her comfort where it is not wanted. "It is not a crime to be human."

Hysterical laughter bubbles up my throat. "I have made many mistakes, Helen. This was not one of them."

A frown cuts across Helen's brow. "What are you saying?"

"She knew." Andromache's gaze is a spear, skewering me to the wall. "You knew the escape would fail. And still you let me place my son into another woman's arms so that she could ride him to his doom."

I was wrong. Andromache's rage is not hot. It is a deep freeze spreading through this room on winding tendrils of ice.

Burning. Cutting. Cold.

"Yes. I knew."

"Why?" Helen's voice reaches me from somewhere far away.

I do not look at her. My words and my attention are fixed solely on Andromache. "For the same reason you let your son go. Because it was the only way."

Andromache's stillness is by far the loudest thing in this room. "I could kill you." She cocks her head to the side and watches me as I have felt the Hawk watch his prey before he snares them in his talons.

She is stronger. It wouldn't take much. A little squeeze. A few steps backward to the balcony ledge. I watch both scenes play out in the flat blackness of her eyes.

"You could, but you won't."

Her teeth bare in a snarl. "You know *nothing*."

"I know that as much as you want to hurt me, you cannot. Not without dishonoring Hector's memory."

At the sound of his name, she rears back.

Helen seizes the moment to place herself between us. "Explain this to us, Cassandra. Help us understand it." Even now, her voice is full of compassion.

"There was only one road open to Andrius that led out of the city, but it was twisted. Bent in places. I knew none of you would have taken it had you realized where it would lead." Helpless, my hands stir the air.

Searching. Always searching. "The things I see . . . They come to me in bits and pieces. I don't always know how they will fit together."

"Just as you did not know it was Patroclus in Achilles's armor whom you sent Hector to kill that day, damning us all?"

Pain cuts like a lash, drawing a whimper from my throat.

A sound I have not made in twelve years.

Andromache smiles the way she fights. Utterly without mercy. "He trusted you. He believed you when nobody else did, and you sent him to his death just as you sent his son to the slaughter." Her rage flash-boils the air between us. "He loved you, and you betrayed him."

The Crone. The Child. The Fury. The Wraith. The Hawk. Their voices are a howling gale, battering me from all sides. I step into the stillness at its center.

"You're right. When Troy falls, she will fall because of the things I did and those I failed to do." Invisible hands close around my neck, but I force the words through them. "But I never betrayed Hector. I would have paid any price to save him, but as much as I loved him, I knew him too. He would have died a thousand times to buy his son one chance at life. So that is what I gave him."

"I do not believe you."

I look to the balcony where it waits. Three feet of ledge. Four inches wide. Half a dozen steps away.

I close my eyes. "I am not asking you to believe me. I am asking you to let me save your son."

"All the words you speak are lies," Andromache hisses.

"Ask the herdsmen who guard the east wall. They will have seen a horse with a coat of flame run across the plain and into a chariot force of Achaeans. Ask them where the horse fled if you can't take me at my word."

"What do we do?" Helen seizes the leads of the conversation, though it is already far past anyone's control. "How do we help Rhea if she is trapped in the Achaean camp with the entire army between us?"

All the grief and tension flood out of me at once. "I don't know."

Andromache's laugh is an ugly, broken thing. "There was a time when I felt pity for you. A time when I believed you were merely sick or haunted." Her jaw hardens. "But there is only one thing wrong with you, Cassandra. You are a liar."

"Andromache, please." Helen reaches for her but thinks better of it. "Cassandra isn't the enemy here."

"No. Enemies face you across the battlefield, spear or bow in hand. They do not thrust hidden daggers into your back. Cassandra is a *traitor*."

Andromache's words are arrows. One after another, they hit their mark. I sag against the wall as she turns to leave.

"Wait!" Helen places herself in the doorway, blocking her path. "Where are you going?"

"To Priam and Hecuba. My husband's blood is on her hands. My son's. She will not go unpunished."

My head presses against the wall. Cold. Hard. "You can't go to the king. He will inform the Five of Andrius's flight."

Andromache freezes. Helen lets out a strangled sound.

"The traitor would send word to the Achaeans," she rasps. "They will pull their camp apart looking for Rhea."

I nod. "And when they find her and Andrius, they will show them the same mercy Achilles showed Hector."

35

RHEA

I CRADLE ANDRIUS'S sleeping body and press my back against the warm stones. Flies buzz over the tall grasses, droning in my ears, blending in with the beat of my drumming pulse.

There's no sign yet of the Achaean army, but they won't be long now. Even with Hector's best efforts to draw it out, the fight can't have lasted far into the afternoon. Once Hector won, the Achaeans would have gathered Achilles's body to bring it back here. And if Achilles . . .

No, don't.

Andrius makes a sound in his sleep. My eyes run wild over the circular shrine. Everything about this place is familiar, but it's as if the days and seasons have run backward until it appears as menacing to me as it did the very first time I saw it.

He is yours now, Rhea.

He is yours.

Andrius jerks his head before slamming it back down into my shoulder. Helen's draught is wearing off. When Andrius wakes, he'll be hungry. Wet. Missing his mother. And he'll express all these things the only way he knows how.

Just a few hundred paces away, the camp is alive with movement. Even emptied of the Achaean armies, there are people busy about their daily duties. The men won't know the difference between one baby and another, but the women . . . Some will have noted my absence, as they're sure to mark my sudden reappearance with a strange infant in my arms.

Sounds echo in the distance, carried by the wind. Beyond the swamp the Achaean army approaches across the plain. If I'm going to slip into the camp unnoticed, this may be my only chance.

Tall grasses tickle my arms as I make my way to the edge of the latrine huts. A band of carpenters passes by, pulling two wagons full of timber. I hold my breath, and then I slip out from the grasses and into the tail of their procession.

People rapidly fill the open spaces of the camp. I follow their gazes to the Kesik Cut, where the bridge has been lowered to make way for the armies. Agamemnon's and Menelaus's men cross first. What I see on their faces knocks the air from my lungs.

Not fear. Confidence.

Not defeat. Victory.

Hector.

The camp wavers like a mirage. I turn away from the savage cheers of triumph, and something twists inside my chest. Andrius starts to cry. He roots into my neck. His soft, wet mouth seeking someone else's warmth. Someone else's smell. But Andromache isn't here, and she isn't coming. I am all he has now.

Andrius's cries grow louder. Holding him tight, I walk without knowing exactly where I'm going. Not the living tents. There are too many women there, including Calis and several suspected Achaean informants. The bathhouse is too open. The infirmary no place for a child.

More cheers rise up behind me. Unable to help it, I look over my shoulder. A lone chariot crosses the Kesik Cut. Something bumps and pitches in the dirt track behind it.

The world wavers. Acid burns up the back of my throat. Staggering against the gathering crowd, I make for the bathhouse. The arched entryway beckons, but I head around the back to the small stream. I've barely reached the banks when the heaving starts. Spasms rack me. Over and over again till there is nothing left. Several pots of water lie on the muddy bank. I reach for one, but the handle slips from my shaking fingers. I sit down on the bank next to the broken shards of clay.

My shoulders quake with the effort of holding back this storm. It batters my rib cage, threatening to break me apart from the inside.

Andrius rubs his face into my neck. I pull him into my warmth.

His cries turn shrill.

"It's all right." I rock him gently. "I'm here. I'm not going anywhere."

My words do nothing to soothe him. I reach for the leather skin in my pack. My fingers fumble the flask to his mouth, but he's having none of it.

"What are you doing?"

I spin around.

Calis stands over me, her mouth set in a hard line. Many times I've felt her cold, beady eyes watching me in the camp. Out here by the stream, there is no hiding from them.

"Children are not allowed in the bathhouse," Calis snaps. "You know the rules. Soldiers enjoy the making of babies. They don't much care for the aftermath."

"We were just leaving." I make my way past, but Calis's fingers close around my wrist.

"Where have you been?"

Dread coils in the pit of my stomach. "What do you mean?"

She studies my blotchy face. "There's been no sign of you for days."

I suspected Calis had been tracking my movements. Now there is no doubt. "You're mistaken." When I try to free myself, her grip only tightens. "I've been busy with my duties. Just like everyone else."

"And what might those duties be? I've asked about you in the bathhouse and in the infirmary, and nobody seems to know."

Her words are a trap. I can't allow myself to be drawn into it. "Take it up with Ven or Isola, or even Lissia. Any one of them will tell you where I've been."

"They'll cover for you, more like." Calis's lips twist. "If you're truly a member of Odysseus's household, you're the only one the Pig King from Ithaca allows to work outside his settlement. What if I were to bring you there and ask him? What do you think he'd say?"

It's a bluff. My gut says she wouldn't dare address the king of Ithaca, not even to expose me. But if I'm wrong, it won't be long before Odysseus discovers who I am and exactly what I've been doing. And then Andrius...

My eyes move to the jagged pots of clay at my feet. Calis is larger than I am, but not by much. If I could grab that pot and strike before she cried out, maybe I could—

Calis grabs my hair and yanks. I fall forward, catching my weight on my hands before I crush Andrius beneath me. Pain burns my scalp.

"Let her go."

Calis releases my hair.

Tears of pain stream down my face. I blink them back and find Calis and Ven facing each other on the muddy bank of the stream.

"Stay out of this, Ven," Calis warns. "She's hiding something. I intend to find out what it is."

"Careful where you go digging," Ven warns. "Or you'll end up with dirt on your face."

"If you have something to say to me, spit it out."

Ven smiles. It's frightening. "Rhea isn't the only one with things to hide."

Calis blanches. "I don't know what you mean."

Ven tilts her head. "Does Agamemnon know you report to his brother, Menelaus? That you feed him information in exchange for status?"

Calis hisses. "Stupid whore. Don't speak about things that don't concern you."

"I have no intention to," Ven says easily. "So long as you return the favor."

Even backed into a corner, Calis does not cow. "You are every bit the liar she is. And what of the child? Whose business is he, then?"

Ven's eyes flick to mine briefly, asking for an explanation I can't give. "You were right when you said that Rhea is more than what she seems," Ven says calmly. "The girl runs personal errands for the king of Ithaca. That child in her arms is of Odysseus's blood. Begotten on one of his servants. Everyone knows how highly the king of Ithaca values his wife's opinion. Were the faithful Penelope to find out about the child, Odysseus's welcome home would be less warm than he might hope. Rhea is tending to the problem on his orders." Ven's lips tilt upward. "If you don't believe me, perhaps you should ask him. I wonder how he'd take to having such a private matter made public knowledge."

Calis turns white with rage. "Fine. But know this: I am watching you."

I wait until she is gone before I speak. "Do you think she believed you?"

Ven lets out a breath. "No. But she loves her own hide more than she hates either of us, and she isn't likely to risk it."

My body sags against the ground.

Ven takes in all the things I am trying to hide. "We haven't seen you days."

I adjust my hold on Andrius and busy myself with the skin of milk. "I was stuck behind the walls when the attack came."

"We thought you'd left us."

My cheeks flame because that is exactly what I tried to do.

"I hoped you'd gotten far from here by now," she says, surprising me.

"I tried." It is a whisper.

Andrius fusses, drawing both our gazes.

"Who is he?"

I could lie. I *should*. Instead, I am struck by a memory of Ven the first time I saw her. Tied and battered in a slave wagon bound for a foreign city. Her grief as heavy as her swollen breasts, leaking milk for the child who was taken from her. A boy like the one in my arms.

"Prince Astyanax. Hector's son."

Ven's eyes grow huge. "How . . ."

"It doesn't matter. We had a plan, and it failed. Now we're stuck here until I can come up with a better one."

I raise the skin to his mouth again. Milk streams down Andrius's face, making him gag. His coughing causes a swell of panic. I yank the skin free from his lips. One look at his sweet face, and despair fills me.

Andromache never should've asked me to do this. Cassandra never should've put the idea into her head. I can't protect Andrius. I can't hide him. I can't even feed him.

Hands wrap around mine. Gentle. Firm. Ven moves the milk back to his mouth but tilts the skin so that it lies horizontally.

"He is used to the breast. The milk from the skin is coming too fast. If you hold it this way and pinch the end, he will have to work harder to draw it."

Andrius drinks. Relief loosens every one of my limbs.

When I glance up at Ven, gone is the cold, ruthless woman who has held together our fragile web of shadows. In her place is the broken girl I met in that cart. The pain is fresh in her eyes when they meet mine.

"They can't find him," I say. "Whatever happens, we can't let them find him, Ven."

She studies the sleeping child. "There's only one place you can hope to hide the prince of Troy."

"And where would that be?"

The scars on Ven's face seem to glow. "In plain sight."

AN HOUR AFTER leaving us, Ven returns to the stream. She gestures for me to follow, and I do, too exhausted by the weight of my thoughts to ask questions. It isn't until we are standing in front of a small building near the west side of the camp that my mind summons sufficient strength to be wary.

"Ven?" I stare at the closed door to the weaving hut that sits beside the women's sleeping quarters. This part of the camp also holds the public cookfires and the second drinking stream. It's the only place in the camp that isn't dominated by men. Beyond the hut, the sea crashes against the white beaches of Sigeum Ridge.

"They are waiting."

They? My gaze moves between Ven and the small wooden structure. I've been inside a handful of times. Enough to know there are twelve looms, and at any given moment, exactly twice as many hands working them under Calis's hawk-eyed gaze.

"Calis has gone to make her nightly report to Menelaus," Ven says. "I've sent the others to prepare the many dead for their pyres, but we will not have long." When I do not move, Ven says, "This is not the kind of secret that can be kept without help."

Before I can respond, a commotion starts up on the far end of the cape near the Myrmidons' camp. Most of the Achaean soldiers have long since put away their weapons, but the Myrmidons remain in full armor. They gather around a single chariot, drawn by a man in flashing gold armor.

As if sensing my distress, Andrius snuggles closer.

"I don't want to involve anyone else in this," I say.

"They are already involved. Every woman inside that hut is there of her own free will."

"Because they don't know what we would ask of them."

Ven lifts her chin. "So tell them the truth and let them decide. The

Achaeans have already taken their freedom. Would you take their choices too?"

Her words cut through the fog surrounding me. I can't shield Andrius on my own. But revealing who he is means trusting others to protect the secret of his identity with nothing less than their lives. Lives they've already risked for months just by helping me.

Ven steps into the weaving hut. Letting out a breath, I hold Andrius tightly and follow.

"Why all the secrecy?" a familiar voice snaps. "You've better have a damn good reason for dragging us out—"

Salama stops short when I step into the room. The dozen women behind her wear similarly shocked expressions. Isola moves first. She breaks toward me, wrapping me up in her herb-scented arms. She steps back when Andrius makes a startled sound.

A wrinkle forms between Isola's brows. "We thought you might have gotten caught when the Achaeans surrounded Troy."

"I made it behind the walls just in time."

"Clearly." Salama smooths out her robes. Her words are glib, but the relief on her face warms me every bit as much as Isola's embrace.

"What is the word from Troy?" This time, it's Briseis who speaks. At her side, Lissia and Zeyra nod in silent greeting. Beyond them, more women. All of them sisters in this shadow war we have been waging.

"The Lower City has been ravaged," I say. "The people are crowded into the Citadel."

"Troy's walls will hold." Lissia offers it as if she's trying to convince herself as much as the rest of us.

"Her walls, perhaps. But what of her people?" Briseis asks. "Hector was more than their sword and their shield. He was their spine. They won't know how to stand without him."

None of the women speak.

"So the city will fall, and all of this will have been for nothing." There is anger in Salama's voice. Worse yet, despair.

"No. Not for nothing." I shift the child in my arms.

"Who do we have here?" Lissia smiles though her cat eyes are red-rimmed.

Ven nods. Placing the choice in my hands. My gaze moves over each person in the hut. Most faces are familiar to me, but a few belong to newer recruits I've not yet fully come to know.

All of them women who've trusted me.

Perhaps it's time to return the favor.

"This is Andrius," I say, giving them the name used by those who love him most. "Hector's son. And he needs your help."

36

HELEN

"MAMA. WHERE ARE YOU?"

The dreamy plea launches me from a dead sleep, thrusting me forward in the chair. Darkness consumes the tower's room, except for a thin shaft of moonlight. Outside, its glow reaches for a mountain that remains dark.

The light that was promised us has not appeared.

Andromache sleeps like her soul has long departed this world. Her fully dressed body is flung carelessly across the bed, and an occasional moan assures me she is plagued by nightmares. The hours of our vigil offer nothing but the promise of coming destruction. Not only for my friend who has lost everything—for all of us.

"Mama?"

Again, my body stiffens at the small voice. It does not come from the streets below, where the wailing of Troy's women persists. Laments that echo through the tower, carried up its cylinder core like a trapped breeze that twists into a cyclone.

"Hermione," I whisper. Though I know she is a grown woman now, my heart still reaches for the small girl who must have uttered such a cry. Night after night. A cry that will soon fill the mouth of every child in Troy.

Leave the little ones to me. I will gather them when the time comes.

Everything tightens, within and without. Normally the whisper of the wind is a comfort, but this time, something hardens. I am tired of being patient. Of pleading for the lives of innocents and for those I love.

I rise from Cassandra's chair, my aching back a sign I am not as ageless as the winehouse ballads claim. From the balcony's edge, my eyes fall to stones splashed with tears. So many tears for so many stories, all broken by Time's harsh sickle. How many have been tempted by this promise of a hard-won peace? Lured to a final fall that would put an end to their suffering once and for all?

Years ago, I might have jumped. A part of me longs to still.

And if you had, there'd be one less verse.

One less verse in a Song you did not compose and cannot fully understand. Because you do not see its ending.

And yet . . . *why?* Why all this needless suffering?

Love is not born without labor pains. Every mother knows this.

"Yes," I admit, shaking my weary head.

It is a love that burns, yet why must it burn so thoroughly?

The underbrush must be cleared so the path forward can be followed.

"Only there *is* no path through this!" I cry to the wind.

My aching hands open and close. I turn from the mountains in the east to the sea in the west, my gaze falling to a long line in the dirt. A black streak that stretches from Troy's walls, across the plain, and toward the enemy ships occupying the shoreline.

A scorch in the earth dug by Hector's dragged corpse.

My fingers tingle like they do when I've spent too many hours at the loom. The slick trail of blood shines beneath the moonlight. A sharp pain steals the breath from my chest. Could Hector be leading the way, fighting to protect his child, even from the grave?

The loving father brought low is the only way for his son to rise.

The whisper makes something at the back of my mind spark. Hunched shoulders. A weathered face. A kind if trembling word.

Andromache stirs angrily on the bed behind me. A reminder of how she behaved toward me for years, and of how much we've both changed with the arrival of Andrius.

All the words of reassurance I gave to Andromache, the promises of higher purpose and hope, ring hollow in my own ears. What if there is no meaning to any of this? No reason I was dragged from the daughter who was my home. From the healing work that gave pointless days some greater end, until I was thrust into the belly of a ship like stolen treasure.

No. Not treasure.

A *stowaway*.

The word sizzles like the sky after a summer storm. Hector's tracks glow silver as I pull the final thread through the void, an image forming from what were once worn, fraying fibers.

There is still someone who can save Andrius. If he will listen. If he will finally *hear* us.

If he will stand on his own two feet before kneeling in the dirt.

"NO, HELEN. HE will not listen," Cassandra insists. "He has *never* listened."

"He has. Once," I say. "He listened to Hector. Before the duel with Ajax. I saw it."

"Yes. The king heard Hector. *Hector.*"

Every time Cassandra cries her brother's name, Andromache retreats further into herself. She does not say a word, which is more terrifying than if she spoke volumes.

"And *we* are the ones who hold Hector's memory. Priam will hear us out. He must," I say, reaching for a headscarf. To wear it tonight feels not like a burden but rather like a reminder that the most sacred things are often veiled.

Despite her protests, Cassandra joins us for the journey to the palace. It is clear she is starving for Andromache's forgiveness. Yet Andromache will not give it. She walks beneath a threatening silence, fully veiled in midnight blue, her fiery eyes the only part of her face that is visible. We take to the Citadel streets, where refugees line every wall, taking in fresh air now that the fighting has paused so the Achaeans can prepare for Patroclus's funeral games. I place myself between Andromache and Cassandra, poised to receive any blows the Amazon might deliver, verbal or otherwise.

"Do what you can to help them. But do not give me any more false hope."

That was Andromache's only reply when I told her of my plan. She'd sat on the edge of Cassandra's bed, sharpening a sword Hector had left behind. At first, I feared she intended to use it on herself. Now I'm convinced Andromache means to use the blade on every Achaean she can find before one of them returns the favor, granting her the death wish she makes with every ragged breath.

"*Hector's worst fear was knowing I'd be dragged away in chains,*" Andromache said as she slowed her sharpening and lifted her chin. Tears long dried, all grief consumed by wrath, her nighttime transformation that of a chrysalis. Only in her case, she'd become something far more deadly than beautiful. "*I won't endure the life of a slave, Helen.*"

"*Then begin your struggle for justice by giving Hector the burial he deserves.*"

At that, Andromache's eyes had misted over.

"*We can still give Hector this one thing, Andromache—peace. It is the only way to get Andrius out of the camps. At least then you will be together, no matter what happens.*"

"*The only way,*" Andromache growled. "*Tell that to Cassandra.*"

The mother-turned-Amazon then wrapped her hair in cloth the color of night, sliding Hector's blade into a thin sheath at her hip. "*So be it. But if you steer me wrong as Cassandra has, I might just kill you both.*"

Ahead of us, a grunt from our guide's stout form forces our party to take a sharp left to avoid approaching soldiers, men who grieve their fallen prince the only way they know how—with jugs of stale wine and back-alley brawls while they wait for the next round of a war whose ending is decided.

Or maybe not, I wonder, wringing my hands.

When we reach the entrance to Priam's throne room, the Master of Keys approaches two silent figures who wait for us. They are the only men I could send for because they are the only two left in Troy whom I trust. Aeneas and Cyrrian, their eyes crimson and their faces gaunt. With Hector's death, we have all lost so many parts knitted together in one man— heir, son, husband, father, prince, brother, commander.

Friend.

Aeneas doesn't speak, yet Cyrrian gives me a look that could cut glass. "What is this about?" His gaze shifts to the old man accompanying us, a man whose eyes hold the same stormy sea. "We can't afford to leave the walls for long."

The Master of Keys is silent as usual, but I sense a shift in him at the sight of this younger soldier. The old man's twisted back stands a little straighter, even as the lines of his frown deepen. Beside me, Cassandra clicks her tongue, her movements those of a reptile that longs to shed its skin.

"I will explain once we have the audience of the king," I say, summoning the authoritative tone Andromache can no longer find.

We step into the dark throne room. Priam, a dry husk of a king, barely looks up as we enter. Hecuba's chair beside him isn't empty as I'd hoped. Neither is the raised platform the rulers sit upon like lifeless statues. Three of the king's Five are huddled together around their fading power. Laocoon is noticeably absent. So is Paris, though he has his archers to attend to along the walls, ready for when the battle resumes. From Cassandra's tower, I saw Paris rushing his elite force to the ramparts, bow in hand as the horse on the back of his cloak fluttered on the wind.

It almost made me proud of him.

The men of the council stop arguing when we approach. I can tell they are scheming, working tirelessly to spin Hector's death into a web that somehow benefits *them*. That they think there might yet be some escape brings their self-delusion to new heights.

"What do you want?" The queen's voice is hoarse from the hours of ceremonial wailing.

I step forward, knowing I have the least authority to speak, but that I am the one who must. "We require an audience with King Priam. Alone."

Anchises and Antenor, the oldest of the Old Blood, give our small party a cold glare.

Red-faced Polydamas is the one to answer. "Can't you see the king grieves?"

"It takes warm blood to know grief, son," Antenor says. Cassandra and I both stiffen at the accusations beneath his words.

"That's right. And according to Paris, the wife who abandoned him when he needed her most has veins that run with the icy ichor of the gods." Polydamas sneers. "Helen would see this city burn and all of us with it."

How convenient. If a woman who speaks out can no longer be deemed hysterical, simply say that she is heartless instead.

I turn to the only man in this hall who matters. "King Priam, please. Our request will take only a moment. Yet it must be made in private."

The old king's face softens at my voice. He has much to grieve and much he longs to forget, but maybe he remembers the times we sat together in this chamber. The only daughter by marriage or by blood who has shown him affection rather than apathy or fear.

"Leave us."

There is a firmness in Priam's command that transcends his frail appearance. His diminished Five obey, if begrudgingly. Queen Hecuba, however, does not.

Once the room is emptied of the council, Hecuba speaks, her voice weaker than her words. "Whatever you have to say to my husband, you can say to me."

I roll the option around my mouth like a piece of crystallized resin. Can Hecuba be trusted? The queen became an unlikely ally the day I was summoned before the council. Yet will she be loyal now that the thread is severed from the only son who had a claim on her heart?

Not severed. Only frayed.

"Let her stay. This business is hers as much as it is ours," Cassandra says cryptically.

"Very well, my queen," I continue. "We are here on behalf of Hector's son."

Priam pauses for what feels like a century. "My grandson is his mother's business now." He speaks like he is already resigned to Andrius sharing Hector's fate.

"Scamandrius is no longer *with* his mother."

Priam and Hecuba shift their weathered gazes to Andromache, a column of blue smoke. The entire time we have stood here, her face has not lifted from her sandaled feet.

A flush of color returns to Hecuba's cheeks. "What do you mean?"

I approach their thrones, kneeling on the cold ground. The council members will be held off for only so long, and we are running out of time.

"Your son did not die in vain. He did not run from Achilles out of cowardice. Hector ran to save his child. He ran so Andrius might escape, so the Trojan line might *live on*."

Priam closes his eyes, crumpling into his throne. He reaches for my arm with hands that tremble. "And *did* my grandson escape?"

"We know the prince made it beyond the city gates, but he and the rider who carried him were intercepted before they could reach the safety of

Mount Ida." I glance over my shoulder to where Aeneas and Cyrrian stand. Cyrrian helped Rhea at the east gate, but this is the first time he has heard the outcome. "Our rider sought shelter in the Achaean camps."

Cyrrian's face blanches.

Aeneas's measured voice echoes through the hall. "Then they are as good as dead."

"Not necessarily—"

"How's that?" Aeneas talks over me. "The Achaeans will discover your rider and kill him without asking a single question."

"*Her*," Andromache says, joining me at Priam's feet. "The reason our rider won't be killed on sight is because her face is already well known among our enemies. The girl who rode with my son isn't a mere servant. She's been spying on the Achaeans for months, feeding Hector information about their movements. Still, she won't be able to evade discovery for long."

"Especially not when they notice she carries a baby she did not have with her a week ago," Cyrrian says. There is a desperate edge in his voice that suggests his fear for her comes from a different place than love for Hector's son.

Hecuba throws herself onto the ground, pulling at her veil like she is beginning her ritual mourning all over again. "And who allowed *you* to use these tactics? Who gave you permission to put our grandson, our heir, in harm's way?"

"His father," Andromache replies flatly.

Priam's eyes travel from his overwrought wife to Andromache and back to me. "What are you asking us, Helen?"

"Go to him," I say without hesitation.

Every pair of eyes in the hall turns my way. Hecuba releases a half-mad chuckle. "The king of Troy cannot simply walk into the women's quarters of our enemy and—"

"It is not Andrius he must look for." My eyes hold Priam's alone, conjuring all the stolen tenderness we once shared. "The king must seek out Achilles."

Disbelief and a hundred questions hang heavy in the air.

"Achilles's tent sits on the edge of the Achaean camp," I explain. "Go to him under the veil of darkness and beg him to give Hector's body back."

"Did you not *see* the pleasure that monster took in desecrating our prince?" Cyrrian snaps. "Achilles has no concept of honor, let alone mercy."

"If anyone rides out to retrieve the body, it should be me," Aeneas says, trying to regain control of the conversation. "Hector was my kinsman. I would slit the throats of a dozen sleeping Myrmidons if that's what it takes to grant him eternal rest."

I rise from my supplicant's position, turning to the unlikely troops gathered here. "Have you all forgotten that I am one of them? I have met Achilles. The man. Not the legend spread by poets who are paid to turn mortals into demigods. Achilles ought to be feared, yes. But like all mortal men, he has a weakness."

I turn back to King Priam. "It is his father."

"Peleus," says Priam with a nod. He searches for the Master of Keys across the room. "I met the king of Phthia once. He is a glorious man."

"That's right. King Peleus," I continue. "A noble ruler who respects the long-standing rules of warfare. Unlike his reckless son. He is why our infiltrator into the camps must be Priam, a man, a *king*, who will remind Achilles of his father's long shadow. Cyrrian will accompany the cart as far as the swamp and wait for him there."

"I already said I would ride out," Aeneas protests.

"Your gifts are needed elsewhere," Cassandra, oddly silent until now, says.

I hold the king's gaze as I offer him this last chance at a younger man's glory. "Don't you see? Achilles will accept no one else. Only a loving father and even greater king can remind Achilles of his own father's honor. That is why you must humble yourself before him. Then and only then will Achilles consider returning the body of your son."

"But how will any of this help Prince Scamandrius?" Hecuba demands.

"Once King Priam is admitted to Achilles's household, he must find a way to deliver a message to a woman called Briseis. Rhea told us Achilles's prize has been a loyal friend. Briseis will alert Rhea to meet you at the river's edge. There, Rhea and the baby can join Priam and the cart to ride back to Troy."

"Why?" Cyrrian asks me. Though he does not say it, we all know he is really asking why we'd return Hector's son to a city that will surely burn.

"Because he is better off with us than with the enemy!" Andromache barks.

Priam's chin slumps forward onto his chest. After another long pause, he pats my hand. "The idea has merit. But I cannot help you."

Cassandra's swallowed moan erupts from behind me. "Why not?"

"Because the gods have spoken," Hecuba says. "You've heard the prophecies of Helenus. The star readings of Laocoon. Troy is doomed." She wags a finger at me. "Doomed the moment that woman stepped onto our shores."

"This city will fall," Priam agrees. "My name will die with me, and the memory of our golden Citadel will fade to ruin."

Cassandra flies to the front of the room like a bird of prey, throwing herself at Priam's feet. "Listen to me, Father. Listen *now* for all the times you did not listen before."

Priam shudders, his eyes darting around the room like Cassandra has set a pack of wild beasts upon him. Hecuba turns away from the spectacle in unveiled disgust.

"The gods *haven't* spoken. If they had, none of us would be here. What purpose do we serve if we can play no part? Our fates are never set in stone." Cassandra rises up to claim her full height. "My visions have proven true, yes, but not because they must. Our choices matter. And yet a recitation is always an easier song for mortals to sing. Most lack the courage to go against prophecy by contributing lines of their own."

I shiver as the wind whispers beneath the urgency of her words.

The princess has never looked more herself than she does now, clasping the old king's knee. "If the gods care about our doings, it is because they have given us the ability to act. To contribute our voice. *Please*, Father. Even if Troy is doomed, *this* end, one where Hector's son survives . . . isn't that a better song?"

His withered hand trembling, Priam reaches out to cup Cassandra's chin. "I have no song left in me, child."

A throat clears behind us all. "If I may, my king."

I turn, expecting to see a stranger. Yet the gravelly voice comes from the Master of Keys. He waits at attention, the clenched fists at his sides gripping invisible weapons.

Priam nods. "Go ahead, old friend."

The man stops to cough, his unused voice hoarse. "The only wound that festers worse than losing a child . . ." His eyes flicker across Cyrrian, who stares at the old warrior with the same confusion we all wear. "The only thing worse . . . is the knowledge you might have prevented it. Trust me, King Priam, as you did when we fought shoulder to shoulder. If you do not act now to save Hector's son, death will not spare you the torment of regret that follows."

Even Hecuba cannot look away. "You are a man who sought *kleos* above all else, Phineus. You would have your king go to this tyrant Achilles and *beg* him like a slave?"

"There is no glory in life worth having unless there is someone to pass it on to." The air crackles as the warrior's gaze reaches for the younger man who shares his blue-green eyes. Yet the Master of Keys does not address him.

"Let's not fool ourselves, Priam. If this city falls, we will not go down swinging in a fury of blood and sand like we would have in our youth. One thrust of an enemy spear and our names will be dust. Now, would you rather choke on your pride when the Achaeans slay you in this empty throne room? Or will you give your seed a fighting chance?"

"But how?" Queen Hecuba demands. "How would the king even *leave* the city undetected?"

"The funeral games," Cassandra says.

"She's right, and I know the Achaean kings," I add. "They think this battle is won. They'll be so focused on honoring Patroclus in order to keep Achilles in the fight, they will not be watching the plains closely. This will be the only opportunity."

Priam's head bobs ever so slowly. Without warning, the king grips my hand with his left and reaches for Cassandra's with his right. "I cannot promise I will make it back to Troy . . . but may the gods grant me the swiftness of winged Kairos as I try."

"I will accompany you, my king. As far as the gods allow us to go," vows the Master of Keys.

"All well and good, but who *are* you?" Cyrrian's question is one we have all wondered.

"I am merely an old man who has made too many shadows."

"And you will not seek to redeem yourself by sending my husband to an undignified death!" As Hecuba rises from her throne, she transforms from mourning mother to harrowing queen.

Cassandra stands in response, their mirrored profiles locked in a stalemate. "Will you not take our side just this once, Mother? This is about bringing home *Hector,* the only one of your children you ever loved."

The muscles in the queen's cheeks tighten. "Hector was the only baby I was *allowed* to love. For a short time, at least. The rest of you were handed off to wet nurses before I'd even risen from the birthing bed."

A flicker of compassion. An assurance that for all her sight, Cassandra never saw this.

The prophetess lowers her voice. "Then perhaps you will find a shred of mercy for Andromache, who has not only parted with her son while her milk still flows, but has sent him out among wolves. Because that was the only way to save him."

Andromache studies Cassandra as the young woman pleads with the queen on her behalf. Her Amazon's gaze knows no softness, but it no longer threatens murder either.

Hecuba says nothing. She sits back on her throne to resume her ritual weeping.

"Do not get too comfortable, Mother." Cassandra looks down from her tower of triumph at the parents who never once fought for her. "Before this night is done, much more may be asked of you."

37

RHEA

BRISEIS STOPS SUDDENLY on our way out of the weaving hut. I glance around her shoulder toward the beach, glowing golden in the dying light.

Hundreds of Myrmidons are gathered on the shores of the Aegean. Led by Achilles, their chariots cut circular paths around the massive pyre whose construction had just begun before the siege on Troy. Now that pyre is a tower of wood a hundred feet long, surrounded by scattered offerings and charred, bloodstained earth. My gaze climbs to the shrouded body set high on a flat piece of timber before swinging down to Achilles's chariot as it finishes its third and final revolution. Behind the wheels, still drawn by a length of rope, something dark and misshapen jerks across the ground.

My legs give out from under me, but Ven is there at my right. Salama on my left. Together, they hold me up between them.

He lies exposed to his enemies. Bones twisted and broken under tattered skin. Caked in blood and filth. Achilles didn't just take his life. No, Achilles stripped Hector of his armor and his honor, making him as small in death as he was large in life. I pray to any gods that can hear me that Andromache was not forced to watch.

The knife in my chest gives a vicious twist.

"Diomedes says the siege will be paused so Achilles can hold games in Patroclus's honor." Lissia's words are a thinly veiled warning to the rest of us. "There'll be feasting. Contests of strength. The men will be in rare form."

"But why would they stop the siege when they are so close to taking the Citadel?" I ask.

Briseis's striking face is somber. "Grief makes men stupid."

Salama's grip on my arm turns painful. "I care nothing for their grief."

I force myself to look back at the pyre. At the man with the white-blond hair to match his white-hot rage. Even from here the resemblance to Ajax is unmistakable, and yet they are as distant in my mind as the sun is from the moon.

Down on the beach, the Myrmidons stop their procession. In groups of two they slaughter dozens of pale white oxen and a handful of sheep, using the fat from their carcasses to pack the body. The last animals to die are two of Patroclus's hounds. I think the killing is finally over when a line breaks in the crowd. A group of men are dragged through the warriors by the binds on their hands. No, not men. Boys. Trojans. There are twelve of them, and the oldest can't be older than . . .

A cry works its way up my throat.

"Rhea, what is it?" Briseis takes hold of my arm.

I can't speak. I can't do anything but stare at the third boy from the left. His long, skinny limbs naked in the sun. My vision sharpens on his face of sharp angles and smooth cheeks, stark white with fear.

Rough hands pull me back. "Leave it," Salama says. "There's nothing you can do."

Achilles moves down the line of boys. One by one, his sword makes red slashes across their throats. My mouth opens, but there are no sounds. No words in any language for barbarism like this.

Wine and blood soak the earth. Achilles reaches the boy next to Larion, and with dawning horror, I recognize Nekku.

Nekku falls to his knees before the white-haired warrior. The wind swallows his cries for mercy, just as the sand swallows his blood. And then it is Larion's turn.

Next to Achilles, Larion looks like the boy he is, but when Hector's murderer raises his sword, it is a man who stands to meet it. Tears run down my face as I watch Larion square his shoulders. He doesn't make a sound as Achilles lifts his blade, but his gaze drifts to the beach to where I stand. Our eyes connect, and I whisper to him in the only language I have left in me.

I am here.

Larion smiles. The gap between his teeth is the last thing I see before the world turns red.

Grief wrenches a scream from my lips as I crumple to the ground. I don't know how long I lie there before someone helps me up. Long enough that the bodies have all been tossed on the pyre, fuel for the hungry flames.

"Why?" I ask, because if I reach a hundred years, I won't have lived long enough to understand this.

"Because he is suffering," Briseis says. "And suffering makes men cruel."

"So what does it make us?"

"Women." Briseis lets me go but doesn't move from my side. Together, we watch as one by one, the Myrmidons on the beaches take their long tails of hair and sever them with the edges of their swords. Achilles is the last. Climbing the delicate mass of timber, he takes the long, white braid and places it in Patroclus's stiff hands. Offerings made to honor one fallen warrior while another lies facedown in the mud.

Salama sneers. "He deserves to suffer. They all deserve to suffer for what they've done." Her hatred is a seed planted deep inside my chest.

Briseis regards Salama with dark eyes. The few years separating the two women might as well be lifetimes. "Not all Achaeans are monsters. Just as not all Anatolians are heroes. Men are men regardless of where they come from."

Ajax's smiling face flashes through my thoughts, and the hatred sprouting inside me withers and dies. Beside me, Isola's chin trembles. It makes me wonder whose face it is she sees in her mind.

Down on the beach, flame is set to the pyre. The sickly-sweet smell of burning wood and flesh drifts over us from the beach.

Ven's voice rises up in the silence. "Return to your places. If we are to hide Rhea and Andrius we can't afford to attract attention." She turns to me. "There's a woman in the servants' tents with a newborn. Dirga. She'll feed the child when he wakes. I've told her the same thing I told Calis. That the child is Odysseus's bastard and that Rhea is caring for him. If anyone asks, that is the story we spread."

Dread pools in my stomach at the thought of bringing Andrius into those tents full of women. Most of their sympathies will lie with us, but there are a few, like Calis, who'd do anything for the Achaeans' favor. To expose Andrius to their eyes will be dangerous. Almost as dangerous as trying to hide him.

My feet drag as I make my way to the women's tent in the fading light. It's as if Andrius's weight has tripled in the last hour. I'm passing the bathhouse with Andrius in my arms when my name echoes across the camp.

"Rhea!"

My sandals grow roots to the earth.

Ajax makes his way toward me through a throng. He's dressed in full armor. His helmet tucked in the crook of his arm. Towering shield slung across his back. Dozens of soldiers stand between us, but Ajax rises head and shoulders above them. His face is blood-spattered and so handsome, it causes a wrenching inside my chest.

Ajax stops directly in front of me. A small group of warriors stand at his back. I recognize Teucer among them. They regard me with curious expressions as I drink in the sight of Ajax's face.

The space between us shrinks without either of us taking a single step.

One of his men says something that makes the others laugh. Ajax sends them on their way with a word.

Smirks as they pass. Teucer offers me a quick smile I have no heart to return. He claps Ajax on the back before he follows after the others.

Ajax doesn't even look at him.

"I've missed you," he says.

Ajax has taken leave of his senses. There's no other reason he'd be saying such impossible words where anyone might hear them.

"What are you doing?" I whisper.

Ajax blinks. I watch him register where we are. How close we are. I wait for him to move back. He doesn't.

He reaches for my face, stopping short when Andrius makes a sound. A wrinkle forms between Ajax's brows as he studies the contents of my sling. "Who do we have here?" he asks, his voice gentle.

"He . . . he belongs to a friend of mine." My throat threatens to close. "I promised to look after him until she can."

Every line of Ajax's face softens when he bends low, running one massive knuckle over the soft down on Andrius's head. "He's a sweet little thing." The touch elicits a sharp howl from Andrius, who flails pitifully, as if sensing his enemies close. Ajax nods approvingly. "With a warrior's heart."

Just like his father.

Images lash through my head again. Hector's body naked and broken. Left for the dogs and the birds.

A shudder runs through me.

"Are you fond of children?" Ajax's eyes are heated as he raises them to mine.

Unable to speak, I nod.

A smile tugs at the corner of his lips as his hand moves from Andrius's head to my face, brushing a curl behind my ear.

Ajax drops his hand before I can step away. "There are games tonight to honor Patroclus. I want you to come."

"I can't. I . . ."

"Please, Rhea." Hope shines on his face. The knowledge that he and his men are so close to victory, to all the dreams once shared within our stone wall. "Say you'll come." His words bring me back in time to that night outside Agamemnon's settlement. The night Ajax first asked me to meet him inside the old shrine. How different everything would be if I'd said no instead of yes.

The dimple flashes at the corner of his mouth, and I don't regret any of it. After everything that's happened, I would still go back and make the same choice. And it makes me hate myself just a little that even now, a part of me hums with joy just being near him.

I take a step backward. "I don't feel like watching the games, Ajax."

A flash of surprise. Maybe even hurt. And then an expression I know well. The one that means he has set his mind on something and will not stop until it is done.

"Then do it for me."

I shift Andrius in his sling as if I could somehow hide him from all the eyes around us. We can't continue standing out here in the open. Someone will see us. Someone will ask questions. I have to get him to stop talking. I have to get him to—

"Do you trust me?" Ajax asks abruptly.

"Yes," I say. Because I need him to walk away and because it's true. I do trust Ajax. Mother goddess help me.

Ajax grins. A gesture full of hope he's no longer trying to hide. For reasons I can't explain, it scares me.

"Then promise me you'll come."

I close my eyes. My parents. My sisters. Larion. *Hector.* How many more people will I lose? How much more will I be forced to give up before it is enough? Life has no guarantees. No promises beyond this moment. And if I only have a few of those moments left, I know who I choose to spend them with.

I look up at Ajax and I say the same words I said to him all those moons ago.

"I promise."

~⚬~

ANDRIUS SCREAMS IN his sling. He's been like this for hours. The woman Dirga has nursed him several times, and though he finally takes the breast, it's a battle.

I've tried everything. Talking. Singing. Bouncing and swaying until my hips ache. Isola appeared an hour ago with some soothing salve for his chest. Nothing helps. Andrius is inconsolable. Worse yet, his relentless cries are starting to draw notice.

"What's wrong with him?" Salama drops down onto a pallet beside me. A group of women pass us, headed for the funeral games about to begin across the camp.

I pat Andrius's back the way I've seen Andromache do. It only makes him cry harder. "He misses his mother."

He is not alone.

Salama's gaze flits about the room. "If he keeps on like this, they'll take him from you and give him to someone who can handle him."

I grit my teeth. "I've got to find a way to keep him quiet." There's also the small matter of a promise. My gaze drifts back to the open doorway where more girls are leaving for the funeral games. Ajax will be searching the crowd. If he doesn't find me, he may do something foolish, like come looking for me again. More attention we can't afford.

I'd hoped to hand Andrius off to Salama while I went to the games, but one look at her face when I changed his soiled linens cured me of that illusion.

I stand. "I'm taking him for a walk."

Salama looks at me as if I've sprouted horns. I move to the door, supremely conscious of the dozens of eyes boring into my back. Andrius lets out a furious bellow when a gust of sea air hits us. Other than the wind, the night is warm. With the games under way, the nearby settlements stand empty but for the barest number of guards.

As I walk, the shrill pitch of Andrius's wails is slowly drowned out by the noise up ahead.

I hear them before I see them. Thousands of Achaeans forming a half circle facing the northern end of Cape Sigeum. Cheers and jeers blend together in a deep, masculine roar that dwarfs even the sound of the waves.

The men in front of me roll and crash into each other like the sea. Whatever games are going on in the center of the circle, they're only part of the entertainment. Smaller brawls have broken out in the crowd. I've taken a few steps back when something moves in my peripheral vision. A lone figure leaving Odysseus's settlement.

The man's body is mostly obscured by his dark green cloak.

As if sensing my gaze, the man turns. Dark eyes drop down to the child in my arms. His brows draw together, and I forget to breathe.

I know that face.

It knows me too.

I spin on my heels and push into the crowd, weaving between sweat-soaked, vibrating bodies. When I glance over my shoulder, the prince isn't following.

Not just any prince.

Paris.

Paris, who now sits on the Five and wields its power.

Paris, who refused to give Helen back to the Achaeans even when doing so would have made him a hero. But only because he was buying his time.

Paris, who from the launching of that first Achaean ship intended the war to end exactly this way. With Hector lying at his feet.

Tremors travel up my legs as I stay tucked into the mass of churning men. Did he recognize us? No, he couldn't have. In the weak light, it would have been almost impossible to note the telling streak in Andrius's hair.

I shudder. Andromache never trusted him, but she also underestimated him. And now there is no way for me to warn her.

The crowd jostles me forward. I move sideways, circling back toward the hill at the edge of the swamp crowned by ancient stones. Grasses tickle my feet as I climb to the top of the shrine wall. From here, I have a view of both the field of competition and the rest of the camp.

I scan the surrounding area, but Paris has melted into the shadows. I cannot stop whatever he is doing. I can only do my best to remain unseen. Only when I'm sure he's gone do I switch my attention to the spectacle below.

A chariot race has just concluded. The men scream and cheer as Diomedes collects his prize.

Sitting in a chair at the center of the field, Achilles is a bronze statue, the strands of his freshly cut hair dancing in the wind. A golden urn with two ornate handles lies in his lap, where it is gripped tightly by his hands.

At a gesture from Achilles, half a dozen Myrmidons move forward to draw a large circle in the sand. Their voices fade as I eagerly scour the crowd for a familiar mane of golden hair.

A boxing match commences in the center of the circle, but it is over almost before it begins, earning a groan from the men. The air crackles when Achilles signals the next event. Roars of excitement rise from the crowd, making me think that all the contests until now have been mere preludes to this.

Prizes are brought forward from Achilles's ships to be paraded in front of the audience. The first I can't see from here. The second prize draws approval from the men. Even from this distance, I can tell that the girl is uncommonly beautiful. With strong shoulders for carrying water and wide hips for bearing children.

The third prize is a shield. My gaze fastens on the bold flame painted proudly in the upper corner, where a scrap of white fabric has been lovingly tied over the stylized image of the *alev*. From the end dangles a signet ring.

My head fills with images. The razor smile of the warrior who wielded that shield. His war cry cutting through the camps as he charged over the Achaeans' wall. The way his whole being seemed to glow with life the morning of the festival when Sarpedon won that veil and that ring from Andromache. A story Andromache recalled often with laughter in her eyes.

Tears fill mine.

Down below, the competitors jostle each other for a chance to claim the prizes. Their excitement is doused when Odysseus steps into the circle. His posture dares anyone to meet him. For a moment, it seems as if nobody will answer his challenge. Then the crowd parts, and a giant joins him.

Ajax strips to the waist. Oil and sweat gleam across his wide chest, making him look like molten gold poured into the shape of a man. One that towers over his opponent.

Odysseus smiles as he watches Ajax approach, but Ajax doesn't notice. He is too busy studying the hill where I stand.

Achilles's men bring the prizes. Ajax inspects the girl briefly before he nods. Pain slices my chest. I almost turn around and walk away, but something stops me.

The match begins. Ajax and Odysseus attack each other with brutal savagery. Blood spatters the sand. Ajax scores a point before Odysseus clips the back of his leg, forcing him down to one knee.

Ajax slams Odysseus to the ground, but the Ithacan wiggles out of his grasp. Odysseus drives his head into Ajax's nose. Blood spatters. Ajax roars and retaliates with a vicious takedown that leaves Odysseus momentarily stunned. Ajax is stronger and faster, but Odysseus fights as if he can see every one of the younger man's moves before he makes them.

Blow after blow. Wound after wound until they are both covered in blood.

I watch until I can't bear it anymore. Until the child in my arms is screaming the way I wish I could. I swallow the rising bile, and I do what I should've done in the first place. I walk away.

* * *

NIGHT DRAGS ON dark and heavy. The wall of rock at my back is a shield against the world, but still, the sounds of revelry reach us from outside the stone circle.

Cold seeps into my skin. Beside me, Andrius sleeps soundly on the bed of my cloak. I gave him the rest of the goat's milk and rocked him for an hour before he finally succumbed to exhaustion. It's a battle I'm also in danger of losing when a disturbance in the air forces my eyes open.

Ajax lands in the dirt at the far side of the circle.

I'm on my feet before I feel myself moving.

His hair is matted with sweat. Crimson dots speckle the stubble on his jaw, where an ugly bruise is already forming. Fresh blood drips down his chin from a cut on his lip.

I start toward him, drawn by an invisible force. Rocking forward on my toes, I reach up for the wound. His hand catches mine. Heat where our fingers touch.

Everything inside me goes still in response to some subtle shift. Some turn in the stars I can't see. "Who won the match?"

Ajax's hand spasms around mine. "It was a draw. I would've beaten him, but Odysseus cheated like he always does." His voice is bitter. Hard. "We divided the spoils."

"Who took the girl?" I try to hide how much the question hurts, and I fail.

Ajax's eyes stare down into mine. "I did."

The way he's acting. Guarded. Distant. It's nothing like him.

"What's wrong, Ajax?"

"I spoke to Odysseus tonight."

My heart takes a cold plunge into my guts. "About what?"

"You."

I pull my hand free. "Why would you do that?"

"Odysseus has never heard your name. When I described you to him, he had no idea who you were." His face is etched in marble just like the night we first met. "Odysseus is a conniving bastard, but he wouldn't lie about something like that. Not when there's nothing in it for him."

Dread pools in the pit of my stomach. Odysseus knows the Trojans have an informant in the camp. He's done everything in his power to flush out the shadow. How long before he pieces Ajax's mystery woman together with the spy he's been searching for?

It could be moments or it could be days. It all depends on what Ajax told him.

I glance down at Andrius's sleeping form. Helplessness overwhelms me. "What did you say?"

It's a moment before Ajax answers. "I said that I must've been mistaken, and then I left."

Ajax's gaze holds mine, and I realize that he knows. He *knows*.

Tenderness and sadness mingle in my breast. "Thank you." The words are too small a payment for what I owe.

"You can thank me by telling me who you really are."

"I am Rhea."

Before I can make a sound, he shuts down the distance between us. "You don't belong to Odysseus. You don't belong to anyone in this camp. If you did, you wouldn't need to lie. Whatever your secret, you're risking your life to keep it." He grabs my arm in an iron grip. It hurts, but as angry as he is, he still holds himself back.

"Tell me the truth. You owe me that much." Anger and suspicion swirl in his eyes, but it's the hurt that cuts my legs out from under me. I've wounded him. I've betrayed his trust in a way that can never be forgiven, and still, he didn't turn on me when he so easily could have.

"I can't."

Exasperation paints the strong lines of his face. "*Why?*"

"Because you wouldn't understand!" I scream the words and push at his chest, trying to carve some space between us.

Ajax cages me between his hard body and the rock wall. "You will tell me." His voice is a growl. "Or you'll force me to do something we'll both regret."

"Would you hurt me, Ajax?" I ask quietly. "Because that's what it will take."

He steps back, repelled by my words—an echo of other words once spoken between us. His eyes rake my face, and I have my answer now. Just as I had my answer then. No matter what he says, Ajax won't make good on his threat.

It is the only reason it works.

I draw back, knowing what I have to say and what it will risk. Knowing that I must do it anyway. "My name is Rhea. I am a servant of Prince Hector and Harsa Andromache. Since last spring, I've been making my way into the camp through the swamp to spy for the Trojans."

Ajax's nostrils flare. He takes a clumsy step backward. "Impossible."

His disbelief sends a crack through the dam I've erected inside myself. All the sadness and pain and *rage* I've been holding back come flooding out in a torrent.

"Why? *Why* is that so hard to believe?" The bars of my ribs rattle painfully when I picture Ven's face. The harsh scars on her cheeks. Salama's terrifying smirk. Briseis's broken beauty, and Isola's quiet courage. Or Andromache's . . .

Gods, Andromache.

The way she watched her husband walk to his death and then placed her son in my arms. Because that was the only way she could protect him. Pride and love batter the walls of my heart, because I was there and I *know*.

No warrior has ever been braver.

"Should I have simply accepted the inevitable? Should I have sat and watched as the people I loved were slaughtered?" I fist my hands at my sides—hands that are too small and weak to bring down an enemy but that have still found a way to be useful. The thought drains the last of my rage until there's only sadness. "I watched my home burn once, Ajax. I couldn't stand by and watch it happen again."

A flicker of sympathy, and I realize with amazement that he understands. He understands my reasons even if he doesn't like them. The knowledge leaves me reeling. If I'd told him . . . if I'd trusted him with the truth all those moons ago, perhaps we wouldn't be here. Perhaps everything would be different. But I didn't and it isn't, and now we'll never know what could have been.

Dangerous. Impossible.

Time runs slow as honey. The air is saturated with all the things I've said, and those I didn't. Every conversation. Every laugh and word and touch. Every moment we shared hangs suspended in the space between us.

His face turns stark white beneath his bruises. "You used me. You worked me for information and then you fed it to my enemies."

"The people I love," I say, desperate to make him see that this was never what I wanted. "It might've started that way, but that's not how I feel now. It isn't what drove me to meet you in these stones. I came because I cared. Because I didn't know how not to." This time, I'm the one who steps forward. "The hours I spent here with you were the moments I lived for."

He shakes his head as if this is a nightmare, and he wants nothing more than to wake from it. "You lied to me. About everything."

I love you, Ajax. That was never a lie.

The words stick in my closing throat.

Ajax grabs fistfuls of his hair. Pain flashes across his face as he fights with himself.

At last, his hands fall to his sides. When he looks at me, his massive shoulders are rounded. The darkness is back in his eyes, so deep and black it eats even the light of the distant stars.

I am losing him.

Tears pour down my cheeks. He watches them fall as if they mean nothing to him. As if he is already erasing every moment we shared from his memory. He tears his gaze away and lets it fall on the sleeping child between us. "If I ask you something now, would you give me the truth?" His words are distant. Utterly hollow.

Everything inside me wants to reach for him. "Anything."

Slowly, Ajax lifts his head. "The day of my duel with Hector. It wasn't the gods who guided his sword, was it, Rhea?"

The pain drives me to my knees.

Something dies in his eyes. He turns away. His throat bobs as if it's costing him everything to speak. "I didn't enter the wrestling match tonight for the sake of any prize. I fought for the same reason I went to speak with Odysseus. I did it for you. I thought that if I won the girl, Odysseus might take her in exchange for you."

His movements are heavy when he lifts himself up onto the shrine wall. He starts to lower himself down the other side but stops at the last moment. "You said you couldn't bear to watch your home burn again. I think you should know . . ." The barest hint of his profile. "You were home for me."

38

ANDROMACHE

THE CLOAK FLUTTERS on the wind, a bright ribbon in a city of bones. Any movement in this lifeless tomb we once called the Citadel is enough to capture my attention. My eyes travel slowly up the hooded figure. For a brief moment, the spell cast by my shuffling feet is broken. This section of the city, once a realm of sensory riches, has turned the same dull gray that coats my insides. Streets drained of all color. Every brick and building covered in a layer of ash.

It is the third night of Patroclus's funeral games. King Priam will depart for the Ilium plain as soon as the sun is down. As their party made preparations, I took to these crowded streets. Wandering among the city's refugees as they sleep like the Shade who haunts its stones and howls from the walls.

Waiting.

For this one small victory—the unlikely return of my son. The feeble chance to cradle him close, whispering words of love, as what remains of Troy goes up in smoke.

It is a more merciful end than the tip of an enemy spear.

One deep breath, and I draw closer to the hooded figure. Heavy footsteps in the dark. The faint scent of myrrh riding the breeze.

The cloak rounds a corner, and I follow. A wider street opens in front of us, the slate gray tinted silver in the moonlight. Hundreds of people rest on either side. Most sit erect like statues with backs pressed to walls, but others slump forward like they're corpses already. Once the air began to clear, many abandoned the stink of the crowded homes to sleep beneath the open sky. While they still can.

I watch as the cloaked phantom moves among them. Seeking warmth. Searching for the comfort of a face it knows.

No, it isn't that . . . The frigid wind slices through me. He is *hunting*.

But hunting *what*?

The cloaked figure pauses when he comes across a girl clutching an infant to her breast. He moves up the street to the next woman who has a child. And the next . . .

My insides twist. Clouds pass over the moon, banishing another layer of shadow. As the night brightens, the cloak before me glows anew. A shock of color among muted tones.

A blood-red robe of Apollo.

I follow the crimson cloak into the High Temple's courtyard. It sits unguarded, abandoned by soldiers for the walls. A second red robe slinks out from the shadows like a snake, merging with the first as their arms link. The pair approach the temple's bronze doors with a confidence that suggests the barrier might just part for them.

This scene is one I've witnessed before, only in reverse.

Aethra and Clymene.

I close in on Paris's servants and slip behind a statue of Athena, her spear ready and her shield stamped with the Gorgon's head. Then comes the sound of a lock turning in a door, followed by the scraping of wood across stone. The two women slip inside the High Temple.

I race after them, shoving my arm through the black crack a second before the heavy door slams shut. Pain sends a wail up my throat, but I swallow it. Pressing my body to the inside wall, I hold my breath in darkness, listening for the patter of small feet.

They haven't seen me. At least not yet.

Slinking among the shadows, I move deeper into the temple. Although the oil lamps lining the perimeter burn bright, the dank cavern is empty.

Aethra and Clymene move toward the green pool where Andrius's dedication ceremony took place. The women pause in front of the waterfall fed by an underground spring.

Another sign of life below this city.

Clutching oil lamps, the women climb onto the edge of the lower pool and walk along the narrow shelf toward the waterfall. They disappear behind it.

I wait a few moments, then plunge my hand through the same wall of water. My fingers find no slimy rock, only empty space. A hidden doorway. I slip behind the waterfall and through the narrow gap it hides.

The ground disappears beneath me.

It isn't a far fall. My palms sting as I meet the hard ground of a small chamber. The roar of rushing water fills my ears, echoing in the darkness all around me.

I rise to my feet, and the cool point of a blade kisses my throat.

"You're not meant to be here, Harsa," says a grating voice I recognize.

"You're right. I am not a snake who hoards secrets instead of helping my own people." I raise my eyes from the gnarled fingers on the blade to Laocoon's gaunt face. "Nor am I a traitor."

The age-spotted hand begins to shake, as does the knife. What I glimpse in the old priest's eyes isn't malice. And that . . . surprises me.

So does the wetness trickling down my chest.

Blood.

It isn't mine.

"I *am* helping my people." Laocoon's gaze drifts to the far wall. The sound of weeping greets me over the rushing water.

Gone are the hoods hiding the women's faces. The older one is slumped against the wall, legs extended lifelessly. Her throat slashed and her eyes gaping.

Clymene—the servant who gave birth to Paris's bastard—sits in a crimson pool beside her mother, shaking in shock as she clutches the dead woman's hand.

I stumble backward until I hit a slick wall. None of this makes sense. If these women were working for Paris and Laocoon, why would the priest kill one of them?

"They are searching for the little prince." Laocoon's blade drops to his side. "For Scamandrius."

My son's name on his blood-drained lips makes my stomach turn.

"I couldn't allow them to reach Paris." He nods at Clymene and what is left of Aethra. "They'd tell him the child cannot be found within these city walls, endangering the king's mission."

The truth lands like a blow. Laocoon knows about Priam's journey across the plain to meet Achilles. He knows my son is no longer in Troy.

"How?" My voice is a weak croak.

"The king trusts me with his secrets." The old priest takes a step to the left, revealing a circular stone stamped with a small serpent. Unlike the stone in Kalawashi's kitchen, there was no need to bust this one open. It's been slid away, its mechanism unlocked. As if waiting for someone to emerge from down below.

"Three nights ago, while I held vigil as our men fought for the Merchant Quarter, I saw Paris emerge from this hidden entrance," Laocoon says. "It leads to a labyrinth beneath Troy that is known only to the king and myself. At least, that was what I thought."

"Paris has been using it to reach the Gate of Ghosts," I say, unsure of Laocoon's part in this but almost certain I'm not telling him anything he doesn't know. "To reach his contacts among the Sea Peoples."

The priest's face hardens with a look that resembles despair. "The Sea Peoples are not the only enemy of Troy that Paris has wrapped in his traitor's cloak."

One by one, the walls fall.

Paris's destination was not the Dardanelle Straits. Or even if it was at times, he often made a significant detour.

Riding his chariot right into the Achaean camps.

Trading Troy's secrets to our enemies. Perhaps to Odysseus himself.

But *why*? Why would Paris destroy the city *he* wants to rule?

My eyes fall back to the serpent stone. To the den it conceals, which— according to Laocoon—is no mere tunnel but a labyrinth with multiple chambers. Perhaps some are large enough to hide those in the Citadel . . . at least, before my allies filled that Citadel with survivors from the Lower City.

It hits me all at once.

Paris does not intend to destroy Troy. Merely the parts that are of no benefit to him.

But what is it that Odysseus gains from him in return?

"How?" My mouth can barely repeat the question, but I must understand. How Laocoon discovered that Paris was conspiring with the enemy, especially when I've long suspected the traitor was the priest before me.

"The stars." Laocoon studies me anew. Not with a thinly veiled contempt, but with a concern that feels genuine. "I track their movements along with the phases of the moon, much as our ancestors did. Paris used this passageway to leave the city hours ago, but no merchant ship would sail tonight on account of the tides. So I ask you, Harsa Andromache, where could our Master of Trade be headed instead?"

I gesture to Clymene huddled in the corner, her sobs silenced by terror. "I have a notion she could tell us."

Clymene's wild gaze darts between us. "Don't kill me, I beg you. To survive a master like the prince, I only did what I had to do. *Please*, Harsa. I am a mother too."

And that is all it takes to dampen the blaze within me. There's no time to deal with her anyway. I turn back to Laocoon, who awaits me with an expression of satisfied determination.

"Paris has betrayed Troy." Again, he raises the glinting blade. "I intend for the next time he returns to the city to be his last."

"But how did he access this passageway in the first place?" I ask, thinking of the stones in the Citadel homes that would not budge.

Laocoon bares stained teeth as he lifts his hand of golden rings. The third is a signet ring like the one I gave Sarpedon, its raised serpent meant to leave a stamp.

Or in this case, a key meant to fit into a lock.

"As a guardian of Troy's past and a protector of her future, I hold one of the keys to the serpent stones. King Priam has the other. Paris could have easily traded one ring out for another. I suspect the king would hardly notice."

"The prince will return to the city soon," Clymene says urgently, more than willing to double-deal if it spares her life. "We heard him say so. As soon as Patroclus's funeral games are finished."

"Then why not use this Gate of Ghosts to get as many people out of the city as possible?" I demand.

Laocoon shakes his head. "If the Achaeans attack the city again at dawn, they will surround the plateau to prevent anyone from escaping."

Dread grips my pounding heart. Paris cannot learn about Rhea and the cargo she carries. He can't discover that Andrius hides in the Achaean camps.

You must not lose them, my alev.

The whisper of Hector's unwashed body and unblessed spirit reverberates through this chamber of stale air.

My gaze drops to Laocoon's blade. It is the only way this can end. Even if Rhea escapes the camp and returns to the city, Andrius will never be safe here.

Not unless Paris himself is dead.

"I'll do it." I extend an open hand to Laocoon.

I should have done it years ago.

"No, Harsa." The priest removes his signet ring and presses it into my palm. "Your duty is to your son and to Troy's people. I will handle the traitor who seeks to bring down her walls from within."

I study Laocoon, and he returns my gaze with an expression I've never witnessed. One that speaks of all the values we share despite others that might separate us. Perhaps he was right when he said I've failed to notice the things I've most looked down on. That is my mistake.

"I will always do right by Troy," the priest says.

For the first time, I believe him.

I point to Clymene. "What about her?"

"My dressing room is behind the altar to Apollo. Secure her inside it." Laocoon's eyes find mine one last time. "May the gods grant safe passage to Hector's son."

I nod, my heart begging the same. Clymene yelps when I grab her arm and drag her back through the hidden chamber's entrance.

"Harsa," she whimpers once we're aboveground. "Paris isn't the only one who will be searching the Citadel for your son. They will come for him soon."

The bitter promise stops me in my tracks. "Who will?"

Clymene shakes her head. "I don't know. Prince Paris never revealed his identity. But I assure you that whoever guides Paris's hand, with Hector no longer blocking the path to the throne, he will be eager to eliminate your son."

Fear for Andrius rises up like a two-headed snake, but I push it down. I must keep my wits. Rely on my rage and nothing else.

I shove Clymene into Laocoon's dressing room and secure the door with an iron bar. The priest's serpent ring glistens on the back of my hand as I press my face to the wood and whisper, "If we are able to move people into the den beneath the city, I will do my best to ensure your child is among them."

Though it will not be me who fulfills that promise. Not when I can no longer move through the Citadel openly, thanks to this woman's treachery. If there are others searching for Andrius, they will quickly grow suspicious if they see me without him.

I turn my back on Clymene and move toward the forest of pillars leading back to the temple's entrance. Perhaps the gods will show more mercy, but I cannot afford to.

A voice emerges from the alcove to my right. "You shouldn't blame her."

I step into the shadows of the corner that houses the Great Dog megalith. Along with a dozen Luwian gods whose names will be forever lost if this temple falls.

"The stupid girl schemes to increase her son's standing. That is all."

Words from a woman who has spent her life doing the same.

A searing pain rips through me.

And look where that favored son ended up.

Queen Hecuba rises from where she is lighting incense to Hannahanna. It seems her fear for Priam has moved her to seek childhood comforts once more. The queen's eyes are dry now. Steady and cold. "Where are you going, Andromache?"

"To the tower." I see no reason to hide it. Not when Hecuba knows what this night has in store and all that is at stake.

The queen's nod tells me she heard every word Clymene blubbered. I watch her shrewd mind chewing on its scheme.

"Make sure the tower door is secured. When we barred Cassandra there, we ensured there was no thicker door in all of Troy."

I nod and leave Hecuba to what may well be her final prayers. As soon as I reach the tower, my body explodes up its winding staircase. Cassandra and Helen sit silently beside the hearth. They stare up at me in bewilderment.

Helen stands. "What is it?"

I point to the empty cradle beside the bed. The place I spent my final night with Hector before I became this fury who seeks only revenge.

That isn't all you seek, my alev.

I push away the whisper, wiping a trail of soot and sweat from my brow. "None of us can leave the tower. No one can know Andrius isn't here. *This is how we protect my son.*"

HOURS LATER AND still no one has arrived.

It's the uncertainty that makes me uneasy. If Laocoon isn't the superior mind working behind Paris, then the real phantom will have to show his face. He must. With Hector dead, what's stopping him?

Again, I stare at the balcony's long fall. *What's stopping me?*

The wind that pushes me back into Cassandra's room no longer carries the rumble of racing chariots. Patroclus's funeral games will be over soon, and now the feasting in his honor will commence.

I envision King Priam, guarded by Cyrrian and the Master of Keys, making his way past the smoking remains of the Lower City to depart through the south gate. The Achaeans will be drunk on wine and grief. Hopefully both cause them to lower their guard long enough for one old king to make his way across the plain under a beggar's cloak.

My heart races at the promise of holding my son again, even as it breaks when I think of what he will return to.

But at least we will be together at the end.

Even still, we must hide the truth of Andrius's absence until the dawn. Then it will be over.

Over.

For all the hours I've sat here, I feel as though I've been waiting for the blade to drop.

What if Paris finds Rhea in the camps before Priam does? What if the king is slaughtered by Achilles before he can utter a word of his plea? What if Laocoon fails to slay Paris and he reenters the city to take his crumbling throne?

So many outcomes I cannot control. So many *what ifs.*

But I do not bear these doubts alone. Helen has not left my side. Cassandra sleeps in the bed behind us, curled into the farthest corner. She is staying as far away from me as possible, which is probably wise. Though my wrath has other targets, I can feel her misguidance fermenting inside me like stored wine. If the night's schemes are successful and Andrius is granted safe passage, I intend to pour myself a glass before making a toast to Lelwani, god of death.

Tonight, I protect. Tomorrow, I avenge.

"Will you kill him?" Helen asks from the hearth. She reads my dark thoughts with an accuracy I have come to expect.

"If Paris returns to the city and somehow slips past Laocoon, it may be the last free choice I make . . . unless I turn the sword on myself."

"No. You won't do that."

My chin jerks in her direction. "What makes you so certain?"

Helen's jeweled gaze holds steady. "Because it would mean abandoning all hope for Andrius, and hope is the only currency a mother has to trade."

"*Hope?*" I spit out the word. "Look around you, Helen. What reason do we have to hope? When the city is rubble, we will be parceled out among the Achaean kings like animals. Forced to spend the rest of our days in the stinking beds of our enemies. The only relief we'll be granted is when our bellies swell with one of their accursed children—a constant reminder of everything they've taken from us."

She nods gravely. "And yet we will love them all the same."

"Love?" Acid burns the back of my throat. "Love *who?*"

"Any children who come after." Helen's eyes search for some spark in me that isn't born of hatred. "Hear me, Andromache. I have had two husbands. One weak, the other vile. Both cruel. In the eyes of the world, everything that took place in our marriage beds was lawful, and yet we both know what it was."

I grind my teeth, unable to imagine how she endured it. Any of it.

"Yet I promise you this: I never felt a joy that was also fierce. Not until I gathered Hermione into my arms." Helen pauses, her eyes falling to the embers. "If I'd had another child with Paris, I believe it would have been the same. Nothing can stifle the burning love of a mother's heart if she says yes to it. Not unless we grant darkness power over a bond it can otherwise lay no claim to."

"You are telling me I should look forward to becoming an Achaean's broodmare?"

"No. I am saying that even if you never know another love like Hector, you may yet know another love like Andrius."

I shake my head. "My son can never be replaced."

"Nor can my daughter. Yet if I'd been given another child . . ." Helen lets the thought go. "It is evil that longs to possess. Revenge that imposes limits. But love? Love can only ever expand." The former queen wearing rags looks at me for a long time. "Leave the door to that chamber open a crack, Andromache. That is all I'm saying. You will never replace the loves you have lost. Loves with a depth most mortals will never reach. Then again, I never thought I'd survive my first winter in Troy . . ." She pauses again, breathing deeply. "It is the lot of women to endure."

"You mean it is the curse of women to suffer. Needlessly."

"To suffer, yes." Helen nods. "But do you know of any other route to love?"

I clench my fists. "It is not worth the price."

Her small smile says she does not believe me. "And yet we willingly pay the fare."

A sudden gasp behind us, and Cassandra shoots up stiff in the bed. The black of her eyes swallows the yellow. The voice that leaves her lips is ancient. "*They are here*," says the Crone.

"Who?" I ask a breath before the knock comes. The Master of Keys left with Priam for the plain, so there's no one to defend this tower or the empty cradle it conceals. No one but us.

I reach for my weapon as I rise to answer. Opening the door a crack, I glimpse the large swell of a stomach. The dagger slides back into its sheath.

Creusa enters the room, quickly followed by Bodecca.

"Aeneas sent us to keep vigil with you," Creusa says.

Then Aeneas does not realize he has sent his pregnant wife into danger.

"The king makes his way across the plain," Bodecca assures us.

My heart throbs in my throat. Priam has kept his promise. If Laocoon's stars are on our side, by dawn either Cyrrian and the Master of Keys will return my dead husband and my living son, or every woman in this room will lose all reason to hope. No matter what Helen claims.

Bodecca casts me a steely glance. "We will sit the night with you."

I place a hand on Creusa's shoulder. She is a faithful friend and sister, but unlike Bodecca, the woman is no fighter. Especially not now. "You risk too much, Creusa."

Hands holding her roundness, she offers me a sure smile. This pregnancy has not been as easy as her first. She's dreadfully thin from vomiting.

"What other choice do I have?" says the eldest daughter of Priam. "If the Achaeans breach the Citadel, my children are no safer than yours."

I cannot bring myself to tell her that right now, the Achaeans are the least of our worries.

Behind us, a groan echoes through the chamber. Cassandra's hands clasp her knees as she rocks back and forth on the bed. "He is here. He has come." The Child's eerie voice whispers through her, raising the hairs on the back of my neck.

Racing to the balcony, I peer into the street below. The flicker of torches drawing closer. At the center of half a dozen Citadel guards stands a man in a dark green cloak.

A thousand curses rise up, aimed mostly at myself. Laocoon was too old; I never should have left him to the task.

Just as Paris never should have doled out his trench work to servants. Now he is here to eliminate the final threat that Andrius and I pose to his reach for Troy's throne. A throne he would steal even as it burns.

"Ready yourselves." I toss Helen a spear before sliding the slim knife Cassandra keeps beside the hearth across her bed.

We have gone over this scenario, should anyone come to the tower searching for Andrius. I will meet the guards by the entrance to the staircase. They can only ascend it one at a time, giving me higher ground and a slight advantage. If they make it past me, Cassandra and Helen will bar the door and do whatever they can to prevent the men from entering the bedchamber.

Paris cannot see the empty cradle. He cannot learn that Andrius isn't here and send word to the Achaeans. Not until Priam has time to return.

I want to scream into the wind blowing up the staircase as I race down it.

Grant me an hour.

But even that feels too long.

When I reach a small window in the spiral passage, I remove an arrow from my quiver. From this position, I can target anyone approaching the courtyard, but once they are inside, they'll be too close to the tower and out of my line of sight. Then it will be hand to hand.

I close my eyes and raise a petition to any god that will listen, hoping the queen has readied their ears. When I open them again, the man in green raises both hands to lower his hood. I pull the bowstring taut and wait for Paris to step into my arrow's path. The irony of killing him with the only weapon he was halfway decent at wielding brings the faintest smile to my lips.

Inhaling deeply, I focus my aim, keeping my eyes fixed on the green cloak.

A shock of white glows in the torchlight as the hood lowers and the figure steps close enough for me to distinguish his features.

Skin like a dried fig.

Eyes too close together and the whiskers of a wild boar.

The man commanding these soldiers isn't Paris.

Panic claws at my insides as the face comes into focus. Other than the high priest, he is the only other man King Priam would trust enough to tell him of his midnight errand. I lower my weapon in relief even as my stomach sinks.

Andrius.

Has word of Priam's fate reached the council?

I race down the staircase, every raised hair a sign something has gone wrong. It is too soon for the king to have made it back to Troy. What if they were caught by Achaean scouts before they even made it across the plain?

I rip open the tower's door. "Harsar Antenor."

Every muscle stiffening, I prepare myself for news so horrible, Priam's brother must deliver it himself. Antenor gives the armed men on his left and right the slightest of nods.

They descend on me like raptors.

With a roar, I buck as the guards pin my arms to my sides.

"Search the tower," Antenor says calmly to the men carrying torches.

The tower reels around me. A thousand stars around it. All the signs I failed to see, now burned behind my eyes like sky serpents.

The constellation they create brings a new clarity as the full extent of this treachery unfolds. Paris and Antenor work together to eliminate Hector's line and help the Achaeans take the city. While our enemies dance in the blood-soaked streets, they seek shelter in the serpent's den below ground, along with the Old Blood most loyal to them. Helen's treasure is returned and the Achaeans sail for home with most of Troy's women as their slaves. With their brothers gone and the chaff burned away, Paris and Antenor emerge from the den to begin again. A fresh pot on which to paint a new design.

One with Paris as Troy's king, and Antenor as the hand that moves him.

Antenor's serpentine gaze assures me I have seen it all.

"Bring me Hector's child," he calls after the men heading toward the staircase. "But be gentle."

Antenor's lips twitch in a way that turns me inside out. "We don't want to upset the mother."

Everything burns as I struggle to break free. "Paris will be the death of Troy!"

"I couldn't agree more," Antenor says calmly. "Paris is a shortsighted fool. Be grateful your son will end up under my care instead."

My temples pound with confusion. These vipers may believe they rule this city now that Hector is gone, but the women who loved him best will stand as firm as any of the ranks that fought under his command.

Don't let them in. Don't let them see the empty cradle.

Antenor takes two steps closer, his rank breath on my cheek. "Don't worry, Harsa Andromache. It's fortunate that Hector made Helenus the child's guardian instead of Paris. He and I will guarantee that your son is protected."

Lies. Every last word.

Shouts and muffled scuffling pull my gaze to the tower. The two guards digging their fingers into my arms turn that way too. For a moment, their grips loosen. I take full advantage, throwing my weight forward in one motion as I duck to the ground. My hands grasp the small daggers strapped to the calves above each man's sandal.

Shooting upward again, a blade in each hand, I thrust the daggers into soft bellies. My captors fall to the ground like sacks of grain.

"Brutal and efficient, Harsa Andromache," Antenor says without emotion. "Traits I wish Hector had displayed more often."

I grab the old man's cloak at the collar and thrust him against the tower wall. The point of my blade quickly finds his chest.

"Andromache."

Helen's voice at my back has my grip loosening slightly. I turn and see Antenor's men, worse for the wear with scrapes along their arms and faces. But they've still managed to drag the women from the tower.

For all the expressions that have passed over Cassandra's face, this look of twisted horror is something new. I follow her gaze to Antenor.

My blade rests on an ugly scar high on his chest.

He smiles. "Kill me, and my men kill them."

If they've seen the empty cradle, they might as well get it over with.

"Where is the prince?" Antenor demands.

Before I can answer, a voice rings out across the courtyard.

"The child is here, Harsar Antenor."

In mourning no longer, Queen Hecuba enters the courtyard wearing one of her finest robes and a golden headdress, as if she were about to address the entire city. She holds a chubby baby in her arms. I recognize it immediately as the child who took shelter in Kalawashi's home, the baby girl to whom I lent Andrius's linen.

"What concern of yours is my grandson?" asks the queen of her brother-in-law.

I suck in my breath.

"Apologies, Queen Hecuba. I was concerned about the young prince's safety, given Andromache's current state. I did not realize he was in your care." The old man smooths his ruffled robes as I release him. "His mother failed to mention this. I believe she is quite unwell."

Hecuba gives the pile of bodies at my feet little more than a passing glance. "Would you not expect the same of any woman who had lost her husband? Who had lost my son?" She bounces the gurgling baby on her hip with a maternal affection that is convincing to the untrained eye.

"Of course, but—" Antenor's explanation is cut short by a low moan behind us. Like the mewling of a cat about to give birth.

Cassandra stands in the arched doorway of the stairwell, her hands gripping either side. A chill runs down my spine as I glimpse the unnatural bend in hers. The way her lips move over her teeth.

The Crone's mouth turns to gums. "We should have known," she rasps.

"Known what, my dear?" Antenor's usual condescension gives way to uncertainty.

"*You.*" Cassandra's face transforms again. Rage vibrates through her as the Fury takes her turn. A ripple travels over Cassandra's features before the Crone stares out from her ancient eyes once more. "You have always been the shadow with no face. The danger we could not see until it was too late."

Cassandra slumps against the wall with a whisper. "Why couldn't *I* see it?"

Antenor tilts his head, considering her. "A shame. You had so much promise, Cassandra. Your visions and your life have proven a disappointment to more than just your parents."

"Careful, Antenor." Hecuba clutches the babe so tightly, the child begins to fuss. What she must have paid the infant's mother to borrow her. "Do not presume to speak for me or the king. Cassandra is a Harsa of Troy. You will address her as such."

If only the queen had spoken on her daughter's behalf years earlier.

"As you command." Antenor bows his head, but there is a mockery in the gesture. I cannot claim any special gifts from the gods, but even I should have glimpsed his true nature. All my years in Troy, and I mistook the man's pitiless aptitude for proficiency and protectiveness of his brother. Ambition, yes, but a vintage I knew well. It seems Cassandra isn't the only person here who wears more than one face.

Her eyes narrow to small slits. "Don't worry, uncle. I see things more clearly now than I ever have." The eerie smile on her lips gives way to the jerky movements of the Wraith. Then the Fury again. Words that hiss at us from beyond the Great River. "You know better than anyone that the things I see are true. And that knowledge will cost you greatly."

Antenor's laugh grates with an edge of fear. "Would you have me believe you have foreseen my death, niece?"

The Child again, voice lilting. "No, uncle. Far worse. I have foreseen your life."

Antenor's laughter dies in his throat. He turns to Queen Hecuba. "Now that we know Prince Scamandrius is safe and in good health, I will report back to the Council."

"Yes, you do that," I say.

Antenor starts to walk away, but before he makes it far, the Crone calls out once more. "We will speak again, and then we shall tell you exactly what we have seen. Find us . . ." A throaty laugh erupts from Cassandra's throat. "Find us when the screaming starts."

Antenor retreats with his men. The women in the courtyard climb back to the tower room in silence. I bar the door behind us, nodding to the baby in Hecuba's arms, each flash of dimpled thighs a lash across my breast. "How?"

The queen regards me evenly. "Does it matter?"

Roots of white hair peek out from her layers of false red. I hold Hecuba's bold gaze and again glimpse a version of my future. If only there was one. "No, I suppose it doesn't."

"I never could abide that man." Hecuba's lips pull back to bare teeth. "He isn't what he pretends to be."

"Few of us are," Helen says softly from where she sits beside Creusa, rubbing the woman's swollen feet.

"No, it is more than that," I say. "Antenor was behind Paris's schemes all along."

Hecuba's frown sags further. "Then it was him . . ."

"Antenor was the one who brought Paris back to Troy," Helen gasps. "Even after Cassandra's warnings."

"You see some, but not all." Cassandra returns to rocking back and forth on the bed.

"I will inform the Council of his treachery," Hecuba says.

Cassandra scoffs. "And you think you will be believed?"

"She's right," I say. "The Council is in Antenor's crooked hand. We cannot act against him until Priam returns."

If the king will even believe us over his brother.

My eyes find Bodecca, who is strangely silent. I can tell by her mouth's thin line that she shares my doubts.

The queen concedes with a nod. I lean over the bed and force my hands to unclench the dagger's handle. The blade falls to the blankets, and I make my way onto the balcony.

The wind blows.

"Will it be enough to deter them?"

Hecuba's question at my back leaves me cold. I search a darkened plain filled with countless enemies. A plain that a weary king is crossing for my son. All the breaths I've been holding on their behalf rush from my aching chest.

"We have done all we can," I say finally. "It is up to Priam and Rhea now."

39

RHEA

LIVE, RHEA. YOU must live.

My sister's words reach me through darkness and smoke. When it clears, a man in rich clothing stands above me. Bloated lips peel back over rows of brown teeth. A golden belt strains across his heavy middle. Over his shoulder, a shadow lurks. It takes to the air. Black bird that becomes a serpent of fire, streaking across the starless sky.

The braided noose circles my neck, cutting into my skin. I rear back. Rocks pierce my hands and knees when I stumble. The bright stalls and colorful wares of the market in Cyzicus bleed together until they re-form into the stark lines of the Achaean camp. The scent of waste and rotting meat. The sounds of blades clashing and men dying. Carrion birds, and bodies laid out on pyres that never stop burning.

I run toward the hill crowned by an ancient shrine of stones. My heart leaps when I see the large figure waiting there. With the last of my strength, I throw myself at his feet and wait for his strong arms to gather me up, but he doesn't reach for me. Instead, he moves past me as if he doesn't see me at all.

My fault. All my fault.

He walks away, and my legs give out. Tears fall. I can't stop them anymore. I can't run. There's nowhere left to go.

Hot, moist breath fans the back of my neck.

My scream is cut off by the hand clamped over my mouth.

"Quiet!" comes the hiss.

I blink. In the near perfect darkness of the sleeping hut, it takes a moment to make out the eyes peeking out over the veil.

"Briseis? What're you—?"

"Come quickly. Bring the babe."

The lines of the sleeping hut take shape out of the blackness around me. I throw my legs over the edge of my low pallet. Briseis hovers a few paces away, scanning the rows of slumbering women for any sign of movement. Since Agamemnon and Achilles made peace, Briseis has been returned to Achilles. If she's discovered here, there'll be trouble.

Scurry, scurry little mouse.

Cassandra's ghostly face flickers in my mind. A shiver runs the length of my spine as I lift Andrius from his bed of blankets. The unhappy sound he makes pierces the stillness of the hut. One of the girls to my right rolls over and issues a small snore. Briseis goes rigid. For a moment, neither of us moves.

Ten breaths pass before Briseis motions for me to follow. Our robes rustle loudly as we weave our way between rows of sleeping women and under the flap of hide leading out into the night.

The moon hangs low in the sky, bathing the camp in ghostly light—another echo of my dream that draws an unwelcome shiver. Stars spell out secrets in the heavens above us. I glance across the open ground in the direction of the sea, where the blackness on the horizon is slightly less dense than that in the west, placing the time at a few hours before sunrise.

Hours I once lived for.

My mind runs to Ajax before I can call it back. I've spent every instant since I left him in the stones remembering the shattered look on his face; preparing myself for the arrival of armed men sent to drag me away.

It hasn't happened.

Wherever he is, Ajax hasn't betrayed me. Somehow, that only makes it worse.

A figure steps out of the shadows of the women's hut.

"I've scouted the way to the bathhouse." Ven pulls back the hood of her cloak, displaying her scars. "You shouldn't encounter any difficulties."

"You weren't seen?" Briseis asks urgently.

"There are guards posted in the usual places, but the rest of the Achaean army is passed out drunk," Ven informs us. "The snoring could be heard in Thrace."

"What's happening?" I ask.

"I'd also like an answer to that." Ven angles her body toward the taller woman standing between us.

Briseis lifts her veil. "While the camp was honoring Patroclus and celebrating Hector's death, an old man clothed in rags appeared at the gates of the Myrmidons' settlement and demanded to see Achilles." A tinge of awe. "The soldiers thought he must have flown over the Kesik Cut and past half the Achaean army. They decided he must be a god in disguise, and so as not to incur his wrath, they brought him before Achilles."

"I take it the man was not a god." Ven's tone betrays her utter contempt for gods. And men.

"No, not a god," Briseis agrees. "A king. King Priam of Troy."

Ven releases a sharp breath. Or maybe I do.

"I was there and I saw him. I heard the words that were spoken. Priam came to beg Achilles for Hector's body so that he might send his son across the Great River. At least," Briseis says, pulling a jagged piece of hair out of her face, "that was the reason he gave Achilles."

Gooseflesh breaks out across my skin. "There was another," I guess.

The uneven ends of Briseis's hair brush her shoulders when she nods. When I saw her last, those curls reached to the small of her back. It makes me wonder if she is grieving for Hector or Patroclus. Perhaps she is mourning both. The lines that were once clearly drawn are now scattered in the sand. Loyalties and loves muddled like waters after a flood.

"I was ordered to make a bed for King Priam," she continues. "As soon as we were alone, he called me by name. I had met him once, many years ago in my husband's palace, but that wasn't how he recognized me." Dark eyes hold me in their grasp. "He knew everything. Where to find Achilles. Who I was. How to enter by way of the swamp and approach the Myrmidon camp. And then he told me why he had come."

My heart knows the answer before my mind even recognizes the question. "Andrius."

"You have friends in Troy, Rhea. People who'll risk everything to bring you and the prince back to safety. At this moment, one of them is breaking bread with the man who murdered his son." She places her hand on my shoulder. "When the sun rises, Priam will be given a wagon with Hector's body. I don't know what the king said or how he managed it, but Achilles has promised him safe passage back to Troy. You will sneak out with Andrius by way of the swamp and wait where the swell of the plain meets the bay. When the wagon passes, you'll climb aboard with the body."

The relief that fills me is fierce and brief. As if drawn by some invisible thread, my gaze climbs in the direction of the distant hill, set with a crown of ancient stones.

I close my eyes. "It's nearly morning now."

"It couldn't be helped," Briseis says. "I had to wait until both Achilles and Priam had retired to bed. They spoke much longer than anyone expected." A troubled expression flickers over her features. "I came as quickly as I could."

"How did you get past the guards?" Ven asks.

"With Achilles's blessing. He thinks I've gone to wash Hector's body." Briseis's words turn hard. "He is mad if he believes that sort of damage can be repaired with wet rags and oil."

She is holding something back. I can tell by the way she scans the darkness. Briseis is not easily cowed. If she was, she wouldn't be here.

"What aren't you saying?"

Briseis releases a sharp breath. "Achilles promised Priam safety, but Achilles is not King of the Achaeans. I know Agamemnon better than I care to. If he discovers Priam is within his grasp, he'll stop at nothing to spill his blood."

Her words are like a slap of cold water, bringing me fully out of the dream that still clings to me. "Who knows that Priam is here?" I ask.

"The guards at the gates, though I don't think they recognized him. Two of Achilles's men, myself, and one other servant."

"Are they trustworthy?" My mind is moving quickly, calculating the distance to the meeting spot. The hours until light breaks. No matter how I look at it, there are too many people involved. Too many factors at play. And then there's Andrius. I press my nose into his hair, inhaling his scent. He's sleeping soundly now, but it won't be long before he wakes again. And uses those warrior lungs.

"The Myrmidons are loyal to Achilles, but Agamemnon and Odysseus have spies everywhere," Briseis says. "Hector's corpse can't simply disappear unnoticed. Someone will investigate. If you decide to meet Priam, you'll be risking capture."

"If you stay, it's the same," Ven says. "We've managed to hide you so far, but secrets have short life spans in a place like this. Calis already suspects something. Sooner or later, word will come from Troy that the prince is missing. It won't be long until someone realizes who you are."

And then, all of the women who risked their lives to protect us will suffer with me.

Ven's fingers reach for the colorful threads adorning Helen's blanket. A blanket like another once woven by a mother's hand.

I reach into my robes. My fingers trace the graceful lines of a wooden horse before finding what they seek. I place my offering on Ven's palm.

Emotions send ripples through her scars as her fingers clasp the bit of fabric. All that's left of the son who was taken from her.

"You kept it," she whispers.

"As I carry his name. Simursu. Son of Zulliama and Lyria."

Her eyes squeeze shut. Tears run the twisted pathways down her cheeks. They are there, and then they aren't.

"This isn't the place for a princeling." Gently, Ven tucks the battered piece of her dead son's blanket back into the folds of Helen's offering. "Bring him back to his mother, where he belongs."

"No." The word explodes from the shadows to our left.

Calis steps around the corner of the sleeping hut, wearing thin robes and a pinched expression. Gray hair hangs in a thick plait across her narrow shoulders.

"I knew you were hiding something." Her lips peel back to reveal small, widely spaced teeth. "But I never would've suspected the prince of Troy. I didn't think even you lot could be that stupid."

I take a hasty step backward, but Calis moves faster. She reaches to grab a fistful of my hair. Both Ven and Briseis block her.

"Whatever you think you heard, forget it," Briseis orders with a coldness that would make Queen Hecuba proud. "Wipe the girl and the child from your memory. If you so much as look at them again, I swear you'll live to regret it."

"Your threats are worthless. You think you're so much better than the rest of us, but you're still just Achilles's whore." Calis spits at Briseis's feet.

"When they realize what you've done, the kings will wrap you in a sack like the trash you are and throw you to their men." Her gaze swings to include me and Ven. "The two of you can only hope to be so lucky."

"Careful, Calis." Ven's voice is a warning. "There are no kings here now. There are only the four of us, and we outnumber you."

Calis's features contort. "One scream, and I can bring half the Achaean army running. How would your precious prince fare then?"

She'd do it, I realize. She'd hand us over rather than see us escape.

"Why?" I don't understand this hatred, or what we've done to earn it. "Would you betray your own sisters for scraps from the table of men who made you a slave?"

A shudder runs through Calis, so brief I might be imagining it. "Any family I had is dead. And it wasn't the Achaeans who killed them, but our neighbors. Men who grew up under the same sun and prayed to the same gods. Men who forgot every tie and kindness when hunger came." She sneers. "Bloodshed and bindings. That is how all our stories end."

"Not all," I say quietly. "Not if you help us."

"Why should I care for you or your troubles?"

"Because helping us would be helping yourself," I reason with her. "The things we do here won't be forgotten. If Troy wins this war, we would see to it that you—"

Calis's laugh is a serrated blade. "Trojan? Achaean? What difference does it make who my master is so long as he feeds me?"

Briseis shakes her head in sorrow. "You've let them make a monster of you."

"You don't know what monsters are." Animosity mixes with anticipation in Calis's flat eyes. "But you will before this night is over." She opens her mouth to scream. Ven moves, but there's no hope of reaching Calis in time. Every muscle in my body clenches while I wait for the cry that will doom us.

A glint of bronze in the moonlight.

Calis's cry cuts off before it begins. Her hands lift to her throat. Blood pours through her fingers. She hits the ground on her knees before falling face-first onto the wet grass.

The shadow hunched over Calis's corpse straightens.

Salama's skin is unnaturally pale in the moonlight. "Her scream would have been the end of us." Salama puts on a brave front, but her hands fumble the knife as she attempts to sheathe it back under her robes.

"You did right," Ven says. The catch in her voice betrays her.

Nothing about this is right.

"I heard her leave the hut after you did," Salama whispers. "I didn't know what else to do, so I followed her."

I can't stop staring at the bloody gash in Calis's neck. She was not a friend. She might even have been an enemy, but she was also one of us. And now she's gone.

"There's no way we can keep this hidden," Ven says grimly.

Briseis's nod is curt. "If they discover her before dawn, they'll send up an alarm."

And then it's only a matter of time before Priam is discovered, and Andrius and I with him.

"We can hide her with the washing," comes a quiet voice from behind us.

As one, we spin to see a girl emerge from the sleeping hut. I recognize her as one of the younger ones who works in the bathhouse. Nia.

Nia joins us outside. She is not alone.

More women make their way out of the sleeping hut, drawn by the commotion outside. They are old and young. Some I know through my work in the camps, but many have no reason to trust or help us. All of them stare at the child in my arms with stunned expressions that suggest they've heard more than we wished them to.

"What did you say?" I tear my gaze away from our audience and focus on Nia.

"We can hide her with the washing," the girl repeats. "None of the men would think to look there. Once the prince is gone, we can pretend to find her. They'll suspect one of the warriors before they do any of us."

Two of the stronger girls move forward without a word. Dumbfounded, I watch as they lift Calis's body between them and drag her toward the stacks of dirty linens piled by the streambed.

"Wait!" Salama hisses. "Slit her robes on the side and down the front."

"Why—" I am not given the chance to finish.

Salama's palm is hot and wet when it wraps around my wrist. "Do you still have the knife Andromache gave you?"

"Yes." Andromache made me promise never to take it off, and I haven't.

Salama licks her lips and nods. "Remember our lessons. If the time comes to use it, don't hesitate."

"Is it really him? The prince Scamandrius?" another girl asks. She can't be older than twelve. I recognize her as one of the girls Menelaus fancies. Her eyes are ancient in her young face, and yet they fill with curiosity at the sight of the child in my arms.

"We call him Andrius," I hear myself say as the girl approaches.

Hesitantly, reverently, she reaches out to grasp the copper curl in his hair.

Awed, she twirls it around her fingers. "I've heard the *alev* is a gift from Tarhunt. A sign the son will bold as his mother."

"With all the strength of his father," adds Nia, her tone humble as she too touches the copper flame.

Their words yank me through time until I am back in Andromache's rooms the day she pushed Andrius into the world. The scent of blood and sweat and the joyful smiles on the faces around me.

"He will be the best of both." I give them Cassandra's words. The one she uttered as she held Andrius the way she herself had never been held. Tears burn in my throat. "He will be all those things. And more."

My eyes take in the faces in front of me. Faces drawn with suffering. There must be something I can say, some way to convince them to keep our secret. I am searching for the right words when the girl drops down to one knee. Beside her, Nia does the same.

I watch in astonishment as one by one, heads bow before the prince of Troy.

"Come, Rhea. There's no more time," Briseis says behind me.

I look at the women in front of me. Some are removing Calis's body. Others have taken a washing basin from inside the hut and are busy scrubbing the bloodstains from the ground. They are women with no past and no future. Women with no verses to remind the world they were here at all.

I swear to the Mother that as long as I live, they will be remembered.

"Thank you," I say.

"We could not save our children." Ven fixes on Andrius with an intensity that tells me she is remembering another little boy. One with midnight eyes. "But we will save the prince of Troy."

BRISEIS LEADS THE way inland across the camp toward the swamp. I follow close behind. The Mother goddess must hear my pleas, because other than a few sleeping grunts, Andrius doesn't make a sound.

Briseis's back is arrow-straight in front of me. She walks as if she fears nothing and no one. Not for the first time, she reminds me a little of Andromache.

I slam that door shut in my head, unprepared to face what lurks behind it.

A soldier stumbles past us. A Myrmidon by the looks of his shorn hair. He inclines his head toward Briseis. Every Achaean soldier knows her by sight.

The celebration of Hector's death raged late into the night. Dark shapes squat in groups by floundering fires, as if the soldiers couldn't be bothered to drag themselves to their own beds, but instead lay down wherever they fell.

I wonder if Ajax is somewhere among the men before I pull back the reins on my thoughts.

Male groans and heavy snores echo around us. A few more soldiers stagger past, but nobody stops us as we pass the bathhouse and move out onto open ground. The latrines lie less than thirty paces ahead. Just beyond them, the shadows of the swamp beckon.

We are a few feet from the latrines when I spot something out of the corner of my eye. I think it must be another sleeping warrior, before I realize no soldier, no matter how drunk, would choose to bed down next to this stench.

Something echoes through me. A whisper.

I take a step toward it.

"Rhea." Briseis's voice reaches me from the darkness up ahead. I ignore it and approach the body left to rot in the shallow trench.

He is lying sideways in the mud, his right leg impossibly bent beneath him. His skin is as battered as the tunic hanging off him. The one that never fit quite right, but that he wore out of love for the woman who made it. A braided rope is wrapped around his neck. His hair matted with filth.

His face is so ravaged, it is all but unrecognizable, and still, I know him. I know him with that part of me that hears the horses whisper.

I drop to my knees.

"Rhea, we must move."

Briseis's voice reaches me through a tunnel of wind. Behind her veiled head, the sky bleeds from black to blue at the edges.

The moon slices through the clouds, illuminating the crust of blood and dirt marring Hector's cheek. Without thinking, I wipe at it with the edge of Helen's blanket.

"Leave it, Rhea. You can't fix this."

Tears rain onto the top of Andrius's sleeping head as I grip the blanket tighter. "I can't let her see him like this."

It will kill her. More so than watching him die, seeing Hector defaced will break Andromache. I bend forward, scrubbing helplessly to erase the damage that's been done. Every stroke releases another memory.

Hector's smile. His quiet patience. His broad form swaying gently on the balcony in the dawn light with Andrius cradled in his arms.

Hands wrap around mine. I let out a ragged breath and find Briseis kneeling across from me. "I will come back here once you are both safely hidden. I swear to you, when Prince Hector returns home, it will not be in shame."

Her fingers squeeze mine to the point of pain. A sob rises in my throat. Andrius stirs, and I force myself to swallow it. Briseis pulls me to my feet, but at the last moment, I drop back down again. Gently, I pull the rope free from around Hector's neck. The way he once pulled a rope free from mine.

Everything inside me rebels at the thought of leaving him like this. If only there was something I could do. Something I could give—

I let out a slow breath as I search my robes for the most precious thing I've ever owned. A figurine of a Phrygian mare in full stride. A horse like the ones Hector loved.

I take the figurine Ajax carved for me, and I wrap it in the scarred folds of Hector's hand.

"I will tell your son." I repeat the same promise I made to Andromache, only this time, I say it in the language we shared. In whispers. "I will tell him who you are."

The camp blurs around me when I rise. The stench of the latrines. The buzz of flies. The wind whipping over the bay. All of it fades into nothing as I cross the last few yards toward the swamp.

Scurry, scurry, my father's voice whispers in my ear, where it is joined by Hector's. And my sister's. Until my head is so loud, I can't hear myself think.

The ancient shrine materializes out of the shadows. My stride shortens as I pass the stones, but I steel my spine and press on without a sideways glance.

We stop at the edge of the swamp. "This is where I leave you." Briseis presses a leather skin into my hands. "Sleeping tonic mixed with milk. From Isola. Give it to the prince as soon as you are settled. Isola says it should keep him quiet until dawn."

I grip the skin tightly.

"Go, Rhea. Find your freedom. For all of us."

Briseis turns away before I can summon the words to thank her. She disappears behind the stones, and I face the waiting swamp. The humid darkness embraces me as it has so many nights, only tonight, the familiar shadows hold no comfort. Tonight, they hold only pain.

Silently, I tread past the hidden poles strung with nets of silver fish and up into the grasses on the other side of the Lisgar Swamp. The ground is wet and squelching under my sandals. I take the secret path that brings me to the open mouth of the Scamander where it flows into the moonlit bay.

A single boat lies beached on the sandy shore, hidden by tall reeds. Cradling Andrius, I lower myself into the boat and use the pole to push us across the slow-flowing water and past the island in the middle to the opposite shore. By the time I drag the small dinghy into the reeds, sweat slicks my skin. I glance up at the sky. Dawn is still a ways off. The meeting place Briseis described lies over the next grassy hill. To reach it, I'll have to travel out in the open over the swell of the plain. We'd be exposed for as long as it takes Hector's body to be prepared and loaded onto Achilles's wagon.

Odysseus's spies may still be wandering the plain. Better to stay in the reeds and wait until I hear the horses before I risk moving farther.

Andrius grumbles against my shoulder as we settle down in the tall grass. Wetness seeps through my cloak. Holding the leather skin the way Ven taught me, I raise it to Andrius's rooting mouth. He suckles the milk hungrily. When his little jaws finally stop working, I gently remove the skin and readjust him against my body.

Time wraps around us. Speeding up and slowing down so that an hour passes in a single breath and yet a lone moth floats against the naked moon for what feels like half a lifetime. I watch its wings beat against the wind, and I wish I had wings too. But I don't. All I have is myself and the shrinking moments before dawn when we'll find out if Andromache's plan has worked, or if it's crumbled to dust like all our other schemes.

Violet threads weave through swatches of blue on the horizon. By now so many things might've gone wrong. Calis's body could've been discovered, or one of the women in the weaving hut might've betrayed us, or a clever spy could have noted something familiar about the old man who appeared like a specter at the Myrmidons' gates. If any of those secrets find their way to Agamemnon's ears, King Priam won't leave the camp alive, no matter what promises have been made. And there's nothing that I can do about it but sit here and wait like the girl who once hid in the stables while her family burned. Afraid. Helpless.

A sound echoes through the stillness. I strain to make out the whisper of horses, but the space beyond the hill is silent save for the wind.

The sound finds me again on the breeze. It isn't coming from the direction from which I expect the wagon. It's coming from the darkened swamp behind me.

I creep through the grasses until I am gazing across the mouth of the Scamander back toward the swamp. Man-shaped shadows steal across the hidden latticework. They move carefully, communicating to each other with gestures in the language of men who do not wish to be heard.

Moonlight glints off the wicked edges of their blades.

Terror grips my throat as I watch them work their way across the swamp. The complex latticework is difficult to navigate if you aren't familiar with it, which these men aren't. They also have armor and weapons to slow them down. Several of them fall sideways into the murky waters. But it only serves to delay them.

A hulking soldier is the first to reach solid ground. The way he grips his sword tells me he isn't here in search of one small slave girl and a helpless infant.

He is here in search of a king.

Dread coats my tongue. The lone soldier on my side of the swamp finishes combing the tall grasses with his sword.

Did I hide the boat well? Did I leave a spot of flattened grass where I rested?

Questions burn through my mind as I watch a second soldier reach this side of the swamp. The first moves to the bank of the Scamander. His gaze sweeps the waters, seeming to linger over my hiding spot before he signals for his men to turn back the way they came.

My limbs go molten with relief, and then it happens.

Andrius starts to cry.

The sound slices through the stillness. Every man in the swamp swivels in our direction. I've taken a single step backward when the first soldier walks into the river. For a moment, I hold out hope the current will sweep him out into the bay, but he keeps trudging forward, the water barely reaching his navel.

Grasses lash at my face as I run. Up ahead, the swell of the plain blocks my view of the meeting spot. Every part of me wants to race toward it, but if I do, I'll only lead these men directly to Priam.

Andrius's wails turn keening. I rub my hands over his back, trying vainly to quiet him. As if sensing my distress, he reaches up, his chubby hands resting on either side of my face. I breathe in his sticky sweetness and a touch of rose that is all Andromache, and something rises up to fill the hollow cracks inside me.

He is yours now, Rhea. You must love him enough for the both of us.

I look into Andrius's face, and a fire lights my blood. The same fire that forged Ven's scars and kept Andromache's hands steady as she cut out her heart and placed it into my hands. The fire that danced in my sister's eyes in the shadows of our father's burning barn.

Heat sears my veins as my arms close around Andrius. My gaze flies over my surroundings, searching for a way out. There is only one.

The flask trembles in my hands as I raise it to Andrius's gaping mouth. He chokes on the flow but takes what little is left. I can only hope it is enough.

The empty sling falls to the ground. Shouts ring behind me as I lay Andrius down on Helen's blanket behind a clump of thorny bushes. His cries trail off as he rests his head against the image of a soaring hawk. His eyes gaze into mine before drifting closed. I stare at his sleeping face, so much like his father's, and the fire in my blood reaches my chest.

Behind me, the men hit the riverbank.

I turn to face them. Only two have managed to cross the river while the rest still struggle at the edge of the swamp. If I can distract them long enough, maybe the wagon will come. Maybe . . .

Every thought leaves my head when the first man emerges from the reeds.

Surprise flashes across his face at the sight of me, but he recovers quickly. The warrior covers the distance between us in six long strides. I count every one.

He raises his sword, and the blade flashes in the moonlight. I wait for his swing to reach its apex, and then I dive to the right, my hands reaching into the folds of my robe as I move sideways, drawing him farther away from the bushes.

The warrior grunts and gives chase. I take a few stumbling steps before he catches me. He lifts his sword again, only this time, I spin into him, thrusting my knife up in tempo to the memory of Andromache's voice, mercilessly counting off the steps.

One. Two. Dodge. Three. Four. Thrust.

The tip of the blade scrapes bone on its way between the soldier's ribs. With a gasp, he falls. Blood pours down my arm, staining my hands. I stare at his lifeless corpse, but there's no time to feel anything. The next man is already climbing out of the reeds.

Any advantage of surprise I had is gone. The second warrior runs at me with a roar. I manage to sidestep the first blow of his axe, but he catches me with the second.

The warrior's elbow collides with my temple, sending the stars spinning. The ground smacks the air from my lungs. Sensing him above me, I lift my knife. Pain flares through my wrist as he kicks it aside. The blade disappears into the grass.

Sounds echo toward us from the swamp. The clash of metal and grunts of pain.

The man lifts his axe above his head. A shrill sound pierces the night. He pauses. It comes again. A child's cry.

The axe lowers. I grab for the man's legs, but he's already stepping over me on his way to the bushes. The axe handle slips into his war belt. He reaches for the spear at his back.

A scream cuts through the swamp behind me as I scramble to my knees. Directly ahead, the soldier drags Helen's blanket out from its hiding spot. Andrius looks up at the man in armor who could almost be his father. He does not make a sound.

The soldier raises his spear.

No!

I throw myself over Andrius's body.

When I close my eyes, my sisters are waiting for me in the dark.

The clang of metal reverberates above my head. I wait for the flash of pain, but it doesn't come. My eyes blink open to the sight of a towering shield hovering over me like a wall of ox hide. The shield moves, revealing the giant behind it.

Our eyes meet, and the world seems to contract around us.

Something moves over Ajax's shoulder. With a roar, he lifts his shield and smashes it into the approaching soldier. The Achaean staggers like a new foal. Three more warriors emerge to take his place. They charge. Ajax thrusts his sword into the belly of the first and sweeps the second off his feet with his shield. The third slips between the other two with killing speed. Ajax bats the Achaean's sword aside and rams his helmetless head directly into the man's face.

Bones crunch. Blood rains down on the earth. Then silence.

Ajax walks toward me. Golden hair stained red. Green eyes frantic. His shield hits the ground and then his arms come around my waist, crushing me to him.

We cling to each other. His scent and his heat sink into my skin, banishing the cold. Andrius makes a sound of protest. Reluctantly, I pull myself free and gather the baby into my arms. I'm afraid that when I look back, Ajax will be gone, but he's still there. Like the answer to every prayer I never dared speak.

"What are you doing here?" I ask.

Ajax uses the neck of his tunic to wipe some of the blood from his face. "I've spent the past two nights in the stones."

My traitorous heart leaps. "Why?"

"I was waiting for you." His hands drop to his sides as if he suddenly doesn't know what to do with them. "I needed to beg your forgiveness. For the things I said. I needed to tell you that I . . ." He swallows. "That I understand why you couldn't trust me."

I press my hand flat against his chest. "I would've given you every one of my secrets, but some weren't mine to tell. You've nothing to be sorry for. Nothing. I'm the one who . . ."

His hand traps mine against the bronze plates of his armor. "You were doing your duty. The same way I do mine every day when I step onto that plain. A wise person once told me it doesn't change who I am." The heat in his gaze leaves me breathless.

"If you saw me pass the stones, why didn't you say something?"

"You walked by without looking back." Pain. "I wasn't sure you'd want to see me. Then those men followed you, and so I followed them."

He lay there in the dark. Watching me. Protecting me even when I couldn't see him. Even when he thought I wouldn't want to.

I drag my gaze to the east, where the horizon has turned lavender. "I have to leave."

Ajax studies the child in my arms. His eyes touch mine briefly before running over the swamp. "I killed the first scouting party, but more will come to find out where the others have gone."

I study the dead men around us. "Who are they?"

"Menelaus's men. Something must have turned their heads this way."

Calis was one of Menelaus's informants. He must have others too. It's possible Agamemnon's brother isn't the fool everyone takes him for.

"Do they know?" I don't realize I've spoken out loud until Ajax answers.

"Know what?" The expression on his face makes it clear he doesn't expect me to answer.

But I am done with secrets. Done with lies.

"King Priam stole into the camp last night. He appealed to Achilles to return Hector's body, and Achilles agreed. They're preparing it for transport back to Troy."

Ajax's gaze travels in the direction of the Myrmidons' camp. A shudder works through him before his shoulders sag. "If there is hope for Achilles, perhaps there's hope for all of us."

"You don't understand." I grab his tunic, twisting the fabric in my fingers. "It's a ruse."

"What kind of ruse?"

"One to get us out."

Ajax's eyes widen slightly as they fall to the child in my hands. "Who is he?"

"Hector's son. We're meant to stow away with Priam in the wagon." The truth tumbles off my tongue. "Some of the women have grown suspicious. We can't stay here any longer without being found."

Ajax's throat bobs once. "Where are you supposed to meet the wagon?"

"Just beyond the swell of the plain."

Jaw clenching, Ajax tugs me forward, but I pull back, forcing him to look at me. "If they find out you helped me, it won't matter who your father is or how fiercely you fight."

Ajax surveys the dead men around us. "I think it's past that now."

A thought strikes like a hammer. "Come with us." I reach out to clasp Ajax's hand. "Come with us back to Troy."

He stares at me. "You want me to return with you to the city whose sons I've spent the past ten years slaughtering?"

"Yes."

He shakes his head. "Agamemnon's punishments will be a mercy compared to the tortures your Trojans invent."

"You're wrong," I say with all the conviction left in me. "I'll tell Priam everything you've done to help us. They'll grant you sanctuary." I swear I'll see it done if I have to shed my last drop of blood for it.

Ajax's shoulders tense. "I won't hide behind Troy's walls."

"I don't want you to hide. I want you to live. With me."

Before he can answer, movement draws our gazes back to the swamp. Another group of men approach. Half of them have already reached our side of the river.

The mask of a stranger slips over Ajax's face as he lifts his towering shield. "Get behind me."

The breath catches in my lungs when Ajax charges the men stepping out of the water. One soldier falls to Ajax's sword. Then another. And another. He dances on the bank of the Scamander, a whirl of steel and fury. Not a single movement is wasted. Not one step falls out of balance. He fights like Aries himself, but no matter how many men he cuts down, more of them come. They swarm him on the beach, cutting him off from us.

One more man reaches the shore and wisely bypasses the raging giant in pursuit of an easier target.

He breaks for me.

Ajax's eyes find mine over the edge of his sword. "Run, Rhea!"

I wrap my hands around Andrius and sprint toward the swell of the plain. The sound of heavy breaths rings out behind me.

Closer. Closer. Close.

I am nearing the bottom of the hill when a hand reaches out to grasp my cloak. The soldier yanks me around. I fall to my knees, shielding Andrius with both arms.

I look up just as two wraiths fly out of the darkness behind me.

A muffled cry. Bodies hit the earth. It happens so quickly, I don't even have time to drag myself out of the way. The last Achaean falls, and I watch, stunned, as one of the shadows reaches down to haul me up.

Not a shadow after all.

"Cyrrian!" I throw my arms around his neck.

"Are you hurt?" He holds me at arm's length. Blood coats his face and hair, giving it a black sheen in the moonlight. In the midst of all that darkness, his eyes spark blue fire in my direction.

The man behind him straightens, and I recognize the grizzled Master of Keys.

"What are you doing here?"

Cyrrian opens his mouth to answer but then snaps it closed. His posture goes rigid as he locks onto something over my shoulder. Beside him, the Master of Keys raises his sword.

I sense Ajax before I feel his fingers grip my hip.

Cyrrian's gaze drops to Ajax's hand. A snarl curls his lips. "We came for you."

"What? Why?" It doesn't make any sense. "You couldn't defend us from the entire Achaean army."

"Your friend didn't give the king much choice," a raspy voice says. I stare in shock at the once-mute Master of Keys. "I came in the hopes of one last adventure." A flash of humor plays across the old soldier's lips. "I've not been disappointed."

"When you didn't come to the meeting spot, we thought something had happened to you," Cyrrian says.

"So you decided it would be a good idea to steal into your enemies' camp?" Ajax's tone makes no secret of what he thinks of this plan.

Cyrrian's jaw hardens. "If it came to that."

"But then we heard the little one cry," the Master of Keys offers.

Ajax studies the bloody ground around us. "Wagon or no wagon. You need to leave."

Cyrrian reaches for his blade. "We'll take no orders from the butcher of Achaea."

Ajax steps out from my side, and the two of them square off. Fury paints Cyrrian's handsome face, but Ajax's rage is buried deep, where only I can see it. And what I glimpse there leaves me cold.

"More men will come," Ajax says slowly. "Eventually, one of Agamemnon's dogs is bound to notice the large groups making one-way trips to the latrines. They'll sound the alarm, and then the whole camp will be on top of you."

"Priam will be here soon with the wagon to take us back to the city," I say. He has to come. Because if he doesn't . . .

Ajax looks at me with an expression I can't place. "You won't be safe there." The hand on my waist tightens. "Troy will burn, Rhea. There's no stopping it now."

Cyrrian's blade appears in his hand. "You're as delusional as the rest of your inbred kinsmen. Agamemnon can't bring down our Citadel walls even though he swarmed them with every man in Achaea."

Ajax shakes his head. "It won't take every man. Just one clever enough to get past the age-old defenses that leave you complacent." Ignoring Cyrrian, Ajax turns me so that I'm facing him alone. "You can't go back to the city. When we fight our way inside, I'd do everything I can to find you, but that doesn't mean someone else wouldn't get to you first." The wildness in his eyes lets me know exactly what that might mean.

"She doesn't need your protection." Cyrrian pulls me toward him and the Master of Keys, drawing an invisible line in the earth between us. Trojans on one side. Ajax on the other. "We don't need your help."

Ajax bares his teeth. "It didn't look that way five minutes ago, Trojan."

Cyrrian snarls. I wedge myself between them.

Desperate to make him hear me, I press my palms against Cyrrian's cheeks. His eyes jerk to mine, the pupils dark and fathomless. He covers my hands with his rough palms.

"Ajax isn't the enemy. If you ever cared for me at all, I'm asking you. Leave it. Please."

Cyrrian's muscles tense under my hands, but after a few moments, he steps back to glare over my shoulder. "Do you always let women do your fighting for you, Achaean?"

Ajax's smile would send saner men running. "She is interceding on your behalf, not mine. If it weren't for her, you'd already be dead."

I step in close to Ajax. His familiar heat bolsters me.

Cyrrian stares at us flatly. "You'd have me believe Ajax the Great is prepared to betray his own people to help the heir of Troy escape?"

"Yes." I lift my chin.

"Why?" Cyrrian directs this question to Ajax.

Ajax studies him carefully. "I'm guessing it's for the same reason you insisted on this suicide mission."

Cyrrian's glare could melt tin.

"What do we do now?" I ask, redirecting them both to more pressing matters. Such as how we might all live to see the sunrise.

"We wait here till the wagon comes, and we pray that no men find us in the meantime," Cyrrian answers.

"Pray harder, Trojan." Ajax whirls his sword in his hand and jerks his chin to where another team of scouts is already making its way across the swamp.

Cyrrian pushes me back. "Go. When you see the wagon, get on it. With or without us." I start to object, but he covers my mouth with his hand. "None of your heroics. The prince must make it back to Troy. That's all that matters now." My eyes find Ajax, and he nods. Cyrrian lets me go and reaches for his sword. Beside him, Ajax hefts his shield. He starts to turn away, but I grab hold of his hand.

No more lies. No more hiding.

"I love you."

His dimples flash. "And I love you, Anatolian girl with the name of a Greek goddess."

"I never meant to hurt you."

The smile fades, but the warmth in his eyes turns molten. "I know."

Ajax cups my face in his scarred hands, and then he walks away, falling in next to Cyrrian and the Master of Keys as they meet the men charging at them from the riverbank. I count their shields. Six. Even for Ajax, that is too many.

The sounds of battle explode behind me as I make my way over the swell of land to the plain. It stretches out before me. An empty field of darkness. There's no wagon. Nothing but a sea of grass under an endless sky.

I am searching the ground around me for some miracle, when I see it. Half hidden in the tall grass.

A stone in the shape of a horse's head.

Hector's voice finds me on the wind.

It is our way to burn the dead, but I saw Haskim buried outside the walls of Troy because he once told me that was the custom of your people. It is by the sea. Too close to the Achaean camp, but when the plains are safe again, I'll show you the spot. It is marked with a stone in the shape of a horse's head. I thought it fitting.

Papa.

I sink to my knees beside my father's grave, and the tears I've been holding back water the earth that cradles his bones.

Please. I raise the plea in the language of the whispers. *Please, please help us.*

For a moment, I feel a stirring inside me, but it fades as quickly as it comes. There's no answer. Only the lonely wind blowing across the plain.

Nobody is coming for us.

Staggering to my feet, I run back around the base of the hill and stop abruptly at the sight of two Trojan warriors and the Achaean giant fighting side by side. The ground around them is littered with corpses.

Cyrrian glances over his shoulder. When I shake my head, his expression turns grim. An axe sails toward him from the left. He doesn't see it.

My heart jumps into my throat. Before the axe connects with Cyrrian's skull, a sword hacks it to the side with one vicious blow. Cyrrian takes the opening Ajax provides and finishes the man with his sickle sword. He doesn't thank Ajax, but he nods in his direction. They both go back to fighting.

The last of the Achaeans falls to the sand, buying us a short reprieve.

"We have to retreat." Cyrrian wipes the blood from his face.

By silent agreement, the men circle me and Andrius as we move around the swell of the plain to the desolate meeting spot. I am searching the distance vainly for any sign of the wagon when a spear sails through the air toward Cyrrian's back. With a soundless cry, the Master of Keys steps into its path.

The old warrior falls, the spear lodged in his stomach. Beside him, Ajax lunges into the grass to dispatch the lone assassin. Cyrrian drops to his knees beside the dying man.

The Master of Keys reaches up with a trembling hand. His gnarled fingers find the back of Cyrrian's neck. The old soldier pulls the younger man close. Red foam speckles his lips as he whispers words into Cyrrian's ear. Then his hands fall to his sides and his eyes close. Eyes, I realize with a jolt, that I know well.

Cyrrian staggers away from the body just as Ajax returns.

"More men are coming," Ajax says. "You have to go."

"Where?" I ask. "We can't beat them back to the walls. There's no—"

Something tugs at me in the silence. A familiar humming in my blood.

My heart leaps in recognition. What started as a stirring now grows into a storm. A storm of whispers. And then there he is. A bright burst of flame charging across the plain.

Atesh.

The stallion grinds to a halt, sending a spray of dirt and mud showering over us.

"What is that thing?" Ajax asks, awed.

Atesh prances before us, accepting the admiration as his due.

"Our way out." I smile at my old friend. "Thank you," I whisper, raising my hand to stroke his neck. "Thank you for not listening when I told you to run."

The Prince of Horses paws the ground. A reminder that I am in no position to give orders. Above our heads, a hawk screams into the night.

"Come on." I hold Atesh steady and glance back at the others. Cyrrian and Ajax stare at me with identical expressions that take me a moment to decipher.

Atesh is the finest horse in Anatolia, but magnificent as he is, he can't carry all of us.

Ajax's hand flexes on the hilt of his sword as he studies the party of men closing in. He takes an audible breath.

When Ajax turns, it isn't me he looks at but Cyrrian. Something passes between them in a language I don't speak.

Cyrrian glances at me briefly before meeting Ajax's gaze. He nods once and reaches up for Atesh's mane. In one graceful leap, he climbs onto the horse's back.

Atesh dances in place but holds steady. Cyrrian reaches down to me. My thoughts run together as I place Andrius in his arms.

Grunts echo across the swamp. I reach for Ajax's hand. "I know the fastest way across the plain. If we run now, we can make it."

Lie.

"I can't run from who I am, Rhea."

My fists clench at my sides. "Then we'll wait for the wagon."

"If your wagon comes, it won't be in time to do us any good."

Before I can respond, he circles my waist with his big hands and walks me backward. One step. Then another.

My nails dig into his shoulders. "I'm not leaving you behind. They'll kill you, Ajax."

"Not if they don't find out what I've done." Ajax leans down so that we are eye to eye. "If these men send out a warning, they'll hunt you down. The only way for you to survive is if I stay behind and kill them all."

He presses his forehead to mine.

When he speaks again, it is my dreams in his mouth.

When his chest rises under my hands, it is my breath in his lungs.

"It's time to go now, Rhea. Go," he says fiercely. "And live."

No. I won't.

Living is not enough. Not without him.

Ajax doesn't give me a choice. He dips his golden head. His arms sweep my legs and then he is carrying me. My fists pound his chest, but he just cradles me like I am something precious and he closes the distance to Cyrrian.

Another wordless look.

"Protect her." Ajax hands me up.

Cyrrian pulls me into his lap and shifts Andrius into my arms. "With my last breath."

Tears stream down my face as I draw Ajax in by the bronze plates of his armor.

"You are my home."

"And you're mine." He seals my lips. His kiss tastes of blood and bronze. Stolen nights and sacred stones and beaches strewn with fallen stars.

I cling to him until his hands clamp around mine, forcing me to let go. Then Cyrrian's arms are there, yanking me back.

A shudder racks Ajax's chest as he backs away from me. Wetness glistens on his cheeks. Behind him, three more men appear around the base of the ridge. His name is a scream lodged in my throat as Ajax's eyes lock on mine. He draws his sword.

Atesh bursts into motion, throwing me back against Cyrrian's chest. Ajax's face blurs in my vision. We circle the small patch of earth once before Atesh unleashes his speed, and my cries are stolen by the wind.

SHADE

He finds her in
the day's soft gloaming.
His lifeblood spent,
Shade ceases roaming.

Rejoined in death
each of them seeking,
an end to pain.
Truth without speaking.

Their choices past
a Shadow made,
some call her Wraith,
the others, Shade.

Straight back now hunched
eyes like the sea.
Key bearer come at last
to set Daughter free.

Deep in the Well
a Child's cry
a Fury's hiss
wings take to sky.
A Crone prepares
to say good-bye.

Upon the tower
Shade and her maker
watch the Horse of Fire
blaze every acre.

High on his back
Shade's child now grown
carries the seed
to futures unknown.

They will not be there
to hear his laughter.
But they'll wait for him
in what comes after.

40

ANDROMACHE

MEMORIES OF MY mother are few. One detail I do remember is a story she told me when I was four or five summers old. Back when I had recurring nightmares that our palace caught fire while we slept. The old tale was meant to give comfort, an Anatolian legend of a boy who fell into a pit of flames that left him with burns all over his body. He lay on his deathbed, writhing from the worst pain anyone could imagine. But before he breathed his last, a shimmering goddess appeared at his bedside to rub a charmed salve into his blistered skin.

And the boy was made new. Whole.

Hot tears slide down my face, landing on the flayed flesh that was once Hector's cheek. Foolishly, I hold my breath. I hope, but nothing happens. The man beneath me is not whole. And the boy he was will never be again.

Lies.

My eyes fill and release. Fill. Release. Until not even the sea can rival me in salt.

Why cry now, my alev? asks the ripped remnants of lips that cannot be his. A warm mouth that once traveled the length of me, whispering the song of two made one.

The sob I've kept at bay works its way up my throat.

Priam returned to the city without Andrius, and I discovered greater depths to my misery. New shades of darkness. No one knows what happened to them. To any of them. If Rhea and my child live. If Cyrian and the Master of Keys were slaughtered where they stood or taken captive.

All I know is that I no longer feel Hector or Andrius in the part of me that lived for them alone.

After Priam delivered my husband's body to the bathing house, the once-great king shuffled back to his palace like an animated corpse. I watched him go. With neither gratitude nor resentment. I was merely *there*. A witness to the last of his life force. Utterly spent.

How I long to join the king in the realm of dead dreams. *But not yet.*

First, Achilles must pay. And then Paris will fly to the Underworld on his heels if Laocoon doesn't get to him first.

My eyes search Hector's battered body. Every rib broken. Not a section of skin unmarred. The women in the camps who prepared him for Priam's arrival did their best. They even pulled his hair away from his face in the Luwian style. I would hardly have been able to tell it was Hector otherwise.

Trembling, I pour out water and dip the rag, beginning the ritual washing my hands know by heart, even as my mind begs to travel elsewhere. I set my thoughts loose on the wind, but it only permits me to peer backward. There is no future.

Before long, I almost forget it is *his* body I am preparing. Until I reach the hands. Cold and stiff. Clenched in a way they never were in life. Not when they broke a horse or carved a cradle or held a baby. Held me.

Something sits in the tight prison of his left hand. I unwrap Hector's fingers and hold the object on my bloodstained palm.

Every faint sound in the room, from the water dripping onto the slab to my own labored breathing, grows deafening. The small horse carved of wood shouldn't come as a shock, for I have pressed countless *atamanui* into the palms of Troy's youth.

The shock is that it is there at all.

Atamanui are not an Achaean custom. It is unique to our lands. Only a woman of Troy would know it.

A small flame fans beneath my heart.

Do not dare it. She is lost. They are all *lost.*

And there is only one thing left to do before abandoning this twilight to join them. The shudder starts in my knees as I invite the feeling inside. It works its way up, until my entire body shakes. The way the sky shook in the purple dawn when the serpents first appeared.

Rage.

It comes. It feasts. It vows.

It releases its venom slowly. I place two flat stones, worn smooth by the waters of the Scamandrius, over Hector's lifeless eyes.

My own, I realize, are dry.

I'VE TAKEN TO counting to pass the time. It's a habit I picked up from Rhea. Fifty-seven. The number of deaths I've witnessed since the battle resumed this morning. I do not flinch with grief when they fall. All I feel is the weight of the inevitable. The certainty that lying facedown in the dirt is where we were always headed.

But not yet. Not until the roar of warriors stationed along these walls tells me my man has arrived.

The air around me pulses with heat. Cicadas buzz and sweat drips down my back in a steady current. For hours, I have sat inside this charred alcove. Right above the spot where Rhea and I bade farewell to Hector before he left to face Ajax. The outer wall is badly burned, but it stands. Its baked stone an oven against my back.

He will come. Soon. The part of me more animal than human knows it well.

And he will approach by the Scaean gate. I have no doubt, for that is where Achilles can be seen by the most men. Glory is all that matters to him now. Just as revenge is all that matters to me.

It didn't take long for the Achaeans to make their final push. To their credit, they gave us a few hours for Hector's funeral. But the time for mourning is done. And so, while the rest of Troy's women wailed and tore at their veils, I sharpened my knives.

And then I waited.

A few feet away from my hiding spot, a Trojan archer loads, releases, then reloads. Loads, releases, reloads. His enemy finds his mark first. The Trojan claws at the bloody socket that now holds an arrow instead of an eye.

A horrific sound follows.

I have watched many more than this choke on their own blood. Some caught sight of my alcove while they writhed on the ground below me. A few breaths before their world went black. Their eyes wondering why an Amazon was tucked in along the wall instead of bleeding on the open plain beside her sisters.

And the Amazons *are* dying. After months with no response, Queen Penthesilea finally received my call for aid. My mentor's small band arrived from the steppe just in time to watch the Merchant Quarter fall. Achilles himself slaughtered the Amazon queen. I heard a foot soldier say that when Penthesilea removed her helmet, he fell in love with her on sight— and then Achilles shoved his sword through her heart.

It matters not. I will greet Penthesilea at the river's edge soon enough.

The plain at my back falls eerily silent. Archers along the ramparts drop to their knees to catch their breath. The air thickens as the faint whisper riding the wind grows louder. Just before the familiar creak of chariot wheels.

Mother goddess, grant me your righteous anger. On behalf of all your battered children.

I peer over the wall as the chariots approach, moments before the release of a guttural war cry. A roar as familiar to me as one of Andrius's wails.

More Trojans fall beneath the walls as the Achaeans advance. Even more turn and flee from what is coming. My lungs burn as I grab my bow and leap onto the ramparts, exposed to the elements. There is only one that matters now.

Fire.

He will come. There's no way he could not. Not when this much blood has been thrown into the water.

A painful smile twists my cracked lips when I glimpse a blur of white, gold, and bronze. It leaps from a chariot, streaking toward the Scaean gate. I track Achilles's gleaming armor like a bird of prey. He races below the ramparts faster than I've ever seen a man run, hugging the line of Troy's outermost wall beneath the Citadel. For a moment, Achilles stops at the edge of the defensive trench, staring down at the broken chariots that have led to the slaughter of so many of his men.

It is my chance. He is closer than he has ever been. This man who killed my husband. My mentor. A thousand Trojan boys whose names I'll never know. This monster who took the beating heart of an entire people and lanced it with his spear for no other reason than his wounded pride.

Achilles lowers his shield and stares away from the city. For a lengthy breath, his back is fully exposed. Heart racing, I nock my arrow and take my aim.

The blow from behind takes me out at the knees. Metal fills my mouth as my chin hits the hard stone. I can hear myself groan as the clouds swirl, but the ringing in my head drowns all other sounds.

With a roar, I push myself upright and whirl around, dagger raised.

"I spared you the cheap shot. A man of Achilles's reputation deserves better."

I wipe the blood from my mouth as Paris takes a step closer. He and I stand on an abandoned section of wall. Alone.

My eyes fall to the wound on Paris's arm, dripping blood.

"A parting gift from Laocoon?" I ask.

"That priest should know when he is beaten."

"A common ailment among fools."

Paris sneers. It strikes me that we've not stood this close since Odysseus's first attack on the Lower City, when Paris revealed his selfish stupidity in front of the Trojan army. Hector had responded with a blow—the first and only time he ever struck his brother. The crack of my husband's fist meeting Paris's perfect nose is a distant echo. And a goad.

I will finish this for you, Hector.

"Better that Achilles die by a cheap shot than by the hand of a traitor," I say, hoping Paris will make the first move.

"Traitor?" Paris chuckles and shakes his head. "Weren't you the one who urged Hector to follow his own path instead of listening to our father? That turned out well, didn't it? I suspect that's really why you loathe me."

My grip on the dagger tightens. "The reasons I loathe you are many."

Paris glares, then smiles. "You hate me because I show you what you truly are. Not a woman, but an ugly, unnatural thing."

I shift the spear to my other hand. My better hand. "Then perhaps I should give you the full experience. That way you'll be well informed when you tell the gods how they made such a terrible mistake."

"I am not here for *you*," Paris snarls, eyes returning to the swift-footed Achilles. His one chance to be remembered in this war.

"Ambitious for a man who couldn't even face Menelaus without wetting himself." I beckon Paris forward with one hand. "Come, I'll warm you up."

Paris bares his teeth. "You know, I'm glad my brother isn't here to see the last of your femininity shrivel like your withered tits."

Something inside me pulls to the point of snapping. A final fiber connecting me to this life, even if it is only hatred. There is no time to linger. Achilles is coming close to the walls again, and Paris is about to make his move.

He is mine.

I race along the rampart, my movements in step with Achilles's. The fluid way the son of Peleus fights is a thing of ravenous beauty. A spear in one hand and a short sword in the other, he moves through warriors like a youth twirling virgins at a festival dance. Achilles cuts men down as if he doesn't even see them. As if he doesn't see anything but his own reflection in their dying eyes.

Beside me, Paris nocks his arrow. His wounded arm causes his shaking hands to slip. He curses and tries again. And again. I raise my own weapon high.

Paris releases the arrow right before I launch my spear. At him. It strikes the Trojan prince in the meat of his thigh. He screams like the girl he claims I've never been.

Paris falls off the rampart, rolling to the floor behind me. I've no time to determine if his injury is fatal, not when I'm searching for the bronze smear that is Achilles. I don't see him at first because he is no longer moving. He stands beneath the ramparts, looking up. Looking right at me. Paris's arrow sticks out of his heel, but Achilles does not seem to notice.

I reach for my bow, fingers working with greater skill than they ever found at the loom.

Inhale. Pull. Release.

Achilles sees me loading, and still he does not move. The muscles of my arm tense as I pull the string taut. My enemy glances at the arrow already in his foot. Then back up at me.

For a moment, he starts to lift his spear. As if he believes he actually possesses the strength to throw it all the way up this wall.

As if he thinks himself a god.

Our eyes lock. It lasts only a flash, but that is long enough. Enough time to see the thread of grief that binds us. The love that has made us each a monster. Still, the poisoned cup we've both drunk from does not settle the score. Whatever Patroclus was to Achilles, Patroclus was no Hector.

All that remains is this: Achilles sees me, and I see him.

When Achilles finally lifts his spear, he does not release it. Instead, he closes his eyes and leans back, exposing his chest.

It is an offering. A silent plea.

Horror washes over me.

Achilles is begging for mercy. The same strange mercy he granted Priam. A man stuck in the mire of inaction, but at times a decent king, unlike Agamemnon. And that is when I see it. In the streaks of dirt running down Achilles's chiseled cheeks. In the white fire of his windswept hair. In the way he is giving me his heart now. Decisively, but on his own terms.

This war, *his* war, was never about the things other men claimed.

One more breath and Hector's face flashes before me. First beautiful, then desecrated. And Achilles's reasons mean nothing. I pull the string back as far as it will go.

Achilles gives me a small nod and I send the arrow home. Time slows as it travels the back of the wind. In the wake of its *whoosh*, I can already hear Paris boasting of his kill.

I am the man who slayed the great Achilles, he will sing at a winehouse hearth.

A legend and a lie that will spread long before the sunrise. If we even live to see it.

The son of Peleus will not.

Lips turning in a small, grateful smile, Achilles falls to the dust he will now become.

And still, I feel nothing.

41

HELEN

THE HORIZON GROWS hazy as night settles in. I stare at the fading line of light from Cassandra's balcony, unable to believe what I saw there this morning.

The Achaean ships. *Leaving.*

The celebratory music sails up from the streets below. I can see Troy's people dancing—Lower City and Citadel alike. Together, they paint a dead city in vibrant strokes as their garments twirl across blackened stone.

I see it all, and yet I do not trust my senses. It makes no sense. None of it.

One moment the Citadel is surrounded, with Achilles storming the Scaean gate and the Merchant Quarter overrun. The next, the Achaeans are racing back to their ships, sailing away on the rose-fingered dawn.

I can't understand it. The Citadel walls are the most difficult to breach, yet it would have been only a matter of time. Cassandra and I were preparing to move Creusa to Kalawashi's home and the den beneath it when Andromache stormed up the tower.

"Achilles is dead." That was all she said as she threw her bow to the floor before peeling off her soiled clothes.

The Achaean kings must have taken Achilles's death as a bad omen. A sign from the gods that although they were winning the battle, the war would not end in their favor.

It is the only explanation. Even so . . . nothing about it sits right with me.

Not that I am in a position to give prophecies. Not when I can't even heal the consequences of them. A reminder of my most recent failure stirs as the music grows louder.

I raise my hands, studying them in the fading twilight. A failure marked in blood. Soon, the wail that confirms it will come. A few more breaths, and the cry pierces the darkness of the birthing room behind me. Only this cry comes from the mother, not the child.

Cassandra's stricken face appears in the balcony's doorway. "She's awake. She needs you, Helen."

Returned from a delirious state, Creusa is weeping softly on the bed. She cradles a small bundle of white linen, her tears ones of grief but also gratitude.

The stillborn infant did not suffer. For that, I am grateful too.

"When you are ready, I will take him." It is not the first time I've said such words to a grieving mother who did not want to let go.

Creusa may not stand with Andromache's spine, but when she nods, I know she is just as brave. She clutches the cold infant to her chest. A child who came into the world without having to watch it burn.

When the fighting grew fiercest—that was when Creusa's waters broke. Unlike Andrius's birth, Creusa's labor was easy and fast. As soon as it came time to push, all it took was a few long groans.

Then I saw the blood. Another levee broken.

"I am sorry, Creusa. So very sorry." I move back toward the balcony to give her space to mourn.

"Why must they sing so *loudly*?" is the only response she can manage.

Andromache follows me outside, garbed in a thin tunic and a pulsing darkness. She stares down on the celebration with marked suspicion. Raucous laughter and the pounding of drums as the people sing their praises to Prince Paris, slayer of Achilles and the savior of Troy.

Andromache hears it all, yet she says nothing.

"They claim Paris killed Achilles with a single shot to the heel," I begin, if only to rouse her. Andromache did not have to tell me who was really responsible.

I know it wasn't Paris.

Yet Andromache hasn't said more than a few words. Not since King Priam returned to the city and we learned our rescue mission had failed.

Now, murder is all that animates her.

"Do you trust it?" I ask, my gaze drifting back to the invisible horizon.

"I don't trust any move the Achaeans make so long as Odysseus is alive. To say nothing of Paris." Andromache grips the edge of the balcony and growls. "I need to go."

And I know what she intends to do. Hunt down the traitor who escaped her yesterday. Andromache looks right through me as she turns to leave. I follow her back into the room, where she refits her armor and grabs Hector's spear, her expression utterly lifeless.

"Andromache, wait." I reach for her arm, but she pulls back like my hand is hot. "Revenge is not a reason to live."

"You're right, Helen. All my reasons to live are gone." Andromache tosses a signet ring up in the air like a golden apple, catching it and tossing it again. "But perhaps others feel differently. If you see the widow Kalawashi before I do, tell her to come find me."

With a march that sings of Hector's armored stride, Andromache, battler of men, leaves us.

Creusa and Cassandra hardly notice. The sisters sit side by side on the bed, their bodies forming a nest around the tiny bundle between them. Creusa looks up at me, rivers streaming down her cheeks. She reaches for my hand, pressing a smooth piece of wood into the palm.

A moth.

"His movements felt like little wings." A faint smile kisses Creusa's ashen lips. The flesh along my arms raises with a hundred needle pricks. She is much too pale.

"Now those wings will take him far from here," Cassandra says in a voice that sounds farther still. She begins to rise from the bloodstained bed. "I must find Aeneas."

Cassandra then pulls me to her level so she can whisper in my ear. "When Creusa has the strength to stand, tell my sister to come to the High Temple. Her husband and Ascanius will be waiting there."

I have no chance to ask her why. A violent shudder travels through Cassandra's birdlike features. It makes me grateful the Unnamed One granted me the gift of healing rather than the gift of prophecy. Even if mistakes and failures come with both.

What has Cassandra just seen?

"Your sister has lost a lot of blood," I say, knowing this is the least of Creusa's losses. "She needs to rest."

"The house of Priam is doomed to wander, not rest." Cassandra looks away from her sister weeping over yet another lost boy. "But she must go soon, Helen. There isn't much time."

I nod weakly. I've given up on asking Cassandra to explain herself. When I rejoin Creusa on the bed, she points to the moth in my hand.

"Will you add it to his pyre?" Creusa lifts her face to me, and it shines with the desperate intensity I have glimpsed in every mother, no matter how seasoned or new. "*Please*, Helen."

I nod, firmly this time, and reach for the small bundle. Creusa lets go and looks away. I wrap the infant in a thicker blanket of wool, unwilling to give him over to the chill that has already turned his thin skin blue.

As I descend the tower, the swaddled corpse in my arms seems to grow heavier. I move silently through the courtyard toward a narrow alley that will allow me to avoid the streets where the celebrations are taking place. Smoke scratches the back of my throat. I scan the rooftops, searching for one just beyond the Citadel walls that is still burning. Any alcove along an outer rampart will do, a haven where this tiny moth can cocoon before making its way to the next world.

Each inhale stings, and every step forward aches. The loss of Creusa's baby is painful, yes, but that is only the beginning of my growing disquiet.

For other than the women who saw him born, will anyone else remember this unnamed child but the One who wove him in his mother's womb? I clutch the stiff form to my heart, my own body trembling with determination to give him a proper send-off. Even if the child's time here was as meager as a speck of ash, his spirit is worth no less than any other.

I exit the dark alley by turning a corner, and night becomes day.

His wild mane glows like the sun in the light of the torches lining the wall. Shrewd eyes scan the length of me before returning to the victim he has pressed to the parapet, a wolf spider pouncing on his prey.

Odysseus.

Here. In the Citadel.

All the air inside my chest flees as the city around me blurs.

How?

There is no time to expel the word. The Ithacan has Laocoon in his clutches, and the old priest's head hangs over the outer wall. I stifle a cry as the two Achaean warriors on Odysseus's left and right help to pin their Trojan prisoner down by his arms. Odysseus raises his sword.

Laocoon turns his head. He meets my gaze with a look of sublime acceptance before the bronze blade falls. If the high priest feels the sword slice through his wrist, his face never shows it. One of Odysseus's men removes his leather belt. It writhes on the wind like a snake before the warrior wraps the strap around the old man's neck. Once Laocoon is strangled, the Achaeans flip the body backward over the wall.

Odysseus takes Laocoon's severed hand and begins removing the rings from its fingers, one by one. When he turns from the ramparts, his searching eyes lock onto mine.

Time stops. Songs become screams.

"The Achaeans are inside the city," I whisper to no one but the wind. If only to remind myself that this is *real*. That Odysseus is here . . . and he has seen me.

The burly warrior moves toward me with a purposeful gait, the way I remember him striding through Menelaus's hall. Back when I was a young mother who never could have foreseen how our tangled threads might lead us both to Troy.

Odysseus scans me again, as if verifying my identity, but it isn't the soft shape beneath my robe that he is hungry for. No, he is searching . . . searching . . . for what? My eyes fall to the dead child in my weary arms.

Andrius.

Fear and hope wrestle within me. If Odysseus is searching for Hector's son here in the Citadel, then maybe Rhea was not discovered in the camps.

She and the child might still be alive.

The low thud of my own heartbeat fills my ears. Odysseus is almost upon me. Hunting. Searching. A scattering of steps away from the answer I cling to. The truth he can never learn, not while the winds still blow.

Gather in the threads. Pull them together. What do you know?

My heart responds to the whisper like a hawk to its falconer. I know that Odysseus hates this war as much as he loathes the prideful kings who caused it. I know he missed his son's childhood and longs for his faithful Penelope, a woman worth more than any dowry Paris stole.

Yet what picture do these loose threads form?

The image of a man. One who loves his wife and son above all else.

Sweat pours down my back as Odysseus closes in, sword drawn, arms outstretched for the infant he believes is Hector's son. Yet for all his scheming, Odysseus cannot hide his surprise when I lift the bundle to him like a priestess at the altar.

We are grateful, little one. May your sacrifice buy him a fighting chance.

Odysseus's face softens the instant his hands close around the wool. His eyes meet mine. I nod, not knowing, but trusting, the small flicker of goodness I find there.

"Hector only wanted what every man wants," I say in a steady voice.

Eyes still on mine, the king of Ithaca slowly unwraps the blanket. Odysseus stares, expressionless, despite the advancing men at his back. In the streets beyond, the songs of triumph have descended into chaos. *Terror.* When he lifts his eyes again, I know it isn't the smoke that blurs them. Odysseus is remembering. Reliving the tightening in his chest when he first held his son and felt the weight. A shift in the universe. The burden to protect and guide this one small light through a realm that was dark and uncertain.

Please . . . I beg silently, not knowing what Odysseus sees, or even understands, as he cradles this dead child close.

"Is it him?" shouts another warrior. A younger man who sprints toward Odysseus, his face streaked with soot and blood.

My mouth falls open, and I wonder if I'm seeing a ghost.

Odysseus does not turn from me; he merely raises his arm. "Stay where you are, Neoptolemus."

I suck in my breath. Achilles's son. The man who has married my daughter. One glance and there can be no doubt. Neoptolemus's hair is the same hot white as his father's, but it's his arrogant belief in his own invincibility that resembles Achilles most.

Please. Please don't tell him.

Odysseus's gaze holds my face, the child cupped defensively in his steady hands. His eyes speak questions I cannot begin to answer. All I can do is follow the tug on the thread inside me, pulling us toward the same destination.

Home.

"They did as much to our children," I say quickly but quietly—and only for him. "My daughter. Your son. Both grown without us. They did not have to kill them to do it. All they needed was to tear from us their most precious years, a thousand memories we will never reclaim."

Odysseus says nothing, but he does not look away.

"I would not have abandoned *one moment* of her love, not for the lust of any man. Nor for all the gold in the east," I say, voice quivering. The screams around us grow louder as they blend with the howl of the wind. A gale carrying the smoke of new fires sparked and spreading.

I raise my pale hands high. "It is Paris. It has *always* been Paris. You've seen how he works. You know it is the truth."

Brow furrowed, Odysseus keeps searching my face. On a hunt for someone to blame for the loss of so many golden days. Will it be me? Agamemnon? Or does he finally see who is really behind our woes?

I may never know the answer.

Silently, the king of Ithaca wraps up the bundle and turns toward an eager Neoptolemus. With a casual indifference I would not believe unless I witnessed it myself, Odysseus drops the body of Aeneas's infant son over the burning walls of Troy.

I close my eyes, grateful the thud that is coming will be smothered by the roar of hungry flames.

"Hector's son has been taken care of," Odysseus says coolly to his men. And then he walks back toward the burning Citadel.

ALL THE WAYS forward are blocked. Consumed by flame and mountains of sun-dried bricks from the toppled building in my path. No, not a building. A *home*. A hundred small moments. A thousand priceless memories.

Ashes.

I've no choice but to return to Creusa by a different route. Cuts cover my feet from walking over rubble. Other than Odysseus and his men, I haven't come across any Achaeans. Yet. Thanks to these hidden routes of the Citadel, first shown to me by the Master of Keys.

It will not stay this way for long.

He is coming for you.

The vision of my end has always been the same. Menelaus's flaming red hair forms a lustrous ring around his head as he lowers his sword down onto mine.

A clammy hand grasps my wrist. I fight against its tight grip, catching sight of a whirling green cloak.

A cloak stitched with a Trojan horse.

"P-Paris" I stutter as his eyes flicker back and forth in fear. More than anything else, Paris has always been *afraid*, and insecurity is the clearest path to cruelty. A man who possessed more faith, who knew who he was and what he stood for, would never have ended up on such a debased road.

A man like Hector . . .

"Was it you, Paris? Did you open the gates to the enemy?"

Paris ignores me, wincing down at the nasty wound on his thigh. Whatever he's done, he knows there will be no victory.

An echo of his fear ripples through me.

"We must hurry, Helen." Paris's fingers tighten around my arm. His voice is desperate, but for what? For a way out of this burning maze *he* set alight? "Please, Helen. They are coming for you. It's all been arranged. I know a way we can both escape."

The way he says *both* is a blow to the core of me.

"We can survive this!" Paris's words sprint toward panic. "Your dowry treasure is hidden in the den beneath the High Temple—past the underground spring, in the passageway guarded by the skeleton of a prisoner wearing Hittite armor."

I cut his deranged rambling to the quick. "What are you trying to tell me?"

"Just *listen!*" The wrath I remember well twists Paris's face. "Beneath those haunted remains is where I buried your dowry. It's more than enough for us to begin again. In any land we desire! I'll send my men to retrieve it and they'll meet us at the ship I have waiting in the bay."

The battle around us falls silent in my own ears. Paris is truly mad if he thinks we'll be able to leave this surrounded city by *any* gate, even the Gate of Ghosts. It would not matter what Odysseus promised him in exchange for access to this underground path into the Citadel's heart.

Yet his plea is genuine. Paris actually believes there is an *us* worth saving. And just like that, he is again a lost boy raised by strangers, left to wail on a mountaintop alone. Returned to the city as a broken young man who never felt secure.

Never knew his place.

It does not excuse what he's done and all he intends to do now, but the sad sight arouses a sliver of pity all the same. In spite of everything, I grieve the loss of the man Paris of Troy might have been.

"No."

Paris has a hard time registering the word. "What did you say?"

"No. I won't come with you."

Rage pulls his features even tighter, smothering the little boy beneath a blanket of ash. When the back of his hand meets my mouth, I barely feel the sting.

"You selfish bitch. Look around! *You* are the whore who caused this!" His black eyes alight as he roars. "Everything I've done . . . it has all been *for you!*"

With his remaining strength, Paris drags me through the burning streets of the Citadel, his anger overcoming his limp. An old injury made worse by Andromache's spear.

"Where are you taking me?"

"As I've said, it has all been arranged."

The gluttonous flames and the sounds of fighting fade as we descend the steepest hill of the Citadel.

The High Temple's bronze doors stand unguarded. Statues of Hittite and Luwian gods that once watched over the courtyard are toppled to the ground, their divine faces shattered in a thousand pieces.

Cassandra's warnings, so many warnings, fill my ears. They have all proven true.

Smoke thickens the air. The Citadel is burning down around us.

Paris shoves me hard against a wall near the temple's entrance, his cloak's stallion head fluttering behind him. As he reaches for the bronze door, he casts me the smallest smile. "You'd never think it, would you?"

I wipe my mouth but the copper taste doesn't fade. "Think what?"

"That Troy fell not because her high walls crumbled, but because of a horse. One that passed through a gate large enough for a single chariot."

His chariot.

"*Why?*" is the only word I can expel.

"Because Troy was lost the moment my brother allowed that hag to take his manhood hostage. Because it's always better to let the past burn and start fresh." Paris lifts his hand to stroke the jawline he just struck. "And we *can* start over, Helen. You will rule the new Troy at my side."

I've no doubt he believes every word. Paris has convinced himself that this is his chance to take what he is owed. He has destroyed a city built over countless generations, all so he can design a kingdom in his own image. The hurt of a boy twisted into the destructive power a single man can wield.

"Wherever you plan on taking me, we will never escape. Troy will haunt us to the end of our days."

"No," Paris seethes. "It is *I* who will haunt the memory of Troy."

I slump against the wall, drained of everything.

Paris pulls open the door to the High Temple and his smile widens, then twists in confusion. The sound that comes next sears itself into my memory. Sharp blades entering soft flesh at such a rapid speed, the crooked smile on Paris's face remains frozen there until he falls.

I raise a hand to my mouth and step away from the bloodied pile of fine silk lying at my feet. At least a dozen stab wounds litter Paris's chest and abdomen, his mouth marked by a trickle of blood and his eyes blank.

I lift my own to the temple's gaping doorway. Odysseus and Menelaus stare back at me, each clutching a hooked dagger, panting from their violent efforts.

"Never trust a man who betrays his own." Odysseus slides his blade, still slick with Paris's blood, back into its sheath. "Even if it is a gift."

One look at me and Menelaus releases the roar he's been holding inside for ten years. He rushes at me, hand tightening around my throat. My feet lift from the ground as Menelaus shoves me against the wall, raising his blade to my windpipe. "Tell me why I shouldn't!" he screams, spit flying at my face. "Tell me *why!*"

All I can hear is my own racing heart. It slows as the life starts to leave me.

But then Odysseus clasps a solid hand on Menelaus's shoulder and he relents. "You just saw the reason drop to the dirt."

Menelaus moves his knife from my throat to my cheek, where it draws a trickle of blood. "No. Her beauty is a curse. One I will finally be rid of."

My first husband steps back, nearly stumbling over my second. My veil is gone and so is any fear of what he might see. Despite the blue fury blazing in Menelaus's eyes, the only thing I glimpse when I stare back at him is our daughter. The graceful hands and delicate curve of her chin. *Mine.* The deep red of her hair and bold blue of her eyes. *His.* One old memory surfaces, and my tears flow freely.

"Please tell her, Menelaus." I nearly choke on my words. "Tell Hermione."

His expression softens slightly. "Tell her what?"

"That I never stopped loving her. Or longing for her."

Menelaus studies my face, every inch of it an attack against his resolve. Maybe Paris was right about it being my greatest weapon. Only this time, the one person permitted to use it is *me.*

"Damn all that the gods gave you. Damn my own weakness!" Menelaus takes another step back, as if beauty were something to be feared. "I never could stand to see your tears. Nor the girl's either."

"Is she as lovely as I have imagined?" I ask softly.

Menelaus stands up tall. "Her face does not strike a blow like yours. But yes, she is lovely. Neoptolemus is well pleased."

At the fresh memory of Achilles's son racing toward Creusa's child, so eager to do the evil deed himself, a shudder passes through me.

Menelaus glances at Odysseus. "You know that I can't let her live."

"No . . ." Odysseus watches me, his bushy brows giving the warning to stay silent. "But you must also appear magnanimous. To wage such a long war only to slit the throat of the woman you sacrificed so many lives for? That wouldn't please the people of Sparta."

"Unlike some, I do not make decisions based on the whims of farmers and goatherds." Menelaus turns his head to spit on Paris's body. "What other choice is there? I can't slay her here and keep my honor, but I also can't live with her and save my pride."

Odysseus's eyes flicker to mine before he gives a careless shrug. "Send her away, then. Punish the woman for her crimes by putting those swan hands to work."

Work.

The unbearable weight on my shoulders begins to lighten. Odysseus does not miss a thing. Not a single word.

I leap at the opportunity. "There is an island of lepers called Letois. A group of healing women tend to the thermal pools at a temple to the sun. Banish me there. They will work my hands at their looms until they are brittle bones."

"I know Letois well," Odysseus adds, nodding. "It is on my way back to Ithaca. I am willing to relieve you of your burden, Menelaus, and deliver Helen to her priestesses." His smile spreads slowly. "For a price, of course."

"That's a relief. Or I'd have thought you'd gone soft." Menelaus turns back to me, his voice sharpening like iron as he gestures to the burning Citadel. "Where is the dowry, Helen? I can't return to Sparta empty-handed. Not when all the kingdoms of Mycenae are crumbling. We will take the gold we came for."

"What remains of it is yours." I pause, meeting his gaze with a challenge forged in fire. "That is, if you know where to search for it as the walls of Troy topple down around you."

Springwater . . . Hittite armor.

"The den beneath this city is a twisted labyrinth of tunnels," I explain, "and it seems you've just stabbed the only other person in Troy who knew of my treasure's whereabouts."

"Then tell us, Helen," Odysseus urges. "Tell us where Paris hid the gold and I will deliver you to Letois. I'll even be the last king to leave these shores in order to see the spoils distributed fairly among our warriors. That way you, Menelaus, can be the first to complete your *nostos*, returning to your kingdom in glory."

Clever, clever Odysseus. He knows Menelaus has done nothing noteworthy this entire war. The Spartan is starving for adulation like a poor man salivates over roasting fish.

"And what of your wife and son?" I ask. If Odysseus is weaving some scheme, I must learn what *he* seeks to gain. And what it might cost me.

"What's a few more weeks if they will make me a rich man?" Odysseus grins, shrewd eyes dancing. "I suspect I will need all the treasure I can get to reclaim my homeland."

So it comes down to this. I must trust that Odysseus will be true to his word. And he must trust that I will never reveal he only pretended to kill Hector's legacy.

It seems a fair bargain.

"The treasure's location is not something I can tell you. Yet I can show you." I step into the High Temple and make my way toward the den entrance Andromache described. "Follow me."

42

CASSANDRA

SCREAMS ECHO. NOT in my head. For once, these screams are real. And they are getting closer.

We have run out of time, says the Crone.

"He will come." I search the open space beyond the stone column.

How many times was I dragged here by my mother's priests when I was a girl? I close my eyes, and I can still feel them. Rough hands. Cold water slipping over my head. Burning my lungs even as it ran down the back of my throat.

Back when they thought I might still be purified. When all that was dark in me might be washed away. And so they held me under the prayer pool until the world turned dark and green water streamed from my nostrils. If the truth mattered, I could have told them.

The only evil spirit who ever touched me was watching from the crowd with self-satisfied eyes.

But the past is not the only reason I despise this place. I hate it more for what is to come.

My jaw aches. I force myself to unclench and look at the sacrificial altar. Soon, very soon, I will hide behind its stone. Then he will come just as I have seen him in every one of my nightmares. Fiery hair. Bloody sword. I can feel his hands as they tear at my robes. The cold edge of the offering slab cutting deep into my back.

My body starts to tremble.

You could have hidden with the others. You didn't have to come here, the Crone says.

"Yes, I did."

The seed is buried. The Crone's voice rings with defeat. *The rest does not matter.*

I reach out and take her hand as she once took hold of mine. "It matters to me."

The Wraith nods. The Fury growls her approval. The Child smiles through her tears. Their pride and sorrow fill the well.

Then you know what you must do, the Crone says.

My fingers curl into claws as I peek back out at the open floor of the High Temple. I have been waiting here since Odysseus and Menelaus came through, Helen leading them toward the waterfall. The Achaeans have already been this way. Evidence of their passage is visible in the bodies scattered across the floor. Red robes in pools of red blood. The first casualties of treachery so deep no one would have expected it.

Of my mother's priests, the survivors aren't so sanctified now. They walk over the bodies of their fallen brothers, snatching at the treasures clutched in the dead's stiff hands. Their self-righteousness breached with the walls. Now they bleat like beasts in the fields when the butcher comes. With neither pity nor hatred, I watch the last one scramble out of the temple toward the palace and whatever false security it still provides.

I breathe in deep and step out from behind the pillar as three figures stagger through the temple doors.

Aeneas's tall form is bent under the old man on his back. His father, Anchises. Aeneas's young son, Ascanius, trails behind him, face painted with fear. With his other shoulder, Aeneas supports Creusa's stumbling weight. Her face is bone white. The only color now spatters her red-smeared robes.

My sister's hair is matted, and her arms are clutched to her chest as if to cradle a ghost. At her side, her living son looks lost already without his mother.

Surprise slips past Aeneas's guard when he sees me waiting for them. "You wanted to see me?"

"No, I wanted to show you."

Aeneas's grim face grows grimmer. He takes in the statues all around us and nods. As if to console himself with the knowledge that this is as good a place as any to die. He looks at his wife and child. "Stay hidden here," he tells them. "I must go to King Priam."

"There is no hope left in the palace," I say. "Not since Paris opened the doors to our enemies."

Horse of Ash and Horse of Fire, whispers the Child. *Only one will be remembered.*

It is as it must be, sighs the Crone.

Aeneas's body trembles as he processes my words, but whatever emotion has bubbled up inside him, he reins it in. "Then he deserves whatever fate awaits him."

"He did," I say. "And so do you. That is why you are here."

"I don't understand." Aeneas glances toward the door. More screams. The singing of swords and the acrid stench of smoke. His mind has already fled this temple to join his men making their final stands before the palace doors.

"Hector is dead. So is your youngest son," I say. "There is nothing left for you here."

Aeneas's head snaps toward me.

"No matter how many Achaeans you kill, Troy will fall. Dying with it will serve nothing. And your service is still required."

Fear flashes across his face before he can hide it. Aeneas has always been wary of me. There was an edge of respect to his avoidance. An acknowledgment of the hands of the gods. That is something we have in common. Both of us are more afraid of the future than the monsters lurking in our pasts.

I see his shadows. All of them.

I step up to the altar and press my back against the slab. "Help me."

Confusion flashes across Aeneas's face, but even now, he is too honorable to refuse. He lends his strength to mine, and inch by inch, the stone slab creeps back across the floor, revealing the dark passage beneath it.

"What is this?" Aeneas gazes down the hole to slithering darkness.

I wipe the sweat from my brow. "A way out. Dug by the men who built the first city."

His frown deepens. "If you knew of this all along, why are you only revealing it now?"

"The passage lets out by the tomb of Ilium," I say. "It is too narrow; the exit is too exposed to provide a clean escape for more than a handful of people. One buried so long it has been forgotten by all. At our peril."

"But not forgotten by you," Aeneas says. A statement. An accusation. It hardly matters now.

I have also not forgotten what happens when one thread is pulled, leading to the unraveling of many others. Silence often does the least harm.

"There are places only a shadow can go. Things only a Shade can see."

Aeneas's back straightens. "My family will take the tunnel, but my place is here. I can't leave the Citadel undefended."

"Your father can't walk. Creusa is too weak and your son too young to carry them. There will be Achaeans stationed by the tomb of Ilium. If you want your family to live, you and your sword must go with them, and you must do it now."

Aeneas stares at his wife and son. His father. Sadness mixes with fondness, but I know even before he speaks that it is not enough to bend his rigid sense of honor. There is only one thing that will push Aeneas into that tunnel. And he must go. All the endless paths. All the twisted roots and scattered seeds that form the tree of the future depend on it. And the winds of fate are blowing.

"I said the city would fall. I foretold all that has happened. Over and over again, I spoke the truth but none of you would hear it."

Aeneas's bronze skin goes ashen.

I take a step toward him. "Hear me now. If the seed of Troy still lives, you are the only one who can bring him to the soil where his roots might grow."

"What seed?"

"The acorn of our oak. The son of Troy that lived even as yours was taken from you."

Understanding dawns. "Andrius lives?"

I lick lips that taste of blood. Aeneas will know it if I lie. It is his own gift. Though he does not yet understand how to employ it. "The future is a realm of shadows. But that means there is still a chance." I grip his arm.

"You claim to be the servant of the gods, cousin. Did you not swear to do them honor? Who do you think gave me the gift of prophecy? Who do you think is speaking through me now?"

I don't know where my visions come from. If there are gods, they are not the kind I would wish to serve, but what I believe does not matter. I let Aeneas's faith fill in all the spaces my words leave blank.

"My place is here," he repeats, though with less conviction.

"Your place is where the gods send you," I tell him. "They have plans for you, Aeneas. Plans that will shape the very course of the ages. Limbs stretching far and wide. Through colors and bends of stars you cannot imagine. Will you deny the path set before you?"

A flash of doubt. Of fear and hope mixed with longing. To do something. To matter.

Even before Aeneas shakes his head, I know that I have failed again. I slump against the stone slab. I can't make him save himself any more than I could save Hector.

"We must go. You must go, Aeneas, if Cassandra bids it."

Creusa moves away from her husband to stand on her own two feet. Her features sag with pain and sorrow. The red sea on her robes spreads, and still, she blinks back the darkness and focuses all her kindness and love on the man who could never return it the way she wanted him to. "If there's even a chance he still lives . . ." Her face crumbles under the weight of her own loss. "If this is the gods' will, then you cannot deny them."

Aeneas adjusts his father onto his back. His jaw is locked, but at last, he nods. With a terse word, he sends his son forward into the tunnel and Creusa after him. The boy shudders at the dark but does as he is bid, helping his mother down. Creusa's limbs shake with exhaustion as she finds her feet on the wooden ladder. Before she goes, my older sister smiles at me. A gift.

Love and sorrow squeeze my chest until I have no room left for breath.

I rest my hand against her feverish cheek. She pushes back my hair from my face like the mother I never had.

Creusa. Always considered the weakest among us. The least exceptional. She sees the merciless destiny that awaits her on my face, and unlike many seasoned warriors, she does not flinch from it. Instead, she takes her son's hand and she leads him down into the tunnel on trembling legs.

"Come, Ascanius."

Tears spill over as I watch them fade away in the dark.

"Where do we go?"

My chin jerks to Aeneas, where he waits with Anchises on his back. "Make your way to the mountain of your boyhood."

"Why there?"

"I only know that this is where your path leads." And it will be a long path. Longer than he could ever know. I have seen that too.

My cousin eases himself down the ladder into the tunnel. When he is submerged past the ouroboros on his breastplate, I drop to my knees so that our noses are close together.

"Aeneas."

Colors dance in the space between us, spilling images onto the backs of my lids. So many shapes. So many warnings and dangers and perils he will face. They hang on the tip of my tongue, but knowing doesn't make it any easier. If anything, the knowing only makes it worse.

But there are certain truths we cannot hide from.

"Tell me," he says.

I lean forward and whisper into Aeneas's ear. When his body recoils, I grip his shoulders and pull him back to me. His expression when I finally let him go is that of a man who suddenly finds the weight of the world on his shoulders.

"Never forget."

Aeneas nods once before he descends into the darkened hole. His body has barely disappeared before footsteps approach. My heart races as I listen to them draw closer.

I can feel him coming. Every step he takes toward me tightens the noose around my neck.

It is time. The Crone's voice vibrates through me. Pride and sorrow. Joy and pain. Because we both know what I must do.

"I can't." I force the words through chattering teeth. "Not without you."

You must face him as yourself. You must look into his eyes with your own, or he will have won.

The Fury screams. The Child juts out her stubborn chin. The Wraith shakes her head because we have come too far to let that happen.

Tremors run through my legs until I need the pillar's help to stand.

You must be brave, whimpers the Child, burying her face in the Fury's robes.

The Fury holds the Child close with one hand and raises her sword with the other.

The Wraith puts her arms around them both. She smiles at me. Aegean eyes. Bone and skin that once frightened me, now as dear to me as any living face.

"I don't want to say good-bye," I whisper to the temple.

We were born of your blood and suffering. It was your choice to welcome us and so it must be you who sends us away, says the Crone. *Your choice.*

"I can't do this without you."

You do not need us, says the Crone. *You have other sisters now. Ones that will see you through.*

I close my eyes and the Crone is there. They all are. Huddled together at the bottom of the well. My protectors. My *friends*.

High above the temple, the Hawk screams in the sky.

No more hiding. The Crone takes my hand gently, as she did once, long ago. *The time has come to step into the Light.*

She waits for me to let go, and when I do, she smiles through her tears.

Go, child. Go, and make the darkness tremble.

The well fills with that darkness now. Their images and their voices fade away. The sudden silence makes me catch my breath. Gasping, I reach out to grip the wall.

Alone. So alone.

No, says a voice.

All *mine*.

Helen's face rises in my mind. Beautiful and kind. Andromache's dark eyes, flashing with fire. Rhea's quiet strength, gripping my hand.

I feel them in the temple with me, and I rise to meet him. False god who appeared to me in the Light. He has come again, and this time, he has not come alone.

Helenus starts forward. "Cassandra? What are you doing here?"

I look past my twin. At the one who walks in his shadow.

"Cassandra," says the voice that sent me falling down a well into darkness. The voice that took all the parts of me that were whole and shattered them into slivers of obsidian.

Antenor steps out into the flickering light of a hundred oil lamps. The flames bathe his body in golden fire, and for a moment, he appears to me as he did that first morning. Hungry for what was never his.

My body threatens to collapse. I bite my cheeks till I taste blood, but I stand still as he approaches.

"The screaming has started, uncle. Are you ready to hear what awaits you?" I ignore Helenus's glassy eyes as they dart between us.

"You look different, Cassandra." Antenor's tone is rife with secrets. "You've been a woman for some time, but over the past few weeks you have grown."

His words send spiders crawling across my skin. He has no idea how right he is. "And you've grown old, Antenor."

His smile punches the air from my lungs. A dozen memories flash through my mind. A dozen moments when he smiled at me just like that. Smiled while I cried.

"What is that?" Helenus asks again, pointing to the gaping hole in the floor. This time, Antenor acknowledges him.

"A secret exit that leads to the tomb of Ilium." His forked tongue turns smooth for Helenus's sake. I can see the hooks he has placed in my brother as easily as the glittering murals on the temple walls. Paris may have proven a disappointment who went rogue, but Antenor was prepared for that too. "You are the heir to Troy now, Helenus. We will carry the truth with us, and one day we will return to avenge the wrongs that were done."

Antenor makes for the tunnel.

"*Truth*," I spit as I step in front of him. "You brought this ruin upon us, and now you would run from it?"

Antenor regards me with disdain. "I have given my life for this city. I did not want to see her burned. You have your brother to thank for that travesty."

"Paris was the spark, but you were the hand that kindled it," I say. "You manipulated him as you have manipulated my father for years. As you sought to manipulate me. But you underestimated Paris. His vanity and his hatred. And when the fire burned your hand, you dropped it. Now it will consume us all."

"What is she talking about, uncle?" Helenus shifts from foot to foot.

"Truth," I say again.

"Your sister is raving." A touch of anger slips past Antenor's guard. He collects himself. "The gods are not fair with their gifts. You were blessed with the sight and she with madness. It was no doing of yours so do not lament it."

I look at my brother. My twin. "Who taught you how to see the truth dancing in the spaces between dreams? Who held your hand and walked you from the dark into the light? Have you forgotten the things I showed you, Helenus? All the nights you cried because you could not see the colors dancing until *I* showed you?"

I drop every wall so there is nothing between us. Nothing but the Truth. "Antenor and Paris did everything in their power to bring down Hector. They have used you, and you did not see it because you did not want to. Because they made you feel important." Sympathy swells inside me despite everything. "They tried to strip Hector of his influence, and when that did not work, they worked to send him to his death. They succeeded, but their success came at a price they did not foresee."

"Uncle?" Helenus stares at the man who has become like a second father to him. He does not want to believe, because if he does, everything he has lived for becomes a lie.

Fury flashes across Antenor's face before he can hide it. "I did not plant those omens in your head, Helenus. Do you think I wield the power of the gods?"

My laugh grates against the walls. "The story of Troy was never written by the gods. But by men."

"My patience is at an end, Cassandra. If you promise not to hinder us, you may even come with us if you choose."

So he can dispose of me at a more convenient time? Never.

I place myself in front of the hole in the temple floor and raise my hand. The blade glitters in the lamplight. The same blade that cut the cord to bring Andrius into the world. The one the Fury used all those years ago to carve that scar across my uncle's chest.

Double blade. Life and Death.

At the sight of it, Antenor pales.

Sounds drift into the temple from the courtyard outside. Fighting. Screams of battle lust and pain.

"The Achaeans," Helenus says.

"Go," Antenor orders. "Bar the temple doors. It won't hold them for long, but long enough to slip away and close the entrance after us."

Helenus looks at me, and in this moment, I know he sees it.

If only seeing were enough.

My brother does as our uncle bids him. He walks away.

The temple rings with silence and fury. Anger and shame and regret.

I lick my cracked lips. "Why?"

Antenor knows exactly what I am asking. "The gods gave you a formidable gift. I hoped I could groom you into a servant of Troy, but you would not be controlled."

So he robbed me of my gift instead. He robbed *me*.

My legs shake as I take in the full depth of his treachery.

"My father trusted you. He loved you." Antenor was the other half of his whole. Just as Helenus once was to me. Priam owed Antenor his life and his throne and his loyalty. He loved his brother, and that love would not allow him to see the truth.

"I never led him astray. I advised him to the best of my abilities. Everything I've ever done was for Priam and for Troy."

The shadows flee from the corners of my mind. "It was never the throne you wanted."

Clarity, not certainty.

"True authority does not come from a diadem. It belongs to those who turn the head that wears it. The king has all eyes upon him and a thousand daggers pointed at his back." Antenor's expression goes distant. "Power keeps you safe until it kills you. The key is to possess it without seeming to."

Priam's time was coming to an end. And with him, Antenor's influence. "You knew you could not control Hector or Andromache and so you sought to replace them with more malleable tools."

"Hector was a soldier who knew one thing well," Antenor says. "He relied too heavily on his wife's counsel. Andromache's ideas would have destroyed the city from the inside out."

"Sometimes we must adapt in order to survive," I say bitterly. "You taught me that."

I lift the knife.

He does not give me an opening. He attacks me with deceptive speed, knocking the knife from my hands. The familiar weight of his body slams into mine, pressing me to the floor.

Screams sound over and over inside my head.

Memories blend with the present. Thens and nows all mixed together. Wine breath on my face. Sandalwood oil in my nostrils. Burning in my lungs as his hands cinch around my throat.

Darkness hovers at the edges of my vision.

I tried, I say to the empty well inside me. *I tried.*

Coppery wetness spatters my face. The hands around my neck go slack. Antenor groans and rolls off me. He crawls to his feet, the wound on his head leaking onto his pristine robes.

"Cassandra." Helenus leans over me, his face, so much like mine, creased in worry. With his help, I stagger to my feet.

Helenus gazes at our uncle, moaning on the floor, and I know that he has found the courage to look between the spaces and see what has been there all along.

He grips my hand and studies my face. "They are gone," he says in wonder. Speaking aloud the truth between us. That the inhabitants of my well were always as visible to Helenus as they were real to me. Ghosts I welcomed and that he feared. It was fear of them that drove the wedge between us. He didn't understand how they saved me. He did not want to.

"I sent them away," I tell him. "It was time to save myself."

"I'm sorry," he tells me. "For all of it."

I nod. "We can't leave Troy. If more of us flee, Odysseus will realize we've escaped. He will know there are more underground exits besides the Gate of Ghosts. Aeneas must make it to Mount Ida, and we must close the entrance to the tunnel behind them so that the Achaeans never find it."

Helenus nods, accepting my word with the same pure faith he offered me when we were children.

"She speaks only in riddles and lies," Antenor hisses, clutching his head as he stands with his back to the hole in the floor.

"You won't walk away from here, Antenor," I tell him. "The darkness waits for you. I see it yawning in your shadow." A promise and a curse.

The oil lamps gutter. Antenor shivers. I take a step toward him, and this time, it is he who cringes back.

"You are a witch," he spits at me. "You are cursed."

My laugh grates across the walls. "All these things and more the world will never know. But you will. When at last you meet the dark, you will do so knowing *exactly* who I am."

I grip the knife and take a step forward. "I am the Hawk."

High in the sky above the temple, a lone bird screams. I take another step. "I am the Child."

Antenor flinches, but I do not stop coming.

"I am the Fury."

Satisfaction lights through me as I watch the blade tremble in his grip.

"I am the Wraith."

Every step toward him is matched by one of his back. Until there is nowhere left to go. Only, he does not see it.

"I am the Crone."

I take the final step. His foot moves over the darkened hole in the floor.

Fear flashes across his face. His arms wheel backward, trying to regain his balance, but it is too late. It has been too late since that morning he came and pressed his hand over my mouth.

He screams and screams, until at last, his screams are swallowed by the dark.

"I am Cassandra," I whisper into the silent temple. "And I was here."

43

ANDROMACHE

WAVES LAP THE foamy shoreline to the west as dawn's first light paints the east. A bird screams. The wind carries its echo through the matted threads of my hair. I awaken from one nightmare into another. My eyes dart around me, painfully aware.

So much beauty. So much death. None of it changes what is.

A city smolders behind us. Our coughs rise with the smoke as soldiers force us across the open plain. Over the swell and the bridge that spans the Kesik Cut. A silver-haired woman in front of me trips on a stone, a remnant of what Troy has become, her knees sinking to the earth. She lifts her trembling arms overhead, waiting for the blow from the Achaean who marches beside her, spear ready to serve as a cattle prod. The old woman's ramblings tell her story. How she can't understand why she has survived when so many others have perished. Her husband of fifty years. Any sons and grandsons she'd have swaddled or sung to.

The thought of the Achaeans letting this old woman live just so she can wash their undergarments has me spitting the rancid taste from my mouth. Still, worse realities are in store for the rest of us.

I fought them when they bound me. When Ajax the Lesser finished with Cassandra and his men discovered me inside the temple as I followed his tracks to take revenge. But there were too many of them.

Too little left of me.

My sore wrists itch. Two red rings bound together, the taut rope connected to the waist of the woman in front of me. All of us linked together, the little girls bound as brutally as their mothers, as we are dragged to our common fate.

To a thousand small deaths, one endless night at a time.

The Achaean with the cattle prod, faceless beneath his helmet, uses his spear to poke at a girl beside the old woman. She is a lithe reed with small, budding breasts. He laughs when the little girl yelps. He laughs even more when she begins to cry.

I feel it then. *Rage*, my old friend.

Raising its head from the black mud.

The girl lifts her ash-streaked face and looks at me. I see her. I see *it*. Buried beneath the blood and the soot.

A bright burning fire no spear or prod can touch.

Fresh air fills my lungs. One gulp of sea breeze after another. My rage takes to the wind.

But my regret refuses to flee. Odysseus lives, and I never found Paris in the fray. None of it matters now. A lesson Achilles taught me.

Hold anything too tightly, and it will eventually burn your hands.

And my hands are raw. Bleeding. Smeared with dirt. I open them as the rope tied around my wrists leads me to my end.

A path I did not choose. A route I never wanted. Not for a single breath.

I surrender to it now. Even if a part of me longs to fight and always will.

The hawk cries again. I shake my head to clear the fog until I am back inside my body. Awake for the coming moment. Writhing with a pain that is all-consuming.

We've reached the beach. I haven't seen Bodecca since the tower. Helen and Hecuba are somewhere behind me, and Cassandra walks a few paces ahead. When the Achaeans dragged us from the city, they made sure to keep those of royal blood together so the spoils could be distributed equally.

Cassandra's bloodied tunic clings to her in strips, and yet she strides to meet her fate with her chin lifted high. She walks like the princess she has always been.

We stand before the Achaean ships, loaded with gold and warriors who want nothing more than to leave these shores behind for good. They are waiting only on us. Prizes of war. Shadows whose names will be lost with the dust that was once Troy.

Some look upon us with lust, but most are worn too thin to entertain any longing but the desire for their own kitchen's bread. The Achaean kings stand calf-deep in the foamy surf, their breastplates dulled, their expressions hardly those of the winning side.

There are no victors here.

Menelaus.

Agamemnon.

Nestor.

Odysseus.

Names that will echo across time like the lap of these shimmering waves.

The kings allow us to gather like frightened livestock before they begin dividing up the women one by one. I clench my hands into balls as Cassandra is shoved forward.

"Who wants the crazy one?"

The kings laugh. Every last one.

Agamemnon claims her quickly, and Cassandra is shuffled off to the side, her hair hanging limp like seaweed. Agamemnon cares not for the state of Cassandra's mind; he simply wants a daughter of Priam to lord himself over.

"Not one of you will survive Troy's demise!" says a damning voice from behind the tapestry of black hair. "The serpent will swallow your kingdoms even as it ate the stars. One by one, your lines will shrivel up. Your cities will fall like grains of wheat. Only one seed shall rise from the soil again."

Cassandra spits in the sand at Agamemnon's feet. "All that's left for me to do is live long enough to see you murdered in your own bed."

Agamemnon frowns, but there is fear trembling behind his disgust. Then he does what all men who are afraid of shadows do.

Cassandra does not flinch at the blow. A tiny smile rises even as she wipes away the blood.

"The Trojan princess will board the ship last," Agamemnon announces. "I suspect she will need to feel the sting of sea spray all the way to Mycenae in order to keep calm."

"Hector's memory will outlive you all!" Cassandra screams as two warriors drag her back to the group of slaves where I stand. Despite the fury chasing her words, this face is all hers.

Love that suffers because it knows.

When the warriors turn their backs, I reach down and pull Cassandra up from the sand. Her bruised lips curl into a gentler smile, and I again glimpse the sister Hector adored.

Shouts erupt around us, distracting the kings from their sorting. One of the ships is so weighed down with booty that it's starting to sink in the shallow waters. Men on deck throw fine pottery and exotic textiles overboard. The common soldiers near us rush into the surf to gather up these treasures, giving me time to whirl around, dragging Cassandra with me. My eyes search the throng of filth and sorrow for alabaster skin and a shock of lustrous hair.

The sight of Helen and Hecuba tied together is startling, despite everything I've seen. Two queens, stripped down to their plain tunics, their faces smeared with soot. Helen's high cheekbones and Hecuba's sagging jowls. The Trojan queen's eyes are red from weeping as she watched her husband cut down in his own throne room.

"*You see only the man he is now,*" Hector once told me. "*Not the king he was.*"

Ruins. All of us.

"Andromache." Pale hands reach out from bound wrists to grasp mine. Even Helen has lost some of her radiance. Still, the warmth of her eyes whispers the truth of all she is.

"They say Neoptolemus intends to claim you." Hecuba's voice is as cool as ever, but it has lost its spiteful sting. She shakes her head. "The widow of my Hector, given as a prize to a mere boy."

The name Neoptolemus stirs up nothing within me. Not hatred and not fear, not even loathing. I could be sent with any one of these brutes and it would not change a thing.

Helen sucks in her breath, and the smothered fire flares beneath my chest.

"What is it?" I ask her.

"Hermione. If Neoptolemus takes you, then you will join her household."

Then what she means is I will stand at her daughter's loom. I will wash her bedding and watch over any children her boy-husband gives her.

Something inside me sparks, then burns itself out.

"You gave up much for Hector. For Andrius." The words come from some obstinate part of me still clinging to life. "I will do whatever I can to protect Hermione from harm."

It is the least of what I owe.

"That isn't what I mean." Helen squeezes my hands. "Please. Just *love* her, Andromache."

My eyes drink in Helen's dimmed shine, and I nod. "As if she were my own."

The Achaeans return from reclaiming their treasure. They grab hold of Helen and Hecuba and move them toward Odysseus's ship.

"Tell her," Helen cries out as her pale hand slips from mine. In the strange look she gives me, I can hear the final word that is lost on the wind.

Tell her . . . everything.

The tears washing my cheeks are my promise. I will tell Hermione the story of the mother who loved her because the telling is all we have. I will speak the truth before it dies unsung within me. I will confess my pride and my wrath and my many failures. And perhaps one day, years from now, I will forgive myself, the only person whose reflection in this sea I cannot bear.

The stars above are fading. So is the outline of Hector's face in my memories. The scent of Andrius's milky breath. I drop to the wet sand and dig my fingers deep. As if I might root myself on this beach. This land I will never see again, though it cradles the cremated remains of all I hold dear.

A rush of dread travels the length of me. The most intense sensation I've felt since Helen took Andrius from my breast and handed him to Rhea. The fear that I will forget them. That their spirits will desert me the moment I depart this shore. Along with everything that has made me who I am.

Soldiers jerk me up from the sand, one gripping each arm. My body bucks like the fire horse. My memories take flight like a hawk. A hard blow across the back sends me straight into the cold surf. I consider plunging my head beneath the waves. Until all sounds cease but for the sea's insistent roar.

A scream erupts from my throat instead. Low and long. It is the scream of every woman who has ever pushed a child into this groaning world. Of every woman who knows that this burning love will last not only for the length of her labor but for every day she draws breath.

Is it worth it? the wind sings.

My stubborn heart whispers that it is.

I look up.

The Achaeans drag me away from the shoreline, but I am not looking at them. I am gazing beyond the ruin that was once a promise made to me by a good man. Mount Ida glows purple in the dawn, the fire of the sun consuming all shadows at its base. The very top of the mountain is still draped in darkness.

But for the light of a single flame.

Certain my eyes are playing tricks, I search for Helen and Cassandra, desperate for them to see it too. A guttural cry is all I can manage. Hearing it, they each follow my gaze toward the mountain.

Our eyes lock. What passes between us is a victory no warrior will ever know. Not if he fought a hundred battles over a thousand lifetimes.

But we know.

We *know.*

Helen's face shines. Cassandra smiles. And I see.

I see him as I will always see him. His father's chestnut eyes. My bronze streak kissing his forehead. The boy turns to the young woman, a lioness who did not begin as his mother.

But who has become his mother now.

I see the girl. Humming a song composed by the wind, but whose whispers must be carried by a human voice. Riding a horse made of fire toward a future unknown. As all futures are, no matter what our dreams declare or the seers claim.

Above all, I see the Light. And it burns.

REFRAIN

ON A PLATEAU facing the sea where the Dardanelles meet the Aegean, a crumbling ruin sits. Halls once gilded in laughter and gold now the dwelling place of shades. Naked foundations of mudbrick scattered with bones and pottery shards. All that remains of a once-great city.

A Hawk soars in the sky. Storms and years have battered his wings. Eyes that once saw from Tenedos to Ida now strain to make out an ancient shrine of stones upon the nearby cape.

The Hawk makes a slow circle over the dead city. A flash of bronze glitters down below. He tucks his wings and dives. The Hawk comes to rest on the broken spire of the tower that was once his home, and he remembers. The strange shadow who once rode his wings.

A familiar stirring echoes in the Hawk's mind. One he has not felt in a long, long time.

Hello, old friend, says the Voice.

The Hawk cries out his joy and his anger.

Is that how you greet me after all this time?

You left, says the Hawk. The Voice had come to him. Changed him. The Voice had made him into something he was never meant to be, and then it had left him alone with his strangeness.

I am sorry. I had no choice. But I am back now.

Where? the Hawk asks.

It does not matter. All that matters is where I am going. I have seen it, old friend, and I am ready. I have come to say good-bye.

The Hawk does not want the Voice to leave. He wants the Voice to stay, and so he asks.

Sing to me.

The Voice smiles. *Fly for me and I will sing.*

The Hawk stretches his ailing wings.

No, my friend. This time, it is I who will carry you.

ON AN ISLAND surrounded by emerald waters, the Weaver stands at her loom. The walls of the temple echo with silent prayers. Bunches of herbs hang from the ceiling, and bowls litter the worktables of her small chamber. A place of healing.

The Weaver's face is bare as it has been since she first came to this place. The holy women of the temple wear simple clothes and lead simpler lives. Their servant hands are hardened by work; faces and arms browned by the sun.

Laugh lines ring the Weaver's eyes and mouth. Like the scars on her fingers, they only add depth to her beauty as she stands at the loom, honoring her god the way she has always done. With the diligent work of her hands.

The Weaver weaves in the silence of her chamber. Waiting as she has all these years for the one who is no longer a child.

The call of a bird drifts through her open window, and the Weaver's thoughts sail with it across the sea to the heart she left behind. Peace fills her, knowing that her child is not alone.

And neither are you, says the One who hears the Weaver's prayers. *They are here with you now. As I am.*

"Where?" The Weaver's voice is a whisper through the room.

She looks out her window at the lone Hawk soaring in the sky.

WIND WHIPS OVER the balcony, sending the Spindle's hair blowing about her shoulders. A child sleeps in her arms. She holds her son close but without grasping, for as a friend once said, love does not possess. It can only ever expand.

Her son's heat seeps into the Spindle's breast as she gazes over the walls, not to the sea in the east, but north. Toward another city that once sat high above a plain where the wind never stopped blowing. The Spindle strokes the child's back and remembers. Another child. One with his father's face. Her love for them the fire that forged her.

The ache is still there, but now it is mingled with something else. Because somewhere in the world, her son lives. That she was not there to see it is a small price to pay. Still, she can't help but wonder. What he looks like now. If he is long-suffering like the girl who raised him, or if his blood runs hot like her own. But mostly, she hopes. That his love will be the fiercest thing about him. That he is a good man.

A Hawk dives low across the valley. The breeze blows east, but this strange bird seems to move on his own current. The phantom wind dances through her. The Spindle closes her eyes and finds them waiting for her in the stillness between heartbeats.

The Hawk and his rider sitting in a burned-out ruin.

The Weaver staring out the window of a stone chamber.

The Spindle's mouth bends into a smile.

FAR ACROSS THE sea, a group of weary travelers build sturdy homes on the edge of a new world. The men labor in the beating sun while the women carry water from the rushing river.

The Mouse shields her eyes. In every direction, rolling green presses up against the sea. Seven hills, lush like the steppes where she was raised, beckon in the distance. The Mouse sets down her basket and rests on the banks of the river. A new beginning. Joy fills her heart as she watches her boy dance in the water with a horse of flames. The man standing guard over them both. Aegean eyes meet hers. Little Mouse. Who was gifted not one great Love, but two.

Their silhouettes molten in the setting sun.

A Hawk dives low over the river. The Mouse catches her breath when she recognizes his song. She closes her eyes and finds them waiting for her in the place where the horses whisper.

The Hawk. The Weaver. The Spindle.

Tears fill the Mouse's eyes as she calls the Acorn closer. Seed of great sorrow.

Even greater love.

"Andrius, come."

The boy runs over, all gangly limbs. Serious like his father. Fearless as his mother. He pushes a streak of copper out of his handsome face.

The Mouse pats the ground beside her, and he curls up at her side, resting his head on her shoulder. Already he is bigger than she is.

"What part would you like to hear?" she asks, her voice fraying at the edges.

"From the beginning." The boy leans into her warmth.

The words flow like water from the well of her memories. It is a story that she alone knows. A story not of heroes, but of shadows, and the Mouse tells it not for the world, but for him. For them.

For the prices they have paid.

High above the clouds, the Hawk soars on the Voice's wings.

In her room, the Weaver closes her eyes and leans back in her chair.

Across the sea, the Spindle clutches the child to her breast and cries tears of joy and sorrow.

And then the ring of houses on the river is gone, and the Hawk is again resting alone on the twisted spire of a fallen tower in a city made of bones.

Will you go now? asks the Hawk. He does not want to be alone.

We have sung the chorus that was asked of us. Will you come with me, old friend?

Yes, thinks the Hawk. There is nothing left for him here. Even the silent Shade who once walked the ramparts is gone. Her song set free at last. *I am tired.*

Then let us rest.

The Hawk closes his weary eyes. His chest rises and falls.

Then stops.

Over the Ilium plain, the wind cries with the voices of the fallen.

ACKNOWLEDGMENTS

We would like to thank our fabulous agent, Shannon Hassan of Marsal Lyon Literary Agency, who shepherded *Horses of Fire* and *Daughters of Bronze* into the world. Your guidance has always been ridiculously on point. We'd be lost without you.

Our deepest gratitude to our brilliant editor, Cassidy Sachs, whose passion for these women and their stories matched our own. You are, quite simply, the greatest. Working with you on these books has been nothing short of magical.

Thanks to Sarah Thegeby, Caroline Payne, LeeAnn Pemberton, and the rest of the team at Dutton. From the gorgeous cover to the pages inside, you made these words shine. Our appreciation for all you did to get this book into readers' hands.

To our beta readers: Lisa Maxwell, Olivia Hinebaugh, Maureen Cremin, Julie Cremin, Elena Patel, and Mark and Loretta Cremin, your guidance and early notes were pivotal. Many thanks also to Olivia Hinebaugh for creating yet another lovely map for us to geek out over. Your talents are endless.

Our deepest thanks to all those who read and supported *Horses of Fire*. Your positive messages, reviews, and book club selections have meant the world to us. We hope the ending in these pages was worth the wait!

To our parents, siblings, and extended families. We are who we are because of you.

Thank you to our husbands, Jordan and Josh, for everything you do. And lastly, to our children: Isla and Jack; Uriah, Isaac, Daniel, and Caleb. Thank you for showing us the kind of love this story is ultimately about. Everything is for you. Now and always.

AUTHORS' NOTE

Horses of Fire and *Daughters of Bronze* were never intended to be a direct retelling of Homer's *Iliad* and *Odyssey*. Although we adore these ancient texts and the additional mythology that surrounds them (which also vary widely in how they portray the events of Troy), the question that most interested us when we sat down to write was: Did the Trojan War actually happen and how might it have realistically taken place if it did? We understand that many readers have strong attachments to the myths, and while we tried to be true to the overall spirit of the *Iliad* (in particular), our primary purpose was to take this beloved story and reimagine it as "myth meets historical fiction" told on an epic scale. Most of the time, when we made changes to the mythology and the characters in it, it was not done according to our own whims but in the service of making the story *more* historically plausible. For instance, is it more likely that Troy fell because the Trojans were gullible enough to haul a gigantic wooden horse through their gates, or could the Trojan horse be a mythological element symbolic of more realistic ways an army might infiltrate a great city? Additionally, other changes were intended to highlight an array of Anatolian cultures—the ancient peoples the Trojans were likely based on—which have been overshadowed for far too long.

Andromache's character, for example, may seem to some like an anachronistic insertion of modern feminist values. But this is where the history gets really fascinating! In Homer's version, Andromache is depicted as

Prince Hector's loyal wife and a loving mother (traits we admire and also sought to portray). Why bother making her a military strategist trained by Amazons? Why have her struggle for greater influence in a city that stands at the crossroads of East and West and only becomes her home after marriage? As novelists, our answer could be, "Well, every character needs a conflict," and being a strong woman in a society that does not value your gifts is a tale as old as time. However, as *historical* novelists, things take an even more interesting turn. Evidence suggests Amazon warrior women may not have been just a mythological invention, given that archaeologists have uncovered the remains of ancient women buried with their weapons— nomadic warriors believed to have migrated across the Eurasian steppe around the Black Sea and as far as Mongolia (coincidentally, the same region the Amazons were said to roam).

In classical Greece, such warrior women were sometimes described as "monstrous," "manly," and "unnatural" (which is Paris's view of Andromache in our version). This was probably because they stood in stark contrast to the ideal Greek woman. Homer was, of course, a Greek, and he wrote the *Iliad* hundreds of years *after* an actual war may have taken place. Since he likely did not have access to an archaeological or historical record (or even view "historical accuracy" in the manner that we do today), he did not portray the Trojans as having their own unique culture, or even their own pantheon. It makes sense that the women in these myths, Trojan and Achaean alike, probably reflected the social expectations of royal women in the Greece of later periods.

But Andromache wasn't Greek; she was Anatolian! In our portrayal of her, we were not only inspired by the possibility that warrior women might have roamed this region during the late Bronze Age; we were also compelled by the existence of Hittite queens known as *Tawananna* and other female rulers of the Near East. Often these queens had significant power and independence, ruling *alongside* their male counterparts instead of being subservient to them. For example, the Great Queen Puduḥepa had her own royal seal, which meant she did not need to use the seal of her husband to declare her authority. Given Andromache's Anatolian origins, we felt she would have more in common with the politically strategic and influential queens who existed in the Hittite Empire or even in Egypt, rather than a queen of Mycenae who probably had much less power. (See Barry

Strauss's *The Trojan War: A New History* for more on this contrast.) The mythology may portray a demure Andromache more akin to the queens of Greece, but the history of the Anatolia and the Near East suggests other possibilities that made her character even more compelling. In this instance, we sided with the history. Similarly, we wanted to explore other ways of interpreting Cassandra and Helen. After all, what's more historically plausible: that a war began because of a woman's infidelity or because of the geopolitical pressures that existed in the late Bronze Age? We were dedicated to the aim of empowering Cassandra, one of the most tragic figures in literature, by giving her choices. And so, the voices she hears are not symptoms of mental illness but very real spirits she welcomes and befriends.

Warning: if you haven't finished the novel, there is a major spoiler ahead!

One aspect of *Daughters of Bronze* where we leaned hard into the mythological tradition was the story of what becomes of Astyanax, also known as Scamandrius. His tragic end is referenced in post-Homeric collections where the infant is horrifically thrown from the burning walls of Troy by either Odysseus or Neoptolemus, Achilles's son (the man who takes Andromache as his slave, bringing the horror to new heights). We are mothers, and one of us had a newborn son when we began writing this duology during the pandemic, so you can imagine how relieved we were to discover an entire tradition of medieval legends where the baby survives the destruction of Troy. (And in some versions, goes on to found a kingdom in Sicily or the royal line that leads to Charlemagne!) This felt like a glimmer of hope in an otherwise dark story that ends in utter tragedy for so many characters we have grown to love. Admittedly, it also speaks to our deep shared belief that our individual actions and choices matter, even when those actions occur in the shadows. It was an absolute thrill to join in this tradition by reimagining an alternative ending for Hector and Andromache's son. In doing so, we were able to play with a question that has long haunted us: Why did the noble Hector—consistently portrayed as a courageous warrior until the very end of the *Iliad*—turn away from Achilles and *run* when it was time for their final showdown? This aspect of Hector's story always felt jarringly out of character. We hope the explanation we reimagined in *Daughters of Bronze* brought you as much satisfaction as it brought us.

ABOUT THE AUTHORS

A. D. RHINE is the pseudonym of Ashlee Cowles and Danielle Stinson. The authors are united by their military "brat" upbringing, childhood friendship spanning two decades, and love of classical literature. Ashlee holds graduate degrees in medieval history from the University of St. Andrews and theological studies from Duke University. Danielle holds a master of arts in law and diplomacy from Tufts University. Their epic duology of the Trojan War, *Horses of Fire* and *Daughters of Bronze*, is the story they have always dreamed of writing together.